Lynne Graham was born in
has been a keen romance reader since her teens.
She is very happily married, to an understanding
husband who has learned to cook since she started
to write! Her five children keep her on her toes. She
has a very large dog who knocks everything over,
a very small terrier who barks a lot, and two cats.
When time allows, Lynne is a keen gardener.

Jackie Ashenden writes dark, emotional stories
with alpha heroes who've just got the world to their
liking, only to have it blown apart by their kick-ass
heroines. She lives in Auckland, New Zealand, with
her husband, the inimitable Dr Jax, two kids and two
rats. When she's not torturing alpha males and their
gutsy heroines she can be found drinking chocolate
martinis, reading anything she can lay her hands on,
wasting time on social media or being forced to go
mountain biking with her husband. To keep up to
date with Jackie's new releases and other news
sign up to her newsletter at jackieashenden.com.

DEMAND FROM A GREEK

LYNNE GRAHAM

JACKIE ASHENDEN

MILLS & BOON

First published in Great Britain 2025
by Mills & Boon, an imprint of HarperCollins*Publishers* Ltd,
1 London Bridge Street, London, SE1 9GF

www.harpercollins.co.uk

HarperCollins*Publishers*, Macken House, 39/40 Mayor Street Upper, Dublin 1, D01 C9W8, Ireland

Demand from a Greek © 2025 Harlequin Enterprises ULC

Shock Greek Heir © 2025 Lynne Graham

Christmas Eve Ultimatum © 2025 Jackie Ashenden

ISBN: 978-0-263-34478-3

09/25

MIX
Paper | Supporting
responsible forestry
FSC™ C007454

This book contains FSC™ certified paper
and other controlled sources to ensure responsible forest management.

For more information visit www.harpercollins.co.uk/green.

Printed and Bound in the UK using 100% Renewable Electricity
at CPI Group (UK) Ltd, Croydon, CR0 4YY

SHOCK GREEK HEIR

LYNNE GRAHAM

MILLS & BOON

With warmest love and thanks to my daughter, Rachel,
my port in every storm.

CHAPTER ONE

SEBASTIAN PAGONIS, TECH BILLIONAIRE, vaulted out of his helicopter on the Indonesian island. His big, powerful body sheathed in chinos and a khaki shirt, dwarfed everyone around him by virtue of his six-foot, five-inch height. His shock of black hair was anchored in a messy man bun, thin steel rings glinted in both earlobes, and he turned heads wherever he went because he looked so downright dangerous.

Glittering dark eyes that gleamed like polished swords in the sunshine scanned his surroundings with vigilance and he was greeted in the shadow of the hangar by an old schoolfriend, Andreas Zervas, who ran the Asian manufacturing side of his business. Andreas, his short, somewhat rounded counterpart, in a light summer suit, grinned up at him with familiar warmth.

'I intended to meet you off your jet in Bali but our newborn ignored etiquette and arrived early and suddenly. Why right now do you look as if you're expecting a hitman to be hiding in the shadows?'

'That would literally be the *only* option my relatives haven't yet attempted,' Sebastian retorted in frank exasperation.

Andreas frowned because he knew exactly what his friend was talking about.

Sebastian's paternal grandmother, Loukia Pagonis had died some weeks earlier and her last will and testament had given her family, including Sebastian, a resounding shock. Without any warning, she had made Sebastian, the outcast in the Pagonis tribe and a man already rich beyond avarice, the heir to her vast international property empire. Ever since then, Sebastian had been fighting off lawsuits and enraged and embittered accusations. The family who had long treated him like a curse on their name and an intolerable social embarrassment were currently reaping the rewards of having treated him like a leper throughout his childhood.

'Don't joke about it,' Andreas reproved, an unusual frown on his good-natured face. 'Stranger things have happened and when you're planning a week off-grid without security, it makes my blood run cold.'

'It's a week off and I...*need* it,' Sebastian admitted grudgingly, intense fatigue briefly bowing his broad shoulders and weighting his dark, deep voice. 'Did you make the final arrangements?'

Andreas sighed as he escorted him towards a top-of-the-range SUV. 'I did but I still think it's a crazy idea. You can't go back. You think you can but you *can't*. You're not that seventeen-year-old boy without a home any more. You're not used to roughing it now either. This experience will be a penance for you, which is why I'm breaking your rules and giving you a burner phone to take with you. You'll be screaming for escape within forty-eight hours. Your nature is too driven not to be and you'll be pining for your superyacht even quicker. It isn't easy to move from the fast lane to the slow sailing life.'

'I have to adapt for the sake of my sanity,' Sebastian growled, irritated by that negative forecast from someone who knew him well. 'But I'll take the phone if it makes you worry less…as long as yours is the only number in it.'

'It is,' Andreas confirmed, taking the wheel to drive them out of the private airfield and down a rural road edged by paddy fields contained by low walls. The car entered a small village to thread slowly through narrow, crowded streets with dust flying up to cloud the windscreen. From there they drew into a small, shabby harbour.

'Give my love to Zoe and the children. What gender is the newborn? You still haven't told me—'

'A little girl after our three boys. We are both over the moon,' Andreas told him happily.

'I'll stop in for the night on my way back next week,' Sebastian promised as he gathered his stuff.

'Look after yourself…and try to be a good loser when you're climbing the walls to get back on shore by tomorrow,' Andreas quipped.

'It's not going to happen,' Sebastian asserted with amusement.

'So, who is this guy, Sebastian Whatever-You-Call-Him?' Bunny asked the skipper of the catamaran *Merry Days*.

For the past month, she had been crewing for Reggie, taking daily parties of tourists out to sail round the islands, serving drinks and providing lunch.

Sadly, however, Indonesia was the very last stop on her world travels. She had neither the time nor the money to explore further. Whether she liked it or not, home was beckoning. In just two weeks, she would be starting work back in the UK as a librarian and that was her cue to settle down and concentrate on her career.

Reggie Davis grinned above his imposing long white beard, bright blue eyes sparkling with satisfaction. 'He's Greek born. According to my source he's also *filthy* rich but prefers to be treated like he's ordinary, for goodness' sake. I mean, can you believe that? I'm giving him my cabin because it's more private and I don't think he'll want to be eating with us, so I'm afraid you'll have to serve him his meals.'

'How does that come under the heading of treating him like he's ordinary?'

'Reckon he's one of those odd, reserved types with quirks because who would hire the whole boat sooner than have to share the facilities?' Reggie asked in wonderment, being a man who had never met anyone he couldn't make into a friend and who flourished best in a crowd. 'But what do we care? Take him sailing, diving, fishing, snorkelling, whatever he wants…mostly just a taste of freedom, I suppose.'

'I'd better get your cabin cleared out,' Bunny said abruptly. 'And maybe I should go to the market.'

'No, if he wants to be ordinary, he eats what we eat even if he does choose to eat alone,' Reggie decreed squarely. 'Nothing fancy, just the norm. He'll not be complaining when he's sitting with one of your curries in front of him.'

'Let's hope not,' Bunny agreed, already on her feet, a small, slightly built blonde with luminous green eyes set in a heart-shaped face and a deep tan from her travels over the past year. She was in her last job at her final destination and about to deal with her last customer. Why did that knowledge sadden her? She went topside to access Reggie's cabin behind the wheelhouse, scolding herself for being spoilt. After all, she had finally enjoyed the year of travel she had first craved when she was eighteen and had been denied.

Her family were naturally overprotective. She was the youngest of six and the only girl. As a result, she had been babied long beyond childhood. Her desire to travel alone for a year between school and university had horrified her family. Their preaching, nagging and genuine concern had finally talked her out of her plans and she had gone to university and completed her degree before taking her year out. In truth that had ended up being the better plan, she conceded, because she had spent four years saving up everything she earned in part-time jobs to finance her travels. She had also taken casual work in every country that allowed her to do so, ensuring that she had a safety net of cash available should she need it.

The next day, Bunny was down on her knees scrubbing the deck when their passenger arrived, the fast slap of his booted feet on the steps sending her head rearing up, fine blonde hair flying back from her face because she was hot and damp with perspiration in the humid afternoon heat.

Simply stunned by the vision of the man in front

of her, she leant back and stared at the guy who had boarded. He was so off-the-scales magnificent that he might have stepped out of a Viking fantasy onscreen. Incredibly tall and broad, not to mention jaw-droppingly gorgeous. One look and her mouth ran dry and her brain seized up.

'Could you just give me two minutes until I finish the deck?' she asked breathlessly.

'No,' Sebastian responded succinctly as if he were still in his busy office. 'You're in a service industry and you should be aware that clients expect immediate attention.'

Even as her slender spine stiffened, Bunny smiled brightly at him. So, he was one of *those*, was he? Oh, joy, she thought, pained to the bone by that warning. 'Thank you for the reminder, sir. Please come this way…'

'Where's the skipper?' Sebastian scrutinised her, unimpressed. He had recognised the shellshocked, dazed look of feminine appreciation in her gaze for what it was and it had annoyed him. Not only had he not expected there to be a woman onboard, but he also didn't want her looking at him like *that*, flirting or hovering or aiming to impress. He got enough of that nonsense every day of the week and he wasn't about to put up with it on a tiny boat where there were few places to escape unwelcome attention. The sooner any such notion of hers was nipped in the bud, the better.

On the other hand, she was surprisingly attractive in a girl-next-door way even if she wasn't his type. Did he even have a type, though? She was naturally blonde, naturally everything he suspected. Cute little face, enormous green eyes the colour of fresh spring leaves, freckles on her small nose above a generous pink mouth. Ridiculously pretty but rather small and thin with modest curves. And cheeky, even if she was striving to hide the fact. Didn't she know yet that her eyes blazed green fire when she was angry?

'Skipper Reggie takes a nap mid-afternoon. I'm afraid I'm on service duty. I'll show you to your cabin.'

Awkwardly wiping her hands on the back of her denim shorts, Bunny offered to take his bag. He frowned, spectacular dark eyes hardening. 'Your hands are dirty.'

'Are you willing to wait while I wash them?'

'No, just lead the way. I'll retain my luggage,' Sebastian retorted curtly.

Charming, she thought grimly as she showed him to his cabin. It was the largest on board and benefited from private facilities but it was still pretty small and he was so very tall; he'd be lucky if he could stand upright any place but in the open air. Richie Rich, she labelled him, just dripping with condescension and gilded expectations that were unlikely to be met on a forty-odd-foot catamaran with a crew of two.

'We usually have dinner at seven. I'll bring it to you. Would you like a drink now or anything else?'

'Water, please,' he said flatly. '*And*…don't speak to me unless you have to.'

Bunny nodded in tight-mouthed silence, spun on her heel and left him to it while she went to fetch the cold water. She was a minion, she realised wryly, and minions were not supposed to have a voice that was heard. Returning with the bottle of chilled water, she knocked on the door. He answered with a towel wrapped round his impressively lean waist and she stepped back immediately from that intimacy. Confronted by a masculine torso that was undeniably centrefold material, she was uncomfortable and she extended the bottle in silence, not bothering to speak since he had already told her that speech from her corner was undesirable.

She went back down to the galley to make a start on dinner. She heard male voices, registering that Reggie had emerged from his nap and was getting acquainted with his passenger. Steps moved overhead as the catamaran moved sleekly through the water. Reggie came down and took a couple of beers out of the fridge.

'Sebastian's okay,' he told her cheerfully. 'Very down to earth, no front to him. We're getting on like a house on fire. Oh, remind me to post the change to our route. You'll enjoy it. We're heading somewhere rather remote and I haven't been there in a few years. There's a great fishing spot waiting for us. We'll definitely have the barbecue up on deck that night.'

Bunny kept on smiling. No front to him? *Sebastian?* She gritted her teeth and when it was time she took the men's meals up on deck and left them there to eat, discreetly ignoring Reggie's suggestion that she join them. As she ate alone, she listened to the distant chatter and the laughter and thought that possibly Sebastian just didn't like female crew members. Or maybe it was just *her*, *her* face, *her* personality, whatever, she thought, irritated that she was even thinking about such a thing. Life was too short for her to be that sensitive. What did it matter what a guy she would never see again thought of her? Everybody got on with Reggie though. Maybe she personally needed to work a little harder on that score, she thought next.

As usual she was up at dawn the next morning, taking care of all the little jobs that were hers before making breakfast. By seven she was knocking on Sebastian's door with a tray.

'Come in!' he called.

One arm balancing the tray, with difficulty she got the door open and saw him sitting up bare-chested in the bed. Moving closer, her face hot at that amount of exposure to male nudity, she extended the tray to him. He grasped it one-handed, being better balanced and stronger than she was and then frowned down at the plate. 'What is this gloop?' he demanded.

'It's a Spanish omelette,' she told him curtly on the way back out. 'Reggie's favourite. It's always eggs for breakfast. If you prefer them prepared another way, let me know.'

'Scrambled, plain,' he specified.

In silence, Bunny nodded, her heart-shaped face flushed with annoyance, Sebastian noticed with growing amusement.

'How did you get a nickname like Bunny?' he asked out of sheer badness.

'My family thought it was cute when I was a baby. It's on my birth certificate,' Bunny admitted with a stiff and decidedly grudging smile before she withdrew.

Sebastian grinned. She hated him and she couldn't hide it… Mission accomplished: she would be staying out of his way all week. This was not the right moment to acknowledge that she had fabulous legs and a mouth made for, well, what a man usually hoped a woman's mouth was made for. There was just something surprisingly sexy about her modest curves and prim, quiet movements. That had to be why he had a hard-on. Determined not to think about that weird glitch in his libido, he tucked into his first Spanish omelette and was surprised by how good it was. Possibly he owed her an apology.

Would he admit that? Probably not. A woman who couldn't even give him a first glance without revealing her every reaction to him was not the kind of woman he bedded. Too young, too naïve, too...*soft*. And he didn't *ever* do soft. As he had once learned to his cost, he reflected grimly, decent and honest intentions didn't always win the best results. He had got burned, badly enough burned by Ariana to ensure that he never went near that type of woman again. If he was the kind of guy who believed in love, he might have felt differently, but Sebastian had never believed in love outside familial love. A parent could love a child, and a child could love a parent. While that might not have been his experience, he had seen enough of the world to accept that he had got the birth parents from hell.

Love between a man and a woman? Just *no*. He almost shuddered in disgust at the thought of being caught up in such a lie, such a cruel fabrication, coined to cover greed, lust, infidelity and ambition, all of which he had witnessed within his own *un*-family circles. He wasn't likely to ever be the kind of idiot who fell for that love fantasy with a woman. He was stronger than that, he knew better. He would be alone on his deathbed. Alone, he functioned better. Alone, he was happiest, hence his current solo voyage. When a woman asked him if he was a commitment-phobe, he just laughed because he was something worse than that. He had never *needed* anyone else in his life, not even as a child, and he could not imagine ever wanting a woman beside him for anything other than occasional sex.

Having eaten and set the world to rights inside his head, Sebastian sprang out of bed and went for a shower. True, the boat was tiny, there was a woman on it and he kept on bashing his head on ceilings and in doorways not intended for anyone of his height, but Reggie had promised to share his favourite fishing spot with him today and Sebastian was looking forward to kicking back with a beer, a rod and good company. Something that reminded him of a long-lost past, something so far removed from his usual daily schedule that it beckoned like an idyllic dream…

Bunny cleaned the galley, wondering how that oversized jerk on deck could imagine it was possible for her to provide more elaborate meals or choices in the minuscule space. When they took out a party of tourists, there was one basic lunch and that was that. She was no cordon bleu cook anyway. *Gloop?* And just assuming that Bunny was a nickname? Even though loads of people before Sebastian had assumed the same, she had got more than the drift of his meaning.

It *was* a horribly silly name and she had always been aware of it, even though her wretched family still rejoiced in it to the extent that it hadn't seemed worth the hassle of renaming herself for university as she had once intended. How would she ever have brought friends home who knew her by another name? And, of course, she had brought friends home, even though she hadn't wanted to, even though she would have loved to keep her new student life separate from her family. Finally, something for her and a little privacy, she had fondly believed.

But parents and big brothers who loved you interfered, needed to know, needed to be assured you were safe and she had gradually appreciated that that was the trade-off for all that love. And her family was always going to be like that, up there to their armpits in *her* business. At uni, however, she had met enough other people from less stable and caring families and had slowly learned the lesson that she had been lucky, luckier than she had ever realised with her nearest and dearest. Those from dysfunctional backgrounds could take out their pain on you if you weren't careful to avoid them, she conceded, her flushed face shadowing with bad memories she rarely took out. And she betted there was a bucketful of bad stuff behind Richie Rich with his Viking good looks and cold arrogance. He and she were complete opposites. Bunny liked everybody until they gave her reason to doubt them. Sebastian, it seemed, disliked them on sight.

Only not, clearly, Reggie, she acknowledged later that day, topping up the cool box with beers while the two men laughed and yarned over lazily dangling fishing rods. She was disconcerted, not having expected their passenger to be quite so relaxed with her boss. After all, there was nothing the least refined about Reg-

gie, a hardworking seaman on the brink of retirement
and at least twice Sebastian's age. Had she misjudged
him? Was it a clash of personalities? Had she said some
triggering word that had set him off to be unpleasant?
And why was it *still* bothering her? He was some foreign rich guy, whom she would never see again after
his week onboard ended.

Sebastian's gaze lingered on Bunny's struggle to cart
up and organise a large barbecue. Every fibre of his
being urged him to get up and help and his lean brown
hands tightened into fists as he resisted the urge to behave like the gentleman he had been raised to be, but
which he *wasn't* in any shape or form. Any attention at
all fed women of her ilk and encouraged them. True,
she hadn't looked even sidewise at him since he had
warned her off and he couldn't understand why that
heartening reality was now setting his teeth on edge.
It was as if there were a blank space where he was.
She didn't look, she didn't speak, she didn't even hang
around when her boss tried to engage her.

'She'd shout at you if you tried to help,' Reggie told
him without warning.

'Sorry?' For an instant, Sebastian was bewildered
by that advice.

'Saw you look at Bunny struggling with the barbecue and feel bad, just warning you she'd bite your nose
off if she thought you were treating her as less than a
man in the same job. She's very tough and independent,
not surprising with five brothers and an adoring family
always round her,' Reggie mused absently, stretching

back into his comfy old seat on deck and reaching for his beer again. 'Her mother is still sending her *care* packages every week even though she's on the other side of the world. I'm scared to tell her that every week her father or one of her brothers calls me checking that she's all right. They're smothering her alive and she's a good kid, hardworking, friendly, everything you could want on a boat like this…it's a shame.'

Sebastian did not respond because he was a sympathy-free zone, having no experience whatsoever of family fussing over him, not a one of them, even Loukia, whom he had loved. Too late had his grandmother realised what his childhood had been like and he could only assume that guilt had influenced her groundbreaking decision not to challenge the trust set up by his grandfather, guilt that she hadn't taken Sebastian in personally rather than palming him off on other family members. No doubt that was why he was now even richer than he had ever desired to be.

In his opinion, however, Reggie's little spiel only warned him that Bunny was spoilt and likely a brat if there was the remotest chance of her being rude to a customer or her boss. But even while he was thinking that he was closely watching every move she made as she squatted down to try again to level the legs of the barbecue, bent over it, peachy bottom flexing, plump breasts bouncing under her tee shirt. Not an ounce of fat on her except where a man wanted it, he noted, his zip tightening yet again across his groin.

His reaction infuriated him. There was just something strange about her that attracted him and, of course, he wasn't about to do anything about it, even as he saw the way the sunlight burnished her streaky blonde hair, the delicacy of her profile, the almost fairy-tale points of her ears. And what about what he was now *convinced* was the far from innocent stretching and bending and flexing of that erotic body in his presence? A simple display of the goods, he reckoned impatiently.

'How do your male customers take to her?' Sebastian enquired silkily.

Reggie dealt him a startled glance. 'Well, they *don't*, if you know what I mean. She doesn't encourage that kind of thing. She's a black belt in judo, as one of my over-friendly customers discovered last month. He was flat on his back and stuttering apologies by the time I came on them. Stupid drunk…!' the older man completed, using some Indonesian word that evidently hit the spot for him but which Sebastian, who spoke several languages, didn't recognise.

'I reckon she's too challenging for most young blokes…and then you've got her family to get past into the bargain,' Reggie remarked, vaulting upright with lean vigour and crossing the deck to take charge of levelling the barbecue while Bunny stood by with folded arms and a stubborn, irritated look on her face.

Too challenging? Sebastian concealed a smile, thinking that all he would have to do was snap his fingers and she'd drop into his hands like a ripe peach. Only he wasn't thinking of doing that, was he? No way was he ruining his week off with any of that nonsense! Sex was always available to him wherever he was in the world. In any case, he had made her hate him now and it would require effort to lure her back and he never, ever made an effort with women because that only encouraged their delusions of being important to him. No, Sebastian had tried-and-trusted methods of handling women and he wasn't planning to go off-piste any time soon.

Why the hell was that jerk always watching her? Bunny frowned down at the sizzling fish on the grill and swallowed hard. She was hot and she was tired because she had worked a long day. She shovelled her own meal on a plate and set it aside before carrying the men's plates over to the table already furnished with a bowl of salad, quinoa laced with Indonesian spices and the fresh bread she baked every day.

'You're not joining us *again*?' Reggie queried in surprise as she walked away with her own plate.

'No. Got a book waiting on me and maybe a swim afterwards,' she muttered, shooting a reluctant glance back even as Sebastian, utter hypocrite that he was, pulled out the third chair at the table as if keen to welcome her.

She went down to the galley, which was even hotter and more airless, and ate with more haste than enjoyment. Then she remembered that she hadn't changed the jerk's bed or his towels and she sped back on deck to cover that necessity.

His cabin was a tip of discarded clothes. Did he have servants who usually picked up after him? She tidied up as best she could, gathering up an impossibly soft fancy sweater in beige and noticing that the label was

Dior, momentarily drawing it to her cheek just to feel that incredible softness against her skin. It was probably cashmere and cost more than she had ever earned in a single year. The ridiculously evocative scent of his skin, citrusy, earthy, *sexy*, engulfed her. He smelled incredibly good.

Guiltily, she folded the garment up and put it back where she had found it, not wishing to be accused of snooping. She replaced the towels and cleaned the little bathroom quickly and efficiently, eager to escape even while she wondered why she had sniffed his jumper like some addict. She was embarrassed by that prompting and still questioning it when she emerged from the cabin again and ran slap bang into its occupant.

'Bunny…what were you—?'

'Cleaning and changing the linen. My job,' Bunny told him with a fixed smile.

Actually, he hadn't been challenging what she had been doing in his cabin. 'I don't need frills on this trip,' he told her, faint colour darkening his high cheekbones as he met green eyes cold as charity and conceded that he might have gone a little overboard in his determination to keep her at a distance.

'Changing beds and cleaning is the norm on this boat, sir. Usually there are six to eight passengers to look after, so one is nothing.'

'But you're already doing all the cooking…and other stuff,' Sebastian reasoned, wondering why he was even talking to her, wondering why he sounded as though he was trying to apologise when he was a man who would require torture before admitting to being in the wrong. He had done too much apologising as a kid and an adolescent, striving to meet the expectations of others. Back then he had been too naïve to see that the combination of his great wealth and his sky-high IQ simply rubbed people up the wrong way. With his horrendous background and experiences, those same people had happily expected him to be a loser, a whiner and a waste of space and had thoroughly disliked him for becoming a winner instead.

'That is my job…sir,' Bunny added curtly.

Sebastian folded his arms. 'I think we got off on the wrong foot. When I asked you not to speak to me, I didn't mean that I wanted you to isolate yourself on a boat this size!'

'No problem, sir,' Bunny said woodenly, hating him with such a passion that it was a marvel he didn't spontaneously combust in front of her. He didn't know what he wanted from her, service or normal, friendly assistance, but he had been super quick and keen to banish any prospect of normality.

'You're being oversensitive,' Sebastian informed her, stormy dark eyes flashing gold. 'I'm trying to say that you don't need to keep your distance from me. That day, I was in a mood.'

'Perhaps I prefer to keep my distance from you.' Bunny was getting madder and madder behind her set smile.

'No,' Sebastian contradicted with crisp bite. 'If you hadn't made it so obvious that you found me attractive when I arrived, I would never have reacted as I did. The initial fault was *yours*, not mine.'

CHAPTER TWO

BUNNY'S JAW DROPPED because she couldn't honestly credit that he had said that to her face. Or that he could be so shamelessly confident of his undeniably spectacular dark good looks that he flung it in her teeth full force to shame her.

Stunned green eyes lifted to his face. 'You're not a very nice person.'

'No, I'm not,' Sebastian agreed in a driven undertone, questioning exactly how, when he had approached her in an attempt to make amends, he had ended up losing his temper with her instead and giving her the facts as he saw them.

Bunny gritted her teeth because lying did not come easily to her. 'I do *not* find you attractive…except to look at,' she declared with gathering steam. 'Your personality is seriously wanting on several fronts.'

Sebastian was incensed beyond belief at that condemnation. No woman had ever talked to him like that. She was rude, offensive and…and without warning he was burning for the chance to snatch her off her feet and plonk her down unceremoniously on his cabin bed and prove that personality had nothing whatsoever to do with sexual chemistry. *That*, they had in spades, he conceded, hooded dark eyes keenly raking her flushed and furious face.

'Liar,' he chided softly with his slow-burning rarely seen smile.

Bunny's small face froze and paled as though he had slapped her. For a split second that dazzling smile of his unleashed butterflies in her stomach. She wanted to tell him that he was a four-letter word of a person but she wasn't about to start swearing for his benefit. How could he say that? How could he be so *sure* that she had momentarily looked at him much as if a famous movie-screen star had unexpectedly stepped on-board? Of course he was sure, an inner voice piped up. He was drop-dead gorgeous and thoroughly aware of the fact. Arrogant, vain and self-satisfied—everything she hated in the opposite sex and she had to get stuck with him on a stupid boat!

'Excuse me,' she said stiffly, bending to bundle up the giant pile of laundry. 'I want to get in a swim before dark.'

Sebastian suppressed a groan. Bunny, it seemed, was not easily placated. 'Look, before you make your boss suspicious, start joining us for meals,' he urged with finality before he disappeared into the cabin.

In receipt of that unsought advice, Bunny breathed in, deep and slow, and went down to her own cabin to don her serviceable swimsuit. Minutes later, she was diving into the turquoise crystal-clear water, sunlight dappling the surface and almost blinding her. Soon enough the sun would be sinking and darkness would fold in. Maybe tomorrow she would consider communal meals, she reasoned absently, questioning why she would do that when she knew Reggie well enough to know that he would never question what she did in her free time.

From the far end of the boat, Sebastian watched her slicing through the water with the confidence of a mermaid, the fading light silvering every slender line of her body, accentuating her grace. A breeze whipped across the sea and she turned and headed back to the catamaran. She grabbed up a colourful towel and wrapped it round her, walking past the wheelhouse to say, 'Anyone want anything? Drinks? Snacks?'

Sebastian stood up and tugged out the spare chair for her. 'Join us for a drink,' he urged.

'Just feeling too sleepy tonight,' she said with her easy smile, the most natural smile she had ever given him. 'Maybe tomorrow.'

And something inside Sebastian flipped in reaction to those sparkling green eyes and the oddest feeling of disappointment. That weird sensation shook him and thoroughly alarmed him. He didn't know what to do with it or even what it was. She was a stranger, she wasn't his familiar type of glossy, glitzy woman. She was poor and he was rich and he didn't do Cinderella. He was also never likely to be any woman's prince.

Wide sensual mouth compressing, Sebastian sank back into his own seat. Reggie trimmed the sails on the mast, muttering about there being nothing on the weather about a storm but that, even if it was the wrong season for one, he felt happier taking precautions because the wind was still getting up. Sebastian rose to help because, when he was a teenager, he had spent two years sailing a catamaran of his own. That was when he had come to terms with who he was, what he was and what he really wanted. He had adjusted to the challenge of being out in the real world, rather than in the monied goldfish bowl of privilege and low family expectations he had been raised in.

Below deck, Bunny settled into her bed, achingly tired but for that moment unable to sleep. She saw Sebastian's beautiful lean dark face afresh. Until him, she hadn't realised that a man could be beautiful or even that that single fact could be such a relentless draw for her. That was all that was the matter with her, she decided. It was just a stupid, physical thing. Nothing she need worry about. She didn't like him and that wasn't likely to change because he couldn't help himself and would probably screw up their next encounter. He had that rich, entitled vibe and she knew how a guy like that operated. Tristram had had the same vibe, same kind of fancy, aristocratic name, only she had been a very naïve teenager when she'd met him her first year of university. Shaking off those annoying memories, Bunny fell asleep.

When she wakened, she didn't at first realise why she was awake because it was still dark, only now the boat was rocking violently, and the wind was roaring. A storm, she registered in surprise, jumping out of bed fast and grabbing up her life jacket, throwing on her shoes and hurtling up topside to see if she could help.

A strange scene greeted her. The waves were terrifyingly high. Sebastian was nonetheless standing fully dressed like a statue while Reggie struggled frantically to tie down the mast. The mast had snapped and broken off low down, falling with sails still blowing madly. She was shocked, marvelling that such a thing could've happened, and she hastened over to Reggie, touching his back to let him know of her presence because the noise of the wind and the churned-up water made communication difficult. Why wasn't Sebastian helping? she wanted to ask and, since she couldn't, as Reggie whirled round she gestured at him and mouthed it.

Reggie yelled an answer but she didn't catch most of it, apart from, 'He's…stupid!'

He leant closer to her to make himself audible. 'Freak storm. Get him into the life raft with you. You've both got to get off *now*. She's heading for the reef and could capsize.'

'But what about you?' she shouted back in dismay.

'Staying with my boat. No arguments! Get on the *raft*!' Reggie framed rawly, his urgency and attitude cutting through her anxieties, sending her straight into crisis mode.

The first day she had started work with Reggie he had taught her what to do in an emergency. She sped with care through every step exactly as he had shown her and all the while the catamaran was being pitched through the water like a child's toy. It was the most terrifying experience she had ever had and she could not understand why the only other able-bodied male on board was doing nothing. Or why Reggie was taking her very firmly by the elbow and ensuring that she got off the boat onto the raft safely, although she stumbled and lost one of her shoes in the water. She watched while Reggie sped back in the teeth of the wind to escort Sebastian as if he were a child needing guidance to join her. She supposed some people just froze in an emergency and he was one of them, seemingly quite impervious to the need to protect himself. Reggie thrust Sebastian down to collapse his legs. He had all the self-determination of a zombie.

Reggie tapped his head and looked at Sebastian. She wasn't sure quite what he meant but she nodded and then her skipper cut the line to release the raft and she was crawling under the canopy, so scared she didn't want to even see the rolling height of the waves sending the raft spinning across the water in a manner that put new meaning into the concept of being seasick. Her tummy heaved and she tried every calming method of breathing that she knew, fighting to keep a hold of her brain and not panic. When she finally glanced in Sebastian's direction again, she saw the rain washing away the blood on his neck and she crawled forward in even greater dismay, finally registering that he could be acting strangely because he had been injured before she'd joined him and Reggie on deck.

Guilt filled her because she had judged him for his silent inactivity, she *knew* she had. Dazed dark eyes gazed past her rather than at her. Was he concussed? Where was the blood coming from? Steadying herself on a lean powerful thigh, she used her other hand to reach up but he was too tall and it was too much of a stretch for her in a moving life raft that didn't feel steady or safe. She yanked off her life belt and tossed it over Sebastian's head, tying it, aware that just then he needed it more than she did. She gave up on the immediate need to locate his injury and caught his hand instead, yanking at it to try and get him under the canopy with her and out of the rain and wind. He was in some kind of daze, unable to do what was best for himself, which meant that that role fell on her. And she only had emergency first-aid training.

'Sebastian!' she shouted to him, as loud as she could, and yanked at his hand again with emphasis and, after a pronounced pause, he shifted his hips and edged painfully slowly under the shelter of the canopy with her.

And then just when she thought that she was getting somewhere with him, he slumped down flat as a pancake and closed his eyes. So, it didn't matter when she had to repeatedly throw up over the side of the raft when it went careening across the waves again as if it were a roller coaster. It didn't matter either when nature called because there was nobody to see once Sebastian had passed out.

Dawn was moving in and the sea was no longer so rough when Bunny managed finally to ease his head up and examine what she could with her fingers. A massive bump and swelling, she registered in horror. He was injured and Reggie had known it. Stupid, she had caught that one word, but he could have been saying 'half-stupid', which meant an entirely different thing. She smoothed his long black hair off his brow because his usual man bun had bitten the dust on deck at some stage.

She scrabbled for the emergency rations, tugging

out the water with relief, not even caring about the brackish stale taste, only grateful that it was there. She shook Sebastian's shoulder but there was no rousing him. She rested a nervous hand on his chest, breathing again when she felt a strong, steady heartbeat. Somehow, she had to get water into him as well. She looked around. There was no land in sight, which was quite worrying when Indonesia rejoiced in almost eighteen thousand islands. Where were they anyway? Reggie had veered off his usual tried-and-trusted course, probably at Sebastian's behest, so when he came around, they would have a better idea of where they were, she thought hopefully.

The hours crawled past. She munched through a granola bar slowly and carefully. There were thirty days of rations on the raft. What had happened to Reggie? His wife would raise the alarm but not until the week's trip was officially past. Maybe he had managed to radio or call for help and survive. Her eyes stung. She was fond of Reggie, her father's old army mate. They would be found quickly, she assured herself, although the raft had been flung many miles from where *Merry Days* had lost her mast twelve hours earlier.

Sebastian stirred and instantly she was trying to get water into him. He grunted something and his eyes flew wide, finally focusing on her. He blinked. Still it seemed something of a blank slate.

'You need water,' she told him and his hand came up to grasp the bottle. 'You hit your head. You have concussion.'

He tried and failed to sit up and she guided the flow

of water for him, not wanting any wasted. He wouldn't eat the granola bar she showed him. He was as stubborn as a pig, which wasn't a surprise. His eyes eased shut again but she chose to be cheered by the reality that he was more aware than he had been the night before. And then some hours later finally she saw what she had been waiting for, what she had expected much sooner: the sight of land. She dug out one of the little oars that was more for steering than passage in readiness and then they were coming in closer and, before the current could control them again, she was frantically paddling towards that distant beach.

She felt the raft catch below on the reef. There wasn't much choice, she thought. She hadn't planned to land over a coral reef with sharp points that tore at the raft in shallow water but getting onto dry land was the objective, especially with Sebastian comatose beside her. She yanked at the life belt to waken him and he half lifted, muttering something in some foreign language, belatedly reminding her that although he spoke perfect English, it was not his native tongue.

'Sebastian, we've got to get onto the beach!' she yelled, that having become her natural way of addressing him.

'Why are you shouting?' he asked.

Bunny grinned, delighted that he was that much closer to the real world inside his head. 'We have to get out of the raft onto the beach.'

Sebastian peered over the side and, presumably having estimated the depth, vaulted upright to immediately vacate the raft, which took her aback. For a split second she simply sat there disconcerted by that instant action before paddling more urgently towards the shore because Bunny was in survivalist mode and she wanted what remained of the raft as part of a shelter, reluctant to let it drift off before she had used it to the utmost. Her arms were ready to fall off by the time she beached the raft, aching like the very devil, and, by then, Sebastian had already stalked up the white-sand beach and headed for the shade provided by an outcrop of rocks. She clambered out into the water on the soft sand and thought, as she leant back to pull the raft up onto the shore, Yeah, he's every man for himself in an emergency, just what you would've expected, just what you would've feared.

In shock she watched as Sebastian began to undress, arranging his fancy sweater, a tee shirt and chinos over the rocks to dry in the sun. Nice to be wearing underwear, she reflected, stuck in her soaked pyjamas. But Sebastian sported boxers and even though they were perfectly respectable, she supposed, there was an enormous amount of Sebastian exposed. Her feet faltered in face of all that semi-nude male. The sheer expanse of bronzed, darkly shadowed torso, the big biceps, the map of eight-pack abs and the elusive vee of sheer muscle disappearing into the boxers, along with the long, powerful, hair-roughened thighs, were a traffic-stopping sight. Colour burned her face. If you didn't have boundaries, Sebastian was the guy to be stuck on a desert island with. And if she had the gumption, she would just be stripping off as well, ignoring the fact she'd be naked, simply concentrating on the fact that her clothing was wet.

* * *

Who the hell was she? Sebastian was wondering. Was she a girlfriend, or a stranger? She knew his name so she had to know him but *how* did she know him? After all, *he* didn't know him, didn't know what he had been doing on a life raft, didn't seem to know what day it was, never mind where he was and what he was doing. He lifted his hand to his long loose black hair and that didn't feel right either. When had he grown his hair so long? He traced the swelling at the back of his head and he knew he'd had medical training at that point because a stream of innate diagnoses was filtering into his thoughts. He had concussion, likely severe concussion, a post-traumatic brain injury including some degree of amnesia. Why else couldn't he recall what he had been doing *before* he got injured? And why wouldn't he just instantly come clean with his companion about what had happened to him? Why did he have an instinctive belief that he couldn't trust anybody?

'Why are you not wearing a life belt?' Sebastian asked as she drew close.

'I put mine on you…you weren't in any fit state to be without one. How's your head?'

Just his luck to be shipwrecked with a saint, he thought and then was dismayed by that cynical thought. She had done a kind thing, careless of her own safety, and why the hell would he be judging her for it? No, he wasn't himself, the self he had been the last time he had been in Indonesia, and yes, he was convinced that that was where he was. The smell of the air, the incredible coral reef below the clear water, the jungle landscape behind him. It was all achingly familiar but he also knew that he wasn't the lanky teenaged boy he had been on his last trip. No, he was a fully grown adult male with a big blank inside his head as if a wall had been built the year he reached twenty, shutting him out from his full self.

'Aching,' he admitted.

'You should rest,' Bunny told him anxiously. 'You were unconscious on the raft and you need to take care of yourself.'

'Of course,' Sebastian agreed, scrutinising her in minute detail. She was wearing what he reckoned had to be pyjamas because they had rainbow-coloured little ponies all over them. And she was almost unbearably cute, very small, dainty, bedraggled blonde hair loose nearly to her waist, luminescent green eyes, so frank and open against bare natural, freckled skin. 'But first, I intend to check out this place.'

Bunny stiffened. 'What do you mean?'

'Is this an island or a peninsula? We need to work out where we are—unless you know?'

'No, I don't,' Bunny admitted, taken aback to be faced with full-force Sebastian again, switched back on after being a zombie without self-determination. All that large personality and domineering nature confronting her? It was almost frightening and she took an actual step back from him. 'We were off course and the storm blew us for miles over a lot of hours.'

'Where were we last you knew?'

Bunny winced. 'Reggie didn't discuss the trip with me. It wasn't his usual. As far as I'm aware it was in the direction *you* wanted to go and it was more remote,' she said uncomfortably.

'And Reggie?' Sebastian prompted.

'Reggie opted to stay with the catamaran, which he believed was about to drift onto the reef because the mast had snapped,' she explained dry-mouthed, wondering how many details he could recall, suspecting it would be few of the emergency that had landed them in unknown territory.

'So, you're crew and I was a passenger?'

'Not while we're *here*,' Bunny argued in a sudden urgent outburst. 'Here, wherever here is, we're *equals*!'

His ebony brows pleated. 'I wasn't aware that I was considering anything else. As I said, I'm off for a walk to explore this place.'

'Aren't you dizzy and weak?' Bunny pressed in growing astonishment.

'No, I'm not,' Sebastian lied without hesitation, spinning on his heel to walk down the beach past the rocks.

'What about your head?'

'A bruise and swelling. It'll be gone in a few days,' he said dismissively.

Bunny surveyed his bronzed back view with seething frustration. How was she supposed to let him walk off alone? Suppose he collapsed or fell? Wouldn't she be responsible for not taking better care of him? He wasn't sensible. How was that a surprise? And how was she supposed to control a man with such a dominant, forceful character? With a whip and a chair?

Snatching up a water bottle and a couple of the energy bars, she ran after him, drawing breathlessly level. 'Two heads are better than one.'

'Not in my experience,' Sebastian said smoothly, thinking of all the times during his education when stupid people had tried to misdirect his projects and derail him. He strode back down the beach to the raft and extracted the knife from the basic supplies. 'This should be useful.'

'Yes, I thought that we should stay on the beach and sort out some shelter for tonight.'

'We can still do that when we return.'

'But it could be dark by then!'

'I'll manage,' he assured her with complete confidence.

CHAPTER THREE

THEY FOLLOWED THE SHORE, sidestepping rocky out-
crops in silence, and nowhere out to sea could she see
any sign of other land but there was a misty haze in
the distance and it could be blocking a clear view. Her
legs got tired and keeping up with Sebastian was no
easy task but she refused to ask him to slow down. She
supposed he was right about the necessity of checking
out their surroundings first.

'What year is it?' he shot at her abruptly.

Disconcerted, she told him, and he nodded, pausing
to filch the water bottle from her and taking a swig,
before passing it back to her and fluidly sinking down
on the sand.

'Why did you ask me what year it was? Don't you
know?'

'Head injury,' he reminded her calmly. 'Time is a
bit confused for me right now. So…what's your name?'

'Bunny…no comments, please. You already made
them once before.' But that fast she was also wondering
why he didn't remember her name. 'Do you remember
the catamaran? Reggie?'

'Not yet,' he admitted flatly. 'No doubt it'll all come
back in good time.'

The last memory Sebastian had was of eating in a little bar at a harbour with his friends, who had drifted out to join him at different times that summer. Andreas had been there, his sister, Ariana, and a couple of others.

'Reggie's the skipper of the boat you hired on a private charter for a week. I'm afraid I don't even know how you got hurt. You were in a daze by the time I reached the deck in the storm,' she told him, handing him an energy bar.

Sebastian studied the bar and then accepted the inevitable: for now, it was all they had. He didn't think he had ever eaten anything that tasted like cardboard with grit before. Well, there was always a first time, but then survival on what he already suspected was a very small island would be a challenge even for him and he had cut his teeth on wilderness camping from an early age. Roughing it came surprisingly naturally to him. The horrors his relatives had heaped on him during his adolescence might actually turn out to be the key to survival. But what about her?

What about *Bunny*? Already skinny as a rail, wet clothes, legs trembling with a tiredness she struggled to hide, dark circles below her eyes. She had neither his strength nor, he believed, his high level of physical fitness on her side. Keeping Bunny breathing could be his biggest challenge. And she had given *him* her life belt! How could anyone be that selfless?

They rounded the cliff and then they were out on the far side of the island and Sebastian released a shout that startled her and started running down the beach. Bunny was so exhausted she wanted to fold where she stood but she kept on moving slowly in the same direction until she saw what had excited him. It was a little wooden pier poking out into the sea, an unlikely sign of human involvement in what seemed so far to be a small island wholly abandoned to the jungle and the birds. He disappeared from view, probably in the forlorn hope of finding a boat or a person, she guessed.

Sebastian was already surprising her on every level. He was very controlled and action orientated. He hadn't unleashed a single moan, the smallest hint of panic or even a word of complaint and yet, physically, he still had to be feeling pretty rough. Nor as a rich man could he be accustomed to moving out of his comfort zone. Their situation was hazardous and scary yet, if anything, danger appeared to fuel Sebastian's energy, lending a sharper edge to those shrewd dark eyes. And didn't he just look amazing clad only in a pair of cotton boxers, slung low on his lean hips? Her face burned and she scolded herself for noticing. He was as decent as he would've been in swimming trunks, which was, to be honest, *not* very decent.

Huffing a little from fatigue, she reached the pier and saw a small track leading through the dense overhanging trees. 'Sebastian!' she shouted, suddenly terrified of him vanishing and her being left alone.

'Over here!' he shouted back and then there was a deafening grinding, breaking noise that filled her with dismay and she pushed her woolly, heavy legs to move faster along the overgrown path until she arrived, shellshocked, in a clearing that contained a house, a very fancy house on her terms, with the look of an architect-designed contemporary building and a deck furnished with an array of outdoor seating littered with branches and leaves.

'Right...' Sebastian appeared in front of her and dropped down to scoop her off her feet without the smallest warning. 'Now you can rest and stop quaking with terror.'

'I am not quaking with terror! What the heck are you doing?' Bunny gasped in disbelief as he carried her towards the house.

'Taking care of you,' Sebastian responded calmly, elbowing open a door and carrying her indoors, past an inner courtyard crammed with jungle plants and a strange indoor pool set in marble.

Without hesitation he settled her down on leopard-print velvet sectional seating in what had to be the most luxurious reception room she had ever seen. 'Wh-where's the owner?'

Sebastian squatted down in front of her, brilliant dark eyes level. 'How would I know? I broke in.'

'You...*what*?' she yelped in horror.

'This isn't a game, Bunny, this is survival. Here we will...hopefully...have water and shelter.'

Bunny gaped at him with frank incredulity. 'But you can't just break into someone else's house!'

'If it comes to a choice between living or dying I can.'

'Don't be stupid!' Bunny slung back at him in a temper. 'We'll be arrested and thrown in a cell!'

Sebastian chuckled. 'Someone has to rescue us first. I think I'll take that risk over being stuck here without shelter and the necessities of life. Now wait here until I can hopefully find you something to change into. Right now, in those wet pyjamas, you're asking for pneumonia and there's not enough flesh on your bones to stave it off.'

'We *can't* stay here, Sebastian,' Bunny moaned and with considerable personal regret on her own account. 'It's somebody's home.'

But Sebastian had already disappeared again. She blinked and literally felt herself zone out for a timeless period and it wasn't until Sebastian reappeared and tossed a man's shirt on her lap that she returned to the present.

'Can't stay here,' she mumbled afresh like a vinyl record stuck in a groove.

'Take off the damp clothing and put on the shirt,' Sebastian instructed impatiently. 'Because if you don't, I'm going to do it for you.'

'Like you would dare!'

'I would dare,' Sebastian assured her.

'Well, go away so as I can change.'

'Modesty in this situation is ridiculous,' Sebastian said very drily.

'Give me a break,' she muttered, and he strode over to the windows and slowly and rather ostentatiously turned his back on her. Unconcerned by that display, Bunny ripped off her pyjamas at speed and put on the plaid cotton shirt, shivering as she clumsily did up the buttons to cover her cold, clammy skin. Until that moment, she hadn't realised how cold she actually was.

'Now go for a sleep,' Sebastian told her.

'But—'

'You're dead on your feet and I don't want you getting sick.'

Bunny tugged a cushion under her head and curled up, too tired to deal with Sebastian, in truth too tired to deal with anything at all. The storm, the frightening sleepless night on the raft and the long hours that had followed were just a tangled jumble of shocking imagery inside her head. Something soft landed on top of her and she snaked her icy toes into the warmth it offered, her eyes sliding shut.

Sebastian was tired too, but he wanted to get the solar power on and the water running before he went to sleep and then had to waken in the dark. That achieved, he placed a lamp beside Bunny so that she wouldn't panic when she awoke and then he folded himself down on the opposite leg of the sectional. The more he looked at her, the more beautiful she seemed to be. There was just something about her face, that particular arrangement of features, the delicate arch of her brows, the clarity of her big eyes, the smooth line of her nose and the natural pink of her lips, he reasoned absently, lost in a sense of fascination new to him. At least, it *felt* new.

Why was he so eager to look after her? Was there something crucial that he had forgotten? Had they been intimate on that boat? And what had he been doing on what sounded like a small boat in any case? It didn't make sense…none of it made sense and, on that edge of frustration, Sebastian finally slept.

Bunny opened her eyes and just lay there, listening to the incredibly noisy chatter of birds at dawn and, beyond that, the most glorious quiet, empty of other people's noises and traffic. Just about there she remembered that her student days were finished, and her eyes flew wide on an unfamiliar ceiling before lowering to take in the oil paintings of birds on the wall, the antique-looking bronze statues, carved mask faces and other paraphernalia displayed across a sleek, sealed glass display unit. It was someone's collection of Indonesian artefacts and a sobering reminder that she had spent the night in someone else's home without their permission. She was startled into sitting straight up and standing. There was no sign of Sebastian.

There was no reasonable explanation for why she panicked when he was out of view. Maybe it was because being marooned on a rather small island with few, if any, edible resources was scary, but Sebastian seemed to have survivalist instincts that beat hers hands down. A more pressing need to find facilities, if there even were any indoors, gripped her and she went off to explore and found a door into a cloakroom behind that inside pond thing in the foyer. An ancient, battered man's jacket hung on the single peg. Not an owner with many visitors, she reckoned. In truth, a working facility with running water interested her much more just then. She studied the pond, empty of water, fish or greenery, and shrugged before heading down the corridor to find a staircase, which she climbed.

The whole time she was snooping, she was telling herself that Sebastian was right and they had to make the best of whatever fate had dealt them. There were only two doors, one of which led into a massive bedroom and en-suite bathroom. A door still hung open on a sparsely filled built-in closet, which Sebastian must've rifled through the night before to give her a shirt. The bathroom had a separate shower and bath, the appointments as opulent in finish as the huge four-poster steel bed, festooned with thin silky drapes to keep out insects at night. Giant windows overlooked the island interior and one set opened out onto a balcony with a single seat. The view over the palm trees and exotic jungle vegetation was magnificent and yet, even in the sunlight, it made her shiver and withdraw indoors again, painfully aware of their isolation and disconnection from the modern world.

Wouldn't the owner of such a fantastic house have an Internet connection and a computer? Heart hammering, she opened the second door into a home office with a desk but there was no tech in there of any kind and she left the room again with a grimace. Before she went downstairs again, she couldn't resist switching on the bathroom shower just to see if it worked and when it did, she was out of her borrowed shirt within seconds and stepping beneath that warm, rather than hot, flow. She didn't take her time. She washed and shampooed fast, unsure how much water she dared use. Emerging, she grabbed a towel and dried herself in guilty haste before donning the shirt, which was at least relatively clean even if she had slept in it.

She trod back down the stairs, embarrassed at having used the unknown owner's comb to untangle her long, knotty hair. When she walked through the last downstairs door, she found the kitchen: a gleaming state-of-the-art installation with stainless-steel utilities that looked as if it had never been used. A man's apron hung incongruously on another single peg. It was the cupboards that she was keenest to investigate in her search for food and just when she feared she'd drawn a blank she opened a large larder cupboard and found it packed with dry goods. Flour, coffee, sugar, salt, rice, pasta, quinoa and, below that, shelves of tins. Relief swept her in a wild rolling wave because with water, food and shelter they could manage for weeks, and surely it wouldn't *be* weeks before they were found?

Reggie would've called for help...but had he had time in the midst of that terrifying storm? And if he *hadn't* survived there would be no one alerted to their plight until his absence was noted. So, nothing certain, nothing sure as far as rescue went, she conceded reluctantly. Right now, they were stuck on this island in this house for the foreseeable future. The hungry growl in her stomach reminded her that she had more important things to concentrate on: food, because she was starving.

Sebastian returned from a busy morning on the beach, having gathered up his dry clothes from the rocks on his way, checked out the ripped remains of the life raft and set up a marker bonfire at the foot of the island. He walked back into the house and heaved a sigh, knowing that he had to eat. He was stunned into initial silence when he saw Bunny busily moving round the kitchen, covered in a giant navy apron.

'Who turned you into a Stepford wife?' he quipped.

Bunny froze and then spun round, a smile lighting up her face. 'Where have you been?' she demanded automatically. 'I mean, what is there to do out there? Where is there to go?'

Sebastian grinned with intense pleasure. 'Is this what being married feels like?'

A wash of pink swept over her expressive face and she turned away. 'I'm sorry, I—'

Amusement quelled, Sebastian rested his hands down on her narrow shoulders and turned her back from the sink where she was draining rice. 'It's okay. I was only teasing. You're very sensitive, aren't you?' he murmured, staring down at her with dark eyes lit by shades of caramel in the sunlit kitchen. 'Don't be that way with me. I'm…outspoken, loud, abrasive but I don't mean any actual harm.'

For an instant, Bunny was absolutely frozen where she stood, lost in the hold of those lustrous eyes of his and the kindness she saw there that he had not shown an ounce of on *Merry Days*. It made her feel all warm and soft inside, it made her want to stretch up and kiss him, a prompting that shook the life out of her and made her pull free and return to the rice.

'You're just in time to eat,' she muttered, shocked by the butterflies in her tummy, the clenching deep down inside. 'I'm afraid it's not cordon bleu exactly, it's tinned frankfurters and sauce and rice.'

'I'll go fishing for us.'

'That sweater needs washing,' she scolded. 'Although I doubt you'll ever get the bloodstains out of it.'

Sebastian laughed. 'Could I care less?' He tilted his head to one side, amusement glittering in his eyes and the curve of his mobile mouth. 'I don't think so but there is a washing machine in the utility area.'

'What utility area?'

As she was putting the food out, Sebastian crossed the kitchen to pull open the hidden door in the wall panelling. She finished setting the plates on the table and walked through. A complex array of levers, buttons and controls almost covered one entire wall and on the other sat a washing machine. 'So there's enough water here to use it freely?' she asked.

'Yes, it's a very expensive system, which I got working.'

'You did?'

'The power was off when we arrived and the water pump.'

Bunny nodded as she sat down at the table. 'So, you know how to work that kind of stuff?'

Sebastian shrugged rather than admit that he had been taken aback by how immediately he had grasped how everything worked, that he evidently knew and understood a lot about sustainable energy and, also, tech stuff. Last night he had dreamt of an algorithm that was somehow crucially important and his fingers had been flying over a keyboard. Piece by piece, who he was ten years on was emerging.

'I'd have been lost. I'm great with books, not so great at the practical stuff.'

He frowned. 'Books?'

'Yes, I'm starting my first job as a librarian when I get home… Gosh, it's only days away,' she voiced in consternation. 'Do you think they'll hold the job for me if I don't turn up?'

'You need to relax for now. I doubt if anyone even knows we're missing yet,' Sebastian said and, although she had thought the same thing herself, it still cast her down to hear his confirmation of it.

'My family will be worrying. They're used to hearing from me every day.'

'*Every* day?' Sebastian said in wonderment at such family attention and affection as he lifted his knife and fork. 'You're British, aren't you?'

'Yes.'

'And you're this far from home and they're still expecting to hear from you *every* day?' he prompted. 'What age are you?'

'Twenty-three.' Bunny had flushed with embarrassment. 'We're just a very close family.'

Sebastian quirked an eloquent ebony brow. 'Did I sleep with you on that boat?' he asked without the smallest warning and with the utmost casualness.

Bunny almost choked on the food in her mouth. 'Er…no, that would be a definite no, Sebastian. In fact we didn't take to each other at all at first meeting.'

And then immediately he had to know all about that

and she wished she had kept her tongue still in her mouth and said nothing, because she was forced to recount that story.

A faint flush highlighted his stunning cheekbones. 'I was rude to you...why?'

Bunny actually grimaced. 'Apparently you got the impression that I was attracted to you and you didn't like that.'

Sebastian nodded reflectively as he pushed the empty plate away, not enjoying what he was learning about his current self. Arrogant, rude, hurtful to a subordinate and all the things he had sworn never to be once he grew up.

'And was I right?' he prompted softly.

Bunny compressed her lips and tried to be the bigger, better person, who didn't lie. 'Yes, you were right, but nothing would have happened between us anyway because I'm not that kind of person.'

'And what kind of person is that?' he pressed. 'Considering that most of us have sex in our lives.'

'I wasn't being judgemental. I was just saying that I wouldn't sleep with someone only on the boat for a week's break!' Bunny fielded more sharply, her colour high, her exasperation with him extreme because he had no tact whatsoever. She rose and piled the plates and moved away from the table.

'Why?'

As she settled the plates into the sink, she was ready to scream. 'I'm not interested in one-night stands and I wouldn't embarrass Reggie, who is a good friend of my father's—'

'So, you wouldn't want word of your sex life travelling home? Is this Reggie that indiscreet?'

Bunny whirled round in a fury. 'Drop the subject, Sebastian, before I explode! We did not share anything on the boat but mutual antipathy, I assure you!'

'I appreciate that you find this discussion trying but I had to know how we interacted prior to coming here because I'm *very* attracted to you and I have to know where I stand with you.'

And with that, Sebastian sprang up with infuriating calm and walked out of the kitchen.

I'm very *attracted to you.*

Bunny was astonished. *That* hadn't occurred to her as a possibility on the boat or since. All of a sudden, he was forgiven for being so blunt and mortifying her. She understood now. That was why he had asked if they had had sex. He didn't remember the boat. But was being very attracted to her why he had been rude in the first place? No, that made no sense. He must've realised *after* he boarded. Bunny smiled. Well, fancy that!

Not that anything was likely to happen between them, of course. She and Sebastian were ships that passed and she didn't do casual. And wasn't that unfortunate? Bunny had only one man in her past and she had been in what she'd believed was a monogamous relationship with Tristram for most of the time they had been at university together. And then it had fallen apart once she'd discovered that he had been cheating on her all along. Even worse, she had learned that most of her friends and *all* of his had known that he was cheating. People didn't want to get involved these days but even though she understood that her friends had been afraid of telling her the truth, she still thought they could have hinted in any number of ways that Tristram led a double life. After all, her health could have been compromised by his infidelity.

Sebastian's sheer honesty was remarkably appealing to her at that moment as she relived that past. After what her family called the 'Tristram treachery', Bunny had been well warned not to get too involved with anyone she met fleetingly on her travels. And even though she was twenty-three and no longer an innocent, she had stuck to that rule to protect herself from further hurt. Not quite, though, how an adult woman should behave, she found herself thinking, dissatisfied with that fresh view of herself. Tristram had been a lying, cheating creep but she knew that not all men were the same.

She walked out of the kitchen and eventually walked round the whole house to establish that Sebastian had gone.

But he couldn't go far, she reminded herself as she made her way down to the beach. There was no sign of him and she set off along the shore, bare feet crunching on white sparkly sand in the sunlight. The island was divine from the lush green vegetation to the colourful birds and the empty beach of a dream holiday destination. But because she was stuck there against her will, it somehow felt like a prison. A prison with... *Sebastian*?

That was a whole other story, she conceded with a helpless grin. Few women would complain about being marooned with Sebastian. She would never have dared break into a stranger's house. He'd got them off the beach, he'd got the bathroom working and the power on. Even without his striking resemblance to a screen-star fantasy male, he would deserve an accolade for those accomplishments alone.

She was taken aback by the sight of Sebastian feeding a small bonfire at the bottom end of the island, near where they had arrived the day before. Only the *day* before, she reminded herself, and it was already shocking her that she felt so relaxed with him, as if he were a close friend, rather than a near stranger. Really, Bunny, she castigated herself, is this how you react to a very hot guy who admits that he finds you very attractive?

'So, this is what you've been at…you could've told me,' she remarked, striving not to be affected by the image of Sebastian in sunlight. He stood there so very tall and broad, luxuriant black hair tousled, dark eyes golden enticement in daylight and so handsome he made her teeth clench. 'I could've helped gather wood.'

'There are snakes in the undergrowth.'

And she couldn't help it, she shivered, not being a snake kind of girl. 'Why a bonfire? Hoping for passing shipping to notice?'

'I haven't seen a single boat since we arrived. No, the house obviously has a caretaker and presumably he's not that far away.'

'How do you know it has a caretaker and not just an owner?'

'There's no dust and nothing personal left in the house aside from that collection of his and the paintings. The pool in the foyer has been emptied because, whoever he is, he's not been visiting much, but I believe the house is still being checked on at least a monthly basis,' he contended. 'If the caretaker sees smoke and we're even distantly in view of him, he will visit.'

'He might ask the police to visit.'

'Even better,' Sebastian contended with blazing confidence.

'I can't speak Indonesian beyond hello, goodbye and thanks,' she admitted.

'I speak enough to get by,' Sebastian said carelessly as she drew level. 'I spent a lot of time here sailing and exploring when I was a teenager.'

'With your parents?'

His lean strong features tightened. 'No, they...died years before.'

Embarrassed she had asked, Bunny nodded. 'That's tough.'

'Not really, particularly not when I see the level of supervision you're still receiving from yours,' Sebastian traded scathingly and then he stilled and frowned. 'My apologies, I shouldn't have said that.' In an abrupt volte-face, Sebastian bent down to grab up wood to feed the fire, his lithe, powerful length silhouetted against black swirling smoke.

But he had been deflecting sooner than address the topic of parents, Bunny recognised, wondering why that was such a sore spot apart from the obvious reason of loss, particularly when that loss had taken place years back in his distant past. At most, she reckoned he was in his very early thirties, and it was a little odd to still be *that* sensitive. Only what did she know about such emotions when she had yet to lose anyone she loved?

Surely, she *had* to know about his parents, Sebastian was thinking. Everyone knew that horror story! He was the survivor of his family, a victim, which he hated to acknowledge especially when the relatives treated him as though he were mentally unstable and somehow fatally contaminated like his late father. Arrogant much, Pagonis? Of course, not every chance-met stranger knew his history but, with his inherited wealth, people were usually quick to look him up online and then they found out because it was all still out there for anyone to see.

'How much do you know about me?' Sebastian shot at her without warning.

'Nothing, well…three facts. I know your first name and that you were born in Greece and that there's a rumour that you're very rich,' she told him uneasily.

'Didn't you look me up online?'

'Not on my phone budget on a boat abroad,' Bunny admitted. 'I usually use the bar at the harbour for Internet access and send messages or call home while I'm there. I've lived on the boat since I arrived. What's your surname? Would I know it?'

'A lot of people do… Pagonis.'

'Sorry, not familiar at all. Pagonis…' she sounded out absently.

Sebastian was amused, oddly relieved by her ignorance of his background. For once, it seemed, he was on a level playing field with a woman. 'And yours?'

'Woods…'

Sebastian flung back his handsome head and laughed with appreciation. 'Bunny Woods. Nobody was thinking too hard when they named you, but you are undeniably cute.'

Bunny went pink and collided with smouldering dark golden eyes that burned through her like a shot of adrenalin. She rushed into speech. 'I was thinking that we could make a big SOS message on the beach with stones or shells or something...seaweed?' she asked uncertainly. 'In case a plane flies over. I know we haven't heard any yet, but we should be prepared just in case.'

'That's a good idea,' Sebastian commented, walking over to her, lean hands lifting to rest lightly on her slight shoulders. 'Are you going to feel threatened if I kiss you?'

'Will *you*? No telling what a sexually deprived woman might do to a man without backup on a remote island,' she teased.

'No telling.' Enjoyment gleamed in Sebastian's heavily lashed eyes, whirls of caramel and whiskey shades in the darkness of those eyes that made her heart beat so fast, it felt as if it were sitting right at the back of her throat. Her bare feet felt welded to the sand as though she couldn't have moved even if she had wanted to. She was feeling an excitement absolutely new to her that she had not known even in the heady first days with Tristram, and that sense of thrilling anticipation was uniquely seductive. Of course, deep down inside, she expected to be vaguely disappointed as usual.

Sebastian gazed down into her intent green eyes, a sort of witchy green, he decided. He remembered hanging an old green glass fishing buoy in a window as a kid, daydreaming that it was a magic witch's ball that he could somehow escape his life through. He didn't know what it was about Bunny, but she soothed him in some weird way, made him want to be a better man than he believed he was. The way he had spoken to her when he boarded that boat? As if she were nothing, nobody. He didn't want to be that man but, apparently, he *was* that man ten years at least down the road.

He ran slow fingers across her delicate collarbone, tracing it, following the line of her slender neck, cupping her pointed chin, and then let go, bending to lift her gently off her feet and rest her down horizontally on the sand. 'No way of doing this comfortably when we're standing. You are way too small and I am way too tall,' he sighed, folding down and holding his weight off her with one powerful arm.

'You about to whip out a tape measure or kiss me?'

'I didn't want to scare you.'

'I get that…but *still* waiting here,' she countered with a lively smile of one-upmanship.

And then he just kissed her, kissed her long and deep and slow and every nerve ending in her body came alive as though it was a celebration rather than an experiment on her part. Never had she felt like that before. Never had anything felt so intense that her entire body felt engaged in a cliff-edge scream for more. The delve of his tongue made her spine arch and jack-knifed her up into closer contact. And he came down on top of her in a wildly hungry kiss that sent every nerve ending in her body pulsing and begging. Her nipples tightened into hard buds as his chest shifted over hers and a throbbing helpless heat pooled between her thighs. And it was too soon, way too soon for that and way too *dangerous*, her brain shouted at her, dragging her free of the erotic spell he cast. She liked to think through such actions, to look and ponder before she leapt. Sebastian intoxicated her and on some level that was as scary as it was exhilarating.

Opting out, Bunny tried to shift sideways, which was impossible beneath his weight, but he got the message and folded back onto his knees. 'For one kiss, that was amazing.'

'Who are you trying to kid? That was at least ninety-five kisses. Take your clothes off,' she told him, eying the blood stain on that gorgeous sweater.

For a split second, Sebastian froze and then vaulted upright as Bunny got up as well. He peeled off the sweater and the tee shirt, embarked on his salt-stained chinos, only to freeze as she yelped, 'No, not the boxers too!'

No, not a shy bone in this guy's body, she thought with roaring appreciation as she gathered up the sweater, tee shirt and chinos and turned on her heel to head smartly back to the house.

'Where are you going?'

Bunny flipped him a glance over her shoulder and laughed. 'I'm planning to try out the washing machine…'

She swore that she would cherish the incredulous look on Sebastian's darkly handsome face until her dying day.

CHAPTER FOUR

'YOU'RE CLEVER,' SEBASTIAN commented over an evening meal of freshly grilled fish, which he had supplied, and freshly made bread, which she had baked.

'How?' she challenged although she knew perfectly well, for that afternoon had passed with both of them laying out an SOS message on the beach on both sides of the island. Palm leaves weighted down with stones had worked the best. And Sebastian had been kind of quiet and broody.

'When you told me to undress, you *knew* what—'

'Of course, I did,' she said lightly. 'But it's not that simple, Sebastian. I'm not ready to take that step with you.'

His wide sensual lips compressed hard. 'That's fine.'

'And maybe you haven't thought of it, but I have… Have you any contraception?'

His ebony brows lifted and dropped again, his lustrous dark eyes steady while his lush black lashes dipped. 'As a matter of a fact, no. But surely *you*—?'

'What I was using was left behind on the catamaran.'

In the simmering silence, Sebastian breathed in deep and smiled at her, a level smile that surprised her. 'I should've thought of that aspect. I'm afraid I didn't.'

'And I'm afraid I'm naturally sensible and cautious,' Bunny confirmed quietly.

'As a rule, I am too,' he told her, his brilliant dark eyes narrowing. 'But, *not* with you for some reason. Don't look so anxious. But I will certainly cherish that moment when you told me to take my clothes off for many years…and then took them away to wash them.'

'I didn't want to argue with you. I didn't want a confrontation.'

'Listen…' Sebastian closed a hand over hers with complete casualness and smiled at her. 'A woman doesn't ever have to apologise for being clever when she's saying no. I'm not the type of guy who will ever quarrel with that but, be warned, I *am* the kind of man who will think of all the *other* things we can do.'

'Understood,' she said a little breathlessly, her colour high.

'You've been bitten,' he pointed out, indicating the swelling on her arm.

'Last night,' she said with a shrug.

'You won't be bitten tonight. We're both sleeping with the insect drapes around us upstairs.'

Bunny bit at her lower lip.

'And you will be perfectly safe in that bed with me,' Sebastian assured her smoothly.

Bunny didn't think she would be safe even in an Arctic environment with Sebastian, never mind a big, comfy bed. Furthermore, her pyjamas weren't dry as yet, which meant sleeping in the shirt again. She breathed in deep and asked herself if she was really that concerned. And she wasn't. She trusted Sebastian, didn't know why but she simply did. In her opinion he was too outspoken to be a habitual liar.

'How long do you think it will take for us to be found?'

'It could be a couple of weeks until a search finds us and I doubt if we're even officially missing yet. We'll conserve the tinned and dried goods and I'll fish,' Sebastian informed her.

Bunny tried not to think of the horror that would assail her family when or if they were informed that she had gone missing at sea. In an effort to move on from that thought, she said, 'Who do you think owns this place?'

'A keen birdwatcher with enough cash to build his dream hideaway in the back of beyond,' Sebastian opined with a frown. 'Someone older than us, I suspect, and there's no sign of a woman or guests ever having been here. I'll compensate the owner for everything we've used, broken or ruined.'

'I suppose that's all you can do,' Bunny muttered, thinking that there really wasn't anything else to eat on the island unless they started trapping birds and she recalled Reggie telling one of their hunting-mad passengers that it was forbidden on most of the islands they visited.

She tried to get into a book on birds and soon found herself yawning. Sebastian had taken himself off again. He was like that: restless, always needing an occupation or a challenge. She went upstairs and had a brief shower, put a replacement head on the electric toothbrush and freshened up. Pleasantly sleepy, she unfurled the drapes right round the bed and crept in one side. She wondered if she should put a pillow down the middle of the mattress and grimaced at an idea that would only make Sebastian laugh at her.

A while later, she was vaguely aware of Sebastian's return, the sounds of him undressing, the beat of the water in the fabulous shower and she turned towards him as the mattress gave beneath his weight.

'Go back to sleep,' he whispered.

'My mind is too busy. I was thinking of the last time I shared a bed on a regular basis… Not a happy place to revisit,' she muttered ruefully and ready to kick herself.

Sleepy Bunny was confiding Bunny, Sebastian registered, and he grinned. 'Something bad happen?'

'My ex had been cheating on me from the start and I was with him for over two years before I found out. How sad is that?'

'Are *you* still sad about it?'

'Heavens, no! It's way over a year since we broke up. I'm only sad that I didn't catch on sooner. I wasted a lot of time at uni with him when I could've been out having fun.'

'Learn from it,' Sebastian advised, sliding an arm round her and easing her closer. 'Don't get all your hopes and dreams tangled up with one person. It doesn't work. People almost always let you down.'

And where did that depressing belief come from? Sebastian questioned inwardly, positively chilled by what he had said. People could be fast friends and dependable. Yes. He had collided with a lot of the other sort in life but the few close friends he had he trusted completely.

'Kiss me goodnight,' he said abruptly.

'It won't stop at one kiss.'

Sebastian laughed with rich appreciation. 'Is that me or you you're condemning?'

'Both of us,' she traded, her cheek resting against his shoulder, her body relaxing into the heat and the already familiar scent of him. 'Let's be sensible.'

'I don't think I've ever heard a gloomier piece of advice from a woman.'

'You're more daring than me.'

'Daring is more fun,' Sebastian chided, rolling over and gazing down at her in the moonlight, his tousled dark head descending slowly.

And she knew he was giving her time to pull away if she chose but her brain was preoccupied with wondering if she had had *any* fun since childhood. She didn't think so, aside from the very occasional night out with friends. She had toed the line Tristram had laid out like that Stepford wife that Sebastian had mentioned, and the memory stung. Her ex hadn't liked her going out with friends but most likely, she acknowledged now, that had been because he was afraid of her seeing him out cheating on her. It struck her that she had spent most of her life doing what other people believed she should do, first her family and then her ex.

Irritated by that thought that she had never yet claimed the freedom to be herself, she tipped her head back and trailed her soft full lips over Sebastian's and he took the hint like a trooper. She was a little better prepared for that sensual onslaught than she had been earlier in the day.

Even so, that unfamiliar jolt of pure excitement still shook her up. He was one hell of a kisser. Fingers sliding through her hair, he flattened her to the bed and kissed her breathless. She was conscious of every hard, sculpted angle of his big, powerful physique. A little shiver feathered through her in response to the hard masculine arousal pressed against her. And then before she could even catch her breath, Sebastian was pulling back and settling her back on her own side of the bed.

'Night, Bunny.'

'Night,' Bunny whispered shakily, knowing she wished he hadn't stopped, knowing she had been burning up to touch him and feel him touch her, but clearly the fun had gone out of it for him. Served her right too for holding so fast to her boundaries. She wasn't a teenager any more or a born-again virgin. Tristram had taught her a hard lesson but he hadn't broken her, hadn't reduced her to a timid woman, afraid of her own shadow or her desires.

Why wasn't she being honest with herself? She wanted Sebastian more than she had ever wanted any man and she might never get another chance to explore that side of herself with such a perfect partner. Sebastian was experienced, sophisticated, gorgeous… Tick, tick, tick, he checked every box. In addition, she was never going to see him again once they got off the island and wasn't that even more perfect? Sebastian as a wicked one-off experience? Wasn't that much safer than attaching all sorts of foolish emotions to how he could make her feel? And then another rather frightening thought occurred to her and she burst into speech.

'You're not married or engaged or anything…are you?'

Sebastian froze. 'Absolutely not. I'd be wearing a wedding ring if I was married and I've never seen the point in engagements.'

And all of that was true…totally, sincerely true.

'I didn't think so but I found myself needing to check,' Bunny muttered and, before she could lose her nerve, she slid under the sheet that covered them, small smooth hands travelling across his torso and down a long, powerful, hair-roughened thigh.

And Sebastian jerked rigid with shock, total, complete shock as his somewhat proper, blushing companion set about boldly pleasuring him. Just as quickly he relaxed back in the moonlight, enchanted by her sheer unpredictability and the discovery that she could make him crave her caresses like a narcotic. She wasn't skilled or practised but she made up for that with enthusiasm. It wasn't very long before Sebastian was pushing the sheet back, tossing it back out of reach when she tried to hide below it again and long brown fingers settled into the silky depths of her hair to encourage her as his hips rose. He pulled away from her to climax with a guttural groan and flopped back against the pillows.

'That was unbelievably good. I suspect we're both stressed as hell in this situation,' Sebastian sighed as he tugged her back to him. 'And now it's my turn.'

'Nobody needs to take turns!' Bunny gasped, already embarrassed by the intimacy of what she had chosen to do.

'I'm eager to touch you, so no invitation is required,' Sebastian groaned, leaning down to kiss her with languid expertise, his tongue darting, his fingers releasing the buttons on the shirt she wore one by one.

Bunny dragged in a stark breath, insanely conscious of the tightness of her nipples and the heavy ache at the heart of her. He spread the shirt open, kissed her again, slowly, savouring her response. And she thought, This is not me, I am not a fun girl, I'm serious and I don't fool around.

But is that set in stone? another voice demanded. Or can you go off the rails now and again? She was going off the rails but what did it say about her that she didn't *care* just at that moment?

His big hands covered her breasts, teased at her nipples and a slight sound escaped her lips as he shifted position, moving over her, bringing his mouth down to her breasts, toying with the tender tight peaks until she squirmed, hot liquid heat pooling in her pelvis.

'May I put the light on? I want to see you.'

Her teeth clenched on a negative. She was accustomed to the privacy of the dark but with Sebastian, she reckoned, she should've known better. 'If you like...'

He leant over her and lamplight momentarily blinded her. Sebastian gazed down at her anxious face, stunning black-lashed dark eyes intent on her. 'Stop freaking out.'

'I'm not freaking out!'

'It's in your eyes, *kounelaki mou,*' he commented.

'Yet you didn't freak out on the life raft or during the storm, did you?'

'I was freaking out inside myself.'

'But you handled it, so why can't you handle me doing a perfectly normal thing like admiring these very pretty breasts?' he asked softly, one big hand cupping her pert, swollen flesh while his thumb rubbed at the straining pink tip.

And she shivered with reaction, entrapped by his spellbinding gaze until he dropped his head and laved that prominent peak with his tongue before tugging at it with his lips. She closed her eyes and relaxed a tiny amount because he was moving slowly, gently. She tensed when his hand travelled over her stomach and roamed further south, probing the soft damp curls on her mons, teasing her slender thighs apart and then she literally jerked when he stroked her where she so ached to be touched, and her face burned. The first hints of pleasure were almost all-consuming, her hips lifting and tiny noises escaping her as he teased her sensitive entrance.

'You're so wet, so tight,' he husked, shimmying down her body and disconcerting her more than a little by settling himself between her thighs.

'Oh, you don't need to do *that*,' she muttered in mortification because her one and only lover had cringed at the very prospect.

'I want to. I very much want you to enjoy being with me.'

'Oh?' She had nothing to say to that, hadn't really believed that some men thought like that, and she didn't want him to stop what he was doing. Indeed, just then she was on the edge of anticipation as he explored her where she tingled and *needed*. The pulse of hunger climbed ever higher.

And just there the dialogue died because rather suddenly she couldn't have vocalised a word. Sebastian devoured her like a man at a banquet who hadn't eaten in days and she was shocked by that hungry passion for *her* body while she was overwhelmed by sensation. The pleasure built and built like a knot tightening ever more inside her until all she could do was yield to it as he drove her to a peak and she cried out loud as explosive pleasure gripped her, her fingers lost in the luxuriant depths of his hair as her spine arched and blissful waves of delight convulsed her. The fact that she had reached a climax, that there had been no need to fake it, shook her the most.

'Wow,' she mumbled in a wobbly voice. 'You're pretty good at that.'

'I'm a perfectionist. If I promise to pull out, may I continue?' Sebastian asked, convinced that there would not be that great a chance of an unwanted pregnancy engulfing them.

Bunny stiffened. 'But…that's not foolproof.'

'No precautions are foolproof.'

Long brown fingers framed her chin as she lowered her lashes. 'What you really need to know is that if there *are* consequences, I'll be there for you.'

'Doubtful,' she dared to remark. 'When we leave the island, we'll both go back to our own lives.'

'That doesn't mean I'll behave like a bastard or mistreat you. Whatever happens, you can depend on me.' Brilliant dark eyes held hers fast. 'I will support you. I promise you that. I'm not the least bit irresponsible.'

And that she *did* believe. Impatience and frustration engulfed her as she hesitated and then the reckless impulse that had landed her deep into Sebastian's arms took over again. She was going to bury any last memory of Tristram and the damage he had inflicted so deep that she would never think about him again.

'Yes,' she whispered shakily, proud of herself for wanting to move forward and open herself to new experiences with someone else.

'I'll make it good,' he swore.

He stroked her sensitive nub again, refreshing the desire that had gone into temporary abeyance. Her body jolted back to life, hunger and desire stirring afresh. She linked her arms round his neck, no longer worried about the light, indeed revelling in the glory of Sebastian over her with his long black hair tossed by her fingers, his jawline dark with stubble, his lean, dark perfect features taut with craving for her. Without warning she felt like the hottest woman on planet Earth. *He* made her feel like that where Tristram had left her feeling inadequate and manipulated, stupid and trusting.

Sebastian rearranged her lower limbs like an artist and shifted over her before hoisting her legs over his shoulders. 'The look of dismay on your face is precious,' Sebastian quipped. 'But I'm not going to hurt you.'

'I know that!' she gasped, eyes burning with the

threat of tears because he had read her face and she would sooner he had not.

'If you want to stop, tell me at any stage.'

'Stop fussing,' she urged, her cheeks burning.

He pushed into her slowly and she shut her eyes again, enthralled by that stretching invasion of her channel, and then he sank deep and a little whimper was wrenched from her. It felt so good she was struggling for breath, struggling to stay silent. She had never been a screamer but she suspected that Sebastian had the power to turn her into one. The sensations gathered and pulsed at her core and she melted like honey heated under a grill, the throb of desire a relentless pull on every sense. The scent of his skin, the smooth bronzed satin of his shoulders and back, the raw intensity of his glittering black diamond eyes all held her fast.

He shifted pace, driving into her, sliding out, returning again with a sensual twist of his lithe hips that sent excitement flaming through her. And the erotic thrills only increased when he speeded up, pausing to stroke her again and ensure that she was pitched as high as he was. It was like nothing she had ever experienced, and yet it was everything she had ever dreamt of finding in intimacy.

She opened her eyes to enjoy him again and he stole a deep, driving kiss, his tongue delving in erotic mimicry of his possession. In that moment she felt as though he owned her very soul. A visceral hunger spread as he pushed her to ever greater heights. Her heart was thundering, her whole body given over to the pleasure and she surrendered her control to it, holding back nothing as the burning excitement enveloped her and splintered through her in a wondrous explosion of searing pleasure. She was only dimly aware of Sebastian hitting the same high with a masculine growl and the dampness as he spilled on her stomach and she flopped back boneless on the bed, totally wrecked.

Sebastian slid out of bed, stalked into the bathroom and returned some minutes later to wipe her clean. 'Now you can go to sleep without fear of the big bad wolf pouncing.'

'I quite like you pouncing,' she mumbled round an uncontrollable yawn.

'I like you pouncing on me even better,' he countered and that was the last thing she remembered for some time.

Sebastian watched her burrow under his arm and throw a leg over his. He didn't think he liked that kind of togetherness because he could feel some inner part of him recoil but, for some reason, he rather liked it with her. He felt oddly guilty though, rather as though he had seduced her. He was pretty sure that she wasn't very experienced and that he was *her* walk on the wild side. Nothing wrong with that, was there? Was it because she made him feel oddly protective? But how the hell could he protect her from himself?

He knew the effect that he could have on the wrong kind of woman. He knew that for a reason he would never forget. Years had passed but the trauma of dealing with Ariana had marked him deep, taught him to be careful around certain women. But much more important questions beyond the temporary amnesia afflicting him were gradually driving him crazy. Who was he *now*? Ten years on, ten years more mature? Had he graduated as a doctor? Had he gone on to train as a surgeon? Or somewhere along the road had he fallen by the wayside, distracted by some other discipline, some other interest? Why did he yearn for a keyboard? Why did he dream of strings of coding and did that excite him more?

And was his grandmother, Loukia, even still alive well into her eighties? His stomach churned at the fact that she might not be because she was the only relative he had ever cared about or fully understood. He knew exactly why Loukia had chosen not to raise her orphaned grandson, of course he did. She had raised his father, Jason Pagonis, and that had gone badly wrong for all of them. She had been afraid of it happening again with Sebastian and had stepped back, ultimately failing him by sentencing him to the care of those who despised and resented him because of the blood in his veins and his inheritance. The blood of the eldest and once favourite son, Loukia's heir.

Bunny wakened in an empty bed and headed for the shower straight away. Predictably her thoughts had gone straight to Sebastian, but she didn't censure herself for that truth because she knew that her best chance of surviving being stranded meant relying on him.

After all, she would have let herself almost starve and die before she broke into someone else's house and by then she might've been too weak to do it. If she had thought of a bonfire, she probably would have run at the first sign of a snake or, worse, got bitten. She could've fished but not at the rate Sebastian was fishing, so she wasn't at all surprised to go downstairs and find fish already deboned and ready for cooking. He was very efficient, but he wasn't telling her the whole story about his current condition.

'I'd be wearing a wedding ring if I was married.'

A telling choice of words. Did that mean that Sebastian didn't actually know for sure? Or that he was relying on his lack of a ring to convince him? Did Sebastian not actually remember such facts yet? She recalled him asking what year it was and winced. Exactly how extensive was his memory loss? And wasn't it time she found out?

She had two pairs of old, worn jeans on the table when Sebastian reappeared, bringing with him the scent of fresh smoke. He wore only his boxers and she believed that those were for her benefit because she suspected that without her presence, Sebastian wouldn't be wearing any clothes at all. He was perfectly at home in his own skin and he looked amazing, aglow with bronzed vitality, a walking, lean, powerful temptation of a male with wide shoulders, a heavily muscled torso, lean hips and long, strong legs. In spite of her best intentions, heat surged between her thighs like a betrayal. His stunning dark eyes gleamed like melted caramel in sunshine.

'What are you doing?' he asked, indicating the jeans she had spread out.

'We need clothes. I thought I could cut these jeans

down into shorts so that we had a change, at least,' she said tautly. 'Could we talk before I grill breakfast?'

His lean, strong features tensed and shadowed. 'You've had second thoughts about us last night,' he assumed.

'Yes and no,' she responded awkwardly, unwilling to get into that difficult conversation without having got her thoughts together. 'But it was your memory loss I was keen to ask more about. How much have you forgotten?'

'The past ten years. The last thing I now actively re-call I was heading towards my twentieth birthday and on a sailing holiday here,' he admitted flatly. 'I was a medical student then.'

'Oh, my goodness, I slept with someone who was mentally a teenager last night!' Bunny gasped, taken aback by the amount of time he had lost to amnesia and how carefully he had kept that information to him-self. He might be outspoken but that didn't mean he would ever be a mine of freely offered information, especially not if he deemed it *personal* information, she acknowledged.

'I suspect I must've been unconsciously drawing on knowledge I didn't have at nineteen,' Sebastian in-formed her drily of the night before.

Bunny felt hot colour sweep her from throat to brow and looked at the fish instead.

'A lot of knowledge is still in my head if something jogs my memory,' he confided. 'My dreams are full of flashes of imagery that are unfamiliar to me in the present, a sign, I would imagine, that my memory will soon right itself.'

'And yet you confidently told me that you were single!' Bunny condemned anxiously, switching on the grill, fumbling with the fish to keep her hands busy.

'I am confident of that. I'm a loner. I don't believe in for-ever-and-ever vows. In fact, you could say I was biased against marriage. I don't believe I could've changed *that* much.'

'A lot changes in ten years. Ten years ago, I was breaking my heart for a weirdly dressed guy in a boy-band!'

Sebastian shrugged. 'I was never the idolising sort. I was a nerd. I had sex but I didn't date or have relationships.'

'You sound emotionally repressed,' Bunny remarked. With determination, she moved to hold a pair of jeans up against his long legs and mark them with the pen she had found, so that she would know where to use the scissors. 'Crushes are a healthy step on the way to adult relationships.'

As she straightened up again, the ache between her legs intensified, a reminder of the intimacy *she* had instigated. She had yet to get past that shocking fact, that *she* had practically invited him to have sex with her. Reckless! Or *had* it been reckless? Hadn't it been more a case of her stepping into her future of freedom, unrestrained by other people's boundaries? Her decision for once rather than someone else's choices and beliefs limiting her.

Yesterday's bread was stale, and she had toasted it because Sebastian had put an embargo on using the flour in an effort to slow down their use of the ready food in the larder. She set condiments on the table and made coffee. Black for both of them, sugar in only hers and the sugar was running low. Soon, she would have to go cold turkey, but for all her protests she really wasn't sure that she could go cold turkey on Sebastian, who lit up the room with his energy simply by entering it. His charisma was as unnervingly strong as her own fascination.

'Do you have five minutes free so that I can shout at you?' Sebastian enquired quietly.

'Why would you want to shout at me?'

Sebastian dealt her a grim appraisal. 'Because I found the distress flares unused in the life raft…why the hell didn't you send them up during the storm?'

CHAPTER FIVE

Bunny's smooth brow furrowed and then eased again. Sebastian was studying her with frowning annoyance and her tummy turned over sickly. She decided to be honest. 'I forgot about them.'

'You...*forgot*?' he shot back at her in disbelief, studying her intently. Could anyone possibly be that honest?

Sebastian had little experience of such open behaviour. He was accustomed to lies and half-truths at best. Her candour had blown his anger back on him. He was in a volatile mood and thoroughly unsettled because his memory was returning in snatches. He had recalled being on a surgical rotation at a hospital, so he must have completed his medical degree if he had still been training. But he had also recalled burning the candle at both ends while he struggled to solve a tech security problem. Clearly, his once wholehearted approach to medicine had faltered at some point.

Bunny nodded vigorously. 'In the storm, the raft was pitching about and I was trying to keep my balance and watch yours as well. I was also throwing up a lot and terrified. Reggie never mentioned the flares or told me how to use them.'

'It's simple. You point and fire,' Sebastian incised curtly, exasperated that they might just have missed their chance of an immediate rescue. 'There may have been people on land or shipping nearby.'

'But there just as easily might not have been,' she pointed out in her own defence as she set out the food. 'This island was the first land I saw. Reggie only trained me on how to launch the raft. He never showed me the equipment on it.'

His ebony brows lowered. 'That is as may be but common sense should've urged you to—'

'Well, it didn't, no point crying over what's already behind us,' Bunny said in a deliberately upbeat tone, determined not to have her oversight become the focus for a useless argument. 'Now you've got them to use here at the right moment.'

Sebastian glowered at her. 'I *think*—'

'No, I don't want to hear any more about it,' Bunny told him with brisk finality. 'I plead guilty to a mistake. Now sit down and eat your breakfast.'

Sebastian compressed his wide mobile lips like a grump, but he settled down at the table to lift his coffee. 'You don't like confrontation. That doesn't work with me.'

'We're both trying the best we can to get through this. Let's not make mountains out of molehills.'

His eyes glittered like black ice. 'The homely cliché only sets my teeth on edge.'

'Sorry.' She was disconcerted by that sudden chill in the air and she addressed her attention to her plate. She would've liked to have screamed at him about that horrendous, terrifying night on the raft during the storm, when she might as well have been alone. So, she hadn't been perfect but she had kept them both safe long enough to reach land. 'But you have to accept that I'm not a seawoman or whatever you call it. Reggie gave me my first job on a boat and my *only* experience of sailing and it would take torture and intimidation to get me on *any* kind of a boat again!'

He sprang upright and cleared the table. 'I love being on the water. It relaxes me.'

Bunny said nothing, although she was tempted to remind him that he had been protected from the ordeal by his comatose condition. She wiped down the table before laying down the jeans to cut them.

Sebastian startled her with an intervention because he didn't like the atmosphere he had created. He didn't like arguing or even *trying* to argue with her. He didn't like the distance that was threatening to stretch between them and, in reaction, he curved his hands to her hips and carried her into the opulent reception room, dropping down on the sectional with her splayed across his thighs.

'What are you doing? I was about to cut those jeans down.'

'They'll take a rain check… I'm not as forgiving,' Sebastian contended. 'Let's wind back a few minutes. If you'd still been in bed when I returned, I'd have climbed back into bed with you. If you'd been a little more receptive, I'd have stripped you in the kitchen.'

'Sebastian,' she argued, mortified because she could

fully imagine either scenario. Unlike her, he was very upfront in his attitude to sex.

Without warning, his passionate mouth crushed hers with hungry urgency and her lips parted, instinctively allowing him access. He lifted his head again, dark eyes fiercely intent on her face. 'You want to stop this? Say so now.'

Small fingers reached up to his stubbled jawline and smoothed, her luminous green eyes wide and troubled because she didn't want to wind him up. She wanted him to calm down, although she was still wounded by his criticism of her actions during the storm. 'I don't know what I want yet. We were in that bed before I registered that anything had started.'

In answer to that response, Sebastian swung her off him to set her down with care beside him. 'It's your choice. I'm on fire for you but if you would prefer to call a halt, I won't put pressure on you to change your mind.'

'I've only ever been in one relationship,' she admitted unevenly, embarrassed to admit that lack of experience. 'And you say you don't do relationships at all. I'm not like that. But I do know that what we've got is just for now and is probably only happening because we're stuck here alone together.'

'We don't need to have this discussion. But please don't start imagining that you're falling in love with me.'

Her eyes flew wide. 'Why would you say *that* to me? Am I acting like that?'

'No.' Sebastian vented his breath in an impatient hiss

and then sighed heavily, thinking back to his unfortunate experience with Ariana. 'But once a girl I looked
on like a sister decided she was in love with me and
became obsessive about it.'

Immediately, Bunny was listening. 'Who was she?'

'Ariana, the kid sister of one of my best friends. She
travelled here with her brother and me. I was eighteen.
She was a year younger. There was nothing between us
and never had been. Her brother thought it was funny…
just a silly infatuation, but he insisted that I had to be
frank with her and tell her that I wasn't interested. I
did and she took an overdose and almost died.'

Bunny flinched, clear green eyes flying to his in
dismay and sympathy. 'Oh, no…'

'When Ariana recovered, she was depressed and
her family put her in a clinical support unit because
they were afraid she would try again. I felt responsible even though I hadn't encouraged her. I may not
remember the last few years but I'm always careful to
set that one rule if I see the same woman more than
once. If you should ever feel that you can't live without
me, walk away fast,' he breathed in a raw undertone.
'Because I'm a born and bred loner, Bunny. I don't do
the couple thing. '

'Okay.' Bunny wasn't sure what she wanted. After
Tristram, she had decided that it would be a long time
until she got seriously involved with anyone again, had
dimly pictured enjoying light, fun relationships.

But fate had instead thrown up Sebastian. The force
of his personality could be overwhelming.

I'm on fire for you.'

The very concept of being desired to that extent by Sebastian sent a naked flame racing through her bloodstream. But, just like him, she didn't want any big discussions or complications. There wasn't a nice, neat label for the attraction between them. Lust? She winced but maybe it was only that, yet so many other feelings surged in her in Sebastian's radius. He was so wary, so damaged, she sensed, and she wouldn't have been human had she not wanted to know why. It wasn't solely his experience with an unhappy girl who had fixated on him while he was still a boy, she reckoned.

'Fancy a swim?' she prompted abruptly.

Her suggestion broke the tension. On the beach, Sebastian stripped off everything and laughed when she got into the water in the shirt and the material ballooned up around her. 'Want to borrow my boxers?' he teased.

And she agonised over what she truly wanted because she wanted him, didn't even need to think about it. Did that mean that she was already too keen? Was she asking for trouble when she already knew he was going to walk away? Or was she worrying about tomorrow when *today* was really all she should be concentrating on? A short-term future only, she decided. If she wanted him to back off, he would, but was that what she wanted? She didn't think so.

She watched him in the water, lithe as an otter, unexpectedly graceful for all his size. Backed by lush vegetation, the sunlit beach was sublime. In the distance a slender column of black smoke swirled up from the little bonfire. It hadn't attracted anyone's attention yet, she noted, nor had their painstakingly made SOS messages on the beach.

'You didn't finish the story. What happened to Ariana afterwards?' she asked.

'I haven't remembered that far back yet, but she did have another episode at university and she dropped out.'

Bunny grimaced as she leant back against the wooden pier. 'Why do you take on that guilt? You didn't cause her problems. I would assume she was troubled beforehand even if her family didn't realise that and families often don't. If it hadn't been you who became her focus, it would've been some other boy. It wasn't your fault.'

'It felt like it,' Sebastian countered grimly.

Bunny changed the subject. 'How much wood is there left to keep that bonfire going?'

'I'm reluctant to start felling trees,' he admitted. 'I don't want to do irreparable damage here. I've already combed through most of the undergrowth and removed logs. A nature lover like the owner of that house wouldn't like trees being felled.'

'When will you use the flares?'

'In a few days. I'm hoping we'll hear search planes. We've got to allow that time for a search to begin.'

He settled upright just in front of her and braced his big hands on the pier either side of her. Spectacular dark eyes gazed down into hers.

'You're remembering stuff,' she murmured. 'You're different.'

'How different?'

'More impatient, bossier…bouncing off the walls with surplus energy,' she muttered with rueful amusement.

'I don't like being in situations I can't control.'

'This experience could teach you patience.'

Disconcerting her, Sebastian turned away. 'I'll swim for a while, work off that energy.'

Her brow indented and then she dropped back into the water and swam back to shore.

What the hell was he doing with her? Sebastian was asking himself. She wasn't up to his weight. She wasn't fragile or lacking in confidence like Ariana though. She was her own woman and she didn't trust him. And why should she? Practising withdrawal as a means of contraception? *Really?* He knew how unreliable that was. What had possessed him? And why was he so drawn to her? He needed to give her some space and work out what was happening to him before it all blew up in his face. He wasn't himself, particularly with her. He felt that down to his very bones and the feeling unnerved him. Yet he still couldn't make himself step back from her.

Bunny went back to the house and, to keep occupied, changed the bed. The linen cupboard was full, as if waiting for a full house of guests, and yet there was only that one bed. She missed books. The few books on shelves were of the ornithology variety, not very tempting to someone like her who liked fiction and history. She located the cushions for the outside furniture in a cupboard and grabbed one to sit and survey the tiny view of the beach, which was mostly screened by trees that needed to be cut back. Eventually she dozed off, reflecting that she already missed Sebastian and that there was no way she was going to stop whatever they had started up. Life was simply too short to be that cautious of something or someone new.

'Time to eat,' Sebastian told her, shaking her shoulder.

'You…cooked?'

'Yes, and you're not allowed to criticise,' he warned her, herding her back into the house and the kitchen where he set a plate of pasta in front of her with a flourish.

Still waking up, she ate, deciding that Sebastian could be a little bit annoying because he was good at so many different things. The food was excellent, if spicier than she would have dared to make it.

'I'm going for a shower,' he told her while she was clearing up.

'I'll be in bed.'

He stalked back from the doorway and pulled her into his arms. 'Tell me I can kiss you.'

'You can do anything you like,' she murmured, lifting her head high, clear green eyes striking his levelly. 'And we're not about to stress about that any more.'

'Did it hurt when you fell from heaven?' he teased, dark-as-night eyes glittering like stars as his tension vanished.

For a split second, relief flooded him and he just wanted to grab her and whirl her round the kitchen. It was a weird urge and it knocked him off balance. Possibly he was more stressed than he had been willing to admit but resisting the urge to put his arms round her was still a challenge. Why was he getting these insane feelings of affection that had nothing whatsoever to do with sex? Why wasn't he exasperated with her for playing hot and cold? Why wasn't he offended that she had had to put so much thought into being with him? Had that ever happened to him before?

She groaned and laughed almost simultaneously at that corny line. Her big green eyes sparkled. His big hands cradling her cheeks, he kissed her, fast, hard and full of dark promise, making her shiver with anticipation. 'Later,' he husked with a brilliant smile.

Yes, he wanted her fiercely and she would let herself enjoy that, revel in being desired, truly desired for the very first time. In her one and only relationship, she had been a useful stopgap, a temporary convenience for student life, never the girlfriend Tristram had planned to stay with long term, for all he had once said that she was. After that experience, Sebastian's desire, his bluntness about what he did and didn't want were exceptionally appealing to her. He wasn't telling her any lies, he wasn't faking anything. He didn't want love or commitment. It was honest. They *had* no future! They were having a fling and, goodness knew, she was old enough to have a fling without agonising about it and beating herself up.

There was just something about her, Sebastian reflected in the shower. He wondered how long it would take him to persuade her into the shower with him. He smiled. Having the lights on had been a big enough deal for her. She could be shy. She took for ever to make major decisions, and sex was clearly a major decision for her. She could be impulsive, though, and when she was, she was incredibly sexy. At the same time, she didn't back down with him when he crossed or criticised her and he was beginning to appreciate that quiet, firm, non-combative peace she emanated when he got difficult. She was his polar opposite. So why did they work so well together?

He was volatile, had always been volatile and inclined to brood. He was a science geek and when he was a child his social skills had been abysmal. He wasn't a party person. He didn't do drugs or drink much. His family background had ensured that he knew enough to avoid the obvious pitfalls. He liked sex but he didn't like the complications it brought, the women who demanded more than he had to give, the women who wouldn't give him space to breathe. Thinking about it, and the very idea made him want to laugh at the insanity of it, he realised Bunny was probably his very first relationship.

He had had next to no relationship with the relatives who had sent him away from them rather than take him into their own homes and families. Even his parents had been distant in his memories of them. Nobody had ever got really close to him, certainly not a woman. He had never lived with a woman before, seen her day after day, looked for her when she wasn't there, eaten her cooking, cooked for her. It was scarily intimate, he acknowledged, the sort of set-up he usually avoided like the plague. That in mind, why was he still enjoying being with her? Why wasn't he keeping his distance?

Bunny slid into the cool bed and shivered and a moment later Sebastian rolled over and caught her to him. The heat of him infiltrated every inch of her and liquid warmth stirred between her thighs. Her fingers slid up into his damp hair, the curls of black hair on his chest abrading her tender nipples as his mouth came down on hers with a hunger that both shook and thrilled. She wasn't about to catch feelings for him, she swore to herself, she wasn't going to get attached. Yet deep down inside her a little voice whispered that she was lying to herself and that it was easy to decide to live wild and free, but it would be more of a challenge to hold to that goal.

CHAPTER SIX

'I COULD MAKE COOKIES,' Bunny bargained ten days later.

'Cookies aren't nutritious,' Sebastian countered, sliding a glance over her slender frame as she sat beside him on the pier with her legs dangling. Her delicate features had thinned because they were both losing weight and it worried him. 'Let's conserve the supplies we have.'

'Maybe not but cookies are comforting,' Bunny argued. 'I still remember making them with my grandmother.'

And without the smallest fanfare a sound rather like a click went off inside Sebastian's brain. Click...*his* grandmother, Loukia was dead. For a split second he felt sick as he remembered that. Bang, all of a sudden everything he had forgotten was back in his head where it belonged, everything clashing and crowding together in an ungodly cacophony of demands. Loukia, the will, the onslaught of his relatives and the torturous stress of the latest software he was fine-tuning for the market. Was it any wonder his memory had checked out on him? He hadn't *wanted* to remember what his life was like, had he?

'And then she passed and, six months later, my

grandfather was gone as well. And Mum can't bake for peanuts, so I became the baker at home,' Bunny continued. 'I miss my family. I wouldn't admit that I was homesick the whole year I've been away and I wouldn't let them pay for me to fly home for Christmas because it would've left them short for other things. And now they'll be worrying about me, afraid that something bad has happened and I feel so guilty...'

Thee mou...what had he done? He had never been so irresponsible in his choice of a woman. How he had ended up with someone as unsuitable as Bunny in his bed was a mystery unless it was the sheer novelty of her that had drawn him. The optimistic freshness of the way she saw life, her perpetual, painful honesty, her overdeveloped conscience. The easy affection she offered, the wonderful calm at the heart of her that steadied him. The absolutely amazing sex. Long fingers tightening on the fishing rod, he turned to look at his companion, knowing that he would be judging himself for ever more if he hurt her. 'Go back in the shade... you're burning again,' he told her with the curtness of guilt-stricken concern. 'Your nose is pink.'

'What's wrong?' she asked instantly, alert to the edge honing his dark deep voice.

'I got the rest of my memory back. When you mentioned your grandmother it all simply slid into place and it's sobering stuff,' he grated, checking out fleeting images inside his head and almost flinching from the fallout.

'Don't go back to being the guy you were on the boat,' she warned him ruefully.

'It's too late for that. I'm the guy I was on the boat but I'm also the guy you've been with here for the past two weeks. I'm *both*,' he underlined.

Bunny didn't want to think about him being both because she had loathed the first version of him that she had met. 'You sent up the last flare last night,' she reminded him, suddenly very keen to change the subject.

'Because we heard planes,' he pointed out.

'Only they didn't come near us.'

'What did you remember?' she finally forced herself to ask.

'Everything. That my grandmother passed away last month and it's a few years since I worked as a doctor. I'm in tech development now. I created an anti-hacking security program called Pagekey, which is making me a fortune,' he spelt out quietly and with a significant lack of excitement at the recollection.

'I'm so sorry about your grandmother,' she said quietly. 'Why did you give up medicine?'

'I wasn't compassionate enough. I prefer machines to people. They're more reliable. And I suspect I only went for medicine because all my relatives said I'd never make the grade. Isn't that petty? Let's talk about something rather more relevant.'

'Like?'

'What are our plans if you are pregnant?' he framed softly, choosing the topic that now concerned him most. 'After this length of time, it's possible that you have conceived.'

'Is it? Either of us could be sterile. It doesn't really matter right now anyway, not until we're rescued,' she reasoned awkwardly. 'But I wouldn't want a termination. I'd raise the baby…but I suppose it would wreck my life. Of course, that's a stupid, narrow-minded thing to say.'

'I don't want a child of mine wrecking anyone's life,' Sebastian admitted with glacial candour and a chill ran down her spine.

'I only meant it would wreck all my plans in the short term,' Bunny rephrased immediately. 'My family would fuss and worry. It would mean planning a different future, that's all. Don't judge me for a first passing reaction to a possible crisis. And *don't* freeze me out!'

'I'm not.'

Bunny studied his breathtakingly beautiful face, the new reserve etched into his lean, dark, perfect features, the absence of his easy smile, the taut and wary narrowing of his stunning black-lashed eyes. And she saw the difference in him since he had regained his memory because he hid his emotions. 'You are and you know you are. I know you.'

'You don't. Not the way you think you do,' he assured her smoothly. 'We haven't been living a normal life here.'

'I still know that you want answers right now this minute and solutions at the same time,' she responded flatly. 'And we're not in a position to talk about either, so this is a futile conversation.'

In truth, she had summed up pretty much what he wanted and couldn't have and he almost laughed at how well she had him tabbed. But he didn't laugh because he knew that he needed to back off from the hothouse intensity of their current relationship.

'After this, I *will* walk away…but I won't walk away from my child, should there be one.'

'I'm going for a walk now,' Bunny told him tautly as she scrambled upright in a sudden movement. 'Oh… just one question…*did* you have a girlfriend?'

'No. When I met you, I hadn't been with a woman in months,' he countered.

'So glad I was available for you. Let's hope we'll be rescued soon and then we can escape each other,' she sniped, walking off fast, well aware that right now he would prefer his own company.

Sebastian liked his own space and he especially would dislike if she began shooting twenty questions at him in relation to his returned memories. But she shouldn't have been snide, she scolded herself in shame. If he had only just remembered his grandmother's death, he would be reliving that grief. She was being selfish and insensitive dwelling only on what the return of his memory would mean to her.

'I will walk away.'

What was she supposed to say to that? Could he have shouted the end to their relationship any louder?

He had changed. The minute he had remembered who he was, he had changed so fast her head was still spinning with the shock of it. Sebastian Pagonis, rich tech tycoon. Not a playboy though. She supposed that was a very small comfort. But even so, his very first urge had been to push her away, diminish what they had shared and make it clear that what they currently had was finished the moment they were rescued. Her eyes stung and she blinked furiously, sun glinting off the clear water almost blinding her in the afternoon heat. Her own response to his words made it clear that somewhere down deep she had been hoping that what they had was something more than a forgettable fling.

And now she was upset—well, that had always been on the cards, Sebastian reasoned grimly. If he wasn't prepared to offer the ring, the white picket fence and the family dog, she would be upset and there was nothing he could do about it. Bunny was deeply conventional and he had recognised that early on, so why hadn't he backed off then? A baby? He groaned and felt ashamed of the response. But what did he know about being a father? What did he even know about having a family? Yet he had taken risk after risk with Bunny and once or twice he had even forgotten to be careful. So the odds of her conceiving, when they had been in that bed every day since their arrival, could be pretty high.

Bunny dashed away the furious, over-emotional tears while she reminded herself that she needed to rewrite the last two weeks inside her head. Forget the fling, dial back the emotions, start treating Sebastian like a platonic companion, stop sharing the same bed and ditch all the little intimacies that had begun to seem so natural between them. Why? As he had reminded her, none of what they had shared while stranded was normal. Their life here *wasn't* normal, so how could anything that had grown from their situation be any different?

The distant drone of an engine was sufficient to penetrate her troubled thoughts. After all, they heard no mechanical sounds on the island. She looked back over her shoulder and saw Sebastian running down the beach and beyond him she saw some kind of boat noisily bouncing over the waves towards the island. It had finally happened. Someone had noticed their presence. Not quite able to credit that reality, she momentarily froze and then she began running in the same direction as well.

By the time she arrived, Sebastian was already enjoying an animated conversation with the man, who had tied up his motorboat at the pier. He paused and formally introduced her to Dwi, the caretaker for the 'French house', as it was described, and she noted that Sebastian seemed to speak quite a bit of Indonesian dialect. The owner was a guy named Louis Bernard, an ornithologist and a leading light in television documentaries. A mobile phone was handed to Sebastian with great ceremony.

'Dwi knows that we've been reported missing because it's all over the newspapers. I'm calling my friend Andreas so that the search can be called off. He'll organise everything for us and then I'm going to call Mr Bernard, so that I can explain that we broke into his house to use it. Reggie was picked up last week, by the way,' he advanced. 'But he's in hospital with an injured leg which requires surgery.'

The phone was passed back and forth for Dwi to give the exact location of the island. Sebastian spoke in Greek, laughing occasionally and smiling, and she surmised that Andreas was a close friend. They all began walking towards the house as Sebastian phoned the house owner to offer their thanks for its use as well as assurances that the house would be returned to its original state.

The phone was returned to Dwi. 'We'll be picked

up this evening by helicopter,' Sebastian informed her. 'Your family are already waiting for you. My yacht arrived in Bali last week and I've told Andreas to invite your family to use it for the duration of their stay.'

'My family's here?' Bunny gasped in consternation. 'How many of them?'

'Parents and a couple of brothers, I believe,' Sebastian supplied.

'We can't stay on your…yacht,' she declared uncomfortably.

'Why would you put them to the expense of staying anywhere else?' Sebastian questioned with a frown.

A deep tide of red washed up over her heart-shaped face because that was unanswerable. Her parents were retired and would've dug deep into their savings to fly out to Indonesia. Anything that could lessen the cost of their unexpected stay in Asia would be welcome to them. 'You have a *yacht*?' she said instead of all the many more embarrassing things that she might have said without thinking.

Back in the real world, she was thinking, the differences between her and Sebastian were starkly apparent. He had a yacht! He spoke sufficient Indonesian to have soothed the anxious Dwi and he spoke French fluently while her grasp of the language had advanced no further than the exam she had passed at sixteen. 'I don't want to get on another boat,' she confessed uneasily.

'The yacht won't be sailing anywhere and it's the size of a small cruise ship.'

Bunny swallowed the lump in her throat and nodded obediently because she would have to get over her newly learned aversion to boats to allow her family to take advantage of Sebastian's hospitality. And *his* thoughtfulness on her family's behalf, her conscience slotted in, but she really didn't want to be reminded that Sebastian was that rich and important that his disappearance had been reported in newspapers. Or that, in spite of his wealth and influence, he could still be unexpectedly kind.

While the two men talked, Bunny's memory ranged free.

At dawn that morning, Sebastian had been studying her when she wakened and had informed her that the sun had given her a fifth freckle on her nose. 'So admit it, I notice everything about you,' he had teased, shifting over her, already hard and urgent against her. 'Now you have to say good morning *my* way…'

'Not until I've freshened up.'

'You smell of me and I find that stupendously sexy,' he had husked.

She had gloried in the sensation of having those stunning dark eyes of his locked to her. 'According to you, you find everything about me sexy.'

'So let me take advantage of you again…'

And without hesitation, they had taken advantage of each other, she conceded, her feminine core tingling in erotic recollection of that passion. Although she had not known it at the time, she reflected now, that had been their *last* time together. It was over, done, dusted, soon to be forgotten about, she told herself. She wasn't about to agonise over a stupid, meaningless fling. She wasn't that big an idiot!

For heaven's sake, why was she standing around dreaming when they would soon be leaving? She needed to tidy the house, change the bedding, pick up her few belongings. As she sped indoors, Sebastian caught her by the elbow. 'We'll eat on the yacht.'

'Please tell me there'll be vegetables. You wouldn't believe how much I've missed them!' she sighed, rolling her eyes with determined cheer.

'I have a chef. You can choose your favourite meal,' he promised. 'Roasted veg and cheese? And a dessert?'

'I can hardly wait,' she said brightly, noting that he had tied up his hair again with a length of vine and that miraculously he already looked much more like the guy she had first met. Self-contained, rather remote, his brilliant dark eyes veiled even though his tone was light and casual.

'An official investigation has been opened into the wreck,' Sebastian warned her. 'We'll have to make statements to the police and the shipping authorities. You'll have to watch what you say or you could get Reggie into trouble because that mast should never have come down like that. Either they'll find a reason for it failing or they'll try to blame him for taking out a vessel that wasn't seaworthy.'

Bunny nodded very seriously. 'He wouldn't have done that.'

'No and luckily we're both in good health, which will help matters.'

'But you were hurt.'

'The mast caught the back of my head as it went down. I was fortunate the effects weren't more serious.'

Sebastian paused and studied her. 'Though I would ask you to keep my temporary amnesia a confidential matter. I'm over it. It's no longer relevant. Nobody else needs to know.'

His amnesia was not relevant and she suspected that in his view that covered their temporary relationship as well. 'Understood. I'm not going to talk about you to anyone,' she told him stiffly and turned away.

'There are people who will offer you a lot of money to tell them about your experiences with me here,' he cautioned her tautly. 'If that is likely to tempt you to talk, I would be happy to give you the cash upfront in return for your silence.'

Every scrap of colour evaporated from Bunny's complexion. 'I have no intention of selling you out, Sebastian. But it's interesting how immediately distrustful you've become since regaining your memory.' Bunny's green eyes were reproachful, her tone stiff. 'I may not be rich but I'm happy with what I've got and no matter what I'm offered, I won't be tempted to reveal any secrets that could embarrass you.'

She went upstairs to collect their few possessions and strip the bed.

'You don't need to bother,' Sebastian said from the doorway. 'Dwi says the owner is putting this place up for sale. Apparently, this was once his dream hideaway but he's since got married and his wife doesn't like being so far from civilisation, so he's not using it any more.'

'Even so, I'll put the sheets on to wash,' she murmured. 'It's the polite thing to do.'

She was keeping busy to avoid having to think about what Sebastian had revealed. He had just offered to pay her cash, to *bribe* her to prevent her from talking about her experiences on the island with him. Well, that told her all she needed to know about his opinion of her. Would he have believed ill of her as easily *before* he regained his memory? Was he always this cynical and suspicious? It occurred to her that perhaps she had been lucky to be washed up with a Sebastian who barely knew who he was. To say the least, the fully restored version of Sebastian inhabited a 'them' and 'us' world from which she, by virtue of her economic status, was excluded. He didn't trust her any more but maybe he had *never* trusted her.

It was cool and damp when she heard the helicopter overhead. The late summer weather was definitely on the turn. Although the days remained hot the evenings were getting cooler. As she stepped out of the house, she carried a small bundle and when she reached the beach, she tossed Sebastian's sweater at him.

Frowning, he turned to her.

'You forgot it!' she yelled above the racket of the helicopter settling down on the beach. It had a very sleek paint job in purple and silver and some sort of logo on it.

He strode back towards her. 'I left it for you…it's cold.'

'I'm fine.'

He ignored her assurance and instead ran a reproving finger over the goosebumps on her arm. He dropped his sweater over her head, feeding her hands carefully into the sleeves before stooping to lift her off her feet into his arms to carry her.

'What are you doing?' she demanded in astonishment.

'You don't have any shoes!' he vented in surprise at her reaction as they were approached by the two men who had jumped out of the helicopter. Both were staring and one of them was her eldest brother, John. Her face burned with self-consciousness.

'I'll take her from here,' John asserted, extending his arms to remove her from Sebastian's hold.

Sebastian, however, stood his ground and lifted an arrogant black brow. 'And you are?'

'This is my brother John,' Bunny proclaimed hurriedly.

Sebastian relaxed his hold and handed her over like a parcel. 'Sebastian Pagonis.'

'John Woods.'

'Where's Mum and Dad?' Bunny asked as John moved her into the helicopter.

'There wasn't enough space for more than two of us to fly out here and Mum and Dad are a bit overcome by all this and Mum didn't want to cry over you in front of people.'

'Oh,' Bunny mumbled as the other man leant back over the seat in front and introduced himself as Andreas Zervas. Sebastian's friend, she recalled, and then they were all donning headphones to drown out the noise of the helicopter and there was no further opportunity for conversation. Bunny gazed numbly out of the window as the craft swung in a turn above the island to head back out across the sea. And from that vantage point, the island looked absolutely tiny, the roof of the house only momentarily visible below the trees.

John grasped her hand and squeezed it. Tears prickled behind her lowered eyelids and her throat thickened. What a storm of drama and stress she had created for her family! John would have come without his wife and had probably travelled out to Indonesia with her middle brother, Luke, a corporate lawyer and the highest earner in the family.

It was a longer flight than she was expecting and she couldn't wait to see her parents and reassure them that she was perfectly all right. When the heavy craft finally set down again, she peered out of the window but she could see only technical equipment. She whipped off the headphones and John hissed in her ear, 'Wait until you see this boat...'

They had landed on the yacht? She was hugely relieved that no further travel was required to reach their destination and she moved down the steps onto the helipad, following Sebastian, who told her to watch her feet when she stubbed her toe and then, in exasperation, he lifted her up again. 'You need shoes!' he censured.

'If I hadn't been trying to help you onto the raft, I wouldn't have lost my shoe in the first place!' she snapped back with spirit, colouring when she noticed her brother's surprised glance.

Sebastian stalked through a door and lowered her to a rug. It was a huge reception area and at the very foot of it she saw her parents standing taut and somehow seeming very small against their imposing glass and opulently elegant surroundings. Bunny hurtled down the length of the room into her parents' arms. There was frantic speech and a lot of tears, questions that weren't answered and some harried answers that weren't entirely true. In the midst of it, Sebastian walked up to join them.

'She saved my life,' he told her parents and her brother Luke. 'She got me on the raft and looked after me until I'd recovered my wits.'

'And then he looked after me. He fished and built bonfires and dealt with snakes,' she recalled with a shudder.

Her mother wrapped her arms round Sebastian before Bunny could intercept her and gave him a huge, enthusiastic hug, only separating from him when Bunny's father insisted on shaking his hand while Bunny introduced everybody.

'Let me show you to your cabin,' Sebastian interposed. 'You'll want to get changed and catch up with your parents. I had Andreas organise some clothing basics for you.'

'Oh…er, thanks,' she muttered in a rush as he guided her across a companionway and into an utterly breath-stealing space before stepping out again, leaving her with her family. The cabin was almost as large as the reception area with a very opulent bed on a shallow dais, a snazzy separate seating area and doors out onto a deck. Another door stood ajar on a luxury bathroom that rejoiced in a copper tub, fleecy towels and glorious marble tiles.

'Wow…' Bunny whispered, impressed to death by her surroundings.

'The rest of us are on the deck below,' Luke imparted, frowning at her. 'He's put you next door to *his* cabin.'

Bunny investigated through the third door and rifled through a wardrobe packed with fluttering garments and drawers full of silky underwear. 'Well, I'm not about to complain about being spoiled after the last two weeks,' she confided, lifting her chin. Rather more than 'clothing basics' had been provided, she acknowledged, but she would take that up with Sebastian later in private.

'Of course she's not,' her mother piped up, shooting Luke a reproachful glance. 'Your sister's had a rough time.'

'Exactly how friendly are you with our generous host?' John enquired quietly.

Bunny shrugged. 'About as friendly as you would expect after two weeks worried we weren't going to make it off that island any time soon,' she replied stiffly.

'That's not telling us anything,' Luke reproved.

'I don't owe you an explanation,' she heard herself say sharply and then her mother was shooing the men out, saying that she was overwrought and that it wasn't the time for a postmortem.

'You tend to get close when there's only the two of you all day every day,' she added apologetically as Luke departed with bad grace.

'Would you mind if I went for a shower and got dressed?' she asked her mother as she gathered underwear, a long silky skirt and a light top from the dressing room. 'I need to freshen up.'

'You've changed,' the older woman remarked, her brow furrowing. 'I'm not criticising. You're more confident. Naturally the experience you've had and a year away from home has changed you.'

Bunny stripped and sped into the shower, revelling in the shampoo and the conditioner for her hair and then dressing in haste, all fingers and thumbs as she combed her hair, ran a dryer through it and finally thrust her feet into leather sliders that must've cost the earth. The garments were classy and chic and pleasantly soft and silky against her skin. When she reappeared both her parents were in the seating area chatting and, minutes after that, a stewardess knocked on the door to say that dinner was about to be served.

'Only Bunny is having the roast vegetables because it's her favourite,' Sebastian announced, sending her a fleeting smile. He had changed as well but only into well-worn jeans that fitted his big muscular body as if they had been tailored for him and a loose white linen shirt, bright against his bronzed skin. He had shaved, his strong jawline exposed without the covering black stubble she had grown accustomed to seeing there. His amazing dark good looks had never been more obvious. His brilliant dark eyes gleamed as they rested on her with satisfaction.

'So looks like you've got very friendly with our host,' her brother Luke remarked, his hand at her spine to guide her into a chair at Sebastian's elbow and at a very long polished table.

Drinks were served first but Bunny was hungry enough that her tummy felt as though it were meeting her backbone and as soon as she was able she ate with appetite, cherishing the luxury touches of melted cheese and some sort of moreish chutney.

Most of the conversation centred on their escape during the storm and the island.

'Apparently the caretaker, Dwi, checks the house once a month and he spent the last few weeks away from home visiting relatives. His neighbour phoned him to say that he had seen smoke coming from the island but he didn't believe him. The neighbour was known for telling tall stories but that's why Dwi came out to the island today.'

Stifling a yawn, she cleared her plate. Several times, Sebastian stepped in to answer questions because she was flagging and she wished he would quit his self-appointed role acting as her protector. Evidently, Reggie's catamaran had been saved but it was now official evidence and, bearing in mind his injury, it would probably be weeks, if not months, before his boat was returned to him. Her father had already visited his old friend in hospital and he told her that Reggie's wife, Eka, had been with him. Her family had waited several days after the alarm of her disappearance had been raised before deciding to fly to Indonesia because they had wanted to be on the spot if there were any developments during the search.

'You're exhausted,' Sebastian told her.

'Yes, but I'm too wired to go to sleep yet,' Bunny confided.

'Do you want to call it a night? Or would you like to join me for coffee?'

'Coffee,' Bunny selected.

'We'll have coffee on deck. Coffee with cream,' Sebastian said with a sudden grin and, for a moment, it was as though they were the only two people in the world. His spectacular dark eyes were bright as starshine and held hers fast.

'And biscuits?' she pressed hopefully.

'Play your cards right and there might even be a dessert. I told my chef that you had a sweet tooth.'

Even aware that her family were watching her like hawks, Bunny still let Sebastian draw her neatly away from the table and guide her towards the deck doors.

'Right now, you're overwhelmed,' Sebastian murmured soft and low. 'Too many people around you, too many questions at once. We were living on a very quiet island and we'll both need time to adjust to the change.'

Sometimes he got everything right, she conceded, but sometimes he got it dreadfully wrong: as when he had offered her money in an effort to persuade her not to discuss him with the press. As if she would ever have contemplated doing that! She shifted away from him and took a deeply upholstered seat behind a fancy table in a trendy S shape. She breathed in the sea air with surprising pleasure, seeing the lights of the Bali nightlife in the distance while reassured that the giant yacht would not be moving while she was onboard.

'How did you organise these clothes for me?'

'I told Andreas that you had nothing but a pair of pyjamas to wear and no shoes. I gave him your sizes.

I assume his wife helped him,' he responded lazily as a stewardess appeared carrying a laden tray. 'Until you're reunited with whatever remains of your belongings on Reggie's catamaran, you have nothing. Anything you don't want or like from the selection will be returned. Tomorrow you'll be speaking to the police and the shipping investigators and I doubted that you would want to do it barefoot in pyjamas.'

'But the expense,' she protested uncomfortably, only a little mollified by the news that some garments could be returned.

'I want you to be comfortable.'

'You're not responsible for me,' Bunny told him with curt conviction as she poured the coffee and sugared hers and added cream, cupping the warm brew between her palms to drink.

'I will be if you're pregnant.'

Her eyes flew to the deck doors, but the stewardess had closed them again and she turned back to him. 'No,' she corrected. 'You'll be jointly responsible for the baby once it is born…that is *if* there's a baby. You're not responsible for me in any other way.'

Sebastian dropped down beside her in an elegant careless sprawl, long legs sheathed in taut denim stretched out in front of him. 'You need to relax about this or we're going to be arguing constantly. I've organised a blood test for you tomorrow morning, so that we'll know whether or not we're about to become parents.'

'No,' Bunny countered quietly. 'When I do a pregnancy test I will choose the time and the place and

I'm not ready to cross that bridge yet. Anyway, it's too soon.'

'No, it's not and the sooner we know, the better.' Sebastian closed a big hand over hers where it was clenched tight on the table top. 'Stop burying your head in the sand.'

'I'm not but I won't be railroaded into something I don't want.' She finished the biscuit, which had turned to sawdust inside her mouth, and stood up. 'I'm never likely to be a fan of you taking charge of everything— even stuff that isn't, strictly speaking, any of your business. But as far as you're concerned, if I'm pregnant, the baby doesn't exist until it's born and everything prior to that is totally *my* private business.'

Sebastian caught her hand to tug her down on his lap before she could move out of reach and a startled little gasp of dismay parted her lips. 'What are you doing?' she demanded, taken by surprise and struggling to rise off his lean, muscular thighs again.

Long fingers tipped up her chin, his gaze collided with her angry green eyes. 'Isn't it obvious?'

Sparks were flaring in his dark eyes and yet when his mouth came down and ravished hers, it was tantalisingly sweet and sensually tender. Her body ignited, programmed, it seemed, to still respond to him. Her nipples were tight, her breasts swelling, her breath ragged and the space between her thighs ached. But she lifted her hands and thrust them hard against his shoulders to push him back and detach herself.

'No!' she told him fiercely as she scrambled awk-

wardly and clumsily upright again, grasping the edge of the table to steady herself.

'No?' Sebastian queried in apparent surprise, which inflamed her even more.

'*That* is the past, this is the present. We had a fling and now it's done. Nobody was more blunt than you about the fact that we were over the minute we got off the island!' she reminded him. 'You said you would be walking away…well, I *walked* too, Sebastian. And after you offered to bribe me not to talk about you to the press, I didn't just mentally walk. I freakin' sprinted in the opposite direction!'

Faint colour darkened his blade-sharp cheekbones but his bright dark eyes flashed like lasers against the night sky. 'So, we're done…but how can we be if you're preg—?'

'I can be the mother of your child without that including any further intimacy. You know what the real problem is?' Bunny prompted furiously. 'It's *you*, naturally devious and twisty, suspicious you. If I'd clung to you and tried to attach strings, you'd be at the far end of your stupid pretentious yacht right now, *avoiding* me like the plague! But I didn't cling and because I chose to move on fast, now you're offended.'

'I'm *not* offended,' Sebastian grated in raw interruption.

Bunny rolled her eyes because he was totally offended by her rejection. 'I'm going to turn in now, because if I stay we're going to fight.'

'You'd back down before it got that far.'

In a real temper now, Bunny planted her hands on

her hips. 'No, I wouldn't. Why can't you decide what you want? You said you were walking away…why aren't you?'

Sebastian shrugged a wide shoulder. He couldn't answer that question and he admired her in silence. He still wanted her, the same way he had wanted her the day before and the day before that. His need to keep her close only intensified around other people and that was a shock to his system while landing him on unfamiliar ground. He had believed he could walk away and had discovered different. Even the prospect of her moving out of his sight set his teeth on edge. It wasn't logical and it disturbed him, but he couldn't escape those feelings, those urges.

In addition, it astonished him that he had once written her off as merely pretty, because, even without making the smallest effort, she was beautiful. Golden hair shining beneath the lights, her delicate face flushed, green eyes ablaze, soft pink lips lusciously full, her slender little body taut with tension. She was as addictive as a drug. He got within a yard of her and all he wanted to do was pin her to the nearest horizontal surface, *touch* her, *hold* her. That need was a complete novelty to him. No other woman had ever had that effect on him.

'I can't walk away if you've conceived,' he reminded her, wondering why it had become so important that he kept her close. Habit from the island? Had he become attached to her in some way? He didn't get close to women, yet the prospect of even going to bed *without* Bunny was a new challenge.

'No, but you can back off until the baby's born…if there is one,' she said drily.

'Is that what you want?'

'Yes, in the circumstances it would be wiser,' she said stiffly. 'We both have to move on. I'll inform you if I have any news to share.'

'Okay.' Sebastian heard himself agree to what he didn't want and he was troubled by the knowledge. Being reasonable struck him as a fool's game. Yet logic sat at the very heart of him and he could not understand his own behaviour. For some reason he didn't feel logical about Bunny. What he wanted he didn't want to label.

Her brothers walked her back to her cabin and joined her inside without invitation. 'Has he asked you to sign an NDA?' Luke asked. 'He's asked us and we agreed because we're staying on this yacht.'

'No, he hasn't asked me yet but I'll probably say no,' Bunny admitted. 'I've no plans to talk about him but it was my experience too and I will retain the rights to my side of it.'

John grimaced. 'He's very possessive of you. Are you involved with him?'

Bunny sighed. 'I *was* but it's over now.' She had no intention whatsoever of getting into the possibility of her being pregnant and decided to shelve that for another day.

Her eldest brother looked relieved. 'That's probably for the best. I'm no pop psychologist but, with his background, he's got to be messed up to some degree.'

Bunny held her breath, waiting for him to elaborate but he didn't, and she watched her brothers depart in frustration. She got ready for bed, paced the floor, wondering what her feelings were for Sebastian. Whatever, those emotions were powerful and she *had* to know why he might be messed up. She didn't want anyone else's slant on his secrets either, nor, once she had the means to do so, did she want to look him up online, but the idea of snooping struck her as disrespectful.

She tiptoed to the cabin across from hers and gently rapped on the door. It was abruptly answered, swinging wide on a bare-chested Sebastian, barefoot and clad only in his jeans. 'Yes?'

'Sorry to interrupt but I wanted to know why your background might have messed you up...'

Sebastian blinked and then studied her intently. 'Someone's been talking.'

Reproach in her luminous gaze, she murmured drily, 'But not you...'

Without warning, he flung the door wide and stepped back. Lean bronzed muscles rippled as he shifted uneasily. 'You've got a nerve expecting answers after what you said earlier.'

Bunny winced in agreement. 'I don't want to look you up on the Internet and pry.'

A grim laugh was wrenched from his compressed lips. 'Even if that is what everyone else does?'

Bunny nodded in confirmation and stepped over the threshold.

CHAPTER SEVEN

IT WAS TIME that he told her about his back story, Sebastian reasoned heavily. He preferred to tell it in his own words rather than leave it to her to read the dramatic horrors online.

'It's bad stuff,' he warned her.

'I'm a good listener.'

'My grandmother indulged her eldest son, Jason, in every way,' Sebastian imparted wryly. 'He was the apple of her eye, no matter what he did, and when he met my mother, she was equally spoiled and wilful. Together they were a disaster but they married and had me. People thought it was a good match because they were both very rich. But my father never settled down. He was heavily into drugs and eventually my mother turned to other men.'

'Oh, dear…' Bunny mumbled, watching him pour himself a drink on the other side of the cabin.

'Do you want anything?' he asked.

'Water,' she chose, eying the lines of strain grooved round his wide sensual mouth, moving forward to accept the glass from him, belatedly guilty that she had cornered him into telling her what he so obviously didn't *want* to tell her. 'I'm sorry, I shouldn't have pushed you on such personal issues.'

Sebastian lifted her up with firm hands and deposited her on the end of the giant bed. 'You might as well know the facts when everyone else does,' he parried. 'In his twisted obsessive way my father adored my mother, but she'd met someone else and she insisted on a divorce. The lawyers who represented them were soon at each other's throats.'

'What age were you when all this was happening?'

'Six. The divorce fighting went on for months until one day my father just cracked. He'd already moved out of our home but when he arrived one evening, my nanny let him in,' he explained. 'It was her night off. As she left, my mother called the police. They started to argue and I hid behind the sofa. And without any warning—or indeed any prior record of violence—my father pulled out a gun and shot her...'

Bunny stared back at him with wide, horrified eyes.

'He was off his head. He was spraying bullets everywhere, stopping to reload, and then there was this silence for a long time. I was too scared to come out of hiding.' Sebastian was very pale, his lean, dark, perfect features taut as a bowstring in the lamplight. 'I heard one more shot...my father turned the gun on himself. The police found me with them. I was very distressed.'

Bunny stumbled off the bed and went over to him to wrap both arms round him in a hug. 'I am *so* sorry that I forced you to relive that.'

Sebastian gazed down at her, disconcerted by her unhidden desire to comfort him. Something clenched tight in his chest and he set her back from him with newly learned circumspection. 'You'd better head to bed before your family find you missing. I'll see you in the morning.'

Bunny had never wanted so badly to stay with him but he had lived over twenty years with that tragedy and what could she offer him? Pale and taut, she headed back in shock from what she had learned. He must've been traumatised by such an ordeal and the simultaneous loss of both parents. Had his grandmother taken him in and brought him up? She assumed that Loukia, whom he had mentioned with such affection, must've done. What a ghastly past to have to live down, she reflected, shaken even more by that story of his than she had shown him.

She got into bed, reminding herself that, now that she and Sebastian were no longer involved, his upsetting background wasn't anything to do with her any more. So, why did she feel so agonised on his behalf? Why more than anything else in the world did she want to go back to Sebastian and keep on holding him? The time to express that kind of compassion and affection was already behind them. But, she acknowledged, her heart still yearned for him and the closeness they had enjoyed on the island without criticism or watching eyes judging them.

For goodness' sake, why was she thinking like a lovestruck teenager? Two weeks wasn't enough time to fall in love with anyone, she told herself. Love at first sight, well, it certainly hadn't been that. Lust and loathing at first sight, she reasoned, her entire body overheating with shame. And then from that first night when in truth she had thrown herself at him, other bonds had formed quite naturally. She had felt safe with him, she had trusted him, which was ironic when she reckoned that Sebastian did not trust anyone unless they came with a signed NDA.

She had never felt the way she felt now about Tristram. Neither that instant, unreasoning craving and the frightening power of it, nor the strong, deeper emotions constantly pulling at her. Falling for Tristram had been a slow, steady thing, wholly in keeping with her cautious, sensible nature. Falling for Sebastian was like falling into the eye of a storm.

She was neither cautious nor sensible about Sebastian. She had flung herself into his arms with no thought of a future and had assured herself that she could handle a temporary fling. Only now here she was and she wasn't handling the end of their relationship well, was she? But she had to bury her feelings and deal with the future, most especially if she had conceived.

Sebastian had always made it crystal clear that there was no tomorrow for them. He preferred being alone and he didn't engage in committed relationships with women. He didn't believe in happy marriages either and only now could she comprehend that he was damaged by living through his parents' unhappy marriage and its even more traumatic conclusion. But she had to accept all that and the impossibility of being with Sebastian ever again while at the same time embracing her own probably very different future. And if she *did* prove to be pregnant, would she and Sebastian eventually manage to become reasonably friendly co-parents?

And even worse, in the aftermath of his own ghastly childhood experience, how would Sebastian feel about becoming a parent? Clearly, he had suffered from his parents' troubled marriage. She wouldn't be a bit surprised to learn that Sebastian had never planned to father a child.

'You look beautiful,' Sebastian said with unexpected warmth over the breakfast table.

Disconcerted by that unexpected compliment concerning the plain green sun dress and flat canvas shoes she wore, Bunny smiled back at him, ignoring the sudden telling break in her family's conversation as every eye turned to them. 'Thanks,' she said simply.

'We're leaving for the police station in half an hour and we'll follow that up with the shipping team interview.'

'I'd like to visit Reggie in hospital if that's possible. After all, I won't see him again once I go home…and he was good to me. It was only a few weeks but he was a great boss.'

Her father leant across the table to say, 'Did your mother tell you about Tristram turning up on our doorstep?'

Bunny froze. '*Tristram?* Why on earth would he call with you?'

'He read about you going missing in the newspaper and came to us to ask if there was any news or if there was anything that he could do to help,' her mother explained. 'We didn't invite him in. He left his number but I shouldn't think any of us will be making use of it.'

'The nerve of him! It's not as if we parted as friends,' Bunny exclaimed in a combination of annoyance and resentment, for she had neither seen nor spoken to her ex-boyfriend in a long time. To say the least, their breakup had been messy.

'He's still allowed to be concerned over whether you're alive or dead,' John declared mildly.

Sebastian brooded at the suspicion that the ex-boyfriend was hovering and awaiting Bunny's return. He was annoyed that she had refused the immediate blood test that would've told them whether or not there was going to be a baby but, whether he liked it or not, it was her body and her choice. He needed to get out of the habit of trying to intervene and boss her around because she didn't like it. She didn't suffer from his impatience, his need to plan every step in advance and to always know exactly where he was going. Well, she had killed those goals stone dead the same moment she came into his life, he reckoned with grim humour. He didn't know what he was doing, what he was planning to do next, no, he *only* knew that he wanted her.

He had told her that he would walk away. He had believed that he would walk away. He had been wrong. Still wanting her felt obsessional and it unnerved him. Moderation was always his rule with women but there was nothing moderate about the way he felt. From that first night on the island she had felt like *his* in some primal, utterly inexplicable and absurd way. And he had grown attached to that sensation as if some vital part of him had awakened, had changed him, had turned him inside out and upside down, subjecting him to extreme irrational urges. It was unnerving and he had to get a grip on it fast. He had to let her go, he had to let her walk away…for a time, at least. He had to give her the space to catch her breath before he pressed her.

Bunny was ill at ease because Sebastian was quiet, perfectly polite and pleasant when he did speak but mentally miles away. They got into the helicopter, only the two of them because it was only them who had to give statements and answer questions. From the moment they disembarked at the airport to travel by car into the city, they were surrounded by a security team, who prevented the cameramen and the journalists from either photographing them or questioning them.

'I didn't realise that it would be like this,' Bunny admitted, shaken by the excitement that their arrival had caused and the heaving desperation of the press to get closer to them.

'I've arranged for an official statement to be made about our rescue, but they want the whole story and they're not going to get it,' he responded curtly.

Within an hour they were inside the police station and making their statements, an Indonesian lawyer who apparently worked for Sebastian overseeing every step. It was shocking to witness how much attention and deference Sebastian received simply by dint of being an extremely wealthy and powerful tycoon. On the other side of the city, they answered the investigators' questions about the night of the storm, Reggie's actions and what the two of them had seen and done.

Soon afterwards they were visiting the older man in hospital, where he was now recuperating from his surgery. Reggie explained that a tiny fracture had been found in the mast, the result of a collision with another boat months earlier. At the time the authorities had judged the catamaran undamaged.

They wished him well and returned to the yacht, where she found her family packing up to leave.

'We assume that you have to stay another few days to satisfy the officials,' her father told her ruefully. 'But, lovely as it is here, we need to get home and your brothers need to get back to work.'

'You don't need to stay on in Indonesia and neither do I,' Sebastian told Bunny stiffly, fighting his own inclinations to retain her to the last ditch. 'Any further queries will be passed to us or dealt with by my legal reps here. You can travel home with your family today.'

Shock forked through Bunny like lightning and she turned pale. 'But I haven't got my stuff back yet,' she mumbled weakly.

'It'll be sent on to you once it's made available. I did take the liberty of finding you a spare phone,' Sebastian added, handing her a brand-new mobile phone. 'I put my number in there so that you can stay in touch.'

'Thanks…of course,' she mumbled, pale lips compressed at the prospect of leaving him, of possibly never ever seeing him again. 'I hope I still have a new job to start but who knows if they've held it open for me?'

Her mother wrapped a supportive arm round her. 'I'm so glad you're returning with us. The sooner you get back to a normal routine, the better you will feel.'

Bunny couldn't imagine a normal routine at home because she hadn't had one of those since childhood. She had only just moved home after completing her degree before she'd set off on her year of travel. Everything changed, nothing stayed the same and she looked up at Sebastian as if in appeal.

'It will be a welcome break from me,' he said quietly.

Bunny studied him, tracing those tantalisingly beautiful dark male features and mentally kicking herself. She dropped her gaze in haste. No doubt he was in need of a break from her and he was right, there was no reason for her to stay on. She needed to get on with her life and leave him to enjoy his alone, the way he liked it. No clinging, no sighing, no tears, no excuses. She went back to the cabin and packed only what she had worn. At the very last moment, she picked up Sebastian's discarded Dior sweater, buried her nose in it, drank in the faint lingering scent of him and guiltily shoved it in the flight bag her mother had given her to use.

There it was: the result from the *third* pregnancy test and it was another positive.

Light-headed, Bunny left the cloakroom and got back to packing the library van with fresh books and special requests. On one level it annoyed her that Sebastian had been proven right to be convinced that she would be pregnant. She had thought that an unnecessarily pessimistic outlook, had been tempted to tell him that some women took for ever trying to get pregnant and that the likelihood of her conceiving after just two weeks of sex was slim.

Only now all she could recall was the sheer amount of sex they had had, the barriers that had fallen so fast when they were together all day and alone. It all flooded back into her memory: the spicy kitchen encounters, the swimming sessions, the times up against the walls, the doors. Face burning, she reckoned it would be true to say that Sebastian might as well have been chasing an Olympic record and that it would be unjust to blame him when she had been such a willing partner. The wild freedom of such intimacy had been new and crazily seductive to her and Sebastian's lack of inhibition had smashed down her boundaries one by one.

And now there was to be a baby. She was going to have a baby. A split second later she was smiling ear to ear because she mightn't have Sebastian but she would have his child. But how would *he* feel about that reality? Her smile died, the brief bubbly happiness that had blossomed inside her draining away. He didn't want a family. She had guessed that. On his terms, it would be the worst possible news.

'Aren't you away yet, Bunny dear? Been daydreaming again?' her middle-aged boss enquired, popping her head into the van. 'If you don't watch out you'll be late for the stop at Little Moseby and there'll be complaints and then you'll be running behind all day.'

'I'm leaving right now,' Bunny asserted, deciding to text Sebastian at her first stop before she got into any more trouble.

She worked with two very nice ladies but saw little of them because she was always out with the library van touring rural areas, a service that those without transport very much appreciated. Her job had been held open and her late arrival forgiven because nobody had fancied the hassle of readvertising her position, although she was well aware that her colleagues felt that a man would have been a better fit for the post. It wasn't that anyone was being sexist, merely that they had assumed a man would be safer in lonely places and better able to handle the van when it broke down. They had yet to meet men like her brothers, who struggled even to change a tyre.

Once the rush of customers had tailed off in Little Moseby, Bunny pulled out her phone. It was six weeks since she had seen Sebastian. She had received her rucksack back and had texted him with her thanks, only it had not been the start of much of a conversation. He had asked how she was, the polite stuff, and, of course, she hadn't told him the truth because he wouldn't want to hear it. She was miserable, but she couldn't tell him that, couldn't tell him that her much-wanted job wasn't at all what she had imagined it would be and that living back at home was stifling. He had also sent her flowers every week, which had raised hopes that went unfulfilled because he had neither phoned to speak to her nor suggested that they should meet up.

'You fell for him,' her mother had sighed on that very long flight back home. 'Of course you did. He's very handsome and successful and all that stuff, but I expect it's not likely to go any further with him living in such a different world.'

She texted him, deciding to keep it bald and honest.

I'm pregnant.

She was on her third stop of the day by the time she got a response.

What did the doctor say?

I haven't seen a doctor. I did THREE tests.

Sebastian remained unimpressed.

Biting her lip, she typed that it would take days for her to get a doctor's appointment and that her brother worked in the surgery and that everyone would be put in an awkward, embarrassing position.

Sebastian wondered if she hadn't seen a doctor because she preferred to conceal her pregnancy and her past intimacy with him.

Are you ashamed of your condition?

He was clearly furious at that suspicion.

And that was it.

She almost threw her phone, the one he had bought her, through the windscreen in her rage with him. She didn't respond. Her phone kept on beeping with incoming texts and she ignored it. Sebastian was so particular about the details of absolutely everything. Every P and Q had to be minded and every T crossed. Sometimes he infuriated her and she wasn't dealing with that when she was supposed to be working. She just didn't want to let her family know that she was expecting until she had talked to Sebastian.

As if she didn't already know that she was pregnant even before she did those stupid tests, she thought wearily as she drove home in her mother's ancient car. Her menstrual cycle had stopped dead. Her breasts were sore. She was unbelievably tired and nauseous, and her sister-in-law, John's wife, Betsy, had experienced all those symptoms only months earlier. Unfortunately, however, the much-anticipated event of the first Woods grandchild had come to nothing when Betsy had had an early miscarriage. Currently pregnancy was a topic best avoided in the family.

As she parked her mother's car, she checked her texts, noting Sebastian's increasing frustration with her until the final text when he announced that he would be visiting her the next day.

She phoned him for the first time. 'You *can't*. I'm working all day.'

'I'll track down the library van and ambush you,' Sebastian said with remarkable good cheer.

'You're not…furious?' she prompted.

'No. I was expecting this development.'

Whoa, baby, don't get excited but you're a *development*. She rested her hand against her flat stomach and a feeling of warmth filled her.

'I'll organise lunch somewhere,' Sebastian told her briskly.

'I don't get very long…oh, it's a Friday,' she recalled abstractedly. 'I get longer for lunch on Fridays because it fits the itinerary better.'

'Wonderful. I'll see you around noon tomorrow.'

Right, well, that got the necessity of telling Sebastian out of the way. She screened a yawn in the hallway of the comfortable, cluttered bungalow where her parents lived. As she wandered into the kitchen to help her mother make dinner, she was wondering what she would wear the next day. Her last chance to impress before she lost her normal shape and started sprouting curves.

'Sebastian's coming down tomorrow to take me for lunch,' she revealed, looking on that admission as required footwork in advance of the more shocking revelation that she had conceived by a man who would have not the smallest intention or interest in putting a ring on her finger.

'Has something happened?' her mother enquired. 'I thought you weren't planning to see him again.'

'I didn't think I would get the chance,' Bunny said truthfully. 'But we have some stuff to talk about.'

'He's not sending you those extravagant flowers every week for nothing,' her father commented drily. 'Obviously he's still interested in you.'

Bunny tensed. 'Sort of... I think,' she parried uncomfortably.

'He's got a tragic back history but I wouldn't hold that against him,' her father, a retired policeman, said thoughtfully.

'I just don't want you to get hurt,' her mother chipped in.

And after dinner, unable to settle, Bunny told herself that she wouldn't get hurt even though she was already counting down the hours to seeing him again, picturing him, wondering how he would feel seeing her again. Would he feel *anything*? Bunny had never been more wretched than she had been for the past six weeks, missing Sebastian with every breath that she drew. The colour was leached out of her days by the giant black hole of unhappiness inside her. She had told herself that she didn't love him, that she hadn't known him well enough or long enough for love, but, in her heart, she knew that was a lie. For whatever reasons she had fallen for Sebastian Pagonis like a giant ton of bricks pitched off a cliff and having to get by without him weighed on her very heavily.

Sebastian appeared not long after she arrived at her last morning stop. She was busy tidying the shelves and checking the returns when she heard steps and she suppressed a groan because she assumed it was another customer. Instead, when she whirled round she was confronted by Sebastian, impossibly tall and broad and wholly unfamiliar in a very snazzy dark suit. She sucked in a stark breath, her heartbeat thundering.

'I'm a little early.'

'No, that's fine,' she said breathlessly. 'I just have to park the van in the pub car park and I'm free. You're looking very…tailored and elegant today.'

Sebastian gave her his lazy grin. 'I thought I should make an effort for once. I usually dress very casually.'

'Should I be flattered?' she teased. 'Or intimidated?'

'Hopefully not the latter,' he intoned in his smooth, well-bred drawl. 'Just don't be expecting it all the time.'

A huge smile lit up Bunny's face because she thought it was promising that he was already assuming that he would see her again. He looked amazing, black hair in his usual sleek style on top of his handsome head, and he really had gone to town on his appearance because he had teamed the suit with a silver-grey shirt and a red silk tie. Drop-dead gorgeous but never to be hers. Live in the moment, she urged herself, enjoy him for what he is, a luxury and a pleasure. But, ultimately, too rich for her blood.

'Shall we go?' he enquired, supremely proud of himself for not commenting on the fact that she looked as if she had lost weight and wasn't sleeping well. In fact, she seemed fragile, still beautiful though with her delicate face, snub nose and soft mouth, with her glorious golden hair tumbling round her narrow shoulders.

'I'll park the van...' With difficulty she dredged her gaze from him, her colour high, and closed the door to climb into the driver's seat.

When she'd finished locking up, she smoothed down her plain green dress, straightened her cardigan and tidied her hair, wincing because she owned not a single garment smart enough to impress anybody. It would take time and cash to build up a decent working wardrobe. Sebastian was posed beside a sleek sports car and another two cars were parked behind him, having already disgorged their occupants. Men in smart suits and earpieces were all over the place.

'Travelling in style?' she asked.

'The security?' He shrugged a broad shoulder as he ushered her into the passenger seat. 'No, this is the norm for me. My week in Indonesia was an escape week from these trappings and it turned into two weeks of freedom, so I'm not complaining.'

'Have you always lived like this?'

Sebastian swung into the seat beside her and ignited the engine. 'Pretty much for the last ten years.'

'We could have a quick meal at the pub here,' she pointed out.

'I wanted something more special.'

'Oh?' But Sebastian being Sebastian, he didn't take the bait or explain why he was opting for special rather than convenient.

A lean brown hand settled on her slender thigh briefly and she was tempted to put her hand down on top of his, eager for that connection and fighting the desire to deepen it. 'I missed having you around,' he told her. 'What's it like being back with your family?'

Her thigh tingled where he retained contact and then he removed his hand again, killing the buzz she had experienced. 'Pros and cons. I'd like to move out but I don't have a car and—' Suddenly conscious that she was lamenting her financial status to a billionaire, she winced inwardly. 'Well, there's just good reasons to live at home for the moment.'

'I've a feeling that that will change.'

'With me being pregnant?' Bunny shook her head as he filtered his silver Lamborghini down a long lane lined with wonderfully colourful maple trees. 'My family aren't the type to throw me out in the winter snow. Lecture me, maybe, be disappointed, probably, but nothing worse.'

'No, not that,' he said evasively as he pulled the car to a halt below the trees and parked in front of a long traditional farmhouse. 'This is a very exclusive restaurant. I hope it lives up to its ratings.'

'After the island I can eat anything, except not fish… please, no more fish for at least six months,' she pleaded as he climbed out, urging her to remain seated, and walked right round the bonnet to open her door for her. 'What are you doing?'

'Acting like a gentleman. You're pregnant,' he reminded her as he grasped her hand and lifted her gently out. 'You shouldn't be straining a single muscle right now.'

'You told me that you were raised to be a gentleman but that you don't behave like one,' she reminded him.

'I'm also highly adaptable. All my life, I've had to be,' he imparted, leading her through the parked cars, not to the front entrance as she had expected, but to a quieter side entrance. She heard the distant hum of voices and the clatter of china and cutlery. An older man greeted them and ushered them along a cosy panelled corridor into a very comfortable room with a beautifully set single table, two chairs and a big, cushioned sofa by the window. The fire in the old-fashioned fireplace was lit to ward off the autumn chill and decorated with pumpkin lights.

'This is lovely, very seasonal,' Bunny said warmly as they ordered drinks and the menus were presented. They both chose light bites rather than full meals. A private lunch date where they had their own room was unexpected but she assumed that once again Sebastian was conserving his privacy.

Sebastian fingered the tiny box in his pocket and breathed in deep. The server left the room. Sebastian looked at Bunny's happy smiling face with satisfaction and then he rose upright before dropping down fluidly onto one knee. He was being traditional so he might as well go the whole hog, he decided with determination, even if his agile brain was already throwing up a cartoonish image of the old-fashioned gesture. He clicked open the box and extended it and said with all the gravity he could muster, 'Will you marry me?'

CHAPTER EIGHT

BUNNY HAD NEVER been as shocked or unprepared for a surprise in her life. She leapt upright, wide-eyed and conscience-stricken. 'Oh, *no*!' she exclaimed in dismay. 'Please don't say anything more!'

Slanted ebony brows pleating in confusion, Sebastian slowly rose back to his feet and stared down at her in disbelief. 'I wasn't expecting you to immediately say yes but I did think you would be pleased. Instead, you're staring at me as if I asked something untenable!'

'Please sit down,' she urged shakily. 'Can I see the ring? Just out of sheer curiosity?'

Sebastian set the tiny box on the table. Bunny's eyes were stinging, pain and guilt and a whole host of other emotions swimming around inside her and threatening to spill over into the tears that were all too ready to assail her in recent times. She didn't need a doctor to tell her that her hormones were all roaring into pregnancy hyperdrive.

The ring was a glorious glittering diamond surrounded by emeralds in an art deco geometric shape. 'It's gorgeous,' she whispered admiringly.

'Did I say something wrong?' Sebastian demanded in a raw undertone.

'Sit down,' Bunny urged. 'I get dizzy when you stand over me.'

Lean bronzed profile taut, Sebastian sat back down in his seat.

Bunny leant forward and immediately reached for both of his hands. 'You *know* that you don't really want to marry me.'

'I beg your pardon,' Sebastian challenged, sculpted jaw determined.

She squeezed his hands as if to demand his full attention. 'Sebastian, I know how you feel about marriage. You don't believe in it or in relationships or in couples or in love. Let's talk plainly here,' she murmured steadily. 'You're asking me to marry you either because you think you *should* because I'm pregnant or because you think it's what I want and expect.'

'Thank you for clarifying that for me.' Sebastian spoke with sardonic bite.

'I never thought you would be so impulsive.'

'I miss you,' he framed in a driven undertone. 'It's been six blasted weeks. I'm not being impulsive, I'm being practical.'

'Practical isn't proposing to a woman you were only with for two weeks.'

'Two weeks, twenty-four-seven,' he incised the reminder.

'Marrying me would be a mistake for you. You don't want to be trapped into something like that,' she reasoned uneasily, a warm spot inside her spreading at his admission that he had missed her, had counted their weeks apart. 'We could end up hating each other by the time this baby's born, and splitting up always creates bad feelings, so co-parenting would be more difficult after a divorce.'

'And to think that I believed you were Little Miss Sunshine and yet you have made only negative assumptions about me and what I could offer.'

'You said you missed me...' Bunny hesitated and then bravely pushed herself on to go out on a limb and spell it out. 'Are you saying that you have feelings for me?'

She was literally hanging by her fingernails in the hope of an encouraging answer because that would have been a game-changer.

Instead, in a frustrated movement, Sebastian yanked his hands free of hers. 'No, I'm not. I'm *not* in love with you. I've never been in love and I don't want to be. Love can be a nasty, twisted thing and I want nothing to do with it. But I do believe that I can love my child and that my child can love me. If we're not together, though, I'll hardly see that child and that worries me. I also find the idea of being parted from you while you're carrying my baby even more worrying. I feel very strongly that we should be together *now*.'

Just for a moment, Bunny allowed herself to imagine how she would have felt if Sebastian had answered her differently, if he'd thrown out a few flattering lies and sprinkled them with stardust. Had he done that, she'd have bitten his hand off with eagerness to accept his proposal, but that wasn't Sebastian's way. He preferred brutal honesty. He didn't make empty promises or feed her half-truths with a sting in their tail, like Tristram insisting that he loved her even after she found him with another girl and then telling her while she was packing up to leave him that she was boring and dull in bed.

'You're not prepared to marry me and take a chance on me, are you?' Sebastian breathed in an almost savage undertone.

'Not right now. It's too soon and I'm not convinced you've thought it through in enough depth. I can imagine nothing worse than becoming your wife and then you changing your mind about wanting to be married.' Well, actually she could, she reflected reluctantly. Sebastian walking away for ever would be the absolute worst scenario. And he would probably never ask her to marry him again and that was a thought that made her feel a little desperate and fear that she was her own worst enemy.

'We could get engaged,' she suggested in a sudden rush. 'Try that for size first.'

Sebastian was too restive to stay still and he was pacing the small room, swinging back abruptly to her to say, 'You'd agree to that option?'

'Why not?'

'We'd have to live together,' he told her without hesitation. 'I want you *with* me. That's a priority. Becoming a father starts with looking after you.'

Disconcerted by how strongly he stressed that reality, Bunny was relieved when the server entered with their meals. If they lived together, he would soon find out whether he wanted that kind of relationship or whether he preferred his loner lifestyle. If he walked away, she got hurt. If she had him and then lost him again, she would be hurt. It didn't seem to her that she had any true choice.

She sipped her water and then stuck out her left hand. 'You can put the ring on now.'

Sebastian vented a pained groan. 'All sentimental and soppy with bells on, right?'

'Well, you're the one who said he wanted to sign up for this,' she dared.

'Only because it's the only way I get you *and* the baby. I'm basic. I don't need frills.'

'I like frills…in the right place at the right time,' she countered as he slid the ring onto her wedding finger, where it glittered in the firelight. It fitted her very well, which she chose to take as a positive sign. 'It's an antique ring, isn't it?'

'It belonged to my Pagonis grandmother, Loukia.'

'She raised you, didn't she?' Bunny gathered while they ate.

'No, I was passed like a parcel nobody wanted to keep around the Pagonis tribe. Six months to a year with each set. Let's not talk about that now.'

Bunny had paled in dismay at the explanation but she smiled and his brilliant dark gaze lingered on her with approval.

'We'll have to find somewhere to live. I assume you'll prefer to be within reach of your family?'

'If it were possible, yes,' she agreed.

'And your current employment isn't very suitable now that you're pregnant,' Sebastian pointed out. 'I don't want you out alone in some van at the back end of nowhere dealing with strangers.'

'The budget wouldn't stretch to an assistant. It's not

what I imagined I'd be doing but you have to start at the bottom and work your way up the ladder.'

'Unless you're a Pagonis or attached to one,' Sebastian slotted in with amusement. Considering that he already had everything fully planned for their immediate future, he was relieved that he had very little left to do. 'I believe I can come up with a library for you to work in. *Thee mou*… I own an enormous amount of property. I suppose you want to go home to your family tonight.'

Bunny went pink and flashed her ring. 'Yes.'

'All I want is a bed and you and no interruptions.' That was a catchphrase for Sebastian, a mere soundbite. Everything was already organised, everything that would allow him to be the decent parent he himself had never had.

Bunny brushed her hair behind her ear and straightened her spine, a self-conscious smile playing with the corners of her mouth. 'Basic, well, you did warn me.'

His wide sensual lips settled into a smile, the last remnants of his tension evaporating. He had got more or less what he wanted, he conceded, and the bottom line was that he wanted *her*. Engaged, married, what was the difference? As long as she was with him, those frills she mentioned didn't matter. And possibly she was right. Maybe he *would* wake up in a few weeks and want his freedom back. He was as afraid of letting her down as he was of developing feelings for her. He wanted no part of the kind of dangerously possessive feelings his father had had for his mother.

'We'll wait until we've moved in together,' Sebastian decreed, on a roll now that he had achieved his goal. 'I want to take my time. When we get back together it won't be a temporary thing that reminds me of a one-night stand.'

'I want to take my time too,' Bunny sighed as they left the table and headed back outside. No hurried, stolen moments of passion for Sebastian, she thought ruefully. He wanted it *all*. He wanted perfection.

'You'll need to resign from your job,' he pointed out as he walked her back towards the car.

'Right now... I mean, *immediately*?' Bunny frowned in dismay and stopped dead in her tracks. 'I'll still have to work a month's notice. I won't let people down.'

'The longer you wait to leave, the longer it will be until we're living together.'

'You're the most shameless blackmailer!' Bunny snapped furiously, ignoring the turned heads of his hovering security team as she stalked after him. 'But it doesn't mean I'll abandon my principles.'

'Principles have a cost,' Sebastian informed her without hesitation. 'I'm due in Germany to speak at an international conference next week and I also have a lengthy trip to Switzerland lined up.'

'That's perfect, then, isn't it?' Bunny dealt him a huge smile although she really wanted to slap him. He had expected her to fall into line because that was what people did for Sebastian Pagonis. He didn't accept her point of view because it didn't meet his wishes and expectations. 'While you're busy, I'll be busy too.'

'Not ideal though,' Sebastian incised.

'Moving home, resigning from my job, being with you. I wasn't expecting all of that. Six weeks ago, you didn't even hint that you wanted to see me again… It's all a lot to get my head around and you need to be less of a perfectionist.'

'I'm *not* a perfectionist,' he ground out through grated teeth.

'You so *are*. You laid every bonfire in a distinct pattern. You like everything in the correct order. You are never untidy or disorganised. I'm never going to live up to your standards, so you have to accept that now… On the other hand if you would admit to just wanting messy, ordinary, very human me, the sky's your limit!' she proclaimed in desperation, determined to get him out of the brooding mood that had engulfed him as the ramifications of her having refused his marriage proposal sank in.

It shouldn't be like that, not the same day he asked her to marry him and put an engagement ring on her finger, all of it so traditional and so *not* him. He had put on the suit, got down on one knee and it could only have been for *her* benefit and she had disappointed him, which made her feel hugely guilty and sad on his behalf. 'Sebastian…?'

'I'd better take you back to that van.'

Before he could start the car, she just snapped loose her seat belt and grabbed him, one set of fingers spearing into his dense black hair to bring his head down, the other yanking him towards her so that she could find his mouth. She kissed him and then he took over, ramming back his seat and hauling her onto his lap to savour her more passionately. And all the tension evaporated and birthed another kind of tension. It was as though a dam had burst and they were both so hungry for each other that neither one of them had the least control. His tongue delved deep and a growl sounded in his chest as his mouth tasted her delicate jawline and roamed down over the slender length of her neck to the slope of her shoulder. At the same time his big hands roamed over every part of her that he could reach. Bunny gasped and squirmed and tried frantically to get closer.

Sebastian expelled his breath on a hiss and lifted her to settle back into the passenger seat. 'I'll take you to the house we're going to be living in.'

'You already have a house picked?' Bunny demanded in amazement.

'You were right,' he conceded grudgingly. 'I plan *everything* and you gave me six weeks to do it in.'

'I didn't exactly give you six weeks...you kept your distance.'

'I won't be keeping my distance after tonight,' he warned her, laughing and leaning over her, long fingers sifting slowly through her thick silky hair. 'I'll pick you up after work and we'll tell your parents that we've got engaged and that you're moving out. But we won't see the house until tomorrow because I'd like you to see it in daylight first. Are we mentioning the baby?'

'No, not today.' Bunny's head was reeling at the knowledge that Sebastian was about to turn her life upside down. But they would be together. That was the bottom line, she reminded herself, and that was really all that mattered.

She was on a high throughout the afternoon. She put in her resignation but she saw no reason not to work her notice if Sebastian was going to be away on business. She could manage an hour commuting for the space of a month. Even though she would no longer have the use of her mother's car? There would probably be a train, she reasoned.

Sebastian followed her home. She had forgotten that it was a Friday night and the whole family would be there for dinner. Her mother gasped and cried when she saw the ring. Sebastian valiantly withstood being hugged for a solid five minutes and she could see that he was relieved when her father merely shook hands with him. He met her other brothers and their wives and girlfriends. He was much more relaxed and chatty than she would have expected and was predictably cornered by her youngest brother, Noah, who was the family tech whizz and he was eager to hear all about Sebastian's time at MIT.

Bunny ignored her usual wine and had a soft drink instead, reddening when she saw her brother, John, taking note of the fact. When she came out of the bathroom, John was waiting for her. 'So, you noticed,' she said with a rueful little smile.

'Of course, I did. Why didn't you tell me?'

'Because that was Sebastian's news to hear first and I didn't need to get advice on options from you because I already knew what I wanted,' she explained calmly. 'He asked me to marry him but I thought it was too soon for that. I think we should have some time together before we make that leap.'

John frowned in surprise. 'Considering that you've been pining for him since you got back, I'm amazed you didn't just say yes. You're being very sensible.'

'Not really. I'm moving in with him tomorrow. We'll see how that goes.'

'Why so pessimistic?'

'In his heart I'm not sure he's ready for a committed relationship.'

'Time will tell.'

Her parents asked Sebastian to stay and he thanked them but insisted that he would see them in the morning when he collected Bunny.

'Nothing on earth would persuade me to enjoy our reunion sleeping next door to your parents,' he murmured wickedly in her ear when she saw him back to his car. 'You're quite noisy.'

'Am I?' she said, aghast and mortified.

'And I really like it,' he confided, lacing one hand into the fall of her hair and plundering her parted lips with passionate impatience. 'Your enthusiasm only matches my own.'

'Tristram?' Eyes wide, and having answered the bell while awaiting Sebastian, Bunny froze when she found her ex-boyfriend at the door.

He was a well-built young man of around six feet, with cropped blond hair and bright blue eyes. Once she had found him attractive, and his seemingly easy nature had charmed her. But now she fancied she could see the look of entitlement and arrogance in his expectant gaze because he assumed that she would be bowled over by his visit and delighted to see him again. Tristram never doubted the warmth of his welcome.

'I read about your dashing adventure in Asia and

that you were now home. Aren't you going to invite me in?' Tristram asked.

'I'm sorry but there would be no point inviting you in because I'm about to go out,' Bunny advanced stiltedly, but she felt as if she was being rude and stepped outside to seem friendlier than she felt. 'I also don't see what we have to talk about.'

'You look amazing,' Tristram told her, noting the silky conditioned fall of her golden hair and her perfectly made-up face while the grape-coloured fitted skirt and silk shirt she wore enhanced her diminutive curves and small waist.

'Thanks.' Bunny would've liked to have said it was the first thing she threw on but in truth she had made an enormous effort on Sebastian's behalf. She had been waiting at the doors of the nearest local boutique at opening time and had blown everything in her bank account on a decent outfit and some make-up.

'You never made this much effort for me,' Tristram complained, his mouth taking on a sullen curve.

'But then, according to what I was told, you didn't make much effort for her,' Sebastian intoned from behind them both.

Bunny spun in concert with Tristram, who flushed angrily.

'Sebastian Pagonis… Tristram Elsworthy,' Bunny introduced stiffly.

Sebastian was seething, inflamed by the discovery of the ex on Bunny's doorstep. He dropped a territorial arm round her slight shoulders. 'We're running late,' he murmured apologetically.

Tristram backed off a step with a wide understanding smile. 'I won't keep you. I'll call another time, Bunny.'

'I'm afraid I won't be here, Tris. I'm moving,' she said pleasantly.

As her ex headed down the path to return to his car, Sebastian bit out in a raw undertone, 'You should've told him you were pregnant and engaged.'

'I wasn't about to give him private information like that!' Bunny objected.

But it was too late to be talking about what was private because Sebastian had given the game away. A gasp sounded in the hall of her parents' home. Bunny swivelled and saw her mother clamp her hand to her lips below her rounded and shocked eyes.

'Is it true?' the older woman asked.

And that was another hold-up as they went indoors to discuss that subject. Her mother shared the news that John's wife, Betsy, was expecting again, only she wasn't yet telling people, a meaningful restriction that seemed to have escaped her mother-in-law's understanding.

'Well, I must say that went down very well,' Sebastian remarked as they strolled out to the car, her luggage having been stowed while they talked. 'Your mother can't keep a secret.'

'I can't either…not very well or for very long,' Bunny confided guiltily. 'Why were you so angry at Tristram dropping in?'

Sebastian's sculpted jawline clenched. On the face of it, he didn't know why he'd been so angry. He simply didn't want her former boyfriend anywhere near Bunny. Even though the guy had backed off fast, Sebastian didn't like him showing up at Bunny's home and annoying her. That was normal. It didn't mean he was either fanatically possessive or obsessionally jealous, he assured himself. And it would be totally normal for him to check out Tristram Elsworthy and find out who he was.

'What did he want?'

'I haven't a clue. It's probably just one of those random things because he read about me being missing in a newspaper,' she framed. 'But you were so angry when you realised who he was, you went rigid.'

'I don't want him hanging around you,' Sebastian told her truthfully.

'Well, I'm not going to encourage him,' Bunny said cheerfully. 'I can't stand him. He's so fake and I see it now.'

But on one level, Sebastian was still brooding and annoyed that *he* had been annoyed about something so trivial. Even so, Tristram with the uber-short hair and the winning smile was her first love and women were said to be romantic and nostalgic about their first loves. Still troubled by the anger that had engulfed him, Sebastian was quiet.

'So why aren't you telling me anything about this house?' Bunny demanded as Sebastian steered the powerful car off the motorway and back into the countryside.

'It's a surprise. It's not modern but then you like history and old buildings, don't you?'

Her brow furrowed. 'How do you know that?'

'Don't you remember rabbiting on about how much you loved Hampton Court when we were on the island? About how you loved to tour old houses and imagine the people who had lived there? About how you believed that most contemporary furniture lacks character?'

Bunny burned with deep mortification. Certainly she had been guilty of rabbiting on a fair bit, which was why Sebastian was so very well acquainted with her likes and dislikes.

'The location of the house also had to be within reasonable reach of your family for you and close to London for me,' Sebastian added. 'I chose accordingly and I *nailed* it.'

'Did you indeed? What about your own preferences?'

'If a cave came with the usual mod cons I'd live in it. I picked this place based on *your* preferences because I don't really care about my domestic surroundings.'

'Did you buy this property specially?' she asked with a wince.

'*Thee mou*…the last thing we need to do in the Pagonis empire is buy property. I'd never seen the house until I visited it a few weeks ago but it *is* an inherited estate. It belonged to my grandfather's first wife, Rosalie. She was an orphaned only child when they married and she died in childbirth.'

'I didn't realise he'd been married more than once—'

'Neither did I until I grew up. My grandmother must have been a little sensitive about being the *second* wife because she never mentioned her predecessor or as far as I know ever visited this place. It had tenants for decades and I had to throw an army of staff in to put it into order.'

A remarkable turreted and walled Tudor gateway greeted them at the foot of the country lane they were travelling. 'Where on earth are we visiting?' Bunny enquired, assuming this was a detour before the main event.

'Wait and see,' Sebastian urged.

Beyond the gates, long stretches of grass ran between ancient woodland trees and the lane branched to the right. Tall, elaborate chimneys pierced the skyline and then she saw the building. 'Where are we?'

'Our future home… Knightsmead Court.'

Bunny gaped at the ornate expanse of red brick and the lines of mullioned windows, utterly deprived of speech. 'It's glorious,' she whispered, pinching her forearm to be certain that she wasn't fantasising, because Sebastian was bringing her to her dream home. 'But it looks awfully big and not at all your style.'

'But very much yours,' Sebastian pointed out with assurance as he ran the Lamborghini to a halt on the gravel. 'Let's get out and explore.'

They stepped through a doorway above which a date in the sixteenth century was etched. An older woman welcomed them and Sebastian introduced them. Maybelle was the housekeeper. Bunny concentrated as much as she could on the conversation while sidling to the left to gaze into a log fire set in an opulently moulded chimneypiece. Warmth spilled out from the flames, lights flickering on polished oak furniture while flowers from an arrangement in the corner scented the air. To the rear a spectacular carved staircase wended up to the next floor with astonishing sculpted pineapples adorning the newel posts on the way. It was gorgeous while also being unexpectedly homely and warm.

'Let me show you to your new domain…' Sebastian urged, closing one hand over hers and walking her towards the back of the rambling house, his thumb caressing her slender wrist. 'After my grandfather's first wife died, the house was let but only after the most valuable furniture, paintings and books were removed and placed in safe storage. Everything has now been returned and here we have the library.' He flung open a heavy door into a large, very cluttered room, piled with specialist book storage boxes.

'Oh, my goodness!' Bunny exclaimed, scanning the two-tier room with its gallery and solid wooden staircase in one corner, not to mention the plethora of empty shelves waiting to be filled. 'But this room isn't from the Tudor era.'

'Of course not, and we can be grateful that the Victorians built a massive extension at the back of the house to house the library and various other things that were deemed necessities back in their day.'

'Grateful?' she queried in surprise.

'The extension was crumbling and threatening the integrity of the original historic house but it couldn't be demolished because this is a listed building. The trade-off for restoring it at an incredible cost was being allowed to add bathrooms in the Victorian extension to make the house a little more habitable for our tenants.'

'This library is going to be a huge job,' she confided

absently. 'And an absolute joy. Now I understand why you said that you had work for me.'

'As long as you understand that that work only starts when we return from Switzerland,' Sebastian extended lazily.

'We?' Bunny spun round and looked at him, automatically taking in the wickedly hot perfection of him sheathed in jeans and a black shirt that moulded every inch of his powerful torso and long, strong legs. Black diamond eyes glittered back at her in enquiring mode. 'But I'm not travelling to Switzerland with you.'

'Of course you are…and to Germany.'

Bunny blinked in bewilderment. 'No, I *can't*. I'll be working my notice for the next month.'

Sebastian stilled, lean, darkly handsome features tightening. 'Even after I told you how I felt about that?'

'Just a few weeks and then they'll have someone who will take over when I leave. That way the readers won't be left without the service and disappointed,' she reasoned awkwardly, but her conviction that she was doing what was right remained unshaken.

'What about *me* being disappointed?' Sebastian breathed in a bitter undertone. 'Where do I come into this decision?'

Bunny's heart sank on the realisation that they had hit a sticking point, one of those concealed tripwires or triggers that set couples at odds when they didn't know each other well enough to know what the other party wanted. And the awful truth was that Sebastian hadn't come into her decision at all because he hadn't told her that he wanted her with him when he went abroad.

CHAPTER NINE

'WELL, YOU DIDN'T really come into the decision because it's my life and my reputation at stake, not yours,' Bunny proffered tightly. 'And it's only for a month, Sebastian! The way you're reacting, you'd think I'd decided to work miles away for the next year at least. I had absolutely no idea that you were expecting me to travel with you, *be* with you when you're working. You didn't share that wish with me.'

'I didn't,' Sebastian conceded between teeth that sounded gritted.

He had had everything planned but plans fell through, especially with Bunny in the driving seat. She was bone-deep stubborn. She had said no to marriage, which had thrown him onto the defensive. He had dealt with that setback, however, had accepted that he was pretty much on probation as a would-be husband. As a result, he had worked to make everything else perfect for her. However, the simply wanting her with him, wanting her within reach, had fallen apart as a goal as well. And he couldn't believe it because he had made so much effort on her behalf. For the very first time he was really *trying* with a woman, but she hadn't budged an inch from her previous stance. *Was* he being unreasonable? He was willing to admit that he was demanding, but nothing had ever been as important to him as she was.

'I'm sorry that I've disappointed you,' Bunny murmured unhappily in the long tense silence. 'I assumed that you'd be busy working so it wouldn't matter to you if I was working as well.'

'You'll have to have a bodyguard with you when you're out doing those library stops,' Sebastian told her grimly. 'I don't want you alone in quiet places, at risk from any passing pervert or psychopath.'

Bunny rolled her eyes and Sebastian dealt her a slashing glance of reproof. 'These things happen and I won't have it happen to you…or our baby.'

Discomfiture writhed through Bunny as it occurred to her that such a devastating, unforeseen incident had happened to him as a child. 'I wanted to work my notice rather than walk out because who knows what's in the future? I don't want a big black mark on my CV if I were to seek work in the library sector again.'

'Do I really deserve another pessimistic forecast from your corner? Even if we part unmarried, I will make a very generous settlement on you and our child. In all likelihood you will never work for a living again…unless you choose to do so.'

At that information, which merely increased her insecurity about their future as a couple, Bunny hovered uneasily, trying to read his shuttered expression and failing. 'What would I have done with myself anyway while you were working on your business trips? Did you think of that?'

'No,' Sebastian admitted in a roughened undertone. 'I simply wanted you *with* me.'

'And you've got me now for the whole weekend,' Bunny reminded him.

'Aren't I fortunate that you don't work on Saturdays?' he sniped.

At his most basic, he just wanted her with him and that was a compliment, an expression of need and want he would never make more openly. Her heart clenched, sudden tears striking the backs of her eyes, and she cursed those pregnancy hormones turning her into a dripping tap.

'I would've preferred to be with you too,' she muttered, moving closer in slow steps. 'Nothing would have made me happier, but I won't let people down unless I have no other choice. I won't be selfish like that.'

She closed her arms round his still figure, drinking in the rich scent of him like the addict she was. Man and musk, a hint of cologne, and that incredible underlying familiar scent that washed over her in the most enervating, satisfying way. Her hands ran up over his strong back, feeling his slight movements in the ripple of his muscles, registering the instinctive surge of her own response: the tight nipples, the racing heartbeat, the heated ache between her legs, the physical craving that never stopped.

'*Thee mou*... I want you,' he groaned rough and low into the springy depths of her hair. 'I wanted you every night, every morning...'

'So, do something about it,' she whispered in helpless encouragement.

He said nothing. He simply lifted her up into his arms like a caveman and ravished her mouth with raw, demanding hunger. Her fingernails raked and bit into his broad shoulders as she steadied herself as the same urgency rocketed through her like a heat-seeking missile. He carried her out of the library and started up the stairs, talking the whole time.

'I had this fantasy about you last night while you were being so correct and well behaved in front of your family,' he confided. 'You were wearing a corset and black stockings, usually not my thing but stuff like that would suit you…must buy you some.'

'You're much more experienced than me,' she sighed. 'I've never done the lingerie parade for a guy.'

'I'd enjoy it…occasionally. You can be whoever you want to be with me. There are no restrictions. '

'You surprise me. You're such a bossy-boots,' she told him.

'You surprised me the first night. You weren't too shy to go after what you wanted…and you wanted me. It made me feel *amazing*,' he admitted thickly. 'It wasn't the money or the Pagonis name, it was only me as I am and that *did* it for me.'

'Did it really?' she teased as he elbowed his passage into a wainscoted room where the autumn gloom was brightened by lamps with a fire crackling some place out of view. He leant her back against the door and began to inch up her skirt.

'It's too tight for that,' she warned him. 'There's a zip.'

'Should've noticed that,' he grumbled, running down

the zip until the fitted skirt puddled at her feet and he lifted her out of it. It took about thirty seconds for the shirt to fall and then he was tracing the prominent buds of her nipples, fingertips light over the swollen buds visible through the lace of her bra. He tugged down the straps on her shoulders, eased the cups down and bent his dark head. Her head threw back against the door as a moan exploded from her lungs, his tongue lashing the sensitive peaks, need tugging at her feminine core with velvet claws.

Sebastian dropped to his knees, long fingers skimming down the panties she wore, swiping them out of his way. And then he found her with his mouth where she was swollen and damp and throbbing. As he devoured her, she gasped, head falling back again, pleasure seizing her in a fierce grip for long timeless moments until the ultimate high detonated throughout her entire body and she cried out in climax. As her legs buckled, his big hands closed over her hips and he lifted her to lower her down onto a soft, comfortable bed. He detached her bra, cast it aside, smoothed both of his hands up to cup the pouting flesh. His fingers found the sensitised buds, strummed and teased until her back was arching.

Sensation sizzled through Bunny in spasms of tormenting bliss, her body building up, the intense craving tightening again like a knot inside her, making her buck and squirm in delight. She had missed him, she had really, really missed him, not only the sex but the intimacy of being with him, waking up beside him in the morning, falling asleep in his arms. As she writhed, her head tossing on the pillow, she was moaning, gasping his name like a mantra, and then the whole intensity of the experience sent her flying up into the stars in the hold of another breathtaking climax.

'Still with me?' Sebastian purred with his irreverent grin, leaning down over her to kiss her breathless.

'You've still got all your clothes on!' she complained.

His eyes darkened. 'Not for long,' he assured her as he began to strip.

And she watched while the shirt was peeled off, the shoes kicked aside, the jeans tossed aside. It was one of her favourite activities: enjoying the sight of Sebastian's beautiful body naked. Her heart raced a little faster, her inner muscles clenched in anticipation. He came down to her, all trace of his earlier dissatisfaction gone.

'Am I forgiven yet?'

Sebastian frowned. 'You're here now. Only fools sweat the small stuff.'

Bunny threaded her fingers through his tousled long black hair and traced his wide sensual mouth with her fingertips. 'I'm sorry I spoiled the plans you had made but will you please stop talking about the money you intend to give me if we break up?'

'If you faithfully promise to say nothing more about any future you might have that does not include me,' he bargained.

Bunny nodded and smiled at that request, and he tipped her back, rising over her with easy strength, sliding into her hot, tight channel with urgent intensity and then groaning with uninhibited pleasure. 'What a relief it is to no longer have to worry about our lack of birth control.'

Bunny laughed, taking herself by surprise. 'Yes, you weren't very good at the self-denial bit.'

He shifted his lithe hips, sending fresh little tendrils of desire travelling through her, and she moaned, unashamed to show her pleasure. 'Am I allowed to admit that I enjoyed failing?' he confessed.

He had stoked her hunger again. As he began to move more forcefully, she gave herself up to that raw surge of passion again. In the midst of it, he momentarily frustrated her by pausing to put her into another position and then, when that change enhanced her enjoyment, she was thrilled by the wild, exhilarating ride that followed. Her heart thundered, heat and perspiration flushing her skin, excitement gathering and surging through her veins until a supernova explosion of pleasure shattered the last of her control and she slumped, absolutely exhausted.

'That was spectacular,' Sebastian purred in satiated conclusion, releasing her from his weight and gathering her close.

Her drowsy eyelashes fluttered and she snuggled back into him. 'I love you,' she mumbled, and then her eyes opened very wide in dismay and she mentally kicked herself for letting relaxation control her.

'No, you don't,' Sebastian contradicted with succinct bite. 'It's habit, familiarity, a certain amount of affection but it's *not* love. Nobody has ever loved me.'

Bewildered, disconcerted and suddenly propelled

into a new state of alertness, Bunny blinked. 'Your mother...surely?'

'My most common memory of my mother is of her waving as she went out. She was a jet-setter with a giddy social life. I remember my first nanny better than her.'

'Your grandmother, then.'

'Only when I reminded her of the late son she couldn't mention and not so as you would notice while I was growing up without my parents. I stayed with her twice a year, at Christmas and in the summer.'

'Why was that?' she asked with a pained frown.

'Everyone told her she had messed up my father by spoiling him rotten and she felt very guilty and blamed herself for what my father did. It made her take a hands-off approach with me.'

'Was she right to feel guilty?'

'I don't know,' Sebastian mused. 'My grandfather died, leaving her a single parent of five young children. She also had a huge property empire to run. I doubt that a man would be judged so harshly for his parenting flaws.'

'But you still think that basically you're...what? Unlovable?' she pressed.

'No. I think people's feelings change on the turn of a dime.'

'I have parents and grandparents whose long marriages would disprove that. I think you have to work and compromise to sustain a long relationship, but I do think it's possible,' she countered. 'And don't tell me what I feel. That's my business. Only I know how

I feel but I'll keep it to myself in future. If you're still around when I'm seventy-five, I'll be throwing this conversation in your face daily.'

An involuntary smile of relief softened the tense line of Sebastian's lean dark features as her last comment lessened the tension. 'I can imagine that.'

Of course, she didn't love him, he reasoned. Why would she? Right now, she was on a high of great sex, affection and happiness because they were together and she liked the house. And possibly there was even a pregnancy happy hormone? *Was* there? But he had to be honest with her about where he stood and keep it real between them. Better that she understood him from the start than began nourishing hopes he couldn't fulfil. At the same time, he was wondering if she truly believed she loved him and, if she did believe it, what did it *feel* like? And wasn't it weird in such circumstances to wonder what falling in love felt like?

Bunny reckoned that she would never tell him she loved him again. He didn't want her love because he flat out didn't believe in it. There wasn't much that she could do about that. An ache stirred in the region of her heart nonetheless because she, of course, wanted him to love her back. But did love matter if he still wanted her, needed her and treated her well? Only what would keep him with her in a crisis? Their child, whom he believed he *would* love? That suspicion made her heart sink because naturally she needed to be loved for herself and not only for the little passenger she currently carried.

There was no sleeping for her after that stirring exchange. He showed her into a massive contemporary bathroom and through a connecting door into a dressing room already packed with garments. 'You needed clothes. I didn't order maternity stuff because I had no idea what you would like. But there should be enough in the new wardrobe to cover most social engagements.'

Taken aback by yet another giant demonstration of Sebastian's instinctive generosity, Bunny winced. 'Sebastian...er, I don't have social engagements.'

'Your first is only a week away. Next Saturday, we're having a party here for you to meet my friends. Dress formal. There should be a selection of evening gowns in the closets. The week after we're flying to Greece for you to meet my family and won't that be fun?'

'Meaning?'

'Half of them are trying to sue me through the courts at the minute for a share of my grandmother's wealth.'

'Your family's *doing* that to you?'

'Money talks louder than blood in the Pagonis tribe,' he warned her. 'Even better, my uncles and cousins all work for me now.'

Bunny knew sarcasm when she heard it now and she recognised his bitterness too. She had serious questions to ask about his childhood but decided to leave them until later. 'So when do I get the full tour of the house?' she asked instead.

'As soon as you're dressed and we've had lunch.' His dazzling smile engulfed her and she was aware that his extra warmth stemmed from her having restrained her uncomfortable curiosity.

She hastened into the shower to freshen up while wondering with a pleasant sense of anticipation about what lay within those closets. She had never had the money to buy fancy clothes but she loved to dress up. It would be mortifying though to embarrass Sebastian by looking shabby and she was relieved that he had taken care of the problem.

Forty minutes later, she wore light wool trousers, a rather slinky blue top and a cashmere cardigan teamed with soft leather boots. Knightsmead Court had all the drawbacks of a historic listed property. Away from the fireplaces and the background heating provided by a system installed in the twenties, it could be chilly. Pausing only to admire the magnificent four-poster bed, which was enormous and unbelievably comfortable and hung with gorgeous brocade drapes, she smiled at Sebastian.

'How did you know I love four-poster beds?'

'An extensive amount of online snooping. Your footprint is very heavy on four-poster beds. This one is brand new and made to order. I'm too big for an antique bed and I expect a decent mattress,' he told her.

Bunny blinked and went pink at the thought of him going to that much trouble to establish her likes and dislikes. Did it bother her that he admitted to snooping? Not particularly because she had nothing to hide from him. It said much more about him, she reckoned, that he had put her preferences above his own. Pleased, she allowed him to lead her on a tour. There was so much for her to admire. The airy long gallery where the ladies had once taken their exercise in adverse weather, the carved chimneypieces and wainscoted walls, the great hall with its minstrels' gallery and walls hung with shields, medieval weapons and faded flags.

'The perfect backdrop for a party…or a wedding reception,' Sebastian remarked. 'That is assuming we don't go for a guest list of thousands.'

'We're not talking weddings yet,' she reminded him. 'But I would only have friends and family. I should imagine your list would have hundreds of possibilities, business and social.'

'My wedding wouldn't be a business event,' he murmured, opening a door at the end of the hall to usher her into a more reasonably sized dining room where there were a polished table, fine bone china and candelabra, and yet another fire glowed in a giant grate.

'Who's keeping all these fires going?' she exclaimed in wonderment.

'We have a large staff here.'

'Is there an estate with the house?'

'No, there's a home farm and woods and sufficient land to preserve privacy but the majority of the original estate was sold off long before my grandfather met his first wife.'

'Tragic her dying in childbirth and the baby dying as well,' she sighed.

'It's not going to happen with you. You will have every medical exam available and, by the way,' Sebastian continued, 'I organised an appointment for you on Monday to see an obstetrician for the usual checks. I'll go with you before I leave for Germany.'

'I was going to get around to it eventually, but then I

don't really need to think for myself any more with you so happy to do *all* my thinking for me,' she said drily.

'Touché,' he responded without heat. 'I always think ahead. Occasionally it irritates people.'

Their lunch arrived, brought in by an elderly man with a stately manner.

'This is Parker, Bunny. Our butler, who has always worked here and knows everything there is to know about this house,' Sebastian advanced.

'Madam…sir.' Parker executed a slight bow. 'I am happy to still be here.'

'I'm glad you kept him on,' Bunny whispered when he had left them alone again. 'But he must be at least—'

'Seventy-eight, but he doesn't want to retire. He's Maybelle's father,' Sebastian supplied as she shed her cardigan in the heat flowing from the fire. 'And, in what he terms the twilight of his life, presiding over a large staff with an enhanced salary and a large household budget suits him very well.'

Bunny laughed and then her heart-shaped face turned serious. 'It's time you told me about what happened to you after your parents passed away…'

Sebastian flinched. 'The Pagonis family were devastated by the scandal and the shame of what my father did. As the survivor, I was a huge embarrassment and a disappointment. They put out a story that my father had mental health issues, which was untrue. They refused to admit his addiction. They made me see a psychiatrist every week for years and sent me to boarding school in England where I could be forgotten about.' Sebastian toasted her with his wine glass and lounged back in his seat, his lean, darkly handsome features taut. 'Vacation times? They sent me off to wilderness survival camps and places for troubled adolescents because nobody wanted me around.'

'But why was it like that?' she demanded with a frown.

'If I'd died that night, the family wealth would have gone to my four uncles, who had all fiercely resented my father. My grandfather tied everything up in a trust which leaves *everything* to the firstborn son and Loukia didn't challenge her husband's trust arrangements while she was alive. The family thought they would come into her property empire but it had originally been my grandfather's, so it also came to me. I'm already rich beyond avarice. Her will was the last straw, which is why they're dragging me through the courts…and destined to lose. The trust as it currently stands is virtually unbreakable.'

'So what do you plan to do?'

'In the interests of fairness, offer them a decent settlement, continue to employ them and revise that trust for my child's sake and ensure that a daughter will not be discounted. I'm determined to prevent the bitterness revisiting the next generation if we have more than one child,' he proffered calmly.

Bunny nodded thoughtfully. 'That's sensible.'

But she wasn't thinking about the money, she was thinking about a little boy sent abroad for his education because he was an uber-wealthy child and resented for it by those who might instead have shown him love and understanding. And she understood so much more

about Sebastian in that moment. He had been forced to
be a loner, forced into his general attitude of distrust
with the rest of the world because his family had failed
him and if family didn't step up to help and care, why
would you expect anyone else to do so? He didn't believe in love because he hadn't had love but perhaps
that outlook could be softened by time. And was she
prepared to give him that time? The longer she stayed
with him, the harder it would be to leave.

And Sebastian had made it that way quite deliberately whether he saw that or not. He had put together
her dream house and her dream library. He would give
her everything from a four-poster bed to a designer
wardrobe but he wouldn't give her love. Sebastian, she
realised without surprise, was clever enough to also be
intensely manipulative. He made her feel safe but was
that safety an illusion?

CHAPTER TEN

BUNNY DESCENDED THE Tudor staircase sheathed in a red designer halter-neck dress that skimmed forgivingly over the slight new curve of her tummy.

It had been a busy week, starting with her first appointment with the obstetrician, a lovely woman in her thirties who had once worked with Sebastian. The blood test had revealed that their unborn child was a boy. And with that groundbreaking news, she had started working her notice at the library, only that hadn't lasted long because the runner-up for her job had proved to be still available and eager to start as soon as possible. Naturally she had stepped down early to facilitate a transfer that would suit everyone better. Going to work complete with a security team had entailed constant explanations, which had quickly become embarrassing.

'Don't blame Sebastian for having you guarded like the Crown Jewels,' her mother had enthused when Bunny had dared to vent her irritation. 'He lost everything when he lost his parents. Naturally he's terrified of it happening again.'

As that angle had not occurred to her, she had kept her irritation to herself and had accepted her carload of security personnel, who loved it when she visited her parents, where they got treated to cake and coffee.

Sebastian had been in Germany for three days and when he had reappeared had draped a fabulous diamond pendant round her neck and matched it with a pair of stunning earrings. Herding her into their capacious shower clad only in diamonds, he had made passionate love to her and had complained bitterly about how much he had missed her. After only three days apart, she had believed that that was quite promising in terms of attachment. She was starting to think that with Sebastian she needed to pay less heed to what he said and more heed to his actions.

Sebastian strolled out of the great hall, from which the chink of glasses and a low hum of conversation emanated, to greet her. He looked shockingly hot in a tailored black dinner jacket and narrow trousers, having explained that he would dress up because his friends enjoyed 'that sort of thing'. Even if he didn't, he wore that polished sophisticated apparel well. Mentally she kicked herself for not recalling the kind of privileged world that Sebastian had grown up in when there must've been many occasions when he had had to wear such clothing simply to fit in.

She walked into a crowded room filled with gowned women sparkling with precious jewellery and well-groomed men. Her nerves were on high.

'This is Bunny, my fiancée,' Sebastian announced with quiet satisfaction, one hand clasped to her back.

And a literal squeal erupted from a small, bubbly brunette, who sped forward to look at the beautiful ring on Bunny's finger and give Sebastian a warm hug. There was a welter of conjecture. Sebastian admitted freely to having been shipwrecked and stranded with her, being much more open than she was accustomed to him being, and it had the effect of relaxing her. These were people he trusted.

'I'm Zoe, Andreas's wife,' the petite brunette proffered. 'I had to come and meet you. It's a long way to come for a party but we've known Sebastian for so many years that I had to meet the woman who finally cracked his ice heart.'

Bunny recalled the friendly Andreas from their rescue but he had vanished again soon afterwards, and she went pink and muttered ruefully, 'Oh, I hope there was no cracking of hearts, unless it was mine, and mine is certainly not ice.'

'No, you misunderstand,' Zoe assured her. 'I know you are a hundred per cent special because I first met Sebastian when he was seventeen and he has never introduced a woman to us, not *once* in all this time. There've been women—I have no doubt—offstage, as it were, but never one who was a companion, a partner like you. I thought he would be single until the day he died.'

'My word, you're making me feel good,' Bunny said quietly, but, much as she longed to stay with someone who knew Sebastian that well, there were others waiting to meet her and she knew her manners. 'Hopefully see you later?'

'You can bet on it,' Zoe told her warmly.

'Enjoying yourself?' Sebastian asked her later as he

drew her out onto the temporary dance floor laid out at the foot of the great hall.

'Yes. You have some lovely friends, but I was surprised so many were medics,' she confided.

'You get to know people really well when you train and work in medicine. Genuine people, who don't give a damn about my wealth or my dodgy background.'

'It's not dodgy. For goodness' sake, that tragedy wasn't *your* fault!' she exclaimed in annoyance on his behalf.

Sebastian groaned above her head and steered her into a proper dance but she had never learned how to do that and she tripped over his feet several times before surrendering and retiring to the sidelines with a giggle. 'You'll have to give me lessons if you want the fancy stuff,' she warned him.

'I've got family jewellery for you to wear in Greece next week,' he told her.

'Your grandmother's?'

'Yes, the pieces she had to pass down. Her personal collection went to her surviving sons, aside from the engagement ring you're wearing, which she left to me. And I thought that was a bad joke because I never planned to marry,' he murmured soft and low, and they stopped dancing altogether as he lifted his head to stare down at her. 'And then, only a few weeks later, I met *you*...'

Bunny grinned up at him. 'You see, being a loner is not as much fun as you used to think!'

Sebastian rested his hands on her slight shoulders and looked down at her lovely smiling face with smouldering dark eyes. He said something in Greek and then he stretched down to steal a hungry kiss and a flame ignited between her thighs, making her throb, and she pressed her legs together tightly to contain that surge of hunger.

As she walked out to the cloakroom a few minutes later Zoe appeared by her side. 'He's besotted with you,' the Greek woman said cheerfully. 'Have you set a wedding date yet?'

'No, not yet. Sebastian doesn't do love.'

'Maybe not but that's what's written all over his face every time he looks at you, so Eros must not have been listening when he put you two together. I believe in fate.'

Bunny smiled. 'When there's a wedding date—' she chose her answer with care '—you'll be the first to know.'

A week later they were in Greece but with far less relaxing company. Bunny wore an evening gown that would have been fit for a red-carpet appearance. Mostly black, it shone with iridescent crystals that reflected the light in a soft rainbow of colour. At her throat she wore the magnificent Pagonis emerald necklace and the matching drops in her ears and with Sebastian's hand splayed possessively at her spine she walked like a queen, determined not to be 'less' in the presence of the relatives who had treated their nephew so poorly as a child and not much better since.

Everyone was icily polite. They sat down to dine in a giant town house in Athens at a table that seated forty guests. Every eye in the room rested on their every move and she could see that her existence, the underwritten knowledge that Sebastian would marry and presumably have a child someday, was not good news on their terms. But she ignored it, stayed courteous, agonised over what Sebastian must have undergone as a kid in so chilly an atmosphere, and inwardly cursed them all to hell for what they had put him through out of greed and resentment of his privileged position as firstborn of his generation.

When the evening was done, she heaved a huge sigh of relief and accompanied Sebastian upstairs to their bedroom. 'Gosh, that was exhausting…what a horrible bunch of folk! Sorry, I shouldn't say that about family members but when I think of how lucky I've been with mine and how unlucky you've been, it just makes me so *mad*,' she framed furiously.

'You don't need to be mad. The time when it could hurt to be treated that way is far behind me and, if it helps, we only have to see them a couple of times a year,' he assured her wryly. 'I'm head of the family now, like it or not, and we can always hope that the younger generation will be more accepting.'

'Accepting of what?' Bunny exclaimed. 'The fact that you were born rich? That you employ them? That you're a huge success in business? There is nothing unacceptable about you, Sebastian. They are the ones with the problem, *not* you!'

In the act of wrenching off his bow tie, shedding the dinner jacket, Sebastian had paused, and slowly, as she spoke, a smile began to grow at the corners of his handsome mouth, his lean, strong face starting to lose the tension that the dinner party had roused in him.

He began to unhook her elaborate gown, smoothing

her soft skin as he exposed more of it, sending a shiver of awareness through her small frame. 'I like when you defend me with such vehemence. You're so loyal. I appreciate that, having someone on *my* side for a change.'

Bunny turned round in the circle of his arms and stretched up on tiptoe to try and kiss him but it was virtually impossible and, with a chuckle, he lifted her up to him. 'Want something, short stuff?'

'I'm not short. I am average. You're the one topping the excessive scale,' she teased back.

'Is that so?' Her dress, which had left her shoulders bare, fluttered in a cloud of costly fabric to the floor, leaving her clad only in her lingerie. 'I like this view.'

'Put me down,' she urged.

He settled her down on the edge of the bed and studied her closely. 'I want us to set a wedding date. I'm tired of being asked...*when*? I'd also like to be married before the baby's born.'

Colour flushed her cheeks and she threaded a harried hand through the now tousled strands of her long hair, half turning her head away from his glittering dark scrutiny. 'I—'

'And if your answer is still no, I want to know why. We've been together almost a month. You seem happy—'

'I *am* happy!' Bunny broke in, thinking that she had never been happier in her life before. 'But I still think it's too soon.'

'It's not too soon for me,' Sebastian countered with a roughened edge to his dark, deep drawl. 'Why would it still be too soon for you?'

Loathing being put on the spot in such a way, Bunny

got off the bed and said lamely, 'It just is!' As if that were an explanation, when really it was the only explanation she had that she was willing to offer.

She vanished into the en suite to take off her makeup and freshen up. The door behind her opened, framing Sebastian. Faint colour burned along the exotic line of his high cheekbones and his narrowed dark golden eyes were brilliant and focused hard on her. 'Explain,' he told her. 'You didn't foresee this problem when you suggested that we get engaged instead of married, did you?'

'No,' she conceded, squirming at that mistake on her part. 'And that was very shortsighted of me. I just didn't want to risk your idea of being with me changing. I wanted you to have more time.'

Sebastian flung his handsome head back in a sudden movement. 'How much *more* time?' he demanded rawly. 'I feel like I'm on trial here, Bunny. I asked you to marry me, which was *huge* for me.'

'I know… I know,' she began, frantically struggling to think of what to say to satisfy him.

'I'm fully committed to you. It is not unreasonable to ask you for a date,' he ground out.

Anger was poisoning the air, gathering round her like a dark cloud. There was a very slight shake in his dark deep voice. She knew that he was furious with her, striving to control his temper. Sebastian, who almost never lost control of his emotions. She felt like the worst person in the world for making him feel so frustrated with her. She felt as though she had let him down. And then it was as though all the air, toxic or otherwise, had been sucked away from her because Sebastian just turned on his heel and walked away.

'Where are you going?' she gasped, trailing after him.

'I can't stay with you tonight,' Sebastian said gruffly without turning his head as he opened the bedroom door. 'I'm out of patience. It seems like I want much more than you're prepared to give me and I'm banging my head up against a brick wall.'

The door thudded on his departure, and, in a daze, she got ready for bed. Why couldn't she simply agree to marry him? Was it because of Tristram telling her that he wanted her to marry him even though there had been no ring or even a mention of meeting his family? He had strung her along that way for months on end, insisting he cared for her when patently he didn't.

Had she really withheld her consent to marriage because Sebastian couldn't offer her love? After all, he had offered her so many other important things. Like a beautiful home at Knightsmead Court, furnished even to her preferences. He had been unashamedly emotional when he'd viewed their little blip on the ultrasound screen. He looked after her in every possible way. He was everything she wanted, everything she loved. Was she the one with the problem, rather than him? And why was that?

She lay sleepless all night working it out. She didn't feel good enough for Sebastian Pagonis and that basic truth hit her hard. She was an ordinary girl without a pedigreed background, so why would he want her? After all, Tristram hadn't really wanted her when it came down to brass tacks. At least, he hadn't wanted her *enough*. Had she been trying to ensure that Sebastian did want her enough to stay with her for good? But how could anyone prove that in advance?

All she had done was make Sebastian feel as if *he* weren't good enough. He felt as though he were on trial. She shivered at that idea, that she could have subjected him to feeling like that. She was cold in the early morning light filtering through the windows because she hadn't closed the curtains, cold inside and out because Sebastian wasn't with her, lighting up her world the way he usually did. And hadn't she taken that for granted?

That he would keep on trying? Keep on trying to prove himself?

Her heart sank. Love was supposed to be kind and caring and generous but what had she given him? Reaching a sudden decision, Bunny sprang out of bed, weary and heavy-eyed but determined to set that date for Sebastian and apologise for all the insecurities that had subconsciously trapped her. She pulled on a robe and went to look for him.

In an unfamiliar house, that wasn't an easy task. She checked several empty bedrooms, marvelling that such a large property was maintained simply for the couple of annual family get-togethers Sebastian tolerated for the sake of courtesy. If he ever forgave her for infuriating him to such an extent, she would suggest that he found somewhere else for such meetings because he had admitted that he didn't use the Athens house on any other occasion. Unhappily, no bedroom contained him. She returned to her room and showered and dressed, seriously worried that she had no idea where he had gone.

It was one of her bodyguards who let her into that secret by asking her when she wished to head to the airport for their return flight to the UK. 'What does Sebastian want?'

He frowned in bewilderment. 'Mr Pagonis flew to Switzerland at six this morning...'

And belatedly she recalled him mentioning something about that change of flight plan while she had been dressing for that awful dinner the night before. Gloom set in then, over her solitary breakfast. She tried to phone him. The call, unusually, wasn't answered. Convinced he still wasn't speaking to her, she desisted from sending a flood of texts, although it was a challenge when she knew that it would be a week before she saw him again.

She travelled back to Knightsmead, feeling as though she were carting around her own very personal little black cloud. She had been selfish, unreasonable and shortsighted and she wasn't accustomed to seeing such traits in herself, so *that* knowledge couldn't lift her spirits.

She spent a lot of her time with her family that week, until suspicious eyes began to turn in her direction and pretending that everything was fine became too much of a strain. For the first time in her pregnancy, she felt nauseous and reckoned it was simply nerves and a lost appetite. Her brother John called in when she was working in the library.

'Don't be trying to lift that,' he warned her when he found her crouched over a book box.

'No, don't worry, I'm just digging through it. There are books that need restoration and I'm setting them aside first…new bindings, torn pages. Some of them are very old and need special care,' she explained.

'Parker said he'd bring us tea and snacks in here. I've only got an hour before my next appointment. Do you mind if I leave you being industrious and go and have a snoop round your fabulous home for myself?' her brother enquired with amusement.

'Not at all. Go ahead,' she encouraged, because, unlike the rest of her family, John had been too busy to come for the original tour she had offered them. Like her, he was into history and would enjoy browsing alone more.

She rose on her socked feet off the rug. Sebastian had warned her that she was to lift nothing as well. Well, so much for his caring side, she thought painfully, when his polite phone calls had done nothing to mend the breach between them. Did he sulk? This was where you discovered that Mr Perfect wasn't, after all, Mr Perfect, she reflected heavily. But then she hadn't tackled the controversial subject of when they might marry on the phone either, she acknowledged wearily.

She lifted the heavy family bible she wanted to place on the upper gallery table where—according to Parker— it had always sat. Being almost as old as the library, Parker was a font of knowledge about such matters.

She carted the giant book with care in her gloved hands and mounted the wooden staircase. Reaching the gallery, she settled the old family bible back in its former resting place. Flushed with success, she started down the stairs again at speed and, whether it was the socks on her feet or the gloves she wore for handling ancient books, she slid like a sledder at the top of a mountain on a big run. With a sharp cry of alarm, she tried to right her balance, but it was too late. She went bumpety, bumpety bump down the stairs and landed awkwardly with a twisted ankle.

Parker burst in with all the urgency of an ambulance and knelt down by her side, wringing his worn hands in horror and dismay. 'Miss Woods… Miss Woods, what do I do?'

'I'll handle this…' John appeared, frowning down at her. 'You went up those stairs without shoes on, didn't you? And those stupid slippery gloves? Do you have a death wish?' he asked quietly as Parker sped from the room, thoroughly unsettled by her accident.

Bunny didn't rise to the bait, because of course John the ever practical was right. 'I've hurt my ankle, probably going to have a few bruises on my bottom as well,' she groaned as he helped her up and into the nearest armchair.

She withstood a lecture about being more careful now that she was pregnant and hung her head, misery choking her. Just then she didn't care about anything and she knew she had not hurt her baby, only her ankle and her back. She deserved the bruises for being so careless, she thought miserably as her brother bandaged her ankle for her, offered to take her to the hospital if she was apprehensive and looked relieved at her refusal.

Parker brought in the tea with an air of satisfaction. 'Mr Pagonis is on his way home,' he announced.

'But he's not supposed to be back for another couple of days!' Bunny gasped in surprise, underlaid with a strong sense of relief. The sooner she saw him, the sooner she could cross the chasm of the separation she had caused. And she glanced down at herself, noting her ancient comfy jeans, her shapeless sweater, the kind of clothes she put on when she was in a down mood. That wasn't how she wanted to greet Sebastian. Having shared a cup of tea with her brother before he rushed off, she hobbled awkwardly upstairs to shower and change.

Restricted as she was, everything took longer than usual and it hurt hovering on one leg to dry her hair and put on some make-up. The results, however, far outweighed the discomfort. She limped into the dressing room for fresh undies, donning pretty lace pastels in a soft green before rifling in the closet for a dress. It was a little chilly for a dress but she shouldn't be thinking of such practicalities, she warned herself, tugging the stretchy dark green designer garment over her head and shimmying her hips while wondering uncertainly whether going barefoot would be sexier than wearing only one shoe.

Sebastian, as he surged upstairs like a man on a mission, however, had far more pressing concerns. Parker had phoned him while he was in a meeting in Geneva and his brain had gone pretty blank during that brief call, only parts of it staying with him. An accident…a fall…her brother, the doctor, with her. It had traumatised him: the prospect of losing Bunny and the baby, the very idea of them being ripped from his world. Slowly, on the flight back home, he had pulled himself together and another phone conversation with John had reassured him that no great harm had been done, only to Parker, who had panicked.

They were okay, they were okay, Sebastian kept reminding himself, but nothing could dim his urgent need to see Bunny in the flesh. He stopped dead in surprise when he saw her balancing on one leg by gripping one of the posts of the bed, striving to get her foot into one high heel.

'What are you doing?' Sebastian demanded, crossing the room so fast that he left her breathless and lifting her off her feet to lay her down on the bed. 'John said you had to rest it and with the amount of bandaging he's put on your foot, you couldn't get it into a shoe.'

'You're so practical,' Bunny muttered in shaken complaint because popular belief would have suggested that Sebastian should have paused to note how groomed she was looking and to express his appreciation. Unhappily, Sebastian was more interested in probing her ankle and her foot, undoing the bandage, putting it on more tightly and in a different style, his attention wholly directed at her injury.

'We'll have to get those stairs carpeted so that they're less slippery. You're always running round barefoot,' he said in his most prosaic comment yet.

Bunny feasted her eyes on his bent dark head, the gleam of the steel hoop in one ear, the line of his hard jaw, the perfection of his classic nose and wide sensual mouth. Butterflies flew in celebration in her stomach. The core at the heart of her pulsed and her heartbeat quickened. 'I missed you so much,' she said tensely. 'I'll marry you tomorrow if you want.'

'What?' Sebastian glanced up at her in bewilderment, his brain still visualising the potential damage to her foot. Brilliant dark-as-coal eyes assailed hers. *'Tomorrow?'*

Bunny winced because he wasn't making climbing down from her high horse any easier. 'I just meant that I'm happy to marry you whenever you like. I think I was sort of testing you before.'

Sebastian frowned. *'Testing* me?'

'I wanted you to love me before we got married but now I realise that that doesn't matter as much as I thought it did. It's how you treat me that counts and you treat me like I'm something precious.'

'Of course I do, because you *are!*' Sebastian stressed, pushing up his shirtsleeves one after another, strangely shy, now that it had come to crunch time, to say those words he had always sworn that he would never say. But she deserved those words because, even after all he'd said, she had been braver than he was and infinitely wiser when it came to such emotions to say them first. *'Obviously* I love you,' he framed in a driven undertone.

Bunny's beautiful green eyes opened very wide in shock but she deemed it words voiced out of kindness rather than truth, possibly even his attempt to ease the tension that had existed between them since his departure.

Sebastian walked away a few steps and then swung back. 'But how I felt wasn't obvious to me until Parker phoned and told me that you'd had an accident.'

'My goodness, why did he do that? It wasn't a serious fall. He shouldn't have bothered you.'

'*Bothered* me?' Sebastian repeated in disbelief. 'I expect to hear about any accident you have, no matter how minor. You're *my whole world*. If anything happened to you and our baby, I'd lose everything that makes life worth living.'

'I—I didn't realise I was that important to you,' Bunny stammered.

'And the bad news is that I didn't realise either until I was told you had had an accident and I was forced to spend some time thinking about that.' In front of her, Sebastian shuddered in remembrance. 'It was the worst thing that's ever happened to me... The very idea of losing you was unbearable. I couldn't handle it. It knocked me flat. I don't believe I spoke an intelligible word until I was halfway back here and your brother had calmed me down.'

'You spoke to John?' she gasped.

'I knew he was with you when it happened, so naturally I contacted him, assuming you'd be in hospital after the way Parker had spoken of the incident. It was a huge relief to learn that you were relatively unharmed, but I couldn't be content, I couldn't settle, until I saw you for myself,' he confided, approaching the bed to sink down beside her and wrap both arms around her. 'I'm so grateful that you're not badly hurt. I didn't think I could ever love anyone and then you came along.'

Conviction that he meant every word he was saying set into Bunny then and she relaxed for the first time in days. 'And annoyed the hell out of you at first glance.'

'No, I like your feisty side, the way you stand up to me. Very few people challenge me. You *did* and if you hadn't, I'd just have steamrollered over you because that's the way I'm built to react to challenges, so that's really positive for us as a couple,' he concluded.

'You love me,' Bunny recounted softly. 'And you know I love you.'

'Yes, and I was quite happy for you to love me even while I was telling you that I didn't believe in this kind of love,' he groaned. 'That was very selfish.'

'I was selfish too. I always wanted you to love me even though you said you couldn't. I set my heart on the *one* thing you'd told me you couldn't offer.'

'That's your stubborn backbone, but you were pushing me towards a cliff I needed to fall off…to find real happiness,' he breathed tautly. 'And I fell today the minute I had to face the concept of a life that didn't include you. It's good. Now we both know where we are…so you'd agree to marry me *tomorrow*? How did that timeline come about?'

Bunny went red, a little embarrassed even in the midst of that happiness to admit that she had felt kind of desperate and had feared that she was putting him through hoops because of the way Tristram had strung her along.

'I'm glad the little twerp did that if it means I got you instead!' Sebastian teased, not remotely concerned about anything she had done, lying back on the pillows to curve her close. 'Did I tell you that I checked him out and discovered that, far from being in finance as you assumed, Tristram is a podcaster?'

'A podcaster?' Bunny echoed in disbelief.

'Apparently he didn't do well in finance and he decided to interview minor celebrities instead. He's got a decent following but he's basically a paparazzo, which I assume explains why he was chasing after you.'

'He wanted the shipwreck story,' Bunny guessed and shook her head. 'I wouldn't have told him a word.'

The familiar scent of Sebastian flooded her as she buried her nose in his shirtfront and then he tipped up her face and his mouth closed over hers in an unashamedly hungry kiss. Her fancy outfit was tossed on the floor. Sebastian was far too busy telling her how beautiful she was and cupping the very faint swell of her belly with possessive enthusiasm to notice what she had worn. It wasn't very long until both of them were stripped and making passionate love. Bunny cried out his name in release and he groaned in ecstasy, cradling her against him when she was drowsy.

'It's a shame tomorrow would've been too short notice for your family,' Sebastian mused.

'What are you talking about?'

'Our wedding,' Sebastian told her with immense satisfaction. 'Do you think in two weeks' time?'

'You are so impatient,' she complained while hugging him with delight that he really couldn't wait to get that ring on her finger.

'I was scared of falling in love,' he admitted with startling abruptness. 'My father was obsessively jealous and possessive about my mother before she started the divorce and when I first began feeling weird about you I was afraid that his excessiveness might be in my DNA as well.'

'Weird?' Bunny queried. 'Weird about me?'

'Over-the-top possessive and not liking being without you. That's why I believed that, after our rescue, we should both spend some time apart,' he admitted.

'You spent our time apart organising this house for me,' she reminded him. 'How did that fit in?'

'It made me feel better to be making plans for us. I was miserable without you,' he confessed grudgingly.

'I was miserable too,' she whispered. 'And you're not the slightest bit obsessive or possessive. I like being with you too. It's normal when you're in love.'

'You always say the right thing,' Sebastian murmured, replete in his contentment.

In reality, it took Sebastian a whole month to get Bunny to the altar in her family's local church. Her wedding gown, hot off the fashion designer of the year's runway, made the front of many newspapers and several glossy magazines. Her dress was silk scattered with what were rumoured to be real diamonds. The hand-embroidered lace bodice defined her slender curves and then flowed down like some medieval princess gown. Her family surrounded her with Sebastian and it was the happiest day of her life. And *his*.

EPILOGUE

Five years later

'No, THREE CHILDREN is quite enough,' Bunny told her husband, eying four-year-old Argo, two-year-old Sofia and baby Will, named after Bunny's father.

Argo and Sofia were fighting over a toy and Sebastian was separating them while Will was crawling under the table in the great hall while Bunny completed the Christmas decorations for their party. 'Mum had five children only because she was desperate for a girl and I'm not a baby machine.'

'Won't mention it again,' Sebastian told her cheerfully, because Bunny was the broody one of the two of them and he was convinced that, once Will started running around, Bunny would decide on another.

Bunny grinned at him because she knew something he didn't as yet. And he would be over the moon because nobody loved kids more than Sebastian. Being on a high around Sebastian was anything but new to her. She felt like that most days, scrutinising his gorgeous face and tall, superb physique, still barely able to credit that he was hers. All hers, heart and soul and body, she thought fondly while a little skip of heat burned between her thighs.

Had it really been five years since their wedding? So much had changed since then but not the basics. They were still based at Knightsmead Court, although they enjoyed regular trips to other properties abroad. The house's library had quietly become famed among academics, who regularly called to request access to the ancient books and manuscripts that composed the original collection. It was a collection as well that was now being added to on a regular basis since Sebastian had come to appreciate how much his wife delighted in virtually running her own little academic library.

The year before, they had sailed in the yacht to Indonesia and had had a fabulous holiday. Andreas and Zoe and their children and Bunny's family had joined them. Now that the Greek couple were based in the UK again, Zoe had become Bunny's best friend. Andreas and Zoe also accompanied them to those chilly Pagonis gatherings, which Sebastian insisted should continue, and Bunny was beginning to see a definite defrosting of attitude from the younger generation of Sebastian's relatives. Old scandals and resentments had less of a hold on them than they had on his father's contemporaries in the family.

Her own family members were regular visitors. Indeed, Bunny had loved her husband even more when he'd begun to treat her family as if they were *his* own family, finding in them that warmth and affection and interest that he had long been denied by Loukia Pagonis's younger sons.

The children's nanny appeared to take the little ones up to bed and bath. Sebastian cornered his wife against the table. 'So what does that little secretive smile hide?' he asked, both arms firmly closed round her slender body.

Bunny ran her hands up over his splendid torso and slowly up to his shoulders, trying not to smile when she felt the quickening of his body against hers. Sebastian was always ready for de-stressing the natural way. 'Your super swimmers have already done it again. The shower last month when you...' her hands lifted to do little air quotes '...*forgot*. Our fourth is due in the autumn, by which time Will will be a toddler, so it's not a disaster except for my stretch marks.'

'What stretch marks?' he asked, because he only ever looked at her and saw his perfect woman, whom he adored, and as far as he was concerned she had no imperfections. She was the woman who had brought him alive, taught him to feel again and given him so much in the process: a true home, three fabulous children, endless loyalty and love.

'I love you,' she confided, kissing a path up his neck while dragging in the scent of his skin and the burn of her own arousal.

'I love you even more. You're the sun I revolve around,' he told her passionately as he lifted her onto the table, skilled fingers pushing her skirt out of the way.

The silence was slowly broken by little gasps and groans until finally they made themselves respectable again and he carried her over to an armchair to cradle her in possessive arms. 'I bet we have a girl next time.'

He was right but he was also wrong. The fourth pregnancy gave them twins, a boy called Christos and a girl called Annette after her maternal grandmother.

And they all lived happily ever after, in love, and positively boastful about their good fortune.

* * * * *

Did you fall in love with Shock Greek Heir?
*Then don't miss out on these other
intensely romantic stories from Lynne Graham!*

Two Secrets to Shock the Italian
Baby Worth Billions
Greek's Shotgun Wedding
Greek's One-Night Babies
His Royal Bride Replacement

Available Now!

CHRISTMAS EVE ULTIMATUM

JACKIE ASHENDEN

MILLS & BOON

To Bruce, Allan and Dani. Yippee-kai-ay, mfs!

CHAPTER ONE

Ulysses

I KNEW THE moment I saw her that I had to have her.

I'd heard about her through the business grapevine—the ice queen with a facility for numbers, and since I employ no one but the best at Vulcan Energy, the multinational energy conglomerate I own, I wanted to see her for myself. Naturally, with an eye to headhunting her.

She was the CFO of a small but up-and-coming solar energy company, Tanaka Solar—something else I'd had my eye on—so I organised a meeting with their executives.

She was dressed in a pale suit and sat at the meeting table like a queen, white-blonde hair wrapped in a braid around her head like silver rope, her eyes as blue and dark as the north sea.

Katla Sigurdsdottir: Katla, like the Icelandic volcano. Covered in ice with fire at its heart.

Our eyes met and I felt the impact. It had been a long time since I'd experienced such an intense rush of desire for a woman, so I didn't bother to hide my interest from her—I'm always clear about what I want—and she'd flushed, all pretty and pink. Yet her chin came up, she held my gaze and the rest of the world disappeared. A heartbeat passed, and then another. Normally that's when people look away from me, because they find me…intimidating. But she didn't look away. And I could see it then, glowing in her blue eyes—the fire beneath all that ice.

And I knew. Despite her frozen exterior, she would blaze for me.

I'm not a man shy about what he wants, especially when it concerns physical desire, so I wasted no time letting her know that I wanted her. I expected some confusion, some cursory resistance perhaps, the way some women liked to play, and I'm not averse to it. But I didn't expect her to refuse me—not once, not twice, but six times.

I do not take kindly to the word no, but if I'd thought she'd meant it I would have backed off. She didn't mean it, though. So now I'm here, at Tanaka Plaza, the building she works in, ready to deliver her an ultimatum. Because I always get what I want in the end. Many would say that Christmas Eve is not the time for such a declaration, and certainly I have other, better things to do. However, I'm an impatient man and I've waited long enough.

Katla Sigurdsdottir has refused me six times but there will not be a seventh. She will accept me tonight, on Christmas Eve, because if she does not I will take the company she works for, that I've heard she's so loyal to, and make that mine instead.

You can see why they call me dangerous.

Tonight, I've flown into LA from my office in Munich to deliver my ultimatum personally—it would be

crass to deliver it via email—even though LA is a city
I have never cared for. However, I appreciate its raw energy and the greed of the people who live here. They're
hungry for more money, more power, a better life…and
that I definitely relate to. What has my life been, after
all, but the relentless pursuit of all those things?

I'm certainly powerful now so, as I walk into Tanaka
Plaza, my bodyguards flanking me, the man at the desk
on the ground floor presents no obstacle. Xander, head
of my security, explains to him the nature of my business and, proving he knows what's good for him, the
doorman doesn't protest. He quickly ushers us to the
lift that will take us to the top floor.

Five minutes later the sound of music and loud voices
greets us as the lift doors open, and when we approach
the empty reception desk we can see a party going on
through the glass doors that separate the waiting room
from the offices. People are wearing reindeer antlers
and glowing red noses, and there is tinsel around more
than a couple of necks. Everyone is talking and laughing, and some are singing.

A staff Christmas party. How quaint.

I ignore the party, searching the crowd for the woman
I've come for, and eventually I spot her, standing near
the tall, fake Christmas tree in one corner. She is wearing reindeer antlers too, and some kind of unattractive
Christmas-themed sweater, but neither of those things
detracts from her beauty.

She's just as lovely now as she was in that meeting
room. With all her pale hair, pale skin and those North
Sea eyes, she reminds me of an iceberg—cold, frozen,
yet, when the sun touches her, she glows. At least, she

glowed when I looked at her across the boardroom table that day. That's when I knew she was mine.

She's talking to someone I don't care about, the way I don't care about any of the people in that room. They don't matter. Only she does. I'm a dragon and she's the unique gold coin I want to add to my hoard.

Olympia, my younger sister and the only thing I care about it in the entire world, would have something to say about my behaviour—she does not care for my ruthlessness and so I try to restrain myself for her. But Olympia isn't here and this doesn't concern her.

I glance at my bodyguards to let them know that it's time, then I stride past the empty reception desk, through the glass doors and into the gathered party.

At first people are too busy having fun to notice me. But then double-takes start to happen and they're turning around to look, the dark clothes I'm wearing with the black overcoat over the top cutting through all this brightness like a shadow knifes through a bean of sunlight.

I'm not above a little showmanship.

The din of human noise quietens and I leave a trail of silence rippling out behind me as I head straight for her. She is the last to notice, talking to the man standing with her, and only when he glances at me and stops speaking does she turn.

Her dark-blue eyes widen and alarm flares in them before it vanishes under a layer of ice. She glances at my entourage then looks back at me, and her chin lifts, hauteur in every line of her tall, slender figure.

'Mr Zakynthos,' she says, her voice clear as a bell with no trace of her native Iceland in the words. 'I didn't realise you'd been invited to our Christmas party. How nice of you to join us. But I'm afraid we're not allowing guests, so the rest of your group will have to leave.'

She should look ridiculous, standing there with antlers on her head in that awful red-and-green Christmas sweater, ordering me around like I'm the nobody she's decided to treat me as. But I'm not a nobody and she doesn't look ridiculous.

I'm not a fanciful man either, but there's an ethereal quality to her, a sharpness to her features, that makes me think of otherworldly beings: elves; fairies; the beautiful creatures of myth, rare and unique, which was what drew me to her in the first place.

I'm a collector of rare and unique things. Beautiful things. I've never wanted to collect a woman before, so the depth of my initial desire to collect her surprised me. But I hate being denied something I want, so it's probably that which has deepened my obsession. It's galling to be a cliché. Nevertheless, I wasn't deterred when I first asked her to dinner and she refused. I asked her again, politely, courteously. I know the rules of human interaction and I play by them, but if that doesn't get me what I want then I break them. Rules are made to broken, after all. So, after rejection number six, I decided it was time to stop playing.

She wanted me—I saw the fire in her eyes that day in the meeting. And she wouldn't have held my gaze, challenging me, if she hadn't found me compelling, as most women generally do. But she is not most women, and tonight I will not take no for an answer.

I smile, appreciating her little joke, taking no notice of the quiet room and all the people staring at me. 'But

I'm not here for the Christmas party, Miss Sigurdsdot-tir,' I say. 'And neither are my associates.'

The man standing next to her frowns and says in puzzled tones, 'Miss?'

She pays no attention to him. 'It's Ms,' she corrects me coldly, her dark-blue gaze on mine. 'Are you want-ing to speak to Mr Tanaka?'

Of course I do. It's his company I'll be using as le-verage, after all.

'Yes,' I say. 'This does involve him.'

Her eyes narrow. '"This"? Can I ask, what is "this"?'

'You can ask.' I give the rest of the room a glance. 'But you may not want an audience for the answer.'

If she's guessed my intentions, she gives no sign. Perhaps she thinks the reason for my presence is some last-minute emergency, a piece of business that needs taking care of before the Christmas break. She would be wrong.

'The business day is over, Mr Zakynthos,' she says. 'It's Christmas Eve, if you hadn't noticed, and unless you're—'

'I'm not here for business,' I interrupt calmly. 'I am here for you.'

She's not so pale now, a flush tinging her cheeks like dawn light touching a snow bank; her full mouth tightening, the blue ice of her eyes trying to freeze me where I stand. 'In what capacity?' she asks, her clear voice noticeably chilling.

I give her a slow smile. 'I think you know in what capacity, Ms Sigurdsdottir.'

'Kat,' the man next to her interjects, scowling. 'What the hell is going on? Who is this guy?'

Once again, she ignores him. 'Mr Zakynthos…' she begins.

But I don't let her finish. 'Find Mr Tanaka and a room where we can discuss this in private. Though…' I pause for effect '… I'm very willing to talk about this right here, right now if you'd prefer.'

She's angry, I can see it in her eyes, but it's a cold anger, as befits a daughter of Iceland. That's where she's from, and I know that because, after that meeting, I wanted to know everything about her, so I educated myself.

Her mother was a kind of free spirit and left Reykjavik when Katla was very young. They led a peripatetic life in Europe, never settling in one place for too long before moving on. I'm not sure how she managed schooling in a life like that, but she did turn up at a British university that she attended young because of her gift for numbers. She studied finance and maths, graduating with honours and getting positions in a number of different companies, before she was headhunted by Tanaka to be their CFO.

It's a small company, specialising in solar energy, but growing fast and I suspect that's largely because of her. Like I said, she's unique. Rare. And, the more I discovered about her, the more I wanted to know because she fascinates me— I confess, I'm not sure why—and there's only one way to handle such obsessions. You must take the thing you're obsessed with and learn everything about it until you know it inside out.

Only once you know a thing completely can you move on. This is why I have to move on her, and move now. There are other things I need to do, other obsessions to explore, but I can't do any of them until I've sated myself with her.

'There is no need to talk about this at all,' she says icily. 'I have nothing to say to you, except to please leave. Because, if you don't, I'll have security throw you out.'

She's impressive, I'll give her that, and some might find her intimidating. But I don't. I find her exciting. In fact, my muscles are already tightening in anticipation of the fight to come, and she *will* give me a fight— I already know that. Which is good. It's been too long since I've had such an interesting lover.

'There was no security downstairs,' I inform her. 'They must have gone home already. It is Christmas Eve, after all.'

'Kat,' the man says, his voice as annoying as the buzz of a mosquito. 'I really need your attention right now. This is important and I—'

'No, it is not,' I break in, causing him to fall silent. 'Stay quiet, please. No one is talking to you.'

He stares at me for a moment, clearly deciding whether or not to argue, but I hold his gaze, letting him know exactly who and what he is dealing with, and he shuts his mouth with a snap.

Katla mutters something under her breath and Mr Tanaka, who must have been informed of my arrival, abruptly appears at my elbow.

'Mr Zakynthos,' he says, eyeing me warily. 'I hear you wish to speak to me?'

'I don't think…' Katla begins.

'Yes,' I say, ignoring her and turning to him. 'I do wish to speak to you. Do you have an office where we can talk in private?'

Tanaka can't afford to be rude. I'm too powerful. Vulcan Energy would swallow his little company whole if I wanted it to, and I may yet want it to, depending on what answer Katla Sigurdsdottir gives to the ultimatum I intend to put to her.

'Of course,' he says. 'Follow me.'

I smile and hold out my hand to the icy queen currently staring daggers at me, in an 'after you' gesture. The antlers and the cheerful Christmas sweater should be covered in a rime of ice, given the chill pouring off her, but that doesn't faze me. I expected ice from her.

The man beside her moves, reaching to grab her elbow as she goes to follow her boss. 'Kat,' he whispers urgently.

'Let her go,' I say before she can react, and I don't hide the threat in my voice. She is mine now and no one touches what's mine.

He flushes and drops his hand, yet he must have some modicum of bravery, because he glares at me. 'I'm her husband,' he says, as if sensing my intentions.

I know she was married. I also know that she left him six months ago.

'Not any more,' I say.

Then I walk past him, following Katla out of the room.

CHAPTER TWO

Katla

MY HEART IS beating so fast I can barely get a breath and I can feel him following behind me, dark and as full of electricity as a thunder storm.

Ulysses Zakynthos: CEO of Vulcan Energy, a huge energy conglomerate that spans half the globe, and utterly ruthless when it comes to business. Utterly ruthless when it comes to other things as well, or so I'd heard. Not that I'd taken much notice of him before the meeting Tanaka Solar had with Vulcan.

Afterwards, though…

Afterwards, I couldn't think of anything else.

He was sitting opposite me and I could almost feel the energy pouring from him. A seething, electric magnetism that made the breath catch my throat.

He was dressed in black, the way he is now, his suit and shirt perfectly tailored, with a silk tie lying like a thread of gold in the coal seam of his business shirt. His hair was short, as ink-black as his shirt and the straight black slashes of his brows. His features were roughly hewn, as if a sculptor hadn't bothered with the finer details of his proud nose, his imperious forehead, his carved cheekbones and his hard mouth.

It was his eyes, though, that held my attention. They were the same deep-gold as his tie, and molten. He was a furnace, generating heat and throwing out energy wherever he went, a living embodiment of the company he headed.

'Handsome' is too pretty a word for what he was. Compelling, mesmerising and hypnotic are words more suited to him.

He looked at me from across the meeting room table and I felt as if the air was igniting all around us. I tried to ignore it, because if this was Ulysses Zakynthos then indeed every word the media said about him was true. He was dangerous, ruthless, the expansion of his own company relentless. And, if he wanted to swallow Tanaka Solar whole, then we were going to have to be very careful indeed.

Tanaka is a small company, but fast growing, and Mr Tanaka wants to stay in control of it. I support him in that. He took a risk when he gave me this job, because I'm not an easy person to work with. I am outspoken and blunt, and some people don't like that, especially coming from a woman. Certainly my references weren't wholly glowing. But Mr Tanaka only cared about my skill with money and, while I believe I've proved myself in my time working for him, I still owe him.

Anyway, though it was a tense meeting with Vulcan Energy, we managed to emerge from it without giving up anything, and I thought I'd seen and heard the last of Ulysses Zakynthos. Yet, not a day later, he called me and asked me out to dinner. I refused, of course, because, while I might be separated from my husband, I wasn't interested in starting another relationship. Most especially not with him, a man more a force of nature than a human being.

Which is why I have to keep my senses sharp as I follow Mr Tanaka now, heading towards his office, bitterly conscious of the man behind me.

Me—that's what he said he wanted. He was here for me.

He swept into the staff Christmas party like a king sweeping through a crowd of commoners, leaving everyone silent and staring in his wake. I hadn't noticed him, because John arrived unexpectedly and was busy telling me what a big mistake I'd made when I'd walked out on him, and that he wanted me to come back to him. So it wasn't until Ulysses Zakynthos was basically right in front of me that I realised he was there.

He was the last person in the world I either wanted or expected to see and I hated how every muscle in my body tightened in response to his electric presence. Then his golden eyes met mine and instantly I felt it again—the sense that the air around us was so charged that all it would take would be one spark for it to all go up in flames.

I didn't like that feeling one bit, so I wasn't polite to him and I wasn't welcoming. I'm suspicious of people as a general rule—certainly of what they say, because people lie all the time—and actions matter to me. So the arrogance of him swanning into our Christmas party and demanding me, as if I was a possession of his and not the CFO of an up-and-coming solar energy company, instantly got my back up.

I thought he'd feel some shame about how I rejected him, or perhaps even some embarrassment, because I did refuse him six times. Yet when I turned to find him standing there, looking at me as if everyone else in the room didn't exist, it was clear that neither shame nor embarrassment were on his radar. I'd be surprised if he even knows what either of them feels like.

It's intoxicating to be looked at like that by a dangerous, compelling man; I can't lie. Especially when my own husband never looked at me that way. And I do try not to lie, even to myself. But Ulysses Zakynthos has so many red flags around him that any woman would be a fool to get close to him.

And I'm not a fool.

Mr Tanaka opens the door to his office and we file in. Mr Zakynthos sits at the head of the meeting-room table as if this is his office and we're all lackeys waiting for his orders.

I sit at the opposite end, as far away from him as I can get, trying not to think about John still out by the Christmas tree, waiting for me to tell him that I want him back. Expecting me to say that I want him back…

No, I can't think about him now, because Mr Zakynthos is down the other end of the table and he's staring at me with his wolf-gold eyes as if he wants me for breakfast, lunch *and* dinner.

It makes me hot, makes my pulse speed up, makes it difficult to breathe. It's as if he's leaching all the oxygen out of the air, and I don't like how part of me is enjoying the all-consuming way he's looking at me. As if I'm the only thing that exists for him in this moment.

His desire for me is obvious, and part of me appreciates his honesty. He's not a man who plays games, I don't think. Even his persistence is honest and I'm reluctantly admiring of that.

Certainly, John was never honest. He was never straightforward. When we married he told me that he'd never lie to me, but he did. He lied when he said he wanted children, and he lied when he said I was the only one for him. He lied when he said that he'd take care of me and that I'd always be safe with him. He lied to me the way my mother lied to me.

So now only honesty will do. It's why I like numbers—because numbers never lie. Numbers are the cold, bright truth of the universe, and numbers I can trust.

Not like the curious part of me that wants to know what makes a man like Ulysses Zakynthos tick. He's a brilliant businessman, that much I do know, because it was his brilliance that catapulted Vulcan Energy from its humble beginnings in Greece to the world stage, where it's now the biggest provider of renewable energy in the world. His drive is undeniably formidable, and so is his intellect, and there's part of me that finds that…intriguing.

I want to know why he's interested in a woman like me, for example, since I'm not what you'd call typical. Men usually approach me in an attempt to headhunt me, and that's what I thought Ulysses Zakynthos wanted too.

Apparently not.

He doesn't want me for Vulcan Energy, he wants me for…me. And I don't understand why. I have a head for numbers, yes, but I'm not beautiful. I'm not interesting, unless you like mathematics and finance, and I'm terrible at small talk. In fact, many people find me aloof, cold and far too blunt, so I can't think how or why I caught his eye.

'So,' he says suddenly, making everyone in the room jump. 'Let's not waste time. Mr Tanaka, you know my interest in Tanaka Solar, and I've made you a very good offer for your company, which you refused, as is your right.'

'Yes,' Mr Tanaka says, frowning. 'Are you here to make another offer? Because, if so, you've come in vain. I'm going to refuse all other offers you might make, because this is my company and mine it will remain.'

'I can respect that.' Ulysses's deep voice, with its faint hint of an accent, rasps over my nerves and makes something vibrate inside me. 'I too keep what's mine. Which is why I'm here. It largely concerns Ms Sigurdsdottir, but also you by association.'

I'm impatient for him to get to the point, but I hide it the way I hide all my emotions. They're intense, my emotions, and hard to manage, so I lock them away where they can't hurt or anger other people.

'Yes, so you keep saying,' I state coolly. 'Please do enlighten us as to how it concerns me.'

Ulysses gives me that slow smile again, and there's nothing in it but threat, yet it brings warmth to his hard features all the same, like sunlight touches the granite face of a mountain. 'I have decided I don't want your company, Mr Tanaka,' he says, all the while looking at me, as if there's nothing he'd rather look at. 'I have decided I want your CFO instead.'

Mr Tanaka's frown deepens. 'I'm sorry, but Ms Sigurdsdottir is—'

'Very happy in her present position?' Ulysses finishes for him. 'Yes, she probably is. But I'm not here to headhunt her for a position in my company. I'm here to headhunt her for a position in my bed.'

The words fall into the shocked silence like stones in a glassy pond, causing ripples to flow out from where they hit the water.

There's a traitorous heat in my cheeks, shock and anger winding its way through me. How dare he say something like that, out loud and in front of my boss? It's offensive, and I want to tell him so, but I know that will only give him the reaction he's no doubt looking for, so I say nothing and give him my best icy stare instead.

Mr Tanaka looks as mortified as I feel. 'I'm sorry,' he says slowly. 'But…what you…what Miss…'

'That shouldn't concern you, Mr Tanaka.' Ulysses is supremely unembarrassed and gazing steadily at me as if he's navigating across stormy seas and I'm his North Star. 'And ordinarily it wouldn't. But you see, I'm a man who always gets what he wants, and I generally don't like being denied.'

'I still don't understand—'

'I will leave your company completely alone, in other words,' Ulysses interrupts gently. 'On the condition that Miss Sigurdsdottir gives some of her precious time to me.'

More shock echoes through me. He can't be serious. He'd really use Mr Tanaka's company as…what…a bargaining chip? Simply so he can get me into bed?

I don't understand why he's so insistent, but what I do know is that I've just about had it with men. First John and all his lies, and now Ulysses Zakynthos using Mr Tanaka's company against me. Presumably because he thinks I'm a loyal worker and won't toss Mr Tanaka and his company to the wolves. Or, rather, to this particular wolf.

Sadly, he's right. I can't be the reason Mr Tanaka will have the company he started twenty years ago and worked so hard to build up pulled out from under him by Ulysses Zakynthos. Letting that happen would make me no better than the predator sitting at the other end of the table, watching me. He doesn't care about Mr Tanaka's company or about Mr Tanaka himself. He just wants what he wants, and currently that's me.

There's a selfishness to it that reminds me of my mother and how, when she was bored with a place, she moved on and dragged me with her, no matter what I had to say about it. Only her whims and desires mattered, never mine, and she made sure I knew it.

Whatever, I don't like being used in that way, so, keeping my voice calm and cold, I say, 'Would you excuse us a moment, Mr Tanaka? I'd like to speak to Mr Zakynthos alone.'

I start to rise, intending to leave the office, but Ulysses doesn't move from his chair, watching me with open amusement in his eyes, the corner of his mouth curling as if he's enjoying my discomfort.

Instead, it's Mr Tanaka who gets to his feet. 'Stay,' he says to me. 'You can speak to Mr Zakynthos here. I'll go back to the Christmas party and make sure the staff are behaving themselves.' It's clear he's desperate to get out of this hideously awkward situation, so I don't protest, sinking back down in my chair instead. Only to face the wolf at the other end of the table, still staring at me as if he'd like to eat me alive.

The door closes behind Mr Tanaka and my heartbeat gathers momentum. Silence falls and tightens as Ulysses Zakynthos lounges down one end of the meeting room table, completely at his ease.

'You're being very persistent, Mr Zakynthos,' I say finally, giving no hint of my anger. 'These days most men understand that when a woman says no, she means no.'

The dark half-smile curling his mouth doesn't fade. 'True. And if I thought you were totally uninterested I'd get up and leave right now.'

'I *am* totally uninterested. That's why I refused you six times. I am also married.'

'Firstly, you're not totally uninterested. Secondly, you left your husband six months ago, correct?'

Shock ripples through me. How does he know that? It's not a state secret that I left John, but it's not something I like to talk about either.

Initially I thought our marriage was happy—at least the first year of it was. John treated me like a queen and there was nothing he wouldn't do for me. It was only towards the end of the first year that the little criticisms started. Not much at first, just comments about how he'd like me to be at home more, and wished my job wouldn't take up so much of my time. Then he started to make comments about my bluntness, my need for honesty, my social awkwardness, and how he wished I wasn't so 'uptight'. He thought my little collection of special items I'd accumulated over the years 'cluttered up' our apartment, and that I needed to be more interested in what he was interested in.

I should have read the signs back then, and should have known what he'd turn out to be, but I didn't see any signs and I didn't know. I thought he was saying those things because he loved me. But I was wrong.

Anyway, as the shock ebbs, more anger rushes in to take its place. 'How do you know that about John?' I ask, because there's no point denying it.

Ulysses lifts a careless shoulder. 'I have my sources.'

'Well,' I say. 'Your sources are wrong. My husband is out there right now, at the Christmas party. And he wants me back.'

It's true. John arrived about half an hour before Ulysses did, apologising to me for his behaviour that made me leave, telling me that he'd made a terrible mistake and that he still loves me. Except I know now that he's a liar and six months without him has made me realise that it wasn't so much a marriage for me as a prison. And he held the key.

I married him because he seemed steady, stable and honest, the complete opposite of my mother. He told me he'd take care of me, that he'd support me, that he'd never let me down. But he didn't do any of those things.

He broke my trust and I will never give it to him again.

'You mean that man you were talking to?' Ulysses drawls.

'Yes.' I put my hands flat on the table, ready to push myself to my feet. 'So, if you don't mind, I need to—'

'Actually, I do mind,' he interrupts in the same casual, careless tone. 'And my request stands.'

'Your "request"?' I let disdain coat the word. 'You mean, your ultimatum.'

He nods, again without a hint of shame, and again I can't help but admire the way he's so straightforward about it. 'Indeed. An ultimatum it is.'

'So, what?' I demand. 'You're going to blackmail me into bed?'

'It's not blackmail, my ice queen, it's leverage. Also, you should know that the only women I have in my bed are women who want to be there. So, if and when it happens, you'll be there because you want to be.'

No matter what I think about his honesty, it's his arrogance that gets under my skin and burns. I run into a lot of arrogant men in my line of work—finance is a very male-dominated space—and they're often difficult to deal with. So you have to be very blunt, very clear and very firm otherwise they'll walk all over you.

Luckily I have no problem doing that, and I'm certain Ulysses Zakynthos is that kind of man. He's used to being listened to. Used to giving orders. Used to deference. Used to getting his way.

Well, he won't get that from me, no matter how many ultimatums he gives me.

'If you're wanting an answer now,' I say, 'Then how about this one? No, I will not give you some of my precious time. In fact, I will not be giving you *any* of my precious time at all.'

His smile widens. 'Then please send Mr Tanaka in. I need to discuss with him my plans for taking his company and cutting it up into little pieces.'

CHAPTER THREE

Ulysses

KATLA FREEZES, HER GAZE clear and cold. 'You wouldn't dare,' she says. 'You'd destroy Tanaka Solar just because I won't go to bed with you?'

Little volcano. I can see her starting to boil already and I am here for it. She's outraged, which of course she should be. Olympia will have my head when she finds out about my behaviour tonight but, as always, it's better to ask forgiveness than it is to beg permission.

Not that I beg anything from anyone. Ever. I'm aware I am being a petulant child, but that doesn't bother me. What bothers me is that she doesn't seem to understand what I'm saying. I've already told her I'm not going to force her into my bed. I've no need to force any woman, not when I have so many who want to be there willingly.

So I laugh softly. 'You mistake me, ice queen. Yes, I want to go to bed with you. I've made no secret of the fact, and what man wouldn't? But all I'm actually asking for is time. However we spend that time is up to you.'

This doesn't mollify her. I can see flashes of lightning in her eyes, like a thunderstorm over the blue seas of the Mediterranean.

'For the sake of argument,' she says, 'How much time are we talking about here?'

I lean back in my chair and put one foot on the opposite knee, entirely at my leisure, as I like to be. Meanwhile, she sits bolt-upright with her hands clasped on the table, her chin at a belligerent angle. She's all challenge, which looks incongruous with the reindeer antlers and Christmas sweater.

'Well,' I say. 'Let's see. You've refused me six times, so I'm thinking...perhaps one month for every one of those refusals.'

She blinks, shock flickering in her eyes. 'So, six months? You can't be serious.'

'Miss Sigurdsdottir, I am always serious, especially when it comes to women.'

'But...why? Why me?'

I stop lounging and lean forward, put my elbows on the table and clasp my hands, pinning her with my gaze so she can see just how serious I really am. 'Because you are unique. You are rare. You are a mathematical genius and a beautiful woman and it's no lie to say that I'm fascinated by you.'

She's not expecting me to be so honest; I can tell by the way her pretty pink blush deepens. But there's no point hiding my interest. After all, my presence here basically shouts it, so why shouldn't she know she's fascinating to me? That's she's rare and beautiful? That she's unique?

'Well,' she says primly. 'That's very...interesting. But I'm not giving you six months. That's ludicrous.'

'I'm not here to debate the finer points of how ludicrous or otherwise my ultimatum is, Katla.' I taste her name like it's something sweet and hot, melting on my tongue. 'I'm not here to bargain, either. I'm here to get what I want, no more and no less.'

'And you're going to use Mr Tanaka's company to get it?'

'Let's be honest.' I lean forward a little more. 'My intention has always been to take Tanaka Solar. I let you and Tanaka walk away from our first meeting only because you captured my interest and I wanted to take some time to consider my approach. I have considered it now and this is my offer. At least I'm giving you a chance to save the company.'

Her gaze narrows into sharp needles of sapphire. 'Or perhaps you don't take it in the first place.'

I give another low laugh, very much enjoying the run for my money she's giving me. I had no idea this Christmas Eve would turn out to be so...exhilarating.

'Or maybe you could give me your time without arguing,' I suggest.

Her delectable mouth hardens. 'But I'm *not* interested in giving you my time. I don't know how I can be any clearer.'

'Really?' I raise a brow. 'I think you're interested, Ms Sigurdsdottir. In fact, I'd go as far to say that now you can't think of any else.'

'You're wrong.'

'Am I? Care to test that theory—how me just how clear you can actually be?'

She pushes her chair back and rises to her feet. 'I don't care to test anything, thank you.'

'So you'd really throw Tanaka Solar away?' I ask. 'Just so you don't have to spend some time with me?'

There's that pretty flush again, bringing colour to her cheeks. I watch it spread down the elegant column of her neck, making me salivate like a hungry wolf.

'I do not appreciate ultimatums, Mr Zakynthos.' The frost in her voice could rime the table between us.

'Seems petty of you,' I murmur, deliberately goading her. 'All I'm asking for is time.'

'Six months is not—'

'It doesn't need to be consecutive. An hour here, an evening there...' I pause then add, 'Perhaps you'll even give me a night once in a while.'

She is silent a moment, her arms folded, her gaze stern and not a little judgmental. I don't mind. Many people judge me, but I don't care about them. The only person whose opinion I care about—the only *person* I care about—is Olympia, my little sister. I would tear down the world for her if she asked. Luckily, she has never asked.

'I thought you weren't going to bargain,' Katla says and this time she's the one raising an eloquent eyebrow.

Little witch. She's not wrong. I *am* bargaining with her now. Telling her she doesn't have to take my six months consecutively was *not* the plan and I do not like deviating from a plan. The plan is for a six-month relationship—her available whenever I want her—so I can immerse myself fully in her. Experience her absolutely until there is nothing more to experience.

I'm not insisting because she denied me, but because she fascinates me. I have never met a woman so icy on the surface and yet, despite all that ice, hot down deep. There's lava inside her; I can see it glowing in her eyes.

'I'm not doing this because you refused me,' I say,

because perhaps after all I *do* care just a little what she thinks of me. 'I'm doing this because I want you. You, Ms Sigurdsdottir. Your body and your mind.'

She stares, her gaze uncannily perceptive. 'Does that line work with other women, Mr Zakynthos? Because it doesn't work with me.'

Oh, she is delightful. Utterly delightful. I love a formidable woman and she is everything I'd hoped she'd be and more. But I'm conscious that time is ticking away. I promised Olympia I'd be home for Christmas Eve, and I'm already more than late with my little detour to LA. I need to move this meeting along.

I push myself from my chair and stroll down the length of the table. She might not want to test our attraction, but I do. A small demonstration is in order, both to confirm for myself that she wants me and to prove it to her if need be.

She regards me suspiciously as I approach. 'What are you doing?'

'Conducting a test.' I move round to stand in front of her, the meeting table behind her, not too close, not just yet. 'If you can swear that you are utterly unmoved by me, I'll let you go back to your little party. And I'll leave you and Tanaka Solar alone.'

She gives me a belligerent look. 'Alone completely? You won't come back and stage a takeover?'

I incline my head. 'I will not.' And I won't. I'm a man of my word.

She is silent, her expression an icy mask. She's trying to freeze me out, I can see that, but I can also see the glow in the depths of her eyes and that blush... I'm bringing out that colour in her—that's all me.

'I'm not interested in tests,' she says coldly.

'But you are interested in me leaving, are you not?' I take a step closer. 'Just as you are interested in proving how indifferent you are to me.'

She doesn't move, though her mouth is in a hard line. 'Fine,' she says. 'Conduct your little test, then.'

Her condescension is adorable. She clearly thinks she's going to past this test with flying colours and 'that'll teach me'. Sadly, it will not. All it will teach her is the depth of her own self-deception.

I reach out and gently slide the reindeer-antler headband from her head. She doesn't move, but her eyes widen, as if she hadn't been expecting that as my first move. Excellent. The more I surprise her, the better this will be. Leaning forward, I lay the headband on the table behind her then leave my hand resting on the table top. This brings me closer and her eyes go even wider.

She smells as good as she looks, like sea salt and flowers, and I want to taste her skin, taste that luscious mouth. But I'm not going to touch her—not now, not yet. I'm only going to get closer and watch her melt like ice-cream in the sun.

Her gaze wavers, her pupils dilating as I extend my other hand to the table behind her, caging her with my body against the edge of it. We're not touching, not any part of us, but I can feel the heat she's putting out and she can feel mine.

I don't move. I merely look at her, studying the blush that stains her cheekbones, listening to her breathing getting faster.

'Is that it?' She's full of bravado and doesn't look

away. 'Please forgive me if I don't fall swooning into your arms.'

'But you're breathing fast,' I murmur. 'And your pupils have dilated.'

'So?' She isn't making any attempt to get away from me, hellbent on proving exactly how uninterested she is. Except it's not working.

'Do you habitually lie to yourself, my ice queen?' I lower my head a touch, not too close, but close enough to see the growing darkness in her eyes. 'Surely you must know that those are physical signs of desire?'

'Or fear,' she returns.

Except she's not afraid, and I know, because I know what fear looks like. I have an intimate acquaintance with it. It rests in my heart like a sliver of glass and I do everything I can to overcome it.

Fear that someone will hurt my Olympia.

Fear that someone will take her away from me. Again.

But that's not going to happen, not now. I've insulated both myself and her with all the power and money I can get, and I'm not going to stop, because a person can never have too much power and money. Especially when there are people to protect.

'I see,' I say softly, not making any move. 'So are you afraid of me, Katla? Or perhaps it's yourself that you're afraid of?'

Her chin is firm, yet her mouth is soft and her gaze drops to my lips. It's only for the briefest second, but I see it. And I know what it means. The electricity in the air between us builds, as does the heat.

'Afraid of myself?' She tries to sound disdainful, but the huskiness in her voice spoils it. 'Are you kidding?'

'No,' I say. 'I told you—I'm always serious when it comes to women.'

She's looking at me now from beneath her silvery lashes, and once again her gaze wavers. 'I'm not afraid,' she says.

'Then explain your pulse,' I say softly. 'And how fast you're breathing, the way your eyes are darkening and…' I lean down a touch more, her lips a breath away '…the way you keep looking at my mouth.'

'I'm not,' she whispers, very definitely looking at my mouth.

I could kiss her right now. All I need is to bridge that tiny gap and brush her mouth with mine. She'd let me, I can see how caught in this mutual heat she is. She wouldn't protest.

But that would feel like giving away a fine poker hand, and I'm not going to do that. I haven't got where I am today by giving away my best cards.

I smile, slow and hot, then I straighten. 'I think we can both agree that my theory has been proved.'

She flushes like a rose in bloom, with both anger and desire. 'Really? Perhaps I need to do a little test of my own.'

And, before I can move, I feel her warm hand suddenly come down over the fly of my trousers and she grips my cock like she owns it.

CHAPTER FOUR

Katla

SHOCK FLARES IN his amber gaze and I feel a twist of deep satisfaction.

He wasn't expecting that, was he? I didn't expect it myself. It was only that the way he'd come closer and closer…caging me against the table, towering over me like a vast oak tree…made me feel…breathless. Then he came even nearer, his body so hot, like a furnace, and he smelled of cedar forests, warm, dry earth and some kind of masculine spice that made my mouth water. His melted-honey gaze was a trap I couldn't get out of, and when he leaned even closer, his mouth so close to mine…

I have never enjoyed sex. With John, I gave him what he wanted, but I didn't take much pleasure from the act myself. It was being close to someone that mattered more to me.

So it was disturbing to feel the blood rushing hot in my veins when Ulysses came near, and a melting kind of pressure between my thighs. An ache. An insistent… need. Not to mention feeling so out of breath and almost hypnotised by a single look.

Kissing is not sexy to me either, but I kissed John because he liked it. Yet when I thought Ulysses was going to kiss me, I'd…wanted him to. And then, when he pulled away, I felt bereft…then angry.

He was playing with me, I was sure, and it felt as if he was using this strange new desire against me. I didn't want him to be right. I didn't want to fail this silly test of his. I wanted to prove that I was as uninterested in him as I'd told him I was. Yet it doesn't matter how badly I want those things; my body isn't lying, and I don't like lies. Even the ones I tell myself.

Perhaps he's right. Perhaps the person I'm afraid of is me.

Still, I have to do something. I have to take back some of the power he's stripped away from me, so I do the first thing that comes into my head. I grab him where he's the most sensitive.

It's not until I do it, though, that I realise my mistake. I should have pushed him away instead, not touched him…*there*. But I did and now my hand is on him and I can see the reaction in his eyes. That blaze of heat is like a solar flare.

He's long, and very, *very* hard, and my breath catches. And all I can think as I stare up into his amber eyes, watching the look in them burn, is that I have done this to him. This ruthless, powerful man with his insolent ultimatum is hard for me.

He thought he was playing with me but now I'm playing with him, and I don't know why that feels like a triumph, yet it does. Perhaps it's because he doesn't shy away from my touch and he doesn't hide his desire. He's blatant and carnal and the starkness of his honesty takes my breath away. He's not threatened by his own desires and doesn't seem to be afraid that I might use them against him. He's not made vulnerable by them the way I am, and now I wonder what it would be like to feel that way myself.

He's right—you are *afraid.*

'Well?' Again, he lifts an arrogant brow. 'Is that sufficient or do you require more proof?'

An unfamiliar devil in me wants to tell him no, it's not sufficient, that I need more proof than that, but I'm wary. In less than ten minutes this man has got under my skin so completely, mesmerised me so utterly, that I have my hand on him and am contemplating giving him exactly what he wants right here, right now. And yes, he's right—no matter how much I want to ignore it, I am scared.

Desires can be used against you, such as my need for safety and stability. John used that to get me to do what he wanted, and then what seemed safe ended up dangerous, and what looked like love was actually harm. I've been wrong about people too many times before, and I don't want to be vulnerable to anyone ever again.

'Don't play with me,' I tell him flatly, my voice hoarse.

'Is that what you think?' His piercing gaze searches mine. 'I was not playing with you, my ice queen. I told you I was going to test our chemistry and I did. It was enlightening.'

I can't deny he's right. He told me that was what he was going to do and that was exactly what he did. Then again, John was like that in the beginning. He promised me so many things and for the first six months of our marriage I felt safe and secure. Happy. But then came the jealousy about the few work friends I had, and then the controlling behaviours—telling me that I promised to love, cherish, honour and obey him when we got married and that I was doing none of those things.

In the end I didn't feel safe with John, but vulnerable. He manipulated me, manipulated some of the things I'm blind or too literal about, and I ended up feeling stupid. I started questioning as to how I'd missed things about him that I should have seen in our early courtship.

He was a liar, just like my mother and, just like my mother, he hurt me. I do not want to be hurt again.

'A physical response doesn't mean consent,' I tell Ulysses, so he's clear.

'Of course not,' he answers without hesitation. 'But perhaps we can discuss that during our time together. What I can promise is that it will be a very pleasurable conversation.'

I search his face, trying to read it, trying to find the hidden traps, but all I see in his eyes is desire. He's been totally upfront about what he wants—and, yes, perhaps he used this attraction between us to prove a point, but only because I let him.

Perhaps it's not him I should be second-guessing. Perhaps, it's myself. Doesn't mean I'm not angry at his effrontery, though. Or his arrogance.

He doesn't move, his gaze on mine, as if he somehow knows what I'm searching for and is letting me read him. He's not leaning into my hand where it rests on his fly, but he's not pulling away either.

'I like you touching me,' he says softly, and I can see that it's true; I can feel it too. 'But I suggest you stop, not if you don't want me to use Mr Tanaka's meeting-room table as a bed.'

I flush and jerk my hand away, because obviously I don't want that to happen, even though a very small part of me is whispering, *but what if you do?*

'Disappointing,' he murmurs. 'But unsurprising.'

He pulls away and straightens, and it feels as if I can breathe again, even as a newly awakened part of me aches, wanting to pull him closer.

'So,' he goes on briskly, all business now, as if I hadn't just had my hand on the hot, hard length of him. 'When and where would you like our first meeting? New Year's Eve perhaps? I have a bottle of excellent champagne we can open to ring in the new year.'

I haven't even thought about Christmas, let alone New Year. Not that there's much to think about. The only good thing my mother ever did was to buy me a book at Christmas Eve, which is an Icelandic tradition. Then I'd have hot chocolate and read happily by myself for the whole night while she went out to Christmas Eve parties. Those are my best memories of Christmas because, after I married John, we only had one Christmas together and it was with his parents. I spent the whole time being criticised and told how to be a better wife to him by my overbearing in-laws, while he just sat there smiling.

Not that I should think about Christmas when it's clear I'm going to have to give Ulysses Zakynthos what he wants, or else Mr Tanaka will lose his company.

It galls me to have to do it, but I can't be the reason that Tanaka Solar is swallowed up by Vulcan Energy— I can't. Not on Christmas Eve.

Reflexively, I smooth the fabric of my skirt, trying to hide how my hands shake. I don't want to give him any more proof of my susceptibility.

'I need to think about it,' I say, desperately hoping he'll give me this. 'Maybe some time in January.'

He frowns. 'That is not the timeline I was hoping for.'

I give him my frostiest stare, feeling more in control now. 'You've barged into my place of work, issuing demands and threatening the company I work for. The least you can do is grant me some space to think about your offer.'

He is unmoved by this, his mouth going hard. Yet the amber glint in his eyes holds nothing but flames. 'You're right—it was a demand, not an offer. And as such you know what will happen if you deny me.'

'I mean, I need space to think about your timeline.' My voice is quite level now, and I'm determined to keep it that way. I'm also determined not to cede any more ground to him than I have to. 'I have a gap in my schedule for a meeting at the end of January. I can spare you an hour.' It's not what he really wants, and I know that, but all he requires is my time. He didn't state where, how or what kind of time he wants.

The granite lines of his face are as hard as his mouth. 'I will not be put in your diary like a lackey.'

'You wanted my time, Mr Zakynthos,' I say crisply. 'You didn't specify what kind of time you wanted, so I have elected to give you my business time.'

I expect him to be furious for denying him yet again—certainly John always got furious when I told him no—but, strangely, this time his expression softens and his hard mouth curves. His smile is as hot as his amber gaze and something inside me melts at the sight of it.

He looks pleased; even… Is that respect I can see? Or maybe admiration?

'Well, well, well,' he murmurs, the words a soft, sexy rumble. 'You've spotted a loophole. You're right, I did not specify what kind of time I required.' His smile deepens as he searches my face, and I can feel the thing inside me melt still further. He told me I was rare, that I was unique, and the way he's looking at me now almost makes me feel as if I am. I've never been unique to anyone before. I've only ever been a problem.

'I could, of course, insist that it's your personal time I want and make that part of my demands,' he goes on. 'But that seems churlish. Also, I do like a challenge.'

It's a reprieve but oddly it doesn't feel like one. And, while I'm satisfied that I've managed to get one over on him, I'm also strangely annoyed by it too. I can't actually have *wanted* him to win this, can I?

Ulysses breaks my gaze, looking down at his watch, and I feel as if I've been released from some powerful magnet. 'My jet is ready,' he murmurs. 'And I have other appointments.' He glances at me again, hot golden eyes pinning me to the spot. 'I will have a lawyer draw up an agreement and send it to you ASAP.'

An agreement? I'm a little offended. I always do what I say and never lie. 'I told you I'd give you some time, and I will,' I say coolly. 'There's no need for agreements.'

He ignores the offence in my tone. 'Indeed, but you'll forgive me if I require some legal certainty. Sometimes one's word is not enough.'

This is so uncannily similar to the way I view the world that for a moment I can't think of anything to say. Because he's right, isn't he? People say one thing and then do another, so you can never be certain of anyone's word.

It makes me wonder what happened to him, who lied to him...

But, no, that's curiosity and I can't be curious about him, not when I've given him too much already.

'Fine,' I say. 'Send it to me and I'll look over it.'

His smile turns lazy and hot. 'In that case, please don't let me stop you from enjoying the rest of your Christmas party.' He gestures towards the door, indicating I should precede him, but I'm not sure I want to go back to the party quite yet. I need a few minutes to get him out of my head, to collect myself, because I can still feel the shape of him against my palm, feel his heat, and it's doing things to me that I can't quite control.

But I don't want him to know that, so I walk past him, determined to act as if nothing happened between us, and open the door to the communal office space and the noise of the Christmas party outside.

John is waiting for me near the doorway, and he frowns at Ulysses, who is following hard on my heels.

'You were in there a long time,' John says. 'What were you doing?' He's smiling but there's a tinge of familiar jealousy in his voice. It's the same tone he used whenever I worked late, or went out with a friend, or any reason when I interacted with people who weren't him. He always wanted to know who I talked to, where I went and what happened.

I didn't like that tone before I left him and I like it

even less now I've been free of it for months. 'Talking,' I say as Ulysses moves past me towards the exit, his entourage gathering around him. 'About business. That's all.'

John stares after Ulysses, his gaze narrowing. Then, clearly dismissing him, John glances back at me. 'So, do you have an answer for me, Kat?'

'I've already given you one.' I try to be patient, because I told him when he first turned up here that I didn't want to go back to him. 'It's no, John.'

He smiles, but it's sharp, angry and impatient. 'You don't mean that.'

He's always telling me what I do and don't mean, and I hate how it makes me second-guess myself. 'I do mean that,' I insist. 'I'm not coming back, and that's final.'

John has never been physically threatening before, but suddenly he reaches out and grabs my arm. 'Come on, Kat, don't be like that. Don't play hard to get.'

But I'm not playing, I never do. I open my mouth to tell him so, but he pulls me closer, his fingers digging into my arm. He's still smiling, but it's even sharper now. 'I just want you to come home,' he says. 'That's all. Once you're home, everything will all be okay.'

My stomach tightens. During the last month of our marriage, just before I left him, he flung one of my little knickknacks against the wall, a glass paperweight. He was angry I'd agreed to a business trip to Paris with Mr Tanaka and hadn't told him. The paperweight shattered, and as I knelt on the carpet, trying to gather up the pieces, I knew then that I had to leave; there was no other option. He was furious when I told him, and for weeks afterwards he'd send me up to fifty texts a day, venting his anger at me. But he didn't do anything else and I thought I was finally rid of him…

Until tonight. Even then, though, when he arrived at the party, I didn't think he'd try anything as physical as grabbing me. Not in a room full of people. Trying to pull away might involve an altercation, and I don't want to cause a fuss, I don't want to spoil people's enjoyment of the party, so I let him walk me towards the exit.

As he does so, I have a strange thought: I had two men at this Christmas party wanting me, both insistent, and both don't like being denied. Both make me feel afraid. But one makes me afraid of my own desires, while the other makes me afraid, full-stop.

John's hold is painful and he doesn't make it easy as he urges me towards the doors. 'It'll be fine,' he says soothingly. 'Don't worry. I just need you home. It's where you belong, Kat, don't you see that? It's what you want.'

We pass everyone having fun and laughing. They're all saying goodbye, 'Happy Christmas,' 'See you next year,' and John tells me to smile so as not to draw attention. I do, but my face feels stiff and my smile is a rictus. Anger seethes inside me at him and what he's doing to me, but anger won't help my situation, so I swallow it instead.

'I don't want to come home with you, John,' I tell him as we leave the office and approach the lifts. 'Let me go.'

'No,' he replies, his fingers digging in harder as he reaches for the lift button. 'My car's downstairs. We can talk about this there.'

CHAPTER FIVE

Ulysses

AFTER THE MEETING with Katla, I stop to have a word with Tanaka, to assure him that his company is safe and I have no plans to stage a takeover. He's not happy and wants my assurances that no harm will come to Katla. I admire his protectiveness, though he has no reason to fear for her safety with me. I'm a dragon when it comes to protecting those I consider mine and, after her performance in that office, Katla is now definitely mine. She claimed me the moment she put her hand on me, after all.

That was a surprise, I can't deny it. It was the very last thing I thought she'd do, in fact, and the sheer unexpectedness of it made me even harder.

Delicious woman. If she continues to be so surprising, it's going to make her eventual seduction even more pleasurable than I first thought. Interesting, too, that she thought I was playing with her, before getting all offended when I insisted on a legal agreement. It makes me want to know why, which ratchets up my anticipation. There're so many new things to learn about her, so many layers to uncover.

Merry fucking Christmas to me.

I leave Tanaka with some reassurances as to Katla's safety, and then stroll out with my bodyguards to the lifts. We're going straight to the airport, since the jet is ready for my flight to Athens. I've now missed Christmas Eve there, which means Olympia won't be happy, but I'll arrive in time for Christmas Day.

As we approach, I see Katla standing near one of the lifts with the pathetic excuse for a man who's apparently her ex-husband. He's gripping her arm and she looks as if she's trying to get away from him. Clearly not noticing my approach, he pushes her roughly against the wall and leans in to whisper something in her ear.

The expression on Katla's face is familiar. It's the same expression my sister used to wear when I first rescued her and brought her home, when she woke up screaming in the middle of the night, her whole body gripped tight by a nightmare.

It's fear.

Anger, hot and bright, flares up inside me. I spent years fighting to get Olympia back from the abusive foster family to whom she was given after our mother died, but by the time I eventually managed to rescue her it was too late. The damage was done.

I'd been too young, too poor and too powerless to stop the state from taking her and giving her to people who hurt her, and I will never let that happen again. I have power, influence and money now, and no one will take what is mine ever again.

And that includes Katla Sigurdsdottir. She notices me coming and with a quick, violent movement she jerks herself out of her ex-husband's grip and takes a couple of steps towards me. 'Please hold the lift, Mr Zakyn-thos,' she says, her tone calm, though the look in her eyes is anything but.

My anger is savage. I'm a difficult man, a hard man, a possessive man. I have a line, and when that line is crossed I will go to war. This man has just crossed it.

I glance at my bodyguards, a wordless command that they immediately obey, closing in a loose circle around the bastard. They won't hurt him, but they'll certainly prevent him from joining Katla and me in the lift.

'Of course,' I tell Katla calmly.

The ex looks like he might make another grab for her but then notices my bodyguards and clearly has second thoughts. His expression is hostile, and I can tell he's weighing up whether to make a fuss or to let this go. If he's an intelligent man, he'll let it go.

At that moment, the lift chimes and the doors open. Like the gentleman I am, I gesture for Katla to enter first.

'Wait for me downstairs,' her ex tells her quickly. 'We need to talk.'

'She will not and, no, you don't,' I say before Katla can reply.

'Kat.' He ignores me, taking a step towards the open lift. 'We really...'

I step into the lift, placing myself between Katla and him, the thought I'd had the second I saw him manhandling her becoming certainty. She is coming to Athens with me and there will be no argument.

'If you touch her again, if you even speak to her again, I will end you,' I tell him pleasantly before the doors shut in his face.

Once they do, I turn around to Katla. She's gone white and is shaking, though it's not fear I see now, not with those furious blue sparks in her eyes.

Whenever those nightmares chased Olympia, she woke up trapped and screaming. I'd grip her arms tightly, using the pressure to ground her so she knew she wasn't still in her nightmare, but in her bed with me protecting her. I do this now with Katla, taking her upper arms in a gentle grip to ground her and hopefully let her know that she's safe now, with me.

'Are you okay?' I ask her softly. 'Did he hurt you?'

She looks up at me then, the fury gradually receding from her eyes, and there's an unexpected satisfaction to be had from the knowledge that she feels safe with me.

'No,' she says at last, her voice cool, 'Thank you, Mr Zakynthos. You can let me go now.'

I release her. 'Don't thank me quite yet.'

She's remarkably composed, considering what just happened, back in her ice queen's armour once again. 'What do you mean?'

A brave woman indeed. Inside, my fury is still roaring and my hands itch to wreak havoc on the man who thought he could threaten her, but I ignore it. It's been a long time since I let that fury out, because I know what I'm capable of, what damage I can do. I promised Olympia that I would stick to the straight and narrow, and never harm another person again, regardless of whether they deserve it or not. And I keep my promises.

Besides, Katla has no use for my anger and, right now, neither do I. Instead, I let her go and lean back against the rail that runs around the interior of the lift, folding my arms. 'I mean, if you think you're safe from a man who'd physically threaten you at a staff Christmas party, then you're sadly mistaken.'

She eyes me warily. 'Yes, that seems obvious. I'm going to call the police and then—'

'No,' I cut in. 'It's Christmas Eve and too late to organise decent protection for you. Which is why I've decided that you will be accompanying me to Athens on my jet.' It's the most obvious course of action to take. Yes, the police will certainly want to hear about her ex, but it'll take too much time for them to do anything, and she needs protection from him *now*. Therefore, *I* will be her protection.

Her eyes widen. 'Go with you to…to Athens? *Now?*'

I have no need for subterfuge, so I incline my head. 'Yes, now. Tonight.'

'No,' she says, still looking thoroughly shocked. 'Of course I can't come with you tonight. I barely know you and you've just threatened—'

'I will not hurt you,' I interrupt, cutting through her objections, getting right to the heart of what she truly wants to know, since I have no patience with protests and excuses. 'Do you believe me?'

Her stare flickers, as if she hadn't been expecting me to get straight to it so quickly. 'Yes,' she says at last, sounding reluctant, as if she doesn't like the fact that she believes me.

I find that amusing, but I don't smile. 'And do you trust me?'

This time her reply is much quicker. 'No,' she says. 'Not as far as I can throw you.'

'Good,' I say, because I'm not offended. 'I wouldn't trust me either.'

'Well, then, I—'

'However, if you believe that I won't hurt you, then you can believe I will also protect you,' I say, impatient now. 'I'm a dangerous man, it's true, but I'm not dangerous to you.'

Her eyes narrow. 'I can look after myself, Mr Zakynthos.'

'Like you did just then?' My amusement has gone now, and all that's left is will—*my* will. 'Because it looked to me as if you needed help.'

She flushes and her mouth hardens yet again. She doesn't like having her vulnerabilities pointed out, that's obvious—and, to be fair, no one does. However, I have made my decision. She is coming with me and I will not take no for answer, not when her safety is at stake.

'He wouldn't have done anything to me,' she says after a moment. 'He only wanted me to come home.'

'Yes, by being physically threatening,' I say. 'Why are you making excuses for him?'

Her flush deepens and she looks away, her jaw tight.

'I know you don't want to come with me,' I say into the heavy silence. 'But I'm afraid you have no other option.'

She glances back, dark-blue eyes stormy. 'Why? Would you make demands like this to another random woman or am I just special?'

'You are special,' I tell her without hesitation, and that too is the truth. 'I told you that you were rare and unique, and I meant it. Make no mistake, I would protect another random woman, but you agreed to give me your time, Katla. Which means you're now my responsibility.'

She scowls. 'I don't want to be your responsibility.'

I stare back, implacable. 'What exactly is your objection? Is it me? Or is it going to Athens in particular?'

Her gaze doesn't flinch. 'All of the above. But you in particular. Your arrogance, for example, is astonishing.'

'So people tell me,' I murmur and, believe me, I know I'm arrogant. But if there's one lesson I've learned is that this world does not reward diffidence. If you want something, you have to take it. You can't wait for it to be given to you. 'But I believe you can handle it for the sake of staying alive.'

She snorts, glancing away from me once again. I'm right, of course, and she doesn't like that I am. Still, part of me is arguing that she's right to be upset with me, especially after her experience with her ex just before, and that I'm doing the same thing in forcing her to go with me. That the only difference is that I am not physically threatening her.

That part of me has Olympia's voice, and it's true, she wouldn't approve of this—she's never been a fan of my more autocratic decisions—but she knows I won't compromise when it comes to safety. She'd understand why I'm bringing Katla with me and why I will brook no argument.

Still, Katla should have some reassurances, especially when we don't know each other well and I've just told her I want her in my bed. That part hasn't changed. However, I don't want her thinking I'm spiriting her away just to ravage her somewhere else in private.

'Don't fret,' I say into the heavy silence. 'My home in Athens isn't some evil lair. Not with my younger sister also living there.'

Katla's blue gaze is frostier than the Arctic circle. 'I don't care who else lives with you. I don't want to go.'

'Noted.'

'I could have family I want to spend Christmas with.'

'Do you, in fact, have family you want to spend Christmas with?'

There's another flare of anger in her gaze, but she doesn't respond, which tells me everything I need to know about that.

The lift begins to slow, then stops, and the doors open.

'You're no better than him,' Katla mutters as I gesture for her to step out first. She clearly means her ex-husband, and I almost smile at how close to my own thoughts is the observation.

'Two differences,' I say as I follow her out of the lift. 'One, I'm not threatening you physically. And two, you actually want to come with me.'

She stops then and turns to me, her eyes glittering with anger. I stare back, daring her to challenge me, to deny me, to lie to me.

Her soft, luscious mouth firms and I can tell she's desperate to protest. I almost want her to, so I can prove to her yet again why she's lying both to herself and me.

'Well?' I raise a brow. 'Come now, my ice queen. You can tell me. Am I wrong?'

CHAPTER SIX

Katla

ULYSSES IS STANDING in front of me in Tanaka Plaza's foyer, his golden-eyed stare full of challenge, and I desperately want to point out to him that I've already said I don't want to go—didn't he listen?

He's just so arrogant, so *insufferably* arrogant, that I want to punch him in the face, which is *not* like me at all. It's John, that's the issue. John and threat he'd whispered in my ear, just as Ulysses and his bodyguards came striding out of the Tanaka offices, about how I'd better come with him or else.

I don't know why I felt such relief the moment I saw Ulysses or why I'd been so certain he would help me. I'd only seen his sharp golden gaze flare with anger as he took in the situation with John, and when I asked him to hold the lift he agreed.

So my furious reaction to him now is likely because he saw that I was afraid. And I hate that he saw it. I hate that he saw my vulnerability too. Also, I'm not best pleased with myself for not expecting that John might do something drastic, and for letting myself be at the mercy of my fear, like some stupid damsel in distress.

My emotions are always an issue. For my mother they were a problem she couldn't and didn't want to solve, and for John they were something to use and manipulate, so it's easier if I keep them all locked away.

But, where Ulysses is concerned, they seem to escape no matter what I do, not to mention being more volatile than I expect. And right now I don't like how he's put me in a position where I have to give him the truth. Truth I don't want to give up, because I don't want him to know that, the moment he said he was taking me to Athens with him, all I felt was relief.

I was so full of anxiety when Ulysses pulled me into the lift. I had no idea what I was going to do, because John knows where I live. He has my address and I wouldn't put it past him to come to my apartment to resume our 'discussion'.

It's a whisper of the same fear I had as a kid, when my mother suddenly announced that she wanted to move on—go to France, or to Spain, or to Germany, because she was bored with where she was and needed a change. I didn't do that change well, and it happened so often that anxiety about moving soon became part of my life.

John played on that anxiety when we first met, promising me safety and security, that I could trust him with anything. Except I couldn't trust him and, while I know leaving the country will keep me safe from him, who will keep me safe from Ulysses Zakynthos?

He promised he won't hurt me, and I believe that, but I still don't trust him an inch, not given the way he used my desire against me up in Mr Tanaka's office. And I don't want to admit to him that I *do* want his protection.

It's a terrible position to be in—I don't want to lie yet I don't want to tell him the truth. The worst part is that somehow he knows that. Somehow he can see the fight that's going on inside me right now, and is daring me either to tell him the truth or to lie straight to his face.

But the truth will mean allowing him to have a piece of me, and I'm not sure I'm ready to cede that right now. However, I can't lie either, so in the end I decide simply to say nothing at all.

I turn my back on him, heading to the doors that lead out of the building and onto the street. Yet I can feel him behind me. I realise that even staying silent has given him something and that he's pleased about it. I can virtually feel the smugness radiating from him.

Outside, a car is waiting, a chauffeur holding the door. Ulysses indicates I'm to get in, but I baulk. 'I don't have my passport and I don't have any luggage,' I say, irritated. 'We'll have to go via my apartment.'

'No,' he says in the kind of tone that suggests arguing with him will not be tolerated. 'The jet is slotted for departure in an hour and I can't afford to miss the window. I have to be in Athens for Christmas or my sister will have my head.' His eyes gleam. 'Everything you need will be provided for, I assure you.'

It's strange that such an arrogant, self-assured man who doesn't seem to care about anyone else's feelings but his own should be so concerned with his sister. It shocked me when he mentioned her, and I can't deny it makes me feel a bit better about going with him. It humanises him, which I resent, because I don't want him to be humanised. I'm quite happy seeing him as a monster.

I want to protest again, that I need my clothes, and definitely my passport, but arguing isn't going to get me anywhere; I already know that. It didn't get me anywhere in Mr Tanaka's office when he demanded I give him my time, either. Still, I can't let him have all the power. I can't let him walk all over me. I let John manipulate me, I let my mother make me feel broken and I'm tired of other people taking advantage of the way I sometimes miss things.

I need something that I can use against him, something that isn't just me arguing. Something palpable, inarguable—something honest. He's not used to being argued with; I know that much. I saw his surprise when I protested in Mr Tanaka's office, so maybe I need more of that.

Then, as I reluctantly get into the car, I remember something else that happened in Mr Tanaka's office. My hand on his fly. That shocked him; I remember quite clearly.

I give him a sidelong glance as he gets in with me and the door shuts after us, enclosing us in the warm car together. His presence seems to be magnified a thousand-fold in the small space, the air full of his heat and his dark, masculine scent.

Just as when he got close to me in Mr Tanaka's office, I feel short of breath, my skin tight and hot. It's overwhelming, as if I'm not in control of myself, as if I'm vulnerable. After what just happened with John, and how Ulysses took charge of me in the lift, I'm suddenly desperate to prove that I'm strong and in command. Desperate to put *him* on the back foot for a change, rather than me.

'That hour,' I say as the car pulls away from the kerb, the words slipping from me almost before I'm ready to speak. 'It can start now.'

Ulysses, his phone in his hand, looks up from the screen, frowning. 'Excuse me?'

'The hour of my time that you wanted,' I clarify. 'It starts now.'

Surprise flickers over his face, which is very satisfying. 'January,' he says. 'Isn't that what you told me?'

'I've changed my mind,' I say determinedly. 'Since you're insisting I come with you, I'm insisting that the time you wish to spend with me starts and ends when I say so, not you.'

He lowers his phones and directs the full force of his attention at me. As it did in Mr Tanaka's office, it makes the breath catch in my throat. It's very intense to be the object of his focus. It's as if he's reading and learning about parts of me that even I don't know about myself.

'Is that so?' he murmurs, the flames in his eyes glowing hot.

He likes to be challenged, that's clear. Or, at least, he likes it when I challenge him. And I have to admit to the small burst of pleasure it gives me too.

'Yes.' I meet his gaze, daring him to disagree or protest. 'So, you have an hour of my time. How do wish to start it?'

'I wish to start it on the plane after take-off when I can devote my full attention to you.'

'Perhaps I don't want your full attention.'

He smiles that slow, hot smile and it makes my stomach clench. 'Oh, I think you do, my ice queen. I think you're desperate for it.'

I wish I could tell him categorically that I don't, but I can't. He's not wrong. His full attention is intoxicating, and I like it. I want more of it. John saw me as a project he had to undertake, as there were things about me he didn't much care for, so he tried get rid of them. He didn't want to know about my job and had no interest in numbers or in finance. He never wanted to talk about what interested me, only about what interested him.

When we first got together, he told me he liked my precise way of speaking, and thought my little quirks were endearing. It was only later that he started to criticise them and made fun of them. I've collected items over the years that all have the spiral of the golden ratio in them: photos, fossils, pressed plants, paintings and sculptures. They're all different, but they all have that same spiral, and I find it beautiful. But John thought they cluttered up the place, that they were ugly. He didn't see the same thing I did and he didn't care that I liked them. He didn't like the person I was, and tried to make me into someone different, someone more palatable to him.

I don't know if Ulysses is the same—perhaps he is—but what I do know is that he called me rare and unique, and I like that. It makes me feel as if my differences are assets rather than deficits.

The leftover fear that sits inside me now is cold, and the betrayal that comes along with it is acidic, but the man sitting beside me is neither of those things. I don't really know what I'm doing, but I want something warm to drown out the fear and the betrayal that John instilled in me.

So, I put my hand on his thigh. He's wearing black

wool suit trousers and he is as hot as I thought he'd be, the heat of his body scorching my palm. I can feel the scratchiness of the wool and, beneath that, hard muscle and taut sinew.

His eyes flare as I touch him and I can see the hunger in them. Again, there is only truth in his gaze, only honesty. Suddenly I know what I can use to give me power. The thing that's honest, inarguable and palpable: the fact that he wants me.

'I appreciate the thought, ice queen,' he murmurs. 'But I'm not sure this is really what you want.'

'Oh?' I raise a brow, meeting his hot, golden gaze. 'That didn't seem to matter to you half an hour ago. Why is it a problem now?' I'm genuinely puzzled. He didn't care when I told him no before, yet he's reluctant when I initiate contact? Isn't this what he wanted? Please don't say I can't use this after all…

'That was before your ex-husband threatened you,' he says. 'You are under my protection now, even if that means protecting you from me.'

I'm even more puzzled, not to mention annoyed. 'I don't understand you. First you tell me you want me in your bed, despite me refusing you, and then when I touch you you tell me that's not what you think I want.'

I take my hand away, oddly hurt by his rejection. 'I told you—I don't like being played with, Mr Zakynthos.'

Something shifts in his eyes—heat, fire. He reaches for my hand once again, but he doesn't put it on his thigh. Instead, he cups my palm over the front of his trousers. He's hot and I can feel the firm length of his erection beneath the wool. My mouth dries.

'I'm not playing with you,' he says softly, yet roughly. 'Make no mistake, Miss Sigurdsdottir, I want you, and you can feel how much. But you must forgive me for wanting to wait until you've recovered from being threatened. I do not hurt women.'

He lifts his hand, but I don't stop touching him. The look in his eyes is molten, and under my palm he's as hard as iron. He's looking at me as if he wants to eat me alive.

Yes. This *is* what I can use: the power of my sexuality. He wants me, he's made no secret of that, and I can use it against him if I wish. But do I? Or will that be playing with him, the way he's playing with me? Am I that much of a hypocrite?

I don't like games, and I don't like lies, but I very much like how my hand on him is testing him. However, I can feel the pressure between my thighs, the needy ache—a warning that playing with this kind of fire could end up burning me. And that's something that frightens me. I could lose control of myself even as I test him…

I take back my hand, unconsciously curling my fingers against the heat lingering in my palm. 'Very well,' I say coolly, looking away. 'If that's what you want.'

I only have time for a quick glimpse of the lights of the road, before his fingers press into my skin and he takes my chin in one powerful hand, turning my face back to his. There's only time for one quick breath before his mouth covers mine.

I have never enjoyed kisses. They're wet and the sensation always makes me uncomfortable. Even worse, I'm not expecting this one. But something happens to me the moment Ulysses sets his lips against mine. His mouth is warm and firm, and somehow I know that he's good at this. That he knows what he's doing and that he'll make me like it whether I want to or not.

And I feel something wake up inside me, something hungry and hot that wants more. That wants his taste, his touch and his heat that's somehow a match for the heat inside me. Heat I never knew was there.

He holds me firmly so I can't pull away, but... I don't want to pull away. It's sensual, this kiss. He explores my mouth first, as if he's taking just a small taste, then his tongue coaxes and it's not wet and uncomfortable, but hot. And I open my mouth so he can explore me deeper. His flavour is heady and rich, like chocolate and fine brandy, and it's so addictive and delicious that I moan.

He grips my jaw in his big, warm hand, tilting back my head to kiss me deeper, and I let him. My eyes are closed, I can see fireworks behind them and my skin is so tight and hot, I want to tear it off.

Automatically, I reach for him, but as soon as I do he lets me go and pulls back, leaving me aching, hot and bereft.

There is fire in his eyes. 'Be under no illusions,' he says, his deep voice all velvety and rough. 'It's *not* what I want. But you owe me six months, ice queen. We have plenty of time.'

CHAPTER SEVEN

Ulysses

I'M NOT A man who regrets his decisions or second-guesses them, but I know the moment I look into Katla's darkening eyes that I should not have kissed her. That it was a mistake, and mainly because I hadn't planned to do so.

She put her hand on my thigh and I felt the heat of it like an arrow of pure desire going straight to my cock. I didn't expect her to touch me, not so soon after the encounter with her ex-husband, and I didn't expect the momentary flicker of disappointment in her eyes when I told her no.

I didn't expect my own reaction either, which had risen so fast and so intensely that I didn't stop to question whether kissing her was right. I only wanted her to know that I hadn't changed my mind about my intentions towards her. That I still wanted her in my bed.

And also, perhaps, because I wanted to taste her.

It was a mistake, though, because it took much more willpower to draw back from her than it should have, especially when she made a soft moan in the back of her throat. Especially when I caught the flavour of her response, sweet as honey on my tongue. She was a little hesitant, a little uncertain at first, but then she opened her mouth, letting me in, kissing me back and...*fuck*.

I've had a lot of women, indulging myself shamelessly over the years, because I'm not a man afraid of his appetites. So one kiss shouldn't get me hard, yet it did. It's simply the intensity of our physical chemistry, of course, nothing more, but I didn't think it would be so strong or require so much willpower to let her go.

If she was any other woman, I wouldn't. I'd haul her into my lap, hike up her skirt be inside her in seconds flat, my driver be damned. But I couldn't ignore that she'd just been threatened by her bastard ex-husband, and Olympia would definitely find it reprehensible if I had sex with Katla not five minutes later.

I always keep in mind what Olympia would think, because her opinion matters. She's my conscience and without her...

Well. I know my own nature: I'm not a good man. However, a good man wouldn't have been able to rescue Olympia from the people who hurt her, let alone the boy I'd been before our mother died. That boy, that soft-hearted rule-follower, didn't have the will or determination required to extract my sister from her abusive situation, so I put that boy down and became someone else. I will carry to my grave the knowledge that I wasn't able to protect her when it counted, but I'll protect her now and do what I can to mitigate the damage.

Katla's pupils have dilated. Her eyes are so dark, and her mouth is full and red. Her cheekbones are stained with colour and so is the pale column of her neck. My ice queen is melting. The fire at the heart of her is burning bright, and it wouldn't take much to make her molten, to make her erupt.

She wants me—of course she does—but, as I told her, we have time.

'My hour,' I tell her as she blinks, half-dazed by the kiss, which is satisfying in the extreme. 'I will have it on the plane. I have things to organise now.' She draws back slightly and I hear her ragged intake of breath. Then she looks away.

I've frustrated her, that's obvious, and while part of me is also frustrated another part suggests that a little frustration can make for a great aphrodisiac. It won't hurt to make her wait and it won't hurt me either.

I'm often impatient, and waiting for what I want is never my favourite thing, but I can afford to do it now. It will make everything sweeter in the end. So, I don't argue, returning to my phone to handle the necessary arrangements that bringing Katla with me involve. I also text Olympia, begging forgiveness for my absence on Christmas Eve, letting her know I'll be arriving on Christmas Day and that I will be bringing 'a friend'.

I never bring women home with me to Athens. Olympia doesn't need me flaunting my affairs in front of her, so she'll be surprised to see Katla. But she'll understand when I tell her the reason for Katla's presence and, in fact, she'd no doubt agree that Katla needs to be protected.

However, while I don't much care for Christmas myself, it *is* important to Olympia. When in foster care, she never had Christmases or birthdays; never had any celebrations at all. So when I finally managed to get her back I made sure that every holiday or birthday was a big deal, and that we celebrated any achievement, big or small.

It's now the middle of the night in Athens, so Olympia doesn't respond, but she'll see my text when she wakes and by then I won't be far away. After I finish my texts, I run through the usual long list of business tasks to complete before leaving LA and busy myself with completing several of them.

Katla doesn't speak the whole way to the airport, and I decide not to break the silence either. There is a certain challenge inherent in letting her control that. It makes me want to see how far I can push her before she breaks.

At the airport, we finalise customs necessities. One of my staff got Katla's address and went to her apartment to fetch her passport, so that's not an issue. The Vulcan jet takes off quickly and soon we're in the air.

I complete another couple of tasks then get the stewardess to pour me a Scotch, which I take over to where Katla is sitting and I sit down in the seat opposite her.

She's sitting primly, looking out of the plane window with her knees together, and her hands clasped in her lap, and doesn't glance at me as I sit. 'Not yet,' she says, peering at the lights of LA disappearing in the darkness.

She's talking about her hour, of course, and it's interesting that's uppermost in her mind. It amuses me. 'Why not?' I ask. 'We have ten hours to kill. You could get rid of at least one day of those six months you owe me.'

She continues to peer out of the window. 'I told you, I will be the one deciding where and when I give my time, not you.'

'Are you mad because I kissed you, Katla mine?' I drawl. 'Or are you mad because I stopped?' I'm taunting her, which isn't fair, but I want to know why she won't tell me the truth. She avoided answering when I told her she actually wanted to go with me—or rather, she didn't deny it—so now I want her to admit to her desires. Especially after that kiss, which she did rather conclusively enjoy.

'It's not wrong to want me,' I murmur when she doesn't say anything. 'It's just sex.'

She doesn't answer immediately, still looking at the blackness beyond the window. 'I told you, I don't like games.'

Yes, she *did* tell me that before, but as I told her in return I'm not playing any games. 'Why do you think I'm playing with you?'

Finally, she glances at me, her gaze icy. 'Well, aren't you? You said you wanted me, then got close to me on the pretext of "testing our chemistry". Then, when I touched you, you said no, only to then put my hand on your fly and kiss me. So you tell me—if that's not playing a game, then what is it?'

She's so blunt and straightforward, not letting me get away with anything. I have to admit, while I don't like being called out, it's certainly refreshing. It keeps me on my toes, which isn't a bad thing.

However, the way she puts all that makes it sound… not good. Then again, as I've already admitted, I'm not a good man. A good man would have taken her first no for an answer and left her alone. A good man wouldn't have threatened the company she worked for, and a good man certainly wouldn't have kissed her the way I did in the car.

A good man wouldn't have done all those things you did years ago.

I shift in my seat, suddenly restless at the thought. No, a good man wouldn't have obtained an illegal weapon and a couple of heavies and gone to take Olympia back by force from the people who'd hurt her.

Then again, during those years, I couldn't afford to be a good man. I had one goal and one goal only: to get my sister back. So I did what needed to be done in order to achieve that. I have no regrets.

'There's no game,' I say, compelled for some reason to explain myself to her. 'I was actually trying to be sensitive to your feelings in the car. And, believe me, that's not something I ever do.'

She regards me for a long moment, her pale forehead creased, her gaze searching. 'Okay,' she says at length, accepting this. 'If that's the case, then thank you. But, just so you know, I hate lies.'

She really does, too; I can see the conviction burning in her eyes. 'How intriguing of you,' I murmur. 'But what about the lies you tell yourself? You tell yourself you don't want me when the opposite is true, for example.'

Her mouth hardens. She doesn't like me pointing that out to her, not at all. 'Perhaps,' she says with some reluctance.

I tilt my head, studying her. 'Why?' I ask curiously. 'What's so very wrong with wanting me?'

She sits back in her seat, but her posture is still stiff.

'Your arrogance, for a start, and your insistence on pursuing me, even when I said no.'

'Yes,' I allow. 'But, as I told you before, if you truly hadn't wanted me I would have left you alone. Except you did want me, my ice queen. And I'd like to know why that makes you so angry.'

'Because you used it against me,' she says with the same bracing frankness she's employed in all our discussions. 'To get what you want.'

'I didn't use it against you,' I correct mildly. 'I merely wanted you to acknowledge it. And, also, it hasn't got me what I wanted, has it? There you are, sitting in your seat and still fully clothed.'

Her eyes narrow as she takes this in. 'You only want an acknowledgement—that's all?'

'Well, no,' I admit. 'That's not all I want. But an acknowledgement would be a big help.'

'You wouldn't use it against me in some fashion?'

I'm a little impatient with this conversation, but I thrust that aside. For some reason honesty and transparency is important to her, and if it's important to her then it's in my interests for it be important to me too. 'I won't,' I promise. 'Scout's honour. Cross my heart and hope to die.'

Her gaze doesn't waver for even a second. 'Do you hear yourself? Do you hear how it sounds as if you're playing right now?'

A small needle of self-awareness slides beneath my skin. Now that she's mentioned it, yes, perhaps I *do* sound a little…casual. Mainly because I'm impatient and part of me is wondering if *she's* playing games with *me*.

But, looking at her lovely face and seeing the expression in her blue eyes, remembering the tenor of our conversations, it's clear she's not a game player at all. There's an open honesty to her that demands honesty in return.

It's simplistic, in a way, but I've become used to games and manipulation because that's business. And I confess I've brought those same manipulative games to my dealings with people too. Usually, that kind of awareness doesn't bother me, because I don't care much for other people's feelings, but...

There is something brave about Katla, sitting opposite me, so prim and serious. And...genuine. She has a reputation in the business world for being sincere, forthright and loyal, and I can see the evidence of that staring back at me now.

It makes me want to be the same.

'Very well.' I put down my Scotch and lean forward, elbows on my knees, my hands clasped. 'You know the truth of how I feel. I've always been honest about that. But I promise that there will be no more games, nor will I use your desire against you. In fact, I'll go further—nothing sexual will happen between us unless you ask me for it explicitly.'

CHAPTER EIGHT

Katla

I STARE INTO Ulysses's molten gaze, studying him. Is he telling me the truth or is he lying? Yes, he's been honest about his desires and about what he wants from me, but I'm unsure about his honesty now. He said he wasn't playing games, but his promise seemed casual and offhand, as if he thought it unimportant. Yet now he's leaning forward, his gaze pinned to mine, telling me nothing sexual will happen between us unless I ask for it.

Which do I believe—his manner, his words or his actions?

Mr Tanaka and I investigated him when he first started making moves against Tanaka Solar, but the information we found was only about his business practices. 'Ruthless' was the word many people used. 'Brilliant' was another. 'Merciless', a third. That tells me nothing about what he's like as a man and I'm curious now; I can't help it. I want to know why he's so ruthless. Why he seems so honest, yet as if he's playing games at the same time. Why his actions are both aggressive and protective, his manner almost…playful.

Being curious is probably to my detriment, but I want to believe him. I want to tell him the truth. He's asked me about my feelings for him a few times now, point blank, and I haven't answered, which seems hypocritical of me. I also don't like the thought that I've been drawn into his games, that I'm using his desire for me as a way to gain back some power. It feels dishonest.

'I might not ask,' I tell him after a moment.

'You might not,' he agrees, his gaze piercing.

'I still don't trust you,' I warn, just so he knows.

He doesn't seem offended. 'I understand.'

Silence falls and I know I have to answer him. I have to give him the same honesty he's giving me, no matter that I dislike him. No matter that he's arrogant and demanding. No matter about his threats to Tanaka Solar.

'Very well,' I say at last, reluctantly. 'You're right. I am…attracted to you.'

One side of his mouth curves and there's satisfaction in it. But oddly the satisfaction doesn't annoy me. It pleases me that he's pleased.

'You liked the kiss,' he says.

'Is that a question or a statement?'

'A statement.' He leans back in his seat again, picks up his Scotch from the small table beside his elbow and sips it. His long legs are stretched out in front of him, his powerful body at rest, and there's something about him lounging like this, lazy as a panther, that makes my mouth go dry.

'Yes,' I say, because I told myself I'd tell him the truth. 'I did like it. It also took approximately thirty seconds,' I add, which is being unnecessarily pedantic but I want him know. 'You can deduct that time from my six months.'

This time his whole mouth curves and his eyes gleam. It doesn't feel like night in the jet any more, but as if daylight has come and is streaming through the windows. My stomach tightens and my breath catches. He is so very beautiful.

'Were you counting?' he asks, heat in the look he gives me.

'No,' I say candidly, because I wasn't in any position to count when he kissed me. 'It's an estimate. Kisses are usually ten seconds, but in the car it was longer.'

'I see,' he murmurs. 'Who the hell have you been kissing that it only takes ten seconds?'

'John,' I say, then add for completeness's sake, 'Sex takes ten minutes.'

Ulysses blinks and a little arrow of pleasure pierces me that once again I've managed to surprise him.

'Ten minutes,' he says blankly, as if the words have no meaning.

'Sometimes less.' I relax in my seat at last because, as it turns out, I do trust his word. He promised nothing would happen unless I asked and I believe him.

'Less,' he echoes in the same tone.

His reaction is puzzling. He looks almost…shocked. Perhaps I'm wrong; perhaps sex doesn't take that long. Or perhaps it takes longer for other people. I just know how long John takes and ten minutes is quite enough for me. I can't imagine wanting longer.

You wanted that kiss to be longer.

Heat curls through me at the reminder and abruptly I'm back in the car, his hand gripping my jaw, his mouth on mine, his tongue exploring me, tasting me… It occurs to me that, if I liked that kiss, I might tolerate sex with Ulysses. I might even like it.

No, you won't. You'll love it.

'That should be illegal,' Ulysses mutters, his voice soft and deep in the humming quiet of the jet's cabin.

My head is full of hot images all of a sudden—of being in bed with Ulysses. Instead of being naked with John, I'm naked with him. His body is on mine, his hands on me, his mouth on my skin. He's inside me…

Need throbs between my legs, the hungry, desperate ache that rose up when he kissed me and that seems to wake whenever he gets close to me.

I've never thought about sex before. I've never thought about it or even wanted it before. Oh, I know what attraction is, what physical passion is, but I didn't think it was something I could experience because I'd never met anyone who made me feel it. But things have changed. I've met someone I want and things such as lust and desire, things I've only ever heard people talk about, are things I now feel myself for the first time. And I feel them for the man sitting across from me.

I swallow, my mouth dry. 'What should be illegal?'

'Ten minutes for sex—maybe less,' he says, and then focuses on me in that intent way he has that leaves me breathless. 'You should brace yourself, my ice queen. With me, it's all night.'

All night? That sounds exhausting. 'I don't think I'd want that,' I say, frowning.

There is a sensual kind of amusement in his eyes now and I'm getting that tight, hot feeling again. 'Well, if you ever want to find out, you know who to come to, hmm?'

I think about it for a moment. All night in Ulysses's bed… Perhaps it wouldn't be so bad. I'm certainly curious; I can't deny that. John is the only man I've ever been with, and that put me off, but maybe it would be different with someone else…someone I actually wanted?

'That's still too long,' I say carefully. 'An hour seems like ample time.'

The amusement disappears from Ulysses's face and he frowns as he studies me. 'Tell me, is John the only man you've been with?'

'That's a very intrusive question,' I say.

'You were the one who brought up the subject,' he points out quite correctly, which is annoying. 'Also, it's absolutely in context with your concerns about sex, not to mention being quite relevant to me as your prospective partner.'

Again, he's right. He's no doubt used to women who're much more sexually experienced than I am, and probably women who enjoy it more too. It's only fair that he knows this about me if I want to take our connection further.

'Okay,' I say. 'That's fair. Yes, John is the only man I've ever been with.'

Ulysses's golden gaze rests on me 'So—if this isn't too intrusive a question—do you actually like sex?'

It's a strange thing to sit here on a plane talking about sex with Ulysses Zakynthos, but he's got a point about the context. If I'm going to spend time with him, possibly time in the bedroom, he should know my experience or otherwise.

'No,' I say frankly. 'Not really.'

He says nothing for a long moment, only stares at me, and I don't know what he's thinking this time. Have I shocked him, surprised him? Does he think me strange or abnormal somehow? I'm not exactly normal, I know that much, and I also know that not everyone likes sex. But most people do, which makes me the odd one out. Perhaps he finds that unattractive in some way.

It wouldn't be the first time my honesty hasn't been appreciated, and my heart feels tight at that last thought. Maybe I shouldn't have been so frank. I didn't think that I wanted to be in his bed but, now that he's been brought face to face with my quirks, I'm tense and concerned that he'll change his mind and not want me after all.

'If you don't want me any more, that's fine,' I tell him straight out and quickly, before I can second-guess myself, because I'd rather know. 'You can change your mind.'

His gaze narrows to sharp golden points. 'Why would you think I'd change my mind?'

'Because I don't like sex,' I explain. 'That's not what you signed up for, I know, and—'

'Katla,' he interrupts, not without a little roughness. 'No, I haven't changed my mind. I'm just over here being quietly appalled at your husband.'

The tight feeling in my heart eases. 'Why?' I ask. 'It's not his fault.' I don't know why I'm defending John, especially after the incident earlier at the Christmas party, but my lack of interest was the issue, not his.

Ulysses blinks again, his gaze roaming over my face as if the expression on it is a language he can't quite

read. I shiver under the pressure of it, even as something in me basks in the attention.

'So,' he says quietly. 'Do you think the fault is yours?'

I don't know why he's taking this so seriously. It's
just sex and it doesn't matter. 'Of course it is,' I tell
him. 'I've just…never liked it. Even before I met John
I never felt any kind of…desire for anyone.' And it's
true, I didn't.

'Yet you do for me,' he points out.

My cheeks heat. It's hard admitting what I'm feeling, even though I swore I'd be honest. I don't like the
vulnerability of it.

Perhaps sex isn't as unimportant as you think? But it
is. At least, I've never needed it to function in my daily
life. Numbers give me joy and pleasure and they're always honest. They're much more reliable than people,
at least.

*Then why are you so reluctant to tell him you want
him?* Maybe it's a habit I've got into; I'm not sure. Yet
honesty compels the truth out of me all the same. 'Yes,'
I say, forcing out the word. 'I do d-desire you.'

'So, perhaps it's not you.' His voice is patient, calm.
'Perhaps the problem is that you just weren't attracted
to your husband. And perhaps, if you have a different
partner, things might be different.'

He does present an interesting if strangely distress-
ing thought. If the problem wasn't me after all, but
John, then I should have known better. I was stupid to
marry him. I accepted that I wasn't a sexual person; I
never questioned it. I never talked to John about it, he
never asked me, and I let that go on for…far too long.

God, everywhere I've turned these past few hours

all I've done is find out things about myself and about my marriage that I didn't know, and that only make me feel even more stupid than I already did.

My throat is tight and my eyes prickle. I never cry, never ever, and I'm not sure why I'm on the edge of tears now, but everything feels too much. There have been too many shocks, too many surprises—and now I'm flying to Athens with a man I hardly know to spend Christmas with his sister and him, after being physically threatened by a man I hadn't thought was dangerous.

How has this even happened? What did I do to get myself into this mess?

Across from me, Ulysses suddenly sits up and puts his Scotch down for the second time. 'Come here, Katla,' he says, my name sounding strangely sensual and exotic in his deep voice. 'I can prove to you that the fault is not yours if you'll let me.'

'What do you mean?' I ask warily.

'You're a volcano, don't you know that?' His tone is like velvet, soft yet a little rough. 'That's why I want you. Deep down, you're molten. Deep down, you're fire. And all you need is someone to melt your ice. I can do that for you. I can show you what you're actually hungry for.'

My heartbeat is loud in my ears and the hot, tight feeling is intensifying. I'm breathless and there is something needy and desperate in me. My mother named me Katla for the volcano in my home country, but I've never thought of *myself* as one. John once made a joke about my name, saying that I wasn't dormant but extinct. It hurt, though I brushed it off at the time.

But Ulysses doesn't think that, he thinks there's fire in me, and now I want to know why.

'Show me,' I say. 'How?'

The flames in his eyes leap high. 'I think you know how.'

I think I do too. I'm not sure if he led me to this point, or whether I walked myself into it, but I do know that if I go to him right now, if I let him show me how like a volcano I am, I won't be the same woman afterwards.

His kiss changed things for me, it woke me up, and I think this will change me too. But…maybe I want to be changed. Maybe I want to be a different woman from the one who nearly let herself get kidnapped by her ex-husband. A different woman from the one who was constantly criticised and belittled by her own mother. Be a woman more aware of herself and what she wants.

So this time I don't second-guess, and I don't think.

I push myself to my feet, take a step that brings me right in front of him and look down into his golden eyes. 'Show me, then.'

CHAPTER NINE

Ulysses

I DIDN'T THINK she'd do it. I didn't think she'd come to me, not after our conversation and my shock at her confession that she doesn't like sex. She's almost virginal in her lack of understanding, but that's not her fault.

The moment she said it wasn't her husband who was the problem, I knew: *he* was the problem. This woman has fire inside her. I knew it the moment I walked into that meeting and saw her sitting there, watching me. I saw it in her eyes; I watched it burn high as we argued tonight in Tanaka's office, and then in the car on the way here. I tasted it in her kiss. Lack of passion is *not* my Katla's problem. The problem was her husband. Logically, if she's only been with one man and thinks she doesn't like sex, yet professes a desire for me, then yes, the problem is definitely *him*.

I now wish I took the time to punch his head in when I had the chance, but sadly my sister, AKA my conscience, wouldn't like it. I'm still angry that he made this woman feel as though she was at fault, though I don't know why she was distressed when I told her that she wasn't to blame.

And she *was* distressed; I saw how it darkened her pretty eyes. That did something to me—it made me want to know why she was upset, what it was that hurt her and how I can fix it. It's strange. I've only ever cared about the feelings of one person but, apparently, I now care about the feelings of another: Katla.

I'm not sure why or how she's different from any other woman I've wanted in my life, but she is. There is a painful sincerity to her that makes me want to protect her—the world is a harsh place for honest people— and it also speaks to a level of trust she has in me. I know she just told me that she didn't trust me, but the fact is she does, at least a little, or else she wouldn't be sitting here.

Now she's trusting me again by coming to me and, though there's trepidation in her eyes, there's also determination. I told her she's brave, and she is.

'I said nothing sexual would happen between us unless you ask,' I remind her, because she's already made it clear that she's not a game player, so I won't play with her. 'So…are you asking right now, Katla mine?'

A flush has crept into her cheeks, and uncertainty flickers across her face. Maybe the reality of the situation is hitting her and, maybe now it's here, she'll change her mind.

Hunger shifts inside me. I don't want her to—Christ, I don't want her to—but I say nothing, letting her think about it. She's already had bad experiences with her husband, and I want to show her what real pleasure is, but only if she's ready for it.

She draws out the moment, damn her.

'Yes,' she says at last. 'I am.'

I crush the relief I feel, but I don't hide my pleasure. I want her to know that she pleases me.

With a few quiet words, I get rid of the stewardess so we can have privacy, then I look at Katla standing in front of me, her eyes dark with a complicated mixture of fear and desire. She's beautiful. And she is mine.

'Come here,' I order, holding out my hand to her.

She takes it, her fingertips a little cold, but I'll soon get her warm, so I ignore it as I draw her into my arms and onto my lap. She moves stiffly and sits awkwardly, as if she's not sure what to do with herself, so I arrange her so she's sitting in the crook of my arm, her legs across me and over the other arm of the seat, her head against my shoulder.

She's a warm, soft armful, and that flower and salt scent plays havoc with my senses. She belongs here in my lap—that's the first thing that hits me. And it's where she always should have been, not with that coward of a husband who didn't know what he had in her. Who only saw the icy exterior of her and not the fire inside.

My body tightens, my cock getting interested, but I ignore it. This is not about me, this is about her. Olympia would be ecstatic if she knew that I'm considering acting unselfishly but, luckily for me, she'll never know.

'Did your husband ever talk to you about what you wanted?' I ask quietly, hooking an errant curl that's slipped out of her braid back behind her ear.

She shivers, looking up at me from beneath silvery lashes, her North Sea eyes dark and deep. 'No. He thought I was frigid.'

Always so ready to rise, my anger burns hot at what

that fool told her, but I ignore it. It's not the time or place for my anger. 'Well,' I murmur. 'Shall we prove him wrong?'

She gives a stiff nod, but her muscles are tense, and I want her to relax. 'I think you need a drink first, hmm?' I suggest.

She starts to rise out of my lap, but I shake my head. 'No, stay there,' I tell her, and she settles. Then I reach for my tumbler of Scotch sitting on the table. I take a sip, but don't swallow. Instead, I put one hand beneath Katla's chin, tilt her head back against my shoulder and dip my head, placing my mouth over hers.

She stiffens at first, then a second later relaxes, her lips softening. I let her taste the Scotch from my mouth and she makes a small, soft sound. I give her more, letting the heat of the alcohol and the kiss blend into something slow, sensual and hot. If the kiss in the car was a promise, this one shows her that I kept that promise. Shows her that I want her, that I'll make it good for her, that I'll seduce her so completely she won't remember her own name. And I'll take it slowly, teach her that she does indeed like sex but she just hasn't yet had it with the right person.

Her mouth opens beneath mine, letting me in, and I deepen the kiss, the flavour of her mixed with the Scotch so damn delicious. It's all I can do not to completely ravage her, but I keep myself in check.

She makes another sound, beginning to kiss me back, and I can taste her hunger. My anger twists into a sullen fury that this woman thought she didn't like sex, all because her husband made her feel as if it was her fault. Didn't he see the passion in her? Didn't he see her hunger? But chemistry's a funny thing, and clearly for Katla it's the defining thing. She had none with her husband, but with me...

I place my hand on her throat, gripping her lightly, my palm pressed to her warm skin, feeling her pulse which is fast and frantic. I want her to know that she's here with me, no one else, and that she's mine.

She shudders as I caress the side of her neck with my thumb, tracing the delicate cord up and down in a slow stroke, then all the tension rushes out of her, her body melting against mine like warm candle wax.

'More,' she whispers against my lips.

The blaze of satisfaction burns through my veins like a drug. Of course she wants more; she's ravenous for this. She's ravenous for me, and she doesn't even know it, though...perhaps she's starting to get an idea now.

Pulling my mouth from hers, I reach for my Scotch and take another sip. This time she tilts her head back for me, ready to take my kiss, and when I bend my head and cover her mouth she drinks the Scotch straight from my mouth.

My God, she tastes incredible. I can't get enough.

I take the kiss deeper, hotter, stroking the silky skin of her neck, and she moves restlessly in my lap, the curve of her rear pressing against my fly. I'm hard and aching and I want to do nothing more than sink myself inside her, but again I push the thought away. With another woman, I'd already be there, but not with Katla. Not now. I want to give her something that her husband never did: relentless physical pleasure.

I move my hand from her throat, trailing my fingers down over the silly Christmas sweater she's wearing, following the curve of her breasts and then down further. She has on a close-fitting business skirt, very plain and no-nonsense. I put my hand on her hip, sliding it down her thigh to the skirt's hem, before easing my fingers beneath it. I feel her tremble, and she draws in a ragged breath, so I lift my head and look down at her, checking in on her. Her face is deeply flushed, her eyes dark-blue, her mouth red. She's staring at me as if I'm her last hope of salvation and it makes my chest clench tight.

This hold she has on me is mysterious, and I don't understand it. The thing in my chest and the way I'm caring about her feelings... Those sensations are foreign to me. Well, perhaps not entirely foreign. I care about my sister, but she's all I have room for. I don't have the space to care about anyone else, and I don't want to.

Yet Katla...

The way she's looking at me right now, the honesty of our conversation just before, makes me feel as if she's letting me see her soul and she's not even aware of what she's doing. And I want to be careful with that soul. I want to keep it safe, keep it protected...

I hear her gasp as I slide my hand up her thigh. Her skin is warm and smooth, and as my fingers edge higher she trembles and her breathing gets ragged. Her gaze clings to mine and I see the molten heart of her begin to blaze as I stroke her. 'Spread your thighs for me, ice queen,' I tell her softly. 'Let me give you what you need.'

Slowly, hesitantly, she obeys, and she's such a beautiful sight, lying in my lap, her white-blonde hair coming out of its braid, the colour stark against the deep pink flush on her face. Her mouth is open and she looks at me…

My *God* the way she looks at me…

'More?' I ask as I slide my hand higher, feeling her heat.

'Yes,' she whispers hoarsely. 'Yes, more.'

So I slip my hand between her thighs, stroking over the damp cotton of her knickers. She gasps again as I trace the shape of her through the fabric, teasing her, drawing out her pleasure so she knows exactly how good her body can make her feel.

This is going to take longer that ten damn minutes.

'Ulysses…' she whispers, her eyes wide and dark. There's uncertainty there and a kind of shock and wonder. Has she ever felt this before? Has she ever even had an orgasm before?

Good God, she's basically an innocent, and here I am demanding things from her, threatening her now, with my hands on her… I thought I knew what she was, but I really had no idea.

You have made a mistake.

Maybe so. But I can't stop now, not while she's here in my lap, having chosen to be there and giving herself to me. I'm committed to this. Stopping will only hurt her and I don't want to do that.

I ease my fingers beneath the edge of her knickers and slide them through her soft curls. She's hot, so hot, and so very wet and all for me. The satisfaction I already feel deepens and abruptly becomes a savage possessiveness. I want to throw her down on the floor and take her fast and hard, and stopping myself from doing so is so difficult. But I promised that I'd show her just how passionate she truly is. She entrusted herself to me, and I can't break that trust by taking something for myself. I won't.

She lifts her hips against my hand as I stroke her clit, making her tremble and gasp. 'Ulysses…' she murmurs again, her voice full of discovery. 'Oh God…'

I'm so hard, I hurt, but I don't do anything more than stroke her before gently, slowly, sliding one finger inside her. She's so slick and she moans aloud, her eyelashes fluttering closed. I have never seen anything more beautiful than my ice queen melting—melting all over me, because of me.

I kiss her again, sliding another finger inside her, building a rhythm that has her moving restlessly against my hand and kissing me back, frantic and hungry. Part of me wants to take my time, edge her a little, make her even more desperate than she already is, but I don't want to push her.

'Ulysses…' she whispers again, her lips brushing against mine, and I feel her grip my wrist. But she doesn't stop me; she tries to direct me to where she wants my touch most. I smile against her mouth, because I knew this would happen. She's passionate and, now she understands that about herself, she's demanding about what she wants.

I love it. I want to give her everything.

'Shall I make you come, ice queen?' I murmur, teasing her a little. 'Is that what you want?'

'Yes,' she says hoarsely. 'Please, oh, please.'

'You're not really an ice queen, though, are you?' I tilt my hand slightly so my thumb brushes over that tight bundle of nerves between her thighs, even as my

fingers give her the friction she needs. 'You're a volcano, my Katla. And now you're going to explode just
for me.'

I give her that last bit of friction, pressing my thumb
down hard on her clit, and she arches in my lap, her
back bowing, her thighs crushing my hand between
them as the orgasm hits her. She cries out, her eyes
wide, full of ecstasy and wonder as she gazes up at me.

I've watched many women in their moment of climax and they were all lovely. But Katla is transcen-
dent in this moment. Caught in the grip of an intense
pleasure she's probably never felt before, she is utterly
glorious.

I'm not a reformed man. I'm a possessive Neander-
thal and I allow myself to revel in the knowledge that
I'm the one who gave her this moment. I'm the one
showing her what true physical pleasure feels like, and
it pleases me on a level I can't remember feeling before.

I'm painfully hard, but all I do is remove my hand,
smooth down her skirt, and hold her as she relaxes completely in my lap, her eyes closed. She's as sated as a
cat who didn't just get the cream but the whole damn
dairy. I watch her, unable to tear my gaze from her face.
Wisps of hair cling to her flushed forehead like little
white-blonde flames. One is caught across her cheek,
so I gently push it back behind her ear.

Her eyes open then, blue bordering on black. She
looks at me, and I let her. I want her to see what she did
to me. I want her to see my satisfaction and the pleasure
that I got from her. I want her to know that she wasn't
the only one who found this a revelation.

After a long moment, I'm the one who breaks that silence. 'You see, Katla?' I murmur. 'I don't think you like sex at all. I think you fucking love it.'

CHAPTER TEN

Katla

I LIE IN Ulysses's lap, my whole body lax apart from the shivers that move up and down my nerve-endings like tiny electric shocks. I have to admit to myself that, if that's just a taste of what physical pleasure is like with him, then he's right: I do love it. Because that was the single most astonishing experience I've ever had.

It's not that I don't know about orgasms—I'm a grown woman, after all. But to have one requires sexual desire, and I've never felt sexual desire before, let alone sexual pleasure. I even thought I wasn't capable of it, that it happened to other people, and because I didn't know what it felt like I didn't miss it. I can't miss something I've never felt.

But all that has changed now. *Everything* has changed. And I have Ulysses to thank for that. I knew what he was offering me, what he wanted to show me and that it would mean giving myself over to him sexually. And, yes, I was nervous about it. A deep part of me was afraid that John was right—that I was an extinct volcano after all—and that Ulysses would touch me and I'd feel nothing.

But I wasn't afraid enough to refuse him. I wanted to know once and for all if it was possible for me to feel pleasure. I wanted to know if I was the problem.

Sitting in his lap was awkward at first and I wasn't sure how or where to sit or what to do with my arms or my legs. It was very helpful of him to adjust me, though being so close to him was overwhelming. He was so hot, his thighs hard beneath my rear, his chest hard beneath my head. I tensed up, not sure what to expect, but then he took a sip of his Scotch, lowered his head and kissed me.

I knew what to expect, since he'd kissed me in the car, but this…was different. His kiss was slower, with a sensuality to it that stole my breath. Then he let me sip the Scotch from his mouth, which I swear made it even more alcoholic, and that went straight to my head. He tasted so good, the perfect glass to drink from, and the whisky only made it hotter. I found myself relaxing as he put his hand on my throat, which I found unbearably erotic. It felt like a claim, and in that moment I wanted to be his more than I wanted anything in the entire world.

Then he touched me, stroking my body as if he was mapping me, moving down to the hem of my skirt. I knew a moment's anxiety that perhaps this was all in my head—that this lazy, slow build of anticipation would disappear as soon as he touched me further—but it wasn't and it didn't.

His fingers were on my thighs, caressing the sensitive skin there, and I could feel the pressure between my legs growing, the needy ache becoming more intense. Then he stroked me over the cotton of my knickers and it felt like an electric shock, only to become something sharper as he slid a finger beneath the cotton and over my slick flesh.

Even thinking about it now makes me throb, as if I want him to touch me again. The pleasure was incredible. I'd never felt anything like it. And when he pushed a finger inside me…

John never had patience for foreplay, and in the end I told him not to bother, since it never worked for me. He didn't protest and I didn't mind since it only drew the whole process out longer. But now my eyes have been opened. Now I know that I can feel desire, and not only that, but physical pleasure too. I can have an orgasm. The problem was never me but, as Ulysses pointed out, it was that I just didn't have the right partner.

Perhaps it should be galling that it's he who ended up being the right partner. He with his arrogance and his entitlement, his crossing of boundaries. But for some reason it's not galling at all, and I think it's because he listened to me when I told him about John. Because he was gentle and slow, and when I looked up into his golden eyes I saw they were glowing. That he got as much pleasure out of touching me that I got from being touched. There was reverence in that touch, especially towards the end, and I can see that reverence in his eyes now as he looks down at me.

'Yes,' I say, answering his question, even though it probably doesn't need an answer. 'I think I do love it.'

His mouth curves, his smile a blaze of sunlight bathing me in warmth. 'You were never the problem, my Katla,' he murmurs with rough heat. 'What you are is a revelation.'

He means it—I can see the conviction in his eyes—and it makes me feel even warmer. I'm so relaxed it's as if all my bones have melted.

'I'm not sure I am,' I say, being truthful since I've never before been told I'm a revelation to anyone. I've certainly never felt like one. My mother found me frustrating, my interest in numbers baffling and my uninterest in the things that she liked selfish. As for John, he preferred me doing what he said, and taking care of him and his needs to the exclusion of my own. So, no, I was hardly revelatory to anyone.

Ulysses's gaze searches mine. 'What makes you think that?'

Do I want to tell him about my past? About my mother? Do I want to give him more details about my marriage? Part of me wants to, but another part is wary. Honesty compels me to give too much to people and I'm not sure I want to give this man any more. He can have my sexual pleasure, but nothing else.

'Let's just say John was less than…complimentary,' I say, which is nothing that Ulysses doesn't already know, but it's not everything.

That smile of his, it's not lazy or seductive this time, but genuine, and it makes the warmth in my chest press hard against my ribs. He's beautiful when he smiles like that. 'He was an idiot, then,' he says. 'I think when you came under my hand I actually saw God.'

I'm already feeling hot and his plain speaking makes me feel even hotter. It also makes me realise that he is hard; I feel him pressing against me. He's also like a furnace, throwing out heat. I'm getting distracted by his rich, masculine scent and by the shape of his mouth.

Already I can feel my hunger for him growing, but this time I want more. I want to be able to touch him, give him the same pleasure he gave me.

I reach up and touch his face with my fingertips. His skin is rough with the dusting of a five o'clock shadow along his jawline, but very warm, and he doesn't move as I brush my fingers over his carved mouth. His lips are warm, and they feel soft against my skin.

'You are aroused,' I tell him. 'Shall I—?'

'No,' he says, cutting me off before I can finish. 'That was just for you.'

I don't like that. John didn't bother reciprocating during sex, and while I was fine with that, because I didn't want anything from him, I'm not fine with it when it comes to Ulysses. He gave me everything and I want to give him that in return.

I look directly into his burning gaze and hold it. 'You told me that nothing would happen between us unless I asked. So I'm asking. Again.'

'Katla…'

'What? I don't want to do this if only one of us gets what they want. That's what happened with John and I don't want to do the same with you.'

He's clearly not happy with this. Lifting a hand, he shoves it through his black hair and frowns. 'I was trying, for once, to do an unselfish thing.'

'Is that why you gave me an orgasm?' I ask, annoyed. 'So you can feel good about yourself?'

His eyes flash, but whatever temper was there vanishes, and a rueful expression takes its place. 'How do you manage to do that?' he asks. 'Here I am, congratulating myself on being unselfish for a change, and now you're telling me that not letting you give me an orgasm makes me the selfish one?'

'Yes. In that it's all about what you want,' I point out.

He shakes his head, a half-smile curving his mouth, his gaze searching mine, though I have no idea what he's looking for. 'So, in order to be truly unselfish, I should let you give me an orgasm?'

'Yes,' I say, because that seems logical to me.

A laugh escapes him, a soft, sexy rumble, and suddenly I'm starving again. I want to touch him. I want to watch him the way he watched me. I want to see him come apart the way I did, see if I can do to him what he did to me.

'You're a very dangerous woman,' he says. 'Do you know that?'

I shift, adjusting myself so I'm astride his lap, facing him, my skirt hiked up and knees pressing into the seat cushions on either side of his muscular thighs. 'Good,' I say. 'You wanted to prove to me that I'm passionate, and you did. Don't say you weren't warned.'

He laughs again and I shiver as his hands come to rest on my hips, holding me where I am. 'You're infuriating,' he says. 'I love it.'

'Well?' I shift on him experimentally, relishing the way his breath catches. 'Do you want some of this passion or not?'

This time he doesn't laugh. This time he growls and, before I can say another word, he pulls me close and his mouth is on mine, and he's kissing me, hungrily, savagely.

It's a world away from the slow, whisky-soaked kiss of earlier. He's not careful, sensual or lazy now, just hungry, a man who gives no quarter, and I like that. It makes me feel strong and desired, rather than vulnerable. His equal rather than being less in some way.

I slide my fingers into the rough silk of his hair as the heat of his mouth consumes me. He moves fast, desperate almost as he jerks at the buttons and zip of his trousers, opening them up and freeing himself. Breaking our kiss for a moment, he pulls his wallet out from his pocket and grabs a condom from it. I want to put it on him myself, because I'm dying to touch him, but he brushes my hands away, deals with the packet and then sheaths himself. Once he's done, he grabs my hips, lifts me up, pulls aside my underwear and then eases me down onto him.

He's big and thick, and I gasp as he pushes inside me. The feel of him at first is too much, but just when I think I can't take any more I realise it's actually not enough. I shudder as I settle on him at last, holding his gaze and watching his golden eyes turn to smoky amber, glowing like dragon's fire.

He gives another growl and his fingers press against my hips as he begins to move me, showing me how to ride him, a slow up and down that soon has me panting. I want to move faster, harder, but he doesn't let me, keeping me in a languid rhythm that seems to wind everything inside me so tight.

'Faster,' I tell him, chafing at the speed he's setting.

'No,' he says roughly. 'Take what you're given.'

For some reason I find that shockingly erotic, and so is the speed he insists on. I can't believe how quickly the pleasure is building and it takes me by surprise. He sees my shock and bares his teeth at me, triumphant that he's doing this to me.

But it's a triumph we share, because I can see what I'm doing to him as well. The lines of his face are taut, the muscles of his body tense. He's holding himself back, that's obvious, but I don't want that for him. If I'm a volcano, then he is too, and we can't hold back an eruption.

I put my hands on his hard chest and lean forward, kissing him again, using my teeth this time, because I think he'll like the savagery of it. He does. He gives a rough curse and then finally moves faster, harder, and it feels so good. For the first time in my life, I want it to last for more than ten minutes. I want it to last for ever.

But of course it can't, because then he's touching me again, his hand down between my thighs to where we're joined. He's stroking me there, the friction and feel of him inside me making the tight knot of pleasure burst apart, ecstasy flooding my veins like wildfire.

I cry out and he moves twice more, hard and deep, and then he shudders, his own guttural sound of pleasure escaping as the orgasm comes for him too. All the strength has gone out of me so I slump forward against him, turning my face against the warmth of his neck, closing my eyes as my frantic breathing slows. I can hear the strong beat of his heart slowing too. He's still gripping my hips firmly, keeping me in place, the warmth of his breath in my hair.

'Woman,' he murmurs, breathless and rough. 'If that's just a taste of what you're capable of, then you're going to be the death of me.'

This sounds like it's a good thing, and for the first

time in a very long time I smile. I'm pleased with my-self. This feels very much like solving a thorny and complicated equation after many months of hard re-search.

Ulysses shifts and I make a lazy protest as he takes my chin in his long fingers, tilting my head so he can look into my face. 'Stop complaining,' he chides in a lazy drawl. 'Are you okay? I didn't hurt you?'

My body is humming with the after effects of two orgasms and I can safely say I have never felt better in my entire life. 'I'm absolutely wonderful,' I tell him solemnly. 'And what about you? Did I hurt you?'

His expression relaxes, the warmth of his genuine smile lighting his face. 'No, Katla mine, you did not. Perhaps next time you should. I don't mind a little pain.'

Next time? Does he assume we'll be doing this again? 'So…you want to do this again?'

His smile turns sensual. 'What? Do you think a quick fuck on a plane is all I want?'

I flush at the terminology, but not because I'm offended. 'I don't know,' I say. 'You wanted me, I thought. And now you've had me.'

'I said six months and I meant six months.' He runs a lazy finger down the side of my neck, raising goosebumps all over my skin. 'And if we spend those six months entirely in bed then I won't be unhappy.' Amusement glitters in his eyes. 'We can do it in ten-minute increments, if you like.'

I'm starting to recognise when he's teasing me, and he's definitely teasing me now about what I said about sex. It makes me think about my certainty, and how long it took, and then the look on his face as I said it…

Now I really *do* feel stupid, because he's shown me what sex can be like, and the depth of my lack of understanding astonishes even me. God, I hate it when I miss things.

'What is it?' he asks, obviously seeing the change of expression on my face. 'Did I say something wrong?'

He's not teasing this time, he's serious, and it seems ridiculous to be embarrassed after what we just did together, so I say, 'I feel silly now—for telling you about that.'

'Hey,' he says, his voice softening, the gold of his eyes pinning me in place. 'You didn't know. There's no shame in not knowing something.' Again, all I can see in his eyes is sincerity. 'If anyone should be ashamed, it's your husband. He had you and all your passion in his bed, and he didn't do a thing to help you unlock it. But it's there, Katla. It was always there.'

He's genuine. For some reason it's important to him that I understand that, and something in my chest eases. A tight feeling that has been there so long I almost stopped being aware of it at all.

You can believe him. You can trust him.

It seems strange to think that about a man I've known for little more than a handful of hours. But…everything he's said to me has been true so far and I'm starting to think that maybe I can trust him. I can trust him to give me pleasure at least, that's for sure.

I nod slowly and then, because that feels too inadequate, I reach for him and lean forward, pressing my mouth to his. Telling him without words that I appreciate what he's just said.

'There will be a next time,' he murmurs against my

lips. 'There will be as many next times as you want there to be.'

'Good,' I murmur back. Then, thinking about it, I ask, 'How long approximately was that? You know, for future reference.'

He smiles. 'About half an hour. Seems like it might take us a while to get to six months.'

'Excellent,' I say. Suddenly I'm not worrying about those six months. I think we've found a way to spend them all very nicely.

CHAPTER ELEVEN

Ulysses

THE PLANE TOUCHES down in Athens on Christmas Day, and I'm eager to get home—not only to see Olympia, but because I have Katla with me. Katla, who has proven to be every bit the volcano I hoped she was.

I very much want to take her to bed, lay her out on white sheets and spend a long time exploring every inch of her, because the sex on the plane was only an entree and I'm ready for the main course.

We could have done more while in the air—she certainly wanted to—but for once it was me baulking. I want time and privacy for our next encounter and we had neither in the jet. Also I need…some distance to make sure I keep my head—because when she sat astride me on the seat it made me forget every promise that I'd made to myself that this would be just about her. I was already hard enough that it hurt. Then to have her sitting on me, the cotton of her knickers and the fabric of my trousers the only thing between my hard-on and her astonishing heat, her insisting on returning the orgasm favour…

I'm a man who likes control and I've never doubted

my command over myself. Yet she broke that control, snapped it as easily as an old rubber band. It's not a feeling I enjoy. It reminds me of when my mother died, and the state came to take my sister and me into care. I was sixteen, a good boy, a rule-follower up to that point, and my certainty that we'd be placed together with kind foster parents was rock-solid. And why not? It was the right thing to do and surely the state knew that?

Except the state didn't know that and we weren't placed together. No one wanted a sixteen-year-old boy, no matter how good he was, but a quiet ten-year-old girl was an easy sell. And no matter how much I argued, no matter how much I begged, we were split up,

It hurt to watch her get taken away and to know that nothing I did would make any difference. To feel such powerlessness, as the love I felt for her ravaged my soul. It was something I never wanted to experience ever again.

So I turned that love into fury, and it changed me. It made me realise that the only way I could get Olympia back was not to be the boy I once was—the boy who waited for the good things to be given to him. Instead I became a man who took what he wanted, and what I wanted was my sister back.

It was fury that led me to the only way a boy like me could gain enough money and power to rescue her and that was in the criminal underworld. Four years later, I had one of my associates keeping tabs on the foster parents who had her. The 'father' was scum of the earth, the 'mother' little better; they were only in it for the money they got having a foster kid. I was an enforcer for the most powerful crime families in Athens, and by then I had enough clout to organise a raid on the foster parents.

We got her back, but not without cost. She was afraid of me when I first got her back to the terrible apartment I was living in at the time, and she had every right to be. I'd done things that no good man should ever do. And, worse than that, I didn't see anything wrong with what I was doing or with the path I was on.

Then she told me she couldn't stay with me, that I was no better than the people who'd hurt her, and I knew then that I had to change once again. I'd left behind the sweet kid who did what his mother told him, and now it was time to leave behind the criminal enforcer. I became yet another man— I left the feral warrior behind and became the knight, protective, just and honourable. At least, I managed the first one; I'm still working on the last two.

I'm not perfect, not by any stretch, and when I doubt my actions I think of Olympia and what she would say to me, and I do things differently because of that. Except for one thing: I will do anything to keep her safe, anything at all. No one will ever take her from me again and that has been my guiding principle ever since I got her back. It's what my entire life has been about.

It's been a long time since I've been at the mercy of anyone or anything, but up in the air with Katla in my lap, having just watched her come so beautifully under my hand, I took what she offered without a single second thought. And, my God, those moments inside her, feeling her heat squeeze tight… It tests me even to remember it. But I can't be an animal here in the house

I share with my sister. I must be circumspect. So, first I need to see Olympia and apologise for my absence the night before.

My driver pulls into the driveway of the villa I own in Glyfada, on the Athenian Riviera. It's huge, with two stories and six bedrooms, built in the traditional way, white washed and square as it faces the sea. There are stone terraces, gardens and olive groves as well as a big pool area with a hot tub.

It's a beautiful day for December, with the sun shining, and the sea is its usual brilliant, translucent blue, washing the air with salt as I shepherd Katla inside. My staff all have Christmas leave, so I'm not expecting my housekeeper Elena to be around, but I *am* expecting my sister.

She should be in the living area, perhaps putting a few last presents under the tree there. I don't care about a tree myself, but I put one up for her because she loves it. The tree usually has silver and gold tinsel wound around it, and other decorations of many kinds. I buy her a new Christmas ornament every year and this year, while I was in Munich, I bought a delicate, shimmering silver reindeer that I think she'll love.

Yet as I show Katla into the entrance hallway, and close the door after us, my first warning that something's amiss is the utter silence. With the staff being absent, I'm not too concerned, but then as I stride into the living area with Katla at my heels the silence starts to feel…ominous.

'Wait here,' I instruct Katla tersely, then without another word I leave the living area and make my way upstairs to check Olympia's bedroom. She's not there, which is puzzling. As I walk back downstairs, I text her in case she's outside or somewhere else in the house.

Normally she's responsive to texts, and always replies promptly because she knows I worry about her. I have enemies, naturally, so she never goes anywhere without her security detail, and I'm always very strict with her about that. On public holidays, she usually stays home, because she doesn't like the staff to have to give up a day's leave for her, so I'd be surprised if she's gone out somewhere.

In the living area, Katla is still standing by the Christmas tree and looking up at it, eyes wide, oblivious to my growing concern. I call my head of security to find out where Olympia might be, but he tells me that she didn't order any detail for today.

Cold settles in my gut. She didn't respond to my Christmas Eve apology, now that I think about it, but I didn't worry because I thought she might have been annoyed with me and didn't want to answer. She has been more annoyed with me this past year, getting impatient with my over-protectiveness, but I thought we were over that. Yet, with an empty house and no sign of her, I'm worried. I call her, but there's no reply. It goes straight to voicemail.

Katla turns from the tree, her dark-blue eyes narrowing as she takes me in. She's sensing my growing agitation, no doubt, but I keep it contained and force a smile. 'There are four spare bedrooms upstairs and they all have *en suites*,' I tell her. 'Pick one and get some rest. My sister's room is up there too and she won't mind if you need to borrow some clothes. She has far too many for one woman as it is.'

I want her to nod and take herself off up the stairs so I don't have an audience for my deepening concern, and the fury that often accompanies it, but she doesn't move. She only gives me her direct, piercing stare. 'What's wrong?' she asks.

My smile feels more fixed with each passing second, but I keep it in place. This is not her concern. 'Nothing,' I say, my voice carefully casual. 'Don't let me keep you.'

But she still doesn't move, scanning my face, her forehead creasing. 'What is it, Ulysses?'

The way she says my name makes me automatically think of her saying it as she came, her voice husky and thick with the pleasure I gave her, and an arrow of heat shoots clean through my worry, as though it wasn't there.

I ignore it. Sex is not what I need right now. Right now I need to find out where my sister is, and quickly, and I don't have the time or patience to explain to Katla what the issue is. So I shake my head, turn and stride from the living room, walking quickly down the hallway to my office at the other end of the villa where I'll have some privacy to make a few calls.

However, a quick ten minutes of speaking to various employees and associates doesn't make the reason for Olympia's absence any clearer. She's been at home the past week, apparently, but went out on Christmas Eve. She told Elena that she had a few errands to run and would be back later that evening. Yet she then texted to say she'd be later than she thought, and not to wait for her, so Elena went home. The security detail that went with Olympia was also dismissed by her that evening. However, some time after that, she disappeared and no one knows where she went or why.

I stand in my office, staring sightlessly out of the window at the pines that grow close to the house, a ball of cold fear and fury collecting inside me. I have many enemies—I can't live the kind of life I've lived without earning more than a few—and I've always been conscious that Olympia is a potential target. That's why I keep her close and well protected. And, while her disappearance could be innocuous, I don't think it is. In fact, I'm sure it's not, which means that now I'll have to overturn the entire world looking for her.

I can't lose her—I can't. I swore to protect her all those years ago, promising her that she'd never have to go through the horror of what she experienced with that abusive foster family again. I promised that I'd keep her safe. Breaking that promise is unthinkable, unconscionable, and, by God, if anything's happened to her someone will *pay*...

A million plans turn over in my head and I'm busy sorting through them when my phone vibrates in my hand. I look down at the screen and the world stops spinning for a moment.

It's Olympia.

I hit 'accept' and raise the phone to my ear. 'Where the hell are you?' I growl at her in Greek. 'You didn't answer my texts and—'

'Don't get angry, Ulysses,' Olympia interrupts, the sound of her clear, sweet voice sending relief spilling through me. 'There are a few things I need to say to you.'

'Where are you?' I snap, my relief now turning to anger. 'Why aren't you at home?'

'Listen to me,' she says, blatantly ignoring my questions, which only infuriates me more. 'I have something to tell you.'

My fist closes hard on the piece of technology in my hand. 'What?' I demand, graceless now with all the fury, fear and relief mixing like acid in my stomach.

'I…can't spend Christmas with you.'

She sounds unsure and there is trepidation in her voice. I go very still, listening intently. 'Is everything all right?' I try to keep my voice calm. 'Are you in danger? What's going on, Olympia?'

'No, I'm not in any danger,' she says, and this sounds much more firm and convincing. 'So you can stand down the battle stations.'

I grit my teeth at her flippant comment. 'You sounded afraid.'

There's a long silence down the other end of the phone and then I hear her release a breath. 'Look, I really am safe, Ulysses. I'm not in danger at all. I just… can't come to you right now. I've got a few things I need to sort out.'

This does not make me feel any better. 'What things? Come home, Olympia. I have presents for you and the tree—'

'I know, I know.' She mutters a filthy curse that I had no idea she even knew, then goes on. 'I didn't want to have to tell you like this.'

'Tell me what?' I'm furious, worried and frustrated

and none of this is helping. 'I'll come to you, then, and we can have a face-to-face chat.'

'No,' she says, a surprising hint of steel entering her voice. Surprising, because normally Olympia lets me coddle and cosset her. She likes it when I'm protective—or at least she did. Lately, I admit, she's been more impatient with it. 'I'm not going to tell you where I am or who I'm with, because then you'll start looking for me, and I don't need that drama, okay?'

I don't listen, because of course the 'who I'm with' has got stuck in my brain. She's with someone, and I bet I'm not going to like who that someone is. In fact, I'm don't like *anything* about this entire situation. 'Tell me where you are, Olympia,' I order tersely, my tone hard. 'I won't ask again.'

'Ulysses,' she says, ignoring me, 'I'm pregnant.'

For a second all my fury is drowned beneath a waterfall of icy shock, and all I can do is stare out through the window, my mind utterly blank. 'Pregnant?' I echo as if I have no idea what the word means. 'What?'

'You're going to be an uncle,' Olympia says, a thread of something I can't identify entering her voice. 'It's early days, but I wanted you to know, and I didn't want you to worry about me. I'm with the father and I'm safe, but please, please don't come looking for me.'

Suddenly I hear the sound of another voice down the phone. It's deeper, definitely male and Olympia is arguing with him, which immediately sends me into overdrive. I'm about to shout down the phone at her when I hear the man speak, his Greek impeccable, his accent Italian.

'She's with me, Zakynthos,' he says curtly. 'Rafael Santangelo. And I'm the father of her child. Merry Christmas, motherfucker.'

Then he ends the call.

CHAPTER TWELVE

Katla

I HEAR ULYSSES cursing all the way down the other end of the hallway—and it's a long hallway.

I'm standing in the giant living room, admiring the huge Christmas tree that takes up most of one corner, the radiant crystal star on the top almost brushing the high ceiling. It's covered in tinsel and incredibly delicate and expensive-looking ornaments, hand-blown glass Christmas lights in different shapes and colours arranged artfully in the branches.

I'm also admiring the interior of his palatial Greek villa, with its pristine white walls and long, white linen sectional sofas. Folk art adorns the walls, but it's clear the main attraction in this room lies in the floor-to-ceiling windows and their outlook over the vivid green lawn to the deep blue of the Aegean.

My attention has been caught by a glimpse of a particularly lavish pool area, and I'm just on the point of walking to the windows to get a better look when I'm distracted by what sounds like the beginning of a very intense male tantrum. Despite being wary of male anger, I find myself drawn towards the sound by an impulse I can't explain. I feel like a moth constantly being lured towards the light, and Ulysses is that light.

I wanted more of his touch on the plane, but he refused, saying it would be better to be in a bed—more privacy—and, since he was right, I didn't argue. But since we arrived at his villa I've kept myself in check, because I'm not sure how the meeting with his sister will go.

Ulysses obviously adores her, since he spoke a little about her on the plane after we had sex. I had questions for him—mostly about where his villa was and whether his sister would be okay with me being there. He assured me she would be, that Olympia was caring and easy to get along with and that I would love her.

Yet there's been no sign of her since we arrived and now, with Ulysses cursing a blue streak, I wonder if something terrible has happened. Admittedly, he sounds more angry than upset, but I need to see him, to look into his eyes to determine which it is.

The door to what is obviously his office is standing open. The room is large, with big windows facing the tall pines that grow beside the villa, and a desk stands in front of the windows. Book cases line the walls.

It's a tidy office, but not stark, with knickknacks here and there giving hints of the personality of the man who inhabits it. There's a shell on one of the shelves and I want to look at it, because it has the most perfect spiral. A small, beautiful and delicate abstract painting is propped up against some books. What looks to be a very old Grecian vase sits on another shelf.

Ulysses is standing with his back to me, looking out of the windows. He must not know I'm there, because he turns suddenly, picks up an empty water glass from his desk and hurls it at the wall. The glass smashes into a million pieces, scattering all over the floor, and I freeze in the doorway, shocked.

He catches sight of me, his golden eyes blazing, every line of him taut with fury. And I'm suddenly reminded of the day John threw my glass paperweight and it hit the wall and smashed. That terrified me, and the next day I left him, so by rights I should be terrified now.

Yet, as the shock drains away, it's not fear that replaces it. John would simmer coldly for weeks before exploding, but Ulysses is standing there, making no attempt to hide his fury, and he isn't simmering either. He's already boiling over, and for some reason that fascinates me.

'I suggest you not come near me for the time being,' he says roughly.

'Why?' I ask. 'Will you hurt me?'

His anger flares again, his mouth hard. 'No, of course not. I'm not your bastard husband.'

'No, you're not,' I agree. John chose my paperweight to break because he knew it was mine and that it would hurt me. But Ulysses just threw his own water glass, and it's not the same. 'So why should I not come near you?'

'Because I'm furious,' he bites out through gritted teeth. 'And I'm never very pleasant when I'm furious.' His accent has grown stronger, his voice deeper, which I find unbearably sexy. I even find his anger unbearably sexy, though I shouldn't.

He's practically incandescent with it, his hands in fists at his sides, his eyes blazing. He's not afraid of his anger, I think. He feels comfortable expressing it, and part of me wonders what that would actually be like—to be so relaxed about my emotions that I could express them without worrying about hurting someone or making them angry. Without being told that the way I feel is wrong and inappropriate.

'Why are you furious?' I want to know, because it must be something serious, and if so I want to help. It seems like a strange thing to want to do for a man I haven't known very long, but it's true nevertheless.

Ulysses turns back to the windows, as if looking at me is too much for him. 'My sister is not here. She's with someone else. An enemy of mine from years ago.'

I study his tense posture. He loves his sister, that's obvious, but he's furious too, which likely means he's afraid. Anger sometimes stems from fear, so perhaps he's afraid for her—which makes sense, given what he said about an enemy of his.

'You're worried about her?' I ask.

'Yes,' he bites out. 'Of course I'm fucking worried about her.' There's another silence, then he adds, 'She's pregnant.'

I frown, puzzled. Pregnancy is usually a reason for happiness, isn't it? Sometimes it's not, though, and maybe this is one of those times. I take a couple of steps into the room. 'You're not happy for her?' I ask carefully.

Ulysses turns back again, eyes still blazing like a torch. 'What did I tell you about not being near me?'

I realise then, quite abruptly and on a level I haven't felt before, that I'm really *not* afraid of him. Not even a little. Not when I can see that it's the fear lurking beneath the fury that's driving him. 'You said you wouldn't hurt me and you won't,' I tell him simply. 'I'm not afraid of you, Ulysses.'

A muscle leaps in his jaw. 'You should be.'

'Why? Do you hurt a lot of women?'

His tall figure is almost vibrating with tension. 'Yes, many.' He throws the words at me like missiles trying to keep me at bay.

'Physically?' I ask, even though somehow I know deep down that the answer is no.

That muscle leaps again. 'No,' he grits out. 'Never.'

'So, now we've established I have no reason to be afraid of you, perhaps you can tell me why you're so angry about your sister being pregnant.'

He lets out a breath, opening his hands and closing them again, as if he's longing to grab something—a weapon of some kind—desperate to use it against whatever enemy is threatening him. 'This is my problem,' he says with carefully restrained fury. 'And it has nothing to do with you.'

'Well,' I point out logically, 'You were the one who brought me here. So, now you've made it my problem too.'

My frankness is not appreciated, as he stares at me balefully, yet I can't help but be drawn to his intensity, the fire in him calling to the same fire in me, the fire that I know is deep inside me. The fire that, unlike of him, I'm afraid of.

My childhood was unsettled, my mother going from one place to another—living in communes, helping out on farms or wherever her free spirit took her. I hated never being able to settle, never having any routines, everything changing, sometimes every week, sometimes every day. All the changes would often drive me to meltdowns I couldn't control, and which my mother didn't know how to deal with, so sometimes she'd just lock me in a room wherever we were and leave. Once she was gone a whole night, which was terrifying to me at the time.

As a result, I become very adept at controlling my emotions, never getting too angry, never getting too sad. Never getting too happy either, because my mother didn't like how I expressed my happiness, which was to hum. In fact, the way I expressed any emotion at all felt wrong when it came to her, so in the end it was easier to express nothing at all.

But those emotions don't go away, even if they're not expressed. They get stuck inside, boiling away like lava and, if nothing is done about them, they burn a person alive.

Numbers kept my emotions in check. The abstract beauty of them, divorced from anything but logic, was a lifesaver. I did number puzzles, solved equations and number games, anything that would distract me, and it worked.

But…here in this room, Ulysses is furious and he is doing nothing to distract himself. He's not out of control with fury, but it's there, and he clearly feels it, and is not denying it. I find it fascinating and I wish I could be like that too.

'You don't have to be here, Katla,' he reiterates. 'I would prefer that you leave, in fact.'

'But I don't prefer it,' I tell him, because I want to stay with him. I want to help him, even though I don't know how, I just do. 'You might as well tell me what the issue is. I might be able to help.'

His mouth twists, as if me helping is the stupidest thing he's ever heard, and maybe he's right. Maybe me trying to help him *is* a very stupid idea, which of course makes me feel stupid yet again. Except I can't bring myself to leave, not yet. Not without knowing what's making him so afraid.

The desk is between us, his gaze like the sun searing over my skin. I expect him to tell me to leave again, but this time he says, 'My entire life has been spent keeping Olympia safe. It's my duty as her big brother to protect her and that's all that matters to me. Nothing else is of any importance. I failed in that duty once before and I will not do it again.'

'How did you fail her?' I ask. He's a powerful, dangerous man who gets whatever he wants, whenever he wants it, and I can't imagine him failing to do whatever he set his mind to.

'After our mother died, Olympia was taken into state care and I was too young to stop it from happening,' he says tightly, then curses again as he tugs his phone out once more, looking down at the screen. 'If Rafael Santangelo thinks he's safe from me, he's wrong,' he growls, before raising his phone to his ear and issuing a series of what sounds like orders in rapid Greek, his tone hard and cold.

Part of me thinks I should leave him to his fury. I'm not good at dealing with my own excess emotions, let alone anyone else's, and I'm sure I'm an irritant he doesn't need. But… I can't just walk away, not yet. The threat to his sister is upsetting him and, now I have an inkling as to why, it upsets me a little too. I don't like him thinking he's failed, which is ridiculous, given I barely know him. Yet he was kind to me in the jet, he was careful and patient, so I want to be kind to him in return.

In fact, I can't shake the feeling that he needs me somehow, so instead of walking out of the door as he continues his conversation I move over to the shelf where the shell is, skirting round the broken glass sparkling on the floor. I gently pick up the shell, contemplating the spiral: the golden ratio, perfectly expressed, and exquisitely rendered in nature. The shell has that sense of rightness I require from all the items I have in my collection, and part of me wonders if Ulysses would mind if I took this shell to add to them.

Beside the shell is a small photograph of a young woman who looks about my age. His sister, surely? She has the same black hair and amber eyes as Ulysses, the same straight, proud nose, and she's smiling.

'That's her,' Ulysses says from behind me, his tone brusque. 'That's Olympia.'

The sound of his voice so close makes an electric shock jolt through me. I can feel his heat too, smell his intoxicating scent, and it makes me shiver. The memory of what we did in the plane is still so new and incredible. Now I'm thinking about it again, and I can't stop. The pressure between my thighs is an ache, and I can't concentrate. But I can't ask him for sex again, not now. It would be incredibly inappropriate when he's so angry and upset about his sister.

'I thought so,' I say, hoping the heat won't show in my voice. 'She has the same eyes as you.'

'She was ten years old when our mother died,' he says.

I turn round and look up at him, wanting to see his face. He's still blazing with fury, the build of it like a bonfire in his eyes, the air around us crackling with the electricity he's throwing out.

'What happened?' I ask.

He smiles but there's nothing in it but threat. 'She was passed around a number of different foster carers, some of whom physically assaulted her. I wasn't able to get her back until years later.'

I study his face, thinking about his fury and fear. He must love her so very much, which makes me think about what it would be like to be loved by him. It would be too intense and overwhelming, I think, yet part of my soul aches to be loved so completely.

Mothers are supposed to love their daughters, but my mother never said anything about loving me, because there was too much about me she didn't like. Too much that didn't fit with her idea of what a good daughter should be. My social awkwardness, my resistance to change, my blunt way of speaking. It embarrassed her, I think.

It was the same with John. As my husband, he was supposed to love me, and he even said it, but…he lied. And he had expectations of me as a wife, expectations that I failed to meet.

Ulysses is such an intense man, so his expectations of himself must be very high. And, given he's so furious now, it seems the consequences when those expectations aren't met must be very painful for him.

'I'm sorry,' I tell him, wanting to offer him something, as little as it is. 'That must have been very difficult.'

'You cannot imagine how difficult.' The fire in his eyes leaps and flickers, but I can see shadows between the flames, and my chest clenches tight. It hurt to lose her when he was young, that much I can see. It tortured him. 'I fought for years to finally get her back into my care and, when I did, I swore that no one would ever take her from me again.'

The tautness in my chest tightens further and I'm not sure why. Since when did Ulysses's emotions matter to me? I shouldn't want them to matter, especially not when John's emotions were so fragile and delicate that I had to be careful with them in case they broke.

But, no matter how mysterious my own emotional reaction to Ulysses is, it doesn't change the fact that I have one. Perhaps it's because, once again, he's being honest. He's furious and he's telling me why, instead of saying nothing and making me guess, which was always John's favourite tactic. He's not demanding that I be sympathetic to him either, which was what my mother used to do, because she thought I was selfish.

'Do you know where she is?' I ask, trying to think of something useful to say but coming up with nothing.

'No. But she's with Rafael Santangelo, which doesn't bode well.'

The name rings no bells, so I ask, 'Who is he?'

'I took over his company years ago, and it wasn't amicable from what I can remember.' A muscle in the side of his jaw leaps. 'I've just ordered some of my people to find out everything they can about him, and where he might have taken her.'

I wish I could say more, do something for him, but there's nothing I can give him that will ease his anger or his worry. Once again, I feel things might be easier if I wasn't here so he doesn't have to manage me as well as his own emotions.

'Shall I leave you alone?' I offer, belatedly.

His gaze focuses on me, his attention acute. 'Why did you stay?'

The question is unexpected and for a moment I don't know how to reply. I'm not sure I want to tell him the truth, since I'm not sure I can articulate it, yet he's compelled honesty from me so many times now there seems little point in holding back.

'Because you're angry,' I say slowly. 'And I wanted to know why, and I… I want to help you.'

His gaze is relentless. 'So why do you want to leave now?'

'I don't want to leave,' I correct him. 'But I'm not sure how I can help you, and maybe it's easier if I'm not around.'

This time it's his turn to study me, scanning my face with the same intensity he seemingly brings to everything he does. 'I won't get replies for some time,' he says, his tone brusque. 'So what I need now is distraction. That's what you can offer me. Can you do that for me, Katla mine?'

CHAPTER THIRTEEN

Ulysses

HER CHEEKS FLUSH and her eyes glow, and she's so lovely that for a moment I forget my fury. Forget that my sister has been taken by someone who was never on my radar, so I never thought to guard her from him.

I vaguely recall him, and some unpleasantness to do with his company, but I don't remember what it was—a mistake, clearly, since I never saw him coming. He must have put himself in Olympia's way, since I can't think a meeting between them would have been coincidental, but what I want to know is did he seduce her or did he force her?

The rage in response to that thought is like acid inside me, eating away at my insides. Either way, he targeted her in order to hurt me, and unfortunately the bastard's aim is true.

Then again, if he forced her, she wouldn't have told me to stay away, surely? She also said that she was safe, and if she hadn't been she'd have sounded much more frightened tha she did. Still, I have no reason to find that reassuring. Perhaps Rafael Santangelo is holding a gun to her head and is even now preparing to issue a list of demands.

I've had my people do some searching, but of course it's Christmas, so everything will take much longer than it normally would, and now I'm going out of my mind. I want to call some associates of mine and give them his name—take him out. I have the means. I have the contacts.

But I can't get out of my head Olympia's voice as Rafael Santangelo took the phone from her. She sounded more angry than afraid, and I know what that sounds like, because she's been angry with me more often than she used to be. She's thrown around accusations that I'm suffocating her, that she feels like a captive, and all sorts of over-dramatic nonsense. I don't know how many times I've explained that she needs security because of my enemies, that she's my one weak spot and I'm only trying to protect her, but she never listens.

To be fair, she's been a bit more settled this past year, and hasn't argued about anything, but now... My thoughts careen out of control, my blood turning to ice at the thought of what she might be going through right now, and for the first time in my life I have regrets.

I should have been a better man. I should have been a good man. I should have been principled and moral, and all the things I was when I was a boy. But I wasn't, and I'm not, and I have the enemies to show for it. And now my sister has to bear the consequences.

Katla's gaze on mine is wide and dark, and I know exactly what kind of distraction I need—her, naked. On my desk or on the floor, I don't care where. I need the kind of physical distraction only sex can bring and she'll be the perfect cure.

But, instead of coming closer, she turns and for some reason picks up the shell that sits on the bookshelf behind her. It was one Olympia collected from the beach when I first bought the villa. She loves it here, loves the beach and the glittering sea beyond. She often goes for long walks along the sand and that particular shell was from her first walk.

I kept it, because that was the first time she'd smiled since I rescued her, and that's when I knew that she'd be okay. The dread that had felt like a stone in my gut melted away, the dark cloud that had hung over me ever since she'd been taken from me lifting.

Now Katla has that shell in her hand and she turns to me, holding it as if she somehow knows how precious it is to me.

'You see this?' She indicates the spiral pattern of the shell. 'This is the golden ratio. A ratio between two numbers that equals approximately 1.618. I love finding it in nature, because numbers are the truth of the universe, and you can see that everywhere—such as this shell. Its spiral is perfect and pleasing to the eye.'

She gently places the shell in my hand and looks at me. 'Whenever I feel as if things are happening outside my control, I look for the golden ratio, and wherever I find it it's proof that numbers still work. That the universe is still the same and that everything is happening just as it should.'

I stare at her, for a moment so surprised I don't know what to say—a very rare thing for me. She's looking at me all expectantly. There's some uncertainty there too, but also a kind of glowing shyness, as if she's telling me something very precious and important to her.

I know about the golden ratio, but I'm no mathematician; that's not where my skills lie. And somewhere along the line I've forgotten that, behind her beautiful eyes and her silky, curvy body, there's a brilliant mind. I can see it there now, glittering and sharp as cut crystal in the sun. Some men are intimidated by smart, clever women, but I'm not, and what I can see now only interests me more. I want her body, I can't deny that, but her mind looks to be a vast, undiscovered country and I'm interested in exploring that as well.

'The golden ratio is part of the Fibonacci sequence, no?' I ask as I turn the shell over in my hand.

'Yes,' she says, excitement glowing in her eyes. 'Do you know geometry? What about—?'

'No,' I interrupt, but gently. 'I'm a mathematical dunce, alas. But I like that this shell has a perfect spiral, because this shell is important to me.'

Her eyes widen slightly. 'Oh?'

'Olympia gave this to me when we moved into the villa,' I explain. 'It was on her first walk on the beach that she collected it, and when she gave it to me she smiled. It was the first time I saw her smile after I rescued her.'

The expression on Katla's face softens. 'Then it's a perfect shell in every way.'

'Yes,' I agree. 'It is indeed.'

'I…collect things,' she says, sounding hesitant and more than a little shy. 'I collect things that have the golden ratio on or in them somewhere, that perfect spiral: shells, plants, photos, art…' She looks at me for a long moment, then raises a hand and touches me, tracing a spiral over my cheekbone, my brow bone and my nose. 'Your face.'

There is a shift inside me and I don't understand it. But she's looking at me as if I am something special, something to be treasured, and it does things to me. It tightens my chest. Makes my heart beat fast. I like the way she's looking at me. I like it far too much.

I reach for her hand and gather it between my own. It's warm and soft, just like her. 'And am I something you would like to add to your collection, then?' I ask her. It's supposed to be teasing yet it comes out sounding far too serious.

She flushes and I'm struck once again by her beauty, her uniqueness. I hadn't known she was there when I smashed that glass and any woman in in their right mind would have left at that point. But she didn't. Even when I told her to leave, she stayed, because she wanted to help me, she said.

I don't know why my feelings should matter to her, especially when I haven't much considered hers, but I can't remember the last time someone cared about me in that way. Olympia does, I know that, but our relationship has been so…fraught lately. Katla's cool concern feels calming, like cold water over a burn. A balm I never thought I needed until now.

'It sounds silly, doesn't it?' she says quietly, and I can see that she's embarrassed. That maybe someone, some time, has told her that collecting things was a silly thing to do, so she's assumed that, yes, it is. I want to hurt that person, whoever they were.

'No,' I tell her, and mean it. 'You are collecting things

that please you and that's all that matters. Who cares what other people think?'

She stares up at me, as if I've said something revelatory and not self-evident, and I like that look. I like that something I've said means something to her. I want to ask her more but, before I can, she goes up on her toes and presses her mouth to mine. It electrifies me, this kiss. Sends thoughts of my sister and what's happening with her straight out of my head. There's nothing in the world except Katla and her mouth.

'Show me how to please you,' she whispers against my lips. 'Show me how to give you pleasure.'

The soft, husky words send yet more electricity arcing through me. Oh, there are so many ways for her to please me, so many. And yet...

She puts her hands on my chest, her palms warm, and leans against me, pressing the softness of her body to mine. 'You wanted me to distract you,' she goes on. 'So let me distract you.'

There's nothing I can do until I hear back from my contacts, nothing except call Olympia repeatedly. I'm powerless in this situation; I have no control, which has the potential to drive me out of my mind. But here, right now, Katla is with me and what she's offering me is a gift, as if she knows exactly just how out of my mind I am. She's giving me back some control and in this moment all I want to do is take it.

This woman... She's remarkable. How does she know this is what I need? I look down at her, taking in the wide, dark blue of her eyes and the expression in them, an intensity that takes my breath away. She wants this, I can see it, and perhaps just as badly as I do.

I put my hands over hers and I pull them away, turning them over to plant a kiss in the centre of each palm. Then I meet her gaze. 'Get down on your knees, my ice queen,' I murmur. 'And I'll show you exactly how to please me.'

The flush in her cheeks rises, a delicious glowing pink, and she does what she's told, sinking slowly to her knees in front of me. She doesn't look away, her gaze pinned to mine as if she can't think of anywhere she'd rather look but at me. I'm hard now, the blood pounding in my ears, watching this goddess kneel before me. She's mine to do with what I will. But all she wants is to give me pleasure and all I want is to show her the many ways in which she can.

I let go of one of her hands, guiding the other to the clasp of my belt. 'Undo it,' I instruct, then let that one go too.

And she does, her fingers fumbling as her hands shake. But it's not fear that's making them shake, I can see that clearly. It's desire. It's hunger. It's the volcanic heart of her ready to erupt once again. She gets my belt open at last and she knows what to do now as she tears at the buttons of my fly, pulling it open.

'Slow,' I murmur as she reaches for me. 'Let me savour what you're doing.'

She touches me through the cotton of my boxers, tracing the shape of my cock with light fingers, making me grit my teeth. Her caress makes me harder, makes me want to grab her hand and wrap her fingers around me, but I don't. Because I *do* want to savour her and her touch. I want to see the expression in her eyes as she touches me, because I know damn well

I've never seen it in another woman's eyes before—as if this means something to her, and not just physically, but emotionally too.

It's strange that I want that since sex has always been a physical outlet for me. I don't want any emotional entanglements. The one love I have—Olympia—takes everything from me and I don't have more to give anyone else.

Yet now, what is happening with Katla feels like more than simply physical. It feels intimate and, while that's not what I want, for some reason, in this moment it's somehow right.

So I let her touch me, feel the shape of me through the cotton, and when it gets too much, when I want more, I growl, 'Stop playing, ice queen. Time to open your mouth and take me.'

The look she slants me from underneath her pale lashes sends white-hot heat racing through my bloodstream. It looks to me like a challenge of sorts, as if she's testing me, and I love that. She wants me to show her how to please me, and somehow she knows that her little acts of defiance are part of that pleasure.

I reach to shove down the cotton of my boxers, but she's already there, taking me out and touching me as if she can't get enough. But my patience is thinning and every touch is pushing me further and further to the edge of my control. And I don't want to lose that. I don't want be too rough with her, be too harsh, be anything that might hurt her. She has given me this gift and I want to honour that.

I slide my fingers into the softness of her white-blonde hair, making her braid loosen, and I hold her right where I want her. 'Now,' I order roughly, and she stops playing and opens her mouth, as if she can't wait to taste me.

I can't wait for her to taste me either. She grips me tightly and licks me, teasing just a little, running her tongue along my shaft and around the head. Pleasure splinters through me, shards of it catching deep in every nerve-ending.

Then she looks up at me as she takes me right in deep, the heat of her mouth closing around my cock, and I'm gripped by the most intense pleasure. I've done this many times, with many women, but there is an edge here with Katla, a sweetness that I've never experienced before, and it pierces me like an arrow.

She's on her knees in front of me, watching me the way I watched her in the jet, gauging my reactions, seeing what she's doing to me—and I let her see it. I let her see *all* of it.

'Yes,' I murmur as I thrust into her mouth. 'Just like that, my ice queen. Do you see what you do to me?' I hold her gaze, watching all that blue turn to fire. 'Do you see how much pleasure you're giving me?'

She licks me and uses her teeth, experimenting, and I growl deep in my throat with the pleasure of it. She likes doing this, I can see; it's giving her pleasure, and seeing hers makes mine rise even higher.

My fingers clench in her hair, gripping her tightly, holding her to take my thrusts. She grips my thighs, using her mouth to extract as much pleasure as she can from me, and I am lost.

I growl more orders at her: 'Harder, faster… Yes, like that… That's it… That's so good, my ice queen…

Your mouth is heaven… I love it… Keep going and don't ever stop…'

But then the orgasm rushes over me, so fast it's like a tidal wave, and I barely have time to give her a warning before it grips me and pleasure explodes through me, tearing a harsh growl of release from my throat. When I finally come down from the high, she's still on her knees in front of me, her head resting against my thigh, her arms around my legs, as if she's trying to hold on to keep herself from falling.

I adjust myself, tucking in my clothing, and as she lifts her chin to look up at me I reach down, pulling her to her feet and lifting her into my arms. She lies there warm and soft, her head against my chest, her eyes dark.

'Was that okay?' she asks, as if watching me lose it completely wasn't enough of a confirmation.

'No, my ice queen,' I tell her as I stride out of the door, heading for the stairs that will take us up to my bedroom. 'That wasn't okay. That was fucking incredible.'

A ghost of a smile curves her mouth, and for a moment I'm lost in that smile. For a moment there is nothing but the savage satisfaction that I've made her smile in just that way.

I smile back. 'And now it's time for me to return the favour. Any objections?'

'No,' she says, settling against me. 'None whatsoever.'

CHAPTER FOURTEEN

Katla

I OPEN MY eyes and stare at the ceiling, wondering why it doesn't look like the ceiling of my apartment in LA. It seems higher and the water stain in one corner isn't there.

Then I remember. I'm not in my apartment in LA. I'm in Ulysses Zakynthos's house in Greece, in Ulysses Zakynthos's bed, and I am naked. Perhaps I should be unhappy about that, especially considering all that's happened in the past day or so, but I'm not unhappy. In fact, a delicious little thrill arrows through me.

After I 'distracted' him down in his study, he took me upstairs, stripped me naked and then returned the favour he promised me, with 'added interest'—his words—as a 'special Christmas treat'.

It's been a revelation, being in his bed. I've learned more about myself and my physical feelings in these past few hours than I ever learned in a year's worth of marriage with John. John called me frigid and cold, but I know now that I'm not either of those things. Ulysses told me I was a volcano and whenever he's around I certainly feel like one. As if I could erupt at any moment.

He's merciless with his pleasure, though, and quite ruthless in giving it, not that I'm complaining at all. Especially when it's clear to me that he needs something to take his mind off whatever is happening with his sister.

I thought when he said he wanted distraction that he meant something other than sex, which was why I told him about the shell. Which had then involved talking about my collection. I didn't know what had possessed me to tell him, initially, and when I did I then kicked myself for saying it.

My mother hated my collection, because I'd been doing it since I was a child, and it made it difficult when we moved on to the next town. I had to get it all together before we left and even one thing missing made me anxious. Mum would get impatient and annoyed, and she was always throwing bits and pieces of it out, much to my distress.

John thought it was stupid, too, so I was sure Ulysses would think the same. I don't know why his opinion mattered to me, but it did, and I was waiting for him to tell me it was silly too. Yet...he didn't.

If it pleases you, who cares what other people think?

I roll over in the vast bed, piled high with white pillows and crisp, white linen sheets, and stare out of the window instead. It's dark outside and I can hear the roll and crash of the waves on the shore.

Ulysses is a man who doesn't care what people think. I knew that about him immediately, and part of me wants to be like that too. I don't want to care that other people find me quirky, and I don't want to care that they think my little collections are silly.

If it pleases me, he said. And the things I collect *do*

please me. But I got rid of them after I left John. I threw them all away, because I too thought they were silly, and that maybe if I got rid of them that would make me more acceptable to people. That would make me more 'normal'.

Yet every time I went home after work I would sit in my apartment and nothing in it pleased me. Nothing in it made me feel at home. I told myself that it would take time to become a normal person, but now…

Coming into Ulysses's house felt instantly welcoming. He has little collections too and some of those items felt pleasing to me as well—the shell that his sister gave him, with that perfect spiral.

Once again, he thought about my pleasure, about what pleases me, and he made that important I can't remember anyone who felt that pleasing me was their priority. Certainly not my mother or John. I like that feeling a lot.

The bed is empty and so is the bedroom, and I want to find him to tell him how much I like the way he makes me feel. So I slide from the sheets then take a cursory look around the bedroom for my clothes. I can't find them, so instead I pick up his discarded shirt and put it on, rolling the too-long sleeves up to my elbows. The hem reaches the top of my knees, so I'm well covered, not that I care about that right now.

I pad out into the hallway and wait there a moment, listening for any sound. I can hear someone talking, low and deep: Ulysses. I follow the sound down the stairs and into the high-ceilinged hallway. He must be in the living area, so I go down the hallway to the large lounge at the back, with its tall and beautifully decorated tree.

He's standing by the tree, talking on the phone in Greek and looking out of the windows into the dark night beyond the glass. His back is to me and he's wearing a pair of worn jeans that sit low on his narrow hips and nothing else.

My heart clenches. He's beautiful like this, all velvety olive skin over rock-hard muscle, each line sharply delineated. I know how that skin feels against mine now and I know how he tastes—salty, masculine and delicious. I want him again, my hunger for him seemingly endless.

I must give myself away somehow, because he turns abruptly, and his golden eyes meet mine. Flames leap in them and I feel a rush of satisfaction because I know those flame are all mine. I lit them and they burn now for me.

But competing with those flames is a hard, cold edge that makes me shiver. It's the ruthlessness inside him, the piece of him that brooks no argument, and it's dangerous. Strangely, I find that danger exciting, which makes no sense, especially after John. Then again, I know this man won't hurt me. This ruthlessness is for other people, those who took his sister, and part of me finds that incredibly attractive. He will go to any lengths to get her back;I can see it in his eyes, the depth of his feelings for her obvious. The strength of that love is intoxicating. No one has ever felt that way about me and something in my soul longs for it.

Eventually his conversation ends and he lowers his phone, putting it into his pocket. 'You should be asleep,' he says. 'It's late.'

'I know,' I reply. 'But you were gone and I wanted to know where you were.'

A muscle flicks in his jaw. 'You should go back to bed.'

I debate whether I should obey, but behind the flames in his eyes there's something else, something that looks like pain, so I stay where I am.

It doesn't come as a shock to find that I don't like the thought of him being in pain. That, in fact, I hate it. It feels wrong that a man so beautiful, so powerful and so in control should be in pain about something. Yet it also makes him seem more human, and it tugs on my heart.

'You told me that I should do what pleases me and not care what other people think—and, since staying here is what pleases me, that's what I'm going to do.'

The muscle in his jaw flicks again. 'Katla...'

'We've had this discussion, remember?' I come over to where he's standing and look up into his face. 'Are you still thinking about your sister?'

'Yes.' He bites off the word, as if it tastes bad. 'One of my staff has just found out where she is and it's not in Greece. She's in Sicily. I'm going to get the jet ready so I'll be able to leave tonight.'

I frown. 'You're going to get her?'

He nods. 'The man who has her is dangerous and I can't leave her with him—' He breaks off and reaches into his pocket for his phone once again, and this time his expression darkens as he listens to whoever called him. His Greek is sharp and hard as he argues, and then abruptly he tosses the phone onto the lush white sofa and turns away, giving me the powerful, tense lines of his back.

He's angry, his anger bright and intense, yet it seems to burn out quickly.

'What happened?' I ask.

He curses under his breath in a stream of furious Greek. Then he turns back to me, his eyes lambent with fury. 'The jet can't leave. There are weather issues. Some kind of storm happening along the Italian coast.'

I study him for a moment. He isn't a man who sits around waiting for things to happen, he is the one who makes things happen. He's a man of action, so being unable to help his sister or even go to her must make him feel so powerless. And he's not a man used to being powerless, I think.

I want to offer him my help, or something that will make him feel better, but I don't know what. Earlier, he showed me what kind of help I could give him, which was sex. I could certainly offer him that again—I want to, even—but maybe he's had enough of that. Maybe this requires something more.

I think of myself, and what I need when I am feeling powerless against the slings and arrows of the world. For me it's numbers, the sharp edges of the universe. They're dependable and they never change, despite what happens to me or to the rest of the world. They are eternal and infallible. However, I don't think Ulysses would find the same kind of solace in them that I do, so I say, 'The weather is always changeable, and by tomorrow it might be better.'

'She might be dead by tomorrow,' he snaps, running a restless hand through his coal-black hair.

My heart clenches tight at the look on his face, fury and frustration with a cold, sharp edge. Yet my brain is being its usual logical self and sorting through what he said about his earlier call with what's happening now.

'That's being very dramatic,' I say levelly. 'She's pregnant and with the father. He's not going to kill the mother of his child.'

Ulysses's golden gaze locks onto mine. 'I've learned that people are capable of anything,' he growls. 'Even that.'

There's a warning in his tone, and part of me wants to know how he learned that, but I don't want to be dismissive of his concerns now, no matter how dramatic they are.

'Well,' I say reasonably, 'If he wanted to kill her, he would have done already. In fact, if all he wanted was to hurt you, then he didn't need to take her anywhere at all. He could have killed her immediately.'

That muscle in his impressive jaw leaps and leaps. 'That could be true.'

'Did she say she was in danger?'

'No.'

'So, why don't you believe her?'

Ulysses doesn't like that, but he doesn't look away. 'What do you care?'

He's angry, I know this, an animal caught in a trap and lashing out at anyone trying to help him. And I am trying to help him. I'm trying to offer some cool logic and truth in the face of his boiling rage.

'I don't know,' I say honestly. 'But she's important to you and I don't like seeing you upset.'

He gives me one last fierce stare, then turns to face the windows again, his back once again to me. 'I kidnapped you from your office building and forced you to come with me. You have exactly zero reasons for not liking to see me upset.'

'Maybe,' I tell him. 'But I don't like it all the same.'

He says nothing for long moments and I stare up the length of his powerful back and muscular shoulders. I don't know why I suddenly feel so strongly about this, about him, especially considering that he's right. I have no reason to like him, to feel anything for him at all, and yet…in the space of twenty-four hours he's managed to touch parts of me that no one has ever even noticed before.

It makes me afraid to think these things about him, to feel anything for him, especially when people are so unreliable, so changeable, so fallible. And part of me wonders if I'm wrong about him—that he does have the ability to hurt me and, even worse, I've handed him the means to do so.

Go back upstairs. Leave him and save yourself a world of pain.

I should do that. Except I don't. I stand there looking at the graceful curve of his back and, without even thinking, I rest light fingertips on the groove of his spine and trace the line of it, his skin warm and velvety beneath my touch.

'I'm sorry,' I say softly. 'I want to help you but I don't know how.'

He says nothing for a long moment, his muscles rigid beneath my fingertips. Then slowly he turns around, so instead of his back there is the perfect expanse of his bare chest and abdomen, rigid and hard with muscle. He looks down at me, his golden eyes full of an expression I can't read. 'I mean it,' he says. 'Why should you care about this in any way?'

He wants an answer, I can see that, and I know telling him that I have no idea why I feel this way won't work, so I try to think of a reason to give him, and maybe one to give myself.

'You...obviously care about her very deeply,' I say hesitatingly. 'And that... I find that very attractive.' Then I blush because the words didn't come out the way I wanted them too and it sounds stupid. 'I'm sorry,' I say again quickly, 'I'm not very good at talking about feelings. I'm not very good at anything to do with feelings.'

He doesn't move, doesn't say a word, just stares down at me, radiating strength, power and heat. And once again I'm that moth flying towards him, unable to stay away. 'Have you never cared for someone, Katla?' he asks,

The question comes out of the blue and for some reason it feels as if he's pulled a rug out from under me. 'C-care for someone?' I repeat stupidly.

'Your husband?' Ulysses asks. 'Did you care for him? Do you have any siblings? What about your parents?'

I don't know where he's going with this and I feel strange and uncomfortable talking about it. I don't want to tell him about my childhood, or more about my life with John. I don't want to tell him about the difficulties I have in relationships, because I'm afraid of feeling anything too intensely, too deeply. Because I'm afraid of being hurt again, of not feeling good enough. Of not being normal enough.

'Why do you want to know that?' I ask him, taking

an uncomfortable step back to put some distance between us.

He notes my retreat and something flickers in his eyes. 'So you know what my sister means to me,' he says flatly. 'So you understand why I'm so furious about this.'

There's a lump in my throat and no amount of swallowing will make it go away. 'Well, yes,' I say, and don't elaborate, because I don't want to keep talking about this particular topic.

But Ulysses is an observant man, and of course he takes note of my discomfort. 'Who?' he asks. 'Who was it you cared about?'

I can feel my cheeks getting hot, but I've promised him honesty, so that's what I'll give him. 'My mother,' I say. 'I cared about her.'

His gaze sharpens even more. 'Not your husband?'

'No,' I murmur and glance away, not wanting to meet that glowing golden stare that sees too much. 'Not as much as he wanted me to.'

Then all of a sudden his fingers grip my chin and he turns me back to face him, forcing me to meet his eyes. 'What's wrong?' His voice is soft, in complete contrast to the firmness of his grip. 'You're upset.'

I try to pull away. 'I'm not. This isn't about me, this is about—'

'Tell me,' he orders.

He's going to make me tell him, I know that. He's not someone who will let something alone, and I know that too, so there's no point me changing the subject or trying to distract him. And maybe, if I tell him the truth about myself, he'll finally change the subject.

Or he'll walk away.

That thought leaves me feeling cold, as if my stomach has dropped away, and I don't know why, so I ignore the feeling.

'I did love my mother,' I say flatly. 'But she never loved me.'

He frowns. 'How do you know that?'

I let out a breath. 'Because she never said it to me. She was something of a free spirit and found living in Iceland claustrophobic. So, when I was very young, she left the country and took me with her. My father wasn't in the picture so we spent a long time travelling around Europe, staying in communes or working on farms in exchange for free accommodation. It was a nomadic lifestyle and I...'

I swallow, remembering the difficulties I had. 'I hated it. I don't like change, so constantly moving was awful, and since I...find it hard making friends anyway, making friends while on the move was impossible. Also, Mum wanted an easy child who didn't make fusses or throw tantrums; who could just pick up and leave whenever she called, who would follow her without any kind of fuss, but... I wasn't that child.'

The lump in my throat grows bigger. 'Sometimes she'd leave me with friends and go off for months at a time because it was easier for her to be without me, and I used to be afraid that she'd leave me there and never come back. She didn't, of course, but that was my fear.' I don't like talking about this, but I make myself go on. 'I tried to be the daughter she wanted, to not make a fuss or throw a tantrum whenever we moved. But...she wasn't interested in numbers and she hated my little collections and… I think she wanted someone normal…'

I trail off, conscious of how childlike and whiny I sound. My cheeks burn and I don't want to look into Ulysses's gaze again. I don't want to see pity, bewilderment or contempt, because surely a man like him would feel that for someone like me? Someone who has no control over their emotions and who never seems to fit in anywhere; who was unloved by her own mother and by the man who was supposed to be my husband.

This time Ulysses doesn't insist on me looking at him, granting me the mercy of the blank wall instead. 'And your husband?' he murmurs. 'What about him?'

'I don't know why he wanted me,' I say, because I don't. 'But I married him because I thought he loved me and that my life with him would be stable, that I'd be safe with him. Except… I wasn't. He didn't like my collection either. My mother tried to take away my emotions and John tried to take away my intellect. He always downplayed it, made me feel small. Made me feel stupid about certain things.'

I swallow yet again, because I hate saying all this and yet I can't stop. 'I'm different, Ulysses. Not by a lot, but a little. Just enough to not be much good to anyone.' That sounds so pathetic that I can't bear it, so I try to pull away, but he holds me fast.

And, before I can do anything, he bends and covers my mouth in an intense, hungry kiss. It's hot, savage almost, as if he's trying to prove something, and when he lifts his head my mouth feels branded somehow.

He stares down at me fiercely. 'Yes,' he says in rough tones. 'You're right, you *are* different. But that's what makes you beautiful, don't you understand? That's what makes you rare and unique. That's what makes you special. And, if your mother and husband didn't know what they had and didn't appreciate it, then they're fools.'

CHAPTER FIFTEEN

Ulysses

I HAD NO idea it was even possible to stop thinking about what was happening with my sister but somehow Katla has managed to make me forget the impossible situation I'm in.

After hours of me showing her exactly what kind of distraction I needed, we both fell asleep. Only to be woken by one of my staff members calling me with information about Rafael Santangelo. He's Sicilian, the CEO of a massive construction company and, much like myself, he has houses scattered around the globe. However, his main residence is his Sicilian villa and that's where I bet he's taken her.

I wanted to leave immediately, beard the monster in his den and take my sister back, but an operation of that magnitude involved preparation. So I put everything in motion, only for Katla to come downstairs and find me just as I was confirming my orders.

I'd turned around and seen her standing there, white-blonde hair falling in a waterfall down her back, dressed only in one of my shirts, and the most intense feeling of possessiveness had gripped me.

Mine, something inside me roared. *This woman was mine.*

I was all set to prove it to her too, when the bad news came through that my operation would have to be delayed due to weather in Sicily.

I do not do denial well, or at all, in fact, so naturally this made me furious.

Katla only fixed me with her blue stare and told me that my sister wasn't in any danger, and why, and her careful, cool logic calmed the beast in me.

Unfortunately, though, I was still left with the same terrible sense of failure I've been carrying around with me for years, ever since she'd been taken away from me that first time. Except now I kept having fleeting thoughts that maybe I was to blame for all of this. Maybe I was the one who'd made her run.

The thoughts ate at me, as I turned on Katla, which was unfair of me, yet she didn't leave. She stayed despite me growling like a bad-tempered dog, even when I turned my back on her. Then I felt the lightness of her touch tracing my spine and everything in me coiled tight. The caress of her fingers felt like a valve releasing all this pressure inside me, and so I turned, for some reason wanting her to understand.

And then I saw the shadows in her eyes. And I heard the hesitancy in her voice when she talked about her mother, her bastard of a husband and how the people who should have protected and loved her made her feel not good enough, unworthy.

I knew that was what she felt, because I could see the pain in her lovely blue eyes. My rage had awoken once again at that, but this time on her behalf, and I didn't ask myself why I was so furious for her or why it mattered to me so very much. I only wanted her to know that she wasn't unworthy, strange or not good enough. That her differences were what made her so rare and special. What made her the woman she was.

She's staring at me now and I can see the fear and the wary hope mixed in her gaze. She wants to know that I mean it, and she's afraid that I don't, but I've never lied to her, not once, and I don't intend to start now.

'You really think that's true?' she asks, searching my face as if she's half-afraid of what she'll find. 'No one has ever thought that I was any of those things before.'

'That's because you haven't met the right people.' I open my hand where it grips her chin, sliding my fingers down her neck to grip her throat lightly in a possessive hold I can't stop. I can feel her pulse beating against my palm; it's fast and getting faster. 'I think you're every one of those things, ice queen, and I told you that right from the very beginning.'

Her cheeks have flushed and that delicate rose colour is spreading down her neck and under the neckline of the white shirt she's wearing. *My* shirt. And, by God, all I want now is to rip the halves of it apart, baring her. But I also want it to stay on as I press her to the wall and fuck her right up against it. I want her wearing it when she comes, when she screams my name, so she knows I'm all around her. That she's mine.

I stroke the side of her neck with my thumb and I love how she shivers at the caress. 'People lie,' she says softly. 'I used to ask Mum if I was too different, if she was sad she had me, but she said no. I knew that wasn't true, though. And John…' She trails off, but she doesn't need to finish that sentence. I know her husband didn't love her.

'I don't lie,' I murmur, holding her gaze. 'I have never lied to you and I don't intend to start. You can believe what I say, ice queen. If I say you are rare and special, then that's exactly what you are.'

Her eyes have gone luminous and she's looking at me now as if I've hung the moon.

'Why?' she asks, her voice husky. 'Why do you think that?'

'Well,' I say, 'While it's true I haven't known you long, what I've seen is that you're loyal. You're caring. You're very stubborn and forthright, but I like those things about you. You're incredibly intelligent, too, and that fascinates me. You're also the most passionate woman I've ever met, and right now I'd love to give you another lesson in just how much.'

She should be melting right now, yet she's not. Despite the colour in her cheeks and the starshine in her eyes, there's a crease between her brows. 'I want to help you, though,' she says softly. 'I want to make you feel good, the way you made me feel good just now.'

I give her a half-smile. 'I could give you some further instruction…'

But she shakes her head, impatient almost. 'No, not sex, Ulysses. Not this time. I want to know why you feel you have failed your sister so acutely.'

'Because she was hurt,' I explain, still caressing the side of her neck. 'And I couldn't stop it. Because when I was young I was sure that nothing bad would happen to us, and I was wrong.'

'You were so young, though. You were only sixteen, weren't you?'

'I was, yes. But I told her it would be okay. I told her not to worry.'

I remember the fear in her eyes as she clung to me in the car as the social workers took us away. She needed hope, so I gave it to her, sure that I was right.

'But I was wrong. And now...' I pause a moment, not wanting to admit this out loud, yet not being able to help myself. 'I wonder if it's my fault that she's been taken.'

The crease between Katla's brows deepens. 'Your fault? How?'

'I...held her too tightly, I think. I imposed too many rules on her. It was supposed to keep her safe, but she... found it claustrophobic.' I remember the arguments we had, that I dismissed at the time but that now seem prophetic. 'She wanted more freedom. She told me that I kept her prisoner.'

'And did you?'

'My enemies, they're—'

'You need her, don't you?' Katla interrupts, her gaze disturbingly sharp. 'Because you're afraid.'

There's a lump of ice in my gut, and it feels as if this woman has somehow seen it, mapped its shape and knows just how far its tendrils have reached into my soul. I don't like the feeling.

'Of course I'm afraid,' I say, unable to mask my impatience. 'I'm afraid for her, that something will happen to her, and—'

'And you'll lose the last person who loves you,' Katla says in her usual forthright, open way.

My heart stills in my chest. I want to deny it. I want

to tell her she's wrong, that it's my sister I'm afraid for, for myself. And yet…

Isn't there some part of you that knows it's the truth?

There's something cold in me, a sharp, horrific kind of void that sucks everything I am into it: emptiness; nothingness. The same void that swallowed me when they took Olympia away. Where I had nothing and no one, and I was alone. Where all the people who loved me, who thought I mattered, had gone. And I felt, in some deep-down place inside me, as if I deserved it.

I go to turn away, but Katla reaches for my hand and takes hold of it. She grips it tight, the warmth of her fingers and the pressure of her touch somehow grounding me in the way I used to ground Olympia.

I pause, staring at her, hypnotised.

Her gaze is dark and cool, like the sea on a hot summer day. 'It's not wrong to be afraid, Ulysses. It's not wrong to want to be loved, either. Because if it is then I'm wrong too.'

This woman… The way she looks at me, as if she knows the contents of my soul, is discomforting and I don't like it. And I especially don't like how clear-eyed she is, as if what she sees in me doesn't frighten her when it should. She knows nothing of what I became all those years ago, nothing of my early life as an enforcer. Nothing about the man I was who hurt people and got paid for it.

'Don't look at me like that, ice queen,' I murmur. 'You don't know what kind of man I am, what terrible things I've done—and, believe me, I've done terrible things.'

Katla only looks at me perplexed. 'What things?'

I can't tell her all the gory details about myself. She's quite innocent in some respects and I can't put that on her.

Bullshit. You don't want to change the way she looks at you.

That's true, I can't deny it. Once she knows what I really am, she'll see me differently, I'm sure, and I've got used to her looking at me with such wonder and interest.

Except, once again, her honesty compels mine, so I say, 'I was an enforcer for a crime family. I made sure the rules were followed and doled out punishment to those who broke them. I'm sure you can imagine the kinds of things that involved.'

I wait for her expression to change, for disgust or condemnation to appear, but she only frowns. 'That was your job?'

'Yes,' I say steadily, and I don't look away. 'And I was good at it.'

She nods slowly, as if she expected nothing less. 'Of course. I can't imagine you being bad at anything, Ulysses.'

I want to laugh at that. 'That is not a good thing. I hurt a lot of people.'

'You needed to get your sister back,' she points out. 'And I can imagine that job prospects for a sixteen-year-old weren't great.'

'There were plenty of legal jobs I could have taken.'

'But you had to get her away from that family and fast, yes?'

I nod.

'And illegal jobs pay more, I would think,' she goes

on, following her usual searing logic. 'So you didn't really have a lot of choice, did you?'

'I didn't think so at the time,' I say. 'I don't regret my choices.'

'But you don't do that now, do you?' she persists. 'Vulcan Energy is all above board, right?'

'Of course. But I'm still an enforcer, Katla. And, while Olympia draws breath, I will remain one.'

'Well, then,' she says, clearly not understanding me. 'You may have done some bad things in the past, but that doesn't make you a bad man, Ulysses. You wanted to protect your sister and that was the only way you could do it.'

'Don't try to make it sound better,' I say curtly, wanting her to understand. 'There's nothing honourable in what I did. And the way I've been treating her now—keeping her as a virtual prisoner to protect my own heart rather than hers, as you so eloquently pointed out—isn't any better either.'

Katla opens her mouth as if to speak, then shuts it. Then she studies me for what feels like an aeon, before saying quietly, 'Do you know why I'm so drawn to you? It's because you're full of anger and passion, and amusement and laughter. You're full of all the emotions I have difficulty with, all the emotions that I'm too afraid to feel myself. You gave me the honesty I was searching for and the passion I didn't know I needed, and you protected me. A bad man would have left me to John, but you didn't. You saved me from him.'

I want to tell her she's wrong, that she doesn't know me as well as she thinks, but that look in her eyes makes me almost want to believe her. I've always burned hot, it's true, and that heat was useful in my early career. Anger drove me and left no room for gentler emotions, and I was fine with that. Gentleness wouldn't have saved my sister.

So I don't know what to say to this woman who looks at me as though I'm still the boy I once was. The one who wept when the stray puppy I tried to rescue died. The one who refused to steal bread from the bakery down the street even though we needed it and had no money to buy any. The one who was beaten up by other boys because he knew it was wrong to retaliate, that it was wrong to hurt people. The boy who knew right from wrong and who hadn't yet crossed the line.

But I'm not that boy any more. That boy died when Olympia was taken away, and he never returned. Becoming a warrior to save her involved me getting rid of my conscience, and in doing so I damaged parts of myself. Parts that will never heal.

'Only because I wanted to fuck you,' I growl, deliberately blunt.

But she shakes her head impatiently as if the words have no meaning. 'No. Why are you so set on believing that you're terrible?'

'Why are you so set on believing I'm not?' I counter. 'Six months, remember? I have you for six months and that's all. You don't need to know my life story.'

'But what if I want to?' she asks.

CHAPTER SIXTEEN

Katla

ULYSSES'S EXPRESSION IS SET, his mouth a grim line, the burning of his golden eyes steady. He's very set on thinking the worst about himself, as if he's some kind of monster, which he clearly isn't.

He's a complex equation, though, and there are many variables in his make-up that I wasn't aware of such as his protectiveness, his honesty and his capacity for feeling. Especially his capacity for feeling.

There's fury, desire, fear and pain in him and I want to know where all those things come from. I want to know why he thinks the way he does, because I'm starting to wonder if he's actually the kind of equation I'll never get tired of wanting to solve. He has so many complexities and contrasts, but it's not only that. He's interesting to my brain, and it's how he makes me feel about myself too. My feelings matter to him, I think. They're important, and the fact that they are makes my heart feel tight with an emotion I can't name.

I don't know why the way he thinks about himself is so upsetting to me, and it *is* upsetting. It hurts me that he thinks he's a bad person. Perhaps I shouldn't have pointed out that the reason he kept his sister so close was that he didn't want to lose the only person who loved him. I think it's true, but he didn't like me saying so. Probably because, like me, he is alone in the world, or at least that's what I suspect. Unlike me, though, he does have one person who loves him.

He takes a step back from me, as if he wants to put distance between us, so I let him. It's important to have one's own space, even if it feels oddly painful to me.

'I told you the facts,' he says coolly. 'There's nothing more you don't know.'

'You did,' I agree and then add impulsively, 'I'm sorry for saying that losing Olympia would mean losing the only person who loves you. That was very insensitive of me.'

He is silent a moment, then he says, 'Is it true? I don't know. But there are other are reasons I need her.'

'What reasons?' I ask, because I can't think of any others.

'I had to turn off my conscience when I became an enforcer,' he says slowly. 'I had to strip away the boy I'd once been and become someone else—someone harder, colder. And I *had* to or else I couldn't have done what needed to be done.'

I can see how difficult that must have been for him, especially for a man such as him, with so much capacity for feeling. But all I can think is that he did what he had to do to save the person he loved. No more and no less.

'You saved her, though,' I say simply. 'The end justified the means.'

'That's not all, ice queen,' he murmurs. 'You see, when I got her back, I had to become someone differ-

ent again because I couldn't continue in a life of crime
with a little sister to look after. But the damage had
been done, don't you see? The damage had been done
to me. The part of me that I stripped away, the part
that cared about other people, I could never put back.
My conscience never switched on again. It died. But
I needed something to keep me on the right path and
so Olympia became my conscience. And that's why I
can't be without her.'

He believes this, I can see. He's wholly committed
to it and right now, cut off from her, his true north, he's
a compass needle spinning round and round with nowhere to land.

And all at once I understand that I want to be his
place to land. I want to be his true north.

No matter what he thinks, his conscience isn't dead.
It's alive and well, if a little rusty with disuse, and if
it wasn't I wouldn't be standing here right now. I'd be
having to deal with John.

'I don't think that's true,' I say, moving over to where
he stands, so tall and broad. 'A man with no conscience
wouldn't have saved me last night.'

He watches me approach, his golden gaze steady. 'I
told you why I saved you, ice queen. It was out of selfish
need, not out of any purer concerns. Also, I knew my
sister wouldn't like me walking past a woman in danger.'

'So?' I ask him. 'Does needing someone to guide
you make you totally irredeemable?'

He gives a short, bitter laugh. 'You think I'm looking for redemption? No, I don't want that. I don't need
it either. I am what I am. I made my choices and I don't
regret them.'

No, he doesn't, but they've hurt him all the same. Those choices have changed him. 'Who was that boy, then?' I ask him. 'Who were you before you became an enforcer?'

Ulysses lets out a long breath. 'A rule-follower. The kind of boy who always did what he was told and never argued. I hated violence. I was targeted by the neighbourhood boys to be bullied and beaten up because I never retaliated. Our mother taught Olympia and I that violence was wrong. She taught us to be kind to animals and your elders; to show respect, to never lie.'

He pauses and his gaze on me sharpens. 'And then she died and the state came. I was certain that they would take care of us. That we would be together, because that's what they promised us. Only, people don't keep their promises, do they?'

'No,' I agree. 'No, they don't.'

'But I do,' he says. 'And that boy couldn't have saved her. He couldn't be the man I had to become in order to keep my promise. So I killed him.'

He's blunt, harsh, and I think it's because he's trying to push me away. Either that or maybe he's trying to convince himself that the boy he once was is dead. Except, he's not. He was twisted by circumstances and an enduring, fierce love into something he was never meant to be, but he's not gone.

'No, you didn't,' I say to him, just as bluntly. 'That boy is still there. I see him in your kindness to me, how gentle you are with me. The way my feelings matter to you.'

He stares at me fixedly, the fire in his eyes burning brighter and more intensely. 'It doesn't matter,' he says, the words rough on his tongue. 'The past doesn't matter. I am who I am. And it doesn't change what I want from you or what you'll give me.'

He's right—none of this will change what I give him—but he's wrong in thinking it doesn't matter, because it does. He thinks he lost something, something that makes him human and worthy, but he hasn't lost it. It's still there. It's intrinsic to him, it's part of him; I know it is.

He's like me in many ways. Persistent. Stubborn. Committed. We both tried to become something we weren't and, while he has managed to change his world to fit his new view of himself, I've been trying to change myself to fit the world.

But both of us are wrong, I can see that now. Both of us are denying the people we really are. He wasn't born different like me, but trauma has changed him irreversibly. And so, like me, he finds himself on the outside. He's not alone, though, that's what I want him to know. Not now I'm here.

'Good,' I tell him, meeting his gaze head-on. 'Because what you told me doesn't change anything either. What I told you about yourself is still true, and nothing alters that in the slightest.'

This time it's he who closes the gap between us, the fire in his eyes leaping high. He reaches for me, placing his hands on my hips and pulling me close to the intense furnace of his body.

'You really have to stop looking at me like that,' he orders, low and rough.

'Like what?' I challenge, staring up at him.

'Like you think I'm a good man.' His fingers dig into

my hips, and I'm almost on the edge of pain, but I ignore it. He's given me some pieces of himself and now
he regrets it, I think. He's trying to frighten me away,
but I'm not going to let him.

I told him I wasn't afraid of him, and I'm still not.

'You *are* a good man,' I tell him, looking up into his
eyes. 'You're a good man who had to do some awful
things, that's all. And I know this because it bothers
you.' I lift a hand and lay it against his cheek, the roughness of his five o'clock shadow prickling against my
palm.

'It doesn't bother me,' he disagrees.

'Then why are you telling me to stop looking at
you that way?' I ask. 'If it truly didn't bother you, you
wouldn't care.'

His jaw is hard, flames leaping in his eyes. 'You need
to stop talking,' he growls.

'Make me,' I dare him.

So he does, his mouth coming down hard on mine,
hot, hungry and fierce. It's as if he's let himself off a
leash, his kiss savage, giving no quarter. I know what
he's trying to do. He's trying to show me the enforcer,
ruthless and hard, conscienceless. But what he doesn't
know is that, over these past few hours spent in his company, I've seen the boy he once was. I catch glimpses
of him when he smiles, when he touches my face, when
he saved me from John.

He's a ruthless man, and I'm not blind to that. But
he's also a man with a huge amount of empathy and
a tremendous capacity for caring, and I know that because why else would he be so angry?

What he also doesn't know is that I'm stubborn and

persistent, and when I want something I go out and take
it. And, right now, I want him. I want to show him that
the boy he once was and the man he's become both live
inside him, and they can become one. He can be whole.

I kiss him back, just as fiercely, letting him know
that I'm still hungry for him no matter what he's done—
that hasn't changed. I bite his lower lip hard and then
suck on it, making him growl. He slides his hands beneath the hem of the shirt I'm wearing, running them
all over my bare skin before jerking open the front of
it, buttons raining down as they come off.

One hand slides into my hair as he pulls my head
back, his mouth moving down the column of my neck,
his teeth against my skin pressing hot kisses and small
bites all the way down. His other hand cups my breast,
his thumb brushing over my painfully hard nipple, and
I shudder as pleasure sizzles down every nerve.

I want to touch him, but it's all I can do not to lose
myself in what he's doing to me with the slide of his
hand, the pinch of his fingers around my nipple, his
mouth at my throat making me gasp and tremble. He
wants to do this hard and fast. I can already tell. But
I don't want that. I want to show him that he's worthy
of reverence just as much as I am; that he's as unique
and as rare as I am.

I twist out of his grip and he doesn't reach to pull
me back. He only stands there, his breathing fast, his
eyes glowing like twin suns. The shirt I'm wearing—
his shirt—is hanging open and I'm wearing nothing
beneath it. He's a hungry wolf. He's not going to allow
me much more time, I know that.

So I back over to the Christmas tree with the lights

shining down, and I beckon him over. He comes, lithe as a panther, and when I point at the rug in front of me he growls, 'I'm not a dog, ice queen.'

I only stare at him. 'Do you want me or not?'

He lets out another growl, but sits on the floor where I point. He gazes up at me and, when his eyes meet mine, I shrug off the remains of his shirt then step over to him and lower myself down to sit in his lap, facing him.

'Better,' he murmurs roughly, his hands on my hips.

Sitting on him is like sitting on sun-warmed stone; he's so hot and hard everywhere. I want to lick all over his bare chest, but I stop myself. This is important. He was gentle that moment in the plane, when he showed me the passion inside me, and now I want to be gentle with him. I want to show him the kindness and worthiness that lives inside him.

I lift my hands and take his face between them. 'Close your eyes,' I whisper.

At first I think he's going to resist, because he's not a man who does as he's told, not any more. But then slowly his eyes close, the pressure of his gaze veiled for a moment, so I take the opportunity simply to look at him.

He's beautiful, his face the most perfect ratio, with long, silky black eyelashes and a proud blade of a nose; with his high cheekbones and perfectly carved mouth. I lean forward and kiss his closed lids gently, then move on across his cheekbones and his nose, raining light kisses down on his warm skin.

I hear his breath catch as I kiss his strong jawline, and he whispers, 'What are you doing?'

'Honouring you,' I say, moving to the other side of

his face. 'Honouring what you did for your sister and what you gave up for her. Honouring all the things you sacrificed for her and honouring the boy you once were—that you still are, deep inside.' I kiss his jaw again, moving towards his mouth.

'Katla,' he breathes, but by then I'm at his lips and I cover them, a light, gentle taste of a kiss that stops whatever he was going to say.

Then I deepen it, tasting his mouth, because I love kissing now, I love kissing him. He makes a rough sound deep in his throat. His arms wrap around me, my breasts pressed to the hard wall of his chest, the heat of him a fire I continually want to warm myself against.

I reach down between us to the button of his jeans and undo it, freeing him. He's not wearing underwear, and neither am I, so it's an easy thing to lift myself up slightly and guide him inside me.

I'm already wet and needy for him and he makes another harsh, masculine sound as I settle down on him. We had sex like this up in the jet, and then I wanted to watch what I did to him, because I wanted him to be at my mercy the way I was at his. But not this time. This time I want something different.

Now, I'm scared that he can see what he does to me. I *want* him to know. I want to show him that he means something to me, something more than I ever expected him to. He's got himself under my skin so much that I don't think I'll ever get him out again.

His hands slide to the curve of my back and he spreads his fingers apart, as if he wants to touch as much of me as he can get, and then he opens his eyes, staring straight into mine.

The shock of the eye contact with him makes me tremble deep inside, but I don't look away. Instead I begin a slow rise and fall, and he lets me set the pace.

'Katla,' he murmurs, watching me as if he can't see anything else. 'My ice queen...'

Pleasure begins its slow and delicious build as we move together, perfectly in sync. He doesn't take his eyes off me and I can't look away from him. He's all heat, all fire, blazing beneath me and in that moment, in his arms, I'm fire too. We blaze together, he and I, both of us creatures of flame. And, just before the end comes, before I'm lost in the pleasure he's giving me, I am suddenly aware of one thing.

I think I love him.

CHAPTER SEVENTEEN

Ulysses

I POUR COFFEE beans into the grinder and set it to grind. It's morning outside, though it's early. The sun is still pink in the sky across the water and I can hear the calls of the gulls over the roar of the surf and the coffee grinder.

Turning, I lean against the kitchen counter and look down at my phone, checking once again for any messages from my sister, but there are none.

It looks as if the weather in Italy is clearing and yet… The urge to drop everything and run straight to her is not as strong as it was the day before. Instead, my thoughts keep turning to Katla in my arms last night, in front of the Christmas tree, coloured lights sliding over her bare, pale skin.

I remember the brush of her mouth on my skin, the soft rain of kisses that fell on my eyelids, my brow, my nose, my cheeks. And I remember the way she looked at me, as if there's nothing wrong with me at all, as if I'm not what I know myself to be: a lost cause.

She thinks the boy in me is still there and for a moment, as she murmured to me about how she was honouring me, I wondered myself—because there was a tight feeling in my chest, a kind of longing for something I didn't even know I was missing. A longing for what I saw in her eyes, a need for the hope I saw there.

The hope that I actually am the man that she sees.

Hope is deceiving, though, hope can cut deeper than any knife, break more bones than a baseball bat, and hope can be the death of all you hold dear. And I should know by now that hope is always a risk I can't afford to take.

I don't know how this woman sees in me what no one else can, or why I matter to her so much, but I do know one thing: I don't want to hurt her. I can't bear the thought of causing her pain, especially when she's gone through so much already, with a mother who didn't love her and a husband who only loved himself and didn't care about her.

She too has hope—I saw it in her eyes as we made love under the Christmas tree. No, it wasn't a quick screw or anything as crass as a fuck. It was more than that. Her eyes glowed in the light, a blue so deep I could drown there.

Afterwards, I got us mugs of the egg nog my housekeeper had left in the fridge, spiked them both liberally with rum then sat down under the tree with her in my lap and a blanket wrapped around us. We'd had a long conversation about Icelandic Christmas traditions, which then led to her asking me all sorts of questions about my life, and I didn't stop her. I answered all of them.

That hope was in her eyes the whole time. I don't know what she was hoping for, but I know I can't let her hope for anything involving me. Because the facts remain that, while I might have saved her from her husband, it wasn't because my dead conscience had suddenly woken up. I did so for my own selfish needs, because I wanted her in my bed and I wouldn't take no for an answer. Which makes me no better than the bastard who tried to kidnap her.

The man I was, even the day before, wouldn't have cared. That man wouldn't have been concerned with her feelings. I know this because, if he had, he would have taken her first refusal on board and never called her again. But I didn't do that. I persisted and I pushed, and now she's looking at me as if I can give her something—as if I'm special to her somehow, and I don't want that for her.

I don't want her hoping that she can fix me, or heal me, or any one of a number of things some women think they can achieve. Even Olympia couldn't manage that, because if she had I'd never have gone after Katla the way I did.

Six months I wanted from her and insisted on, even last night. But now I know that six months will only make everything worse for her. Six months will ingrain that hope and when I kill it—and I *will* kill it—that will hurt her. The man I used to be wouldn't have cared about hurting her, but I'm not quite that same man now. I'm different, once again changed by a woman I don't deserve. And I don't deserve her—that much I do know.

Somehow the air in the room alters, as if pressure has shifted, and when I look up Katla is standing in the doorway. She's wearing one of my T-shirts, a white one, and I can see the outline of her pale body beneath the thin cotton, the pink tips of her nipples and the shadow of golden hair between her thighs.

Instantly I'm hard, no matter that we spent most of last night exploring each other yet again, but this time I ignore my recalcitrant cock and meet her steady, blue gaze.

'Good morning,' she says and smiles, and my heart catches in my chest. Her smile is the most beautiful thing I've ever seen and the fact that it's for me only makes it better. But then a needle of ice slides into me, because I know what I have to say.

She wanted me to remember the boy that I was, and I have. Just enough to remember to do the right thing, and the right thing is to let her go.

So I don't smile back, because that won't make this any easier, and neither will putting it off. Instead I push myself away from the counter and straighten. 'Katla,' I say, allowing myself to relish her name for a moment longer. 'I need to talk to you.'

She leans against the door frame, crossing her arms over her chest and raising a brow. 'Oh? What is it?'

She has no idea what I'm about to say, and I don't want to say it. This will hurt her but, if I leave it any longer, it will only hurt more, so I need to do this quickly. 'I've changed my mind,' I say. 'I don't think I want that six months after all.'

Her pale lashes flutter as she blinks in surprise. 'What do you mean?'

'I mean, I'm going to let you go. I'll order the jet to take you back to LA today. You don't need to stay with me and I won't ask for any more of your time.'

Her forehead creases, as if she has difficulty understanding me. 'But you were very insistent on six months. You told me that—'

'I know what I told you,' I interrupt, the ice-cold needle slipping deeper inside me. I've hurt people before—broken bones, shattered limbs—and I never felt a single thing. But doing this to Katla feels like the worst kind of torture and part of me hates myself for doing it. Yet I know this is the only way. The right way. So I ignore her pain, just like I always do. 'But I think it's better for you if you leave.'

'Better for me,' she echoes, still frowning. 'How is leaving better for me?'

'Do I really need to explain that to you?' I ask her impatiently. 'You know who I am. You know what I've done. Apart from anything else, being seen with me isn't going to be good for your business reputation.'

'I don't care,' she says without any hesitation. 'Or at least, I don't care about who you are and what you've done. In fact, I already know who you are, Ulysses. And, as far as my reputation is concerned, I'm not sure I care much about that either.'

'You may not,' I say. 'But I do. I don't want to see you hurt or disadvantaged by my ill-timed kidnapping on Christmas Eve.'

Her eyes glitter, sudden anger flaring in them. 'Well, it's too late for that, isn't it?' Her voice is sharp. 'I'm here now and you were so insistent on six months. Why are you changing your mind now?'

I didn't expect her to argue, though why I didn't expect it I'm not sure, especially when all she's done since I met her is challenge me.

'You want the truth?' I say, even though I know she

always does. 'Because last night, under the Christmas tree, you looked at me as if you hoped for more.'

She flushes so beautifully. 'What's wrong with that?'

Pain catches me in the chest. I thought this would be easier, that I'd end this quickly and without a fuss because I've done it before so many times in the past. I didn't expect to be the one who would find this painful. I can't care, though. I can't.

'It's wrong because I can't give you more,' I tell her, brutally honest now. 'I told you, I'm not looking for redemption. I'm not looking to be saved. And I'm certainly not looking for a woman to be anything other than a sex object.'

Her chin lifts. 'I don't want to save you, Ulysses, or redeem you. And I don't care if all you see me as is a sex object. I want that six months you promised me.'

I grit my teeth. 'There was hope in your eyes, Katla. Don't deny it. You looked at me as if I was God. And that means it's impossible for this to continue. I've hurt too many people in my life, ice queen, and I don't want you to be one of them.'

Suddenly there are tears in her eyes, which shocks me down to my core. It's too late for this not to be anything, isn't it? It's too late for me not to hurt her.

'What you saw in my eyes *was* hope,' she says huskily. 'And do you know why?'

'No,' I bite out, and I don't want to know either.

'Because I love you, Ulysses.'

The words are like knives piercing me. Love. No… I can't do love.

Love is the harsh taskmaster who drove me to kill the boy I was in order to save my little sister. Love was the rage that powered me, the rage that made me do the things I did.

Love is cruel and merciless—it brings out the worst in me and I cannot have it anywhere near me.

I move over to stand in front of her and I hold her gaze with mine. Then, hard, fast and cruel, I say, 'I don't care.'

Then I walk out of the door and leave her standing there.

CHAPTER EIGHTEEN

Katla

I HEAR THE front door slam and a car's engine roar, the squeal of tyres as he leaves, and then there's nothing but silence.

The silence of absence.

I can't believe I lost him so quickly. I can't believe that the one truth I thought would save things actually drove him away. It hurts. I feel winded. It's as if he's reached inside my chest and torn my heart from my body.

I should have stopped him. I should have stood in his way in the doorway and not let him leave, but he took me by surprise. And I was still struggling to understand what he was saying even as he disappeared.

I don't care. That's what he said. I told him I loved him and he said that he didn't care.

But he does care, surely? I could see the pain in his eyes…or maybe I didn't see it. Maybe it's true that he doesn't care. Maybe I've been reading him wrong all this time, telling myself things that aren't true.

Believing my own lies…

Perhaps I shouldn't have said anything to him,

shouldn't have made myself so vulnerable, but when I saw him standing in the kitchen shirtless, the morning light lying over his velvety olive skin, for the first time in my life I wasn't afraid of the emotion inside me. I wanted to give it to him, share it with him, because it was a good thing.

A true thing.

Last night he held me in his arms and we talked. He told me about his life, and when he looked at me I felt precious and treasured. I wanted to tell him I loved him then, but I didn't have the courage, not until this morning.

Did you really think he would love you back, though? Did you really think he would care?

He said he didn't want to hurt me, that's why he wanted to break this off so soon, yet he did end up hurting me.

Or maybe I am the one who's ended up hurting myself, because yes—I did think that I mattered to him. I did think that he cared about me in some way...

My throat is thick and my eyes prickle with tears. I haven't cried for years but I can feel the tears sliding down my face now.

I had no idea how much this would hurt. Why did I think anything more was possible between us when I am who I am? Why did I think that baring my heart would make a difference? And why did I think passion would be enough?

But I have nothing else to offer him. I'm only a woman who doesn't fit anywhere, who has a trail of broken relationships behind her, who finds it difficult to make friends and now who has nothing and no one.

Not even him. I could go after him, I think, but then my pride kicks in. And, no, I'm not going to do that. If he doesn't want me, then I'm not going after him to beg. I've got more dignity than that and a lot more strength. I walked away from my mother, I walked away from John and I'll walk away from Ulysses too. I'll shove him in the past, back where he belongs.

Wiping my eyes, I turn and go upstairs to find Olympia's room. Ulysses told me there were clothes of hers there that she wouldn't mind if I borrowed, so I look through her wardrobe. I can't bear to wear anything more of Ulysses's.

I find a dress that fits and I put it on, along with some borrowed underwear, and just as I finish dressing there is a knock on the front door.

My heartbeat shifts, picking up speed. It's him, surely? Perhaps he's changed his mind, perhaps he's come back after all.

I fly downstairs and pull open the door, my heartbeat hammering. But it's not him. It's a man in a uniform and he says, 'I'm here to take you the airport, ma'am. Whenever you're ready.'

There's nothing here for me, I realise. Nothing here for me now he's gone.

'I'm ready now,' I tell him.

As the car leaves, I don't look back.

CHAPTER NINETEEN

Ulysses

IT DOESN'T TAKE me long to get to the airport and even less time for the jet to take off. It's early but I order a Scotch anyway. Anything to blunt the sharp edges of what happened in my kitchen earlier this morning with Katla standing there, so pretty in my T-shirt, smiling at me, her blue eyes luminous. Telling me that she loved me…

I take a healthy swallow of the Scotch, relishing the burn as it goes down, trying to scour away the memory of those luminous eyes filled with sudden pain, her pretty flush paling as I told her I didn't care. Before walking out like the coward I am, leaving her alone in my kitchen.

I'm a bastard for doing that to her. A bastard for letting things between us get to that point. I just hadn't expected the chemistry between us to blossom into something brighter, deeper and so much more intense than I'd anticipated. Or so fast.

In just over twenty-four hours, Katla fell in love with me and…well. I hope it will take her less time than that to fall out of love with me, for both our sakes. Yet, no matter how many swallows of Scotch I take, I can't get rid the memory of her pain or the tears in her eyes. Of her confusion or the lie I told her as I walked out—the lie that I didn't care that she loved me.

And it is a lie. For some reason, I *do* care, and I can feel the pain of that care like an arrow through my chest. She's the only person I've ever met who values the truth so completely, and says it, no matter how hard it is for her. I know it's hard. Telling me that she loved me must have taken a lot of courage and I repaid that courage with a dirty, terrible lie.

I had to, though. I had to ignore her feelings, because I couldn't give her hope that I'd change my mind. Hope that the six months I wanted was starting to look like not enough time instead of too much. I couldn't let her believe that I could give her more than that, because I can't. There's only room in my life for one woman and that's Olympia. She's my sister, my conscience, and I give her all my meagre capacity for caring. I don't have anything left for anyone else.

Besides, love makes me do terrible things and, though I've put those days behind me, I can't be sure that loving Katla wouldn't catapult me right back to the past. If I'd tear down the world to save Olympia, what would I be capable of when it came to protecting and saving Katla?

I can't allow it. I never will.

Pushing thoughts of her from my mind, I give the next couple of hours my complete focus as the jet touches down in Palermo and we take a helicopter to Rafael Santangelo's villa in the south.

I thought I'd take him by surprise but, as the helicopter touches down on the green lawn in front of the villa, I'm shocked to see the slim form of Olympia standing there, ready to meet me. Of Rafael Santangelo himself there is no sign.

I leap out, noting that she's not running to meet me the way she normally does. Instead she stands straight-backed and alone, wearing a form-fitting, long-sleeved red dress that outlines the shape of her growing pregnancy. She looks strong, standing there by herself, stronger than I can ever recall her looking.

My heart catches painfully when I approach and she doesn't smile. Nor does she move to embrace me, the way she normally does.

Instead, she says, 'I told you not to come.'

Even a day or so ago, I would have ignored her, crossed the space between us, taken her arm and drawn her into the helicopter whether she wanted to go or not. But all I can hear is Katla's voice in my head telling me that I was kind, protective. That the boy I once was isn't dead and why can't I see that myself?

What I see now is that, yes, I could take Olympia away with me under the guise of protecting her but, as Katla told me just yesterday, I'd be doing that because I don't want to lose the one person who loves me. Because I'm afraid for myself. Afraid that without her I'm broken and that I'm stuck being a man I despise and don't know how to change. Afraid that, if she's not with me, everything I've done is for nothing.

But that's my issue to deal with, not Olympia's, just as she has her own demons to exorcise. I can only do so much for her, I realise. She has to exorcise then on her own, without me to protect her from them, or else, I'll just become another one of her demons.

So I stay where I am, meeting my sister's gaze, golden like my own. 'I had to come,' I say. 'You think you could tell me you're pregnant, that you're with some bastard—?'

'That bastard is my husband now,' she cuts in. 'And this has got nothing to do with you.'

So, he married her. That's the only thing he's done right. Rage starts to simmer inside me, and I want to tell her that it's got everything to do with me, but I force the fury away. Force myself to find the cool logic that Katla gave me.

Instead, I look at my little sister and see that the strength in her posture is also in her eyes. Strength that I never knew my scared, vulnerable and beaten Olympia had. Is it the prospect of impending mother-hood? Or is it something else? Something that—God forbid—has to do with Rafael Santangelo?

Whatever it is, it comes to me suddenly that anger is not going to solve this. That, in fact, it's not my issue to deal with, not this time. Olympia is alive and well and is expecting a child. She has a life outside of mine, and I know that if I try to take her away from it the re-lationship we have, strained as it already is, will chip and shatter.

The arrow in my heart worms its way deeper with that thought, sending pain spearing through me. I've already left one woman. I can't put at risk my relation-ship with this one, especially when it's the only one I have left.

So all I say is, 'Congratulations, little one. Are you happy?'

Her eyes widen, as if she's not expecting me to say that, then she blinks and her expression eases. 'Thank you. And as to happiness…that's a complicated one. I think so.'

'I hope you are,' I tell her. 'That's all I ever wanted for you, I hope you know that.'

She stands there a moment, staring at me in surprise, then abruptly she walks over to me and puts her arms around me. 'I know this is a shock, Ulysses. But, when it's all over, I promise to tell you everything.' She hugs me tighter then looks up at me. 'You're really not going to drag me back to Greece?'

I hold her slight form gently. 'No. This is your life now, Olympia. You should live it.'

She smiles at last and for a second I feel better, the arrow in my heart blunted for the moment. Then she frowns. 'You look tired. Is everything okay?'

No, it's not okay. I turned my back on a woman I shouldn't have. I let her go even though she told me she loved me. Even though she looked at me as if I was worth something, as if I was precious to her, and it's been so long since I was precious to anyone. Now I'm wondering if I've made a terrible mistake, but it's too late now. It's too late to go back…

'Yes,' I say out loud. 'I'm fine.'

But Olympia's gaze holds mine and I can see she doesn't believe me. It's not the time to tell her about Katla, though, and I know she'd be furious at how I walked out on her. The strong, confident woman she is now would definitely not let me leave without a lecture. And I have no stomach for that now.

'Goodbye, little one,' I say, giving her one last gentle squeeze. 'Keep in touch, hmm?'

'Ulysses,' she says, gently but very firmly. 'What is it?'

For some reason, I say, 'I met someone.'

Olympia's eyes widen as she hears the emotion I tried unsuccessfully to keep from my voice. 'A woman?'

'Yes,' I say. 'But…it didn't work out. I had to let her go.'

Olympia blinks. 'Why the hell not?'

'It's complicated,' I tell her. 'I have you to look after and—'

'Ulysses,' my sister interrupts impatiently. 'Wait. So you met a woman and it didn't work out because… what…you have to look after me?'

My heart is tight and I can't seem to draw a breath. 'Yes,' I force out.

She stares at me, her gaze searching my face, reading me the way Katla reads me. Then she lets out a long breath. 'Oh, my God,' she whispers. 'It's happened. You're in love with her.'

I don't move. I don't breathe. It can't be true. I don't have the capacity to love someone else, not when Olympia takes everything I've got to give.

And yet… I think of the pain I felt when I told Katla I didn't care. The pain I still feel at the thought of her standing in my kitchen telling me her truth, telling me she loves me, and knowing what that must have cost her.

My ice queen. My volcano—rare, beautiful and brave. Cool as water and hot as lava. The only person ever to look at me and see the truth of me, no matter what I did in the past, no matter the boorish bastard I was to her when I met her…

I can't speak, but Olympia reads the truth in my silence.

'You're an idiot,' she says succinctly. 'And I don't appreciate being used as an excuse.'

'I'm not—' I begin, but she doesn't let me finish.

'I'm not the only one who's been stifled by our past,' she says. 'You have been too. You need to get a life, Ulysses, and I mean that quite literally. I've found mine, now it's time for you to find yours.'

I've grown used to not listening to my sister's histrionics, because she's nothing if not dramatic. But there's quiet truth to what she says that resonates inside me. I have stifled her—I know it—and now I can also see that I've stifled myself too. The life I live, the life I have now, is narrow, tied as it is to her, and it is empty. As empty as my villa when I came on Christmas Day to find Olympia gone.

Except it wasn't totally empty. Katla was there with me.

My chest is tight, the arrow in my heart burrowing deep. 'I will hurt her, little one,' I say. 'You know what I was. You know what I've done. I can't drag her into that with me.'

Olympia looks heavenward. 'Men,' she mutters under her breath. 'So don't drag her into that. Leave that behind and create something else with her.'

'It can't be that simple,' I tell her, because it isn't, is it?

My sister looks up at me and her expression softens.

'Actually, I think it is.' She smiles. 'Don't run away from it, Ulysses. If I can be happy, then you can be too, can't you?'

Happy. I can't even remember ever feeling…happy. Except…maybe I do. Watching Katla show me the spiral in that shell… Listening to her give me a piece of her soul as she told me about her little collection… Feeling her kisses on my face as she whispered that she was honouring me…

I was happy. With her.

'Olympia,' I say roughly.

'I know,' she says, still smiling. 'Go get her.'

So I do.

CHAPTER TWENTY

Katla

THE CONFERENCE ON renewable energy sources at which I'm delivering a paper in Reykjavik's Harpa Hall is full of the most forward thinkers in the sector, and I'm quietly pleased that the talk I've just given was to a full house.

It's been a couple of weeks since I returned from Greece and went back to work after the Christmas break. Mr Tanaka didn't ask me what had happened, and I didn't tell him.

I was still concerned about what John might do, considering our last meeting, but he apparently disappeared and no one quite knows what happened to him.

I threw myself into my work, trying not to think about Ulysses and the forty-eight hours I spent with him, which was apparently long enough to fall in love with him and then get my heart broken.

And he's changed me—irrevocably. He showed me what it was like to be accepted for myself. He showed me that I don't have to make myself smaller to fit someone else's expectations of who I should be—that I truly am rare, precious and beautiful all on my own. And that my passion isn't something to be afraid of but embraced wholeheartedly.

I'm trying to embrace it, of course, but over the past couple of weeks that's been difficult. Every time my phone rang, my heartbeat quickened and I answered it, part of me hoping to hear his deep voice down the other end of the line. Except it never was. And, after that first week went by, I stopped hoping.

Perhaps it is for the best, I tell myself. Perhaps relationships are not for me. Perhaps it would be easier to remain alone for the rest of my life. Yet there's part of me that doesn't believe that. Part of me that aches, aches and aches, longing for the only man who ever made me feel good about being myself.

The energy conference has come at a good time. Mr Tanaka wanted me to give a paper on the economic benefits of renewable energy sources, and I was happy to come back to Iceland, where I was born. I don't remember much of it, since my mother took me away very young, but there is something about the crisp, clean air and the stormy skies that resonate with something deep inside me.

I want to do some sightseeing after the conference ends, so I've booked myself a rental car and plan to do some driving around. In fact, once I've answered the questions of the few people who stayed behind after my talk, I plan to get my car and start my drive today.

Except, as I finish answering the last question, I feel the pressure of someone's gaze. It's heavy, making my skin prickle, and I look up, trying to find the source of it.

The atrium is full of people all standing in little

groups and talking. The cool Icelandic sunshine falls through the honeycombed glass of the Harpa's walls, shining on them.

Then my gaze fixes on the man standing in the centre of the crowd. He's alone, and so tall, he tops most of the other people by a head. And he's looking at me as if his world turns on my command. His eyes are the same gold that haunts my dreams, his face the exact ratio that always soothes me, and deep inside I feel something I thought had died bloom again.

Ulysses.

What is he doing here, at this little conference in Iceland, of all places?

Sudden, bitter fury rises in me and I want to turn and walk away from him, the same way he walked away from me, but my feet are rooted to the spot and I can't move. Tears prickle behind my eyes and I desperately try to force my emotions down. This isn't the time or place for them now, not in a conference centre full of my peers.

Then quite unexpectedly he walks towards me and I wish I could move, turn my back on him and leave— do anything but stand there. Yet all I can do is stare at his beautiful face as he gets closer and closer, until he's standing right in front of me.

The gut punch of his stare, the pressure of it, gets me every time, especially when his eyes blaze with the fire that has always lived close to the surface of his skin. His expression is fierce and intent.

'What are you doing here?' I force out, trying to stay in control of my wildly flailing emotions. I can't bring myself to say his name.

'I heard you were giving a paper,' he says, his deep voice so familiar. I hear it in my dreams still. 'I wanted to see it.'

'Well, you're too late.' I lift my chin, wanting him to know that he didn't hurt me, that I'm strong and not at all broken after he walked away. 'I've already given it.'

His gaze never leaves my face. 'I was hoping you'd give it to me again. In private.'

My heart clenches, pain radiating everywhere in my body. I don't understand what he wants now, not when he made it so clear last time that he didn't care. Even though I knew what he told me then was a lie—that he does care—that wasn't enough to make him stay.

'I'm sorry, I can't,' I say, pleased that my voice is so steady. 'I have other appointments today.'

It's too painful to stand there with his golden eyes on me, so I finally manage to make myself turn and walk quickly to one of the exits.

There is sunshine outside, and the sea that the hall stands at the edge of, with boats on the water. My hotel is right next door to the hall, so I walk quickly towards it, desperate to get away.

But then strong fingers wrap around my arm, halting me, and I'm pulled into the ferocious heat of a strong male body, his arms surrounding me, holding me. I shudder as I feel his mouth near my ear, his breath against my neck. 'Don't go, my ice queen,' he whispers.

I am trembling, the tears in my eyes making the sea in front of me swim. 'You said you didn't care,' I say hoarsely. 'So why are you here?'

'I knew you were giving a paper.' His arms are iron bands around me. 'And so I've have been making plans.

I've bought a lodge on the golden circle and I thought I'd kidnap you and bring you to it. And then I was planning to spend a good few weeks apologising for walking away from you.'

I shut my eyes, my heart hammering. 'I don't understand what you want from me. Is it another six months? A night? What?'

He is quiet for a moment, then he says, 'I don't want to demand anything from you or to take anything from you. Especially anything you're not willing to give. But… I did want you to know that I lied back in Greece. I lied when I told you that I didn't care.'

I swallow, my heart hurting, my body waking at the warmth of him surrounding me, his familiar scent making my mouth go dry. 'I know,' I say. 'I know you lied. But you still walked away.'

Slowly he lets me go. I know I should walk away, but I don't. Instead, I turn round and look at him, see the shadows beneath his eyes and the lean, hungry look on his face.

'I had to,' he says roughly. 'I couldn't keep you. I had to do the right thing for you and that was to get me as far away from you as possible.'

This time I don't bother to withhold my tears, I let them slide down my face. Who cares if he sees them? The tears are the truth in my heart, the truth that I find so hard to say, even to myself—that I love him and I always will, no matter how he feels about me.

'So why are you here, then? Why approach me?' My voice is shaking. 'Why are you making this even harder?'

'Because I was wrong.' His gaze tracks my tears and

yet he doesn't move, his hands in fists at his sides. 'I thought I had nothing to give you, that it would be better to let you go, but it's not. It's not better.'

This is the truth, the heart of it—I can see that now.

'I saw my sister,' he goes on. 'And she told me that she's found a life of her own, one apart from mine, and that I needed to find one too. That I can't let the past drag me down; that if she deserved happiness, then so did I. And I realised that the happiness I wanted was with you, Katla Sigurdsdottir.'

He takes a shuddering breath. 'I love you, ice queen. I think I loved you from the moment I first saw you.'

The words are a hot shock, scouring my soul, and I look deep into his eyes—seeing the truth of him, seeing the big-hearted boy he once was, and still is, staring back at me.

My tears continue to fall and I let them. 'I thought… I thought I wasn't good enough,' I say thickly. 'I thought I was wrong to tell you that I loved you, that I was only seeing what I wanted to see, and…'

He moves then, compulsively, as if he can't hold himself back any longer. And before I know it I'm once again in his arms and he's kissing away the tears on my face.

'You weren't wrong,' he murmurs, his lips featherlight against my cheeks. 'And you're more than good enough. In fact, you're too good for me. I know it, yet I love you anyway. I want you to come back to the lodge. I bought it for you, and if you don't want it, I'll get rid of it. And if you want it but don't want me, I'll walk away. But, before you make any kind of decision, I want you to have this one thing.'

He lets me go, reaches into his pocket and then holds out his hand.

In the middle of his palm is a small white shell with the most perfect spiral. My heart clenches tight. It's the shell from his office, the one Olympia gave him, the one he said was precious to him.

'It's yours,' he says. 'For your collection.'

I want to speak, but my throat is tight and there are more tears in my eyes. So I shake my head, though why I don't know, because I want the shell and I want the lodge—but, more than anything in the entire world, I want him.

He seems to know, because he gathers me to him and lets me weep against his expensive overcoat.

'Six months,' I manage to force out once I've got myself under control. 'I want my six months.'

He cups my face in his hands, his golden eyes on mine. 'Not enough,' he says softly. 'How about a lifetime?'

I swallow, my heart expanding, happiness spreading like wildfire all the way through me. 'Perfect,' I say. 'That's absolutely perfect.'

And it is.

Because in him I've found my ultimate golden ratio.

EPILOGUE

ULYSSES

I STAND AT the windows of the lodge that look out over the frozen lake, a feeling of relief sweeping over me. Finally we're back here in Iceland for Christmas and I don't want to be anywhere else.

Warm arms slide around my waist and I turn to find my wife standing behind me, smiling up at me.

We had six months together after that day in Iceland and, at the end of it, I asked her to marry me.

She agreed. We were married a few hours ago in the Icelandic church in the middle of Reykjavik, and now we're honeymooning in our lodge that sits on the edge of a lake, with mountains in the distance. It's snowing and there's a big Christmas tree with lights in the corner of the big living area.

Olympia, Rafael and their new baby will be arriving to join us on Christmas Eve, but for now Katla and I have the place to ourselves. Her eyes are luminous and her smile makes me everything inside me gather tight.

'I have a very special Christmas present to give you,' she says. 'Do you want it now, or on Christmas Day?'

I hold her close, revelling in her warmth. 'Now, of

course. Have you ever known me to actively choose to wait for something?'

She laughs, then brings the hand she has behind her back in front of her and opens her palm. A long, thin item wrapped up in Christmas paper sits in the middle of it. I frown at as I take it. It's not very heavy and I have no idea what it is.

'Open it,' she says, eyes alight.

So I open it with careful hands and for a moment I stare at it, not really understanding what it is.

Then I do. It's a small plastic stick displaying lines in a plastic window. Two lines.

I blink and look at my little Icelandic volcano. 'Katla?' I say.

She's smiling and her face is pink.

'Katla?' I say again, my heart beating fast.

She's nodding now, and then I drop the stick, wrap my arms around her and hold her very, very tightly. Everything I was going to say rushes straight out of my head.

Katla is pregnant. I am going to be a father.

'Merry Christmas, my love,' she whispers in my ear.

It is indeed going to be a very merry Christmas, and next year it will be even merrier.

She is the life I was waiting for, the life I didn't know I needed.

And I can honestly say that I can't wait to live it.

* * * * *

MILLS & BOON®

Coming next month

BUSINESS BETWEEN ENEMIES
Louise Fuller

My heart feels like a dead weight inside my chest.

I stare at the man standing with his back to me beside the window, panic slipping and sliding over my skin like suntan oil.

Only it's not just panic. It's something I can't, won't name, that flickers down my spine and over my skin, pulling everything so tight that it's suddenly hard to catch my breath. And I hate that even now he can do this to me. That he can make me shake, and on the inside too, before I even see his face.

My stomach clenches and unclenches, and my heart starts to pound painfully hard, and I can't stop either happening. This is his doing. Just being near him does things to my body, things I can't control. But I need to control them.

'What's he doing here?' I say hoarsely. Although I don't know why I ask that question, because I know the answer. But I can't accept it until I hear it said out loud.

'Mr. Valetti is the new co-CEO.'

Continue reading

BUSINESS BETWEEN ENEMIES
Louise Fuller

Available next month
millsandboon.co.uk

COMING SOON!

We really hope you enjoyed reading this book.
If you're looking for more romance
be sure to head to the shops when
new books are available on

Thursday 23rd October

To see which titles are coming soon, please visit

millsandboon.co.uk/nextmonth

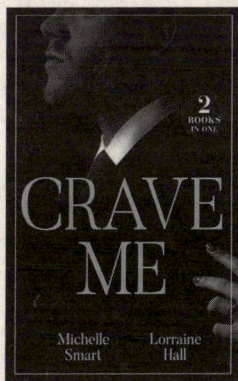

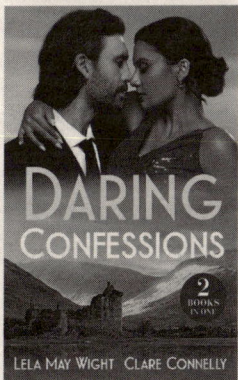

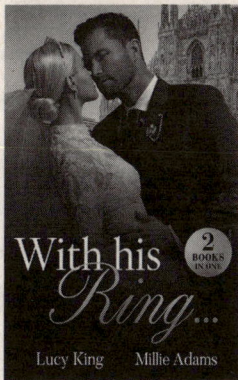

afterglow BOOKS

Afterglow Books is a trend-led, trope-filled list of books with diverse, authentic and relatable characters, a wide array of voices and representations, plus real world trials and tribulations. Featuring all the tropes you could possibly want (think small-town settings, fake relationships, grumpy vs sunshine, enemies to lovers) and all with a generous dose of spice in every story.

♪ @millsandboonuk
⊙ @millsandboonuk
afterglowbooks.co.uk
#AfterglowBooks

For all the latest book news, exclusive content and giveaways scan the QR code below to sign up to the Afterglow newsletter:

SCAN ME

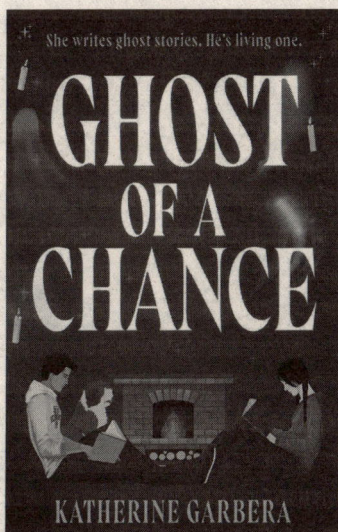

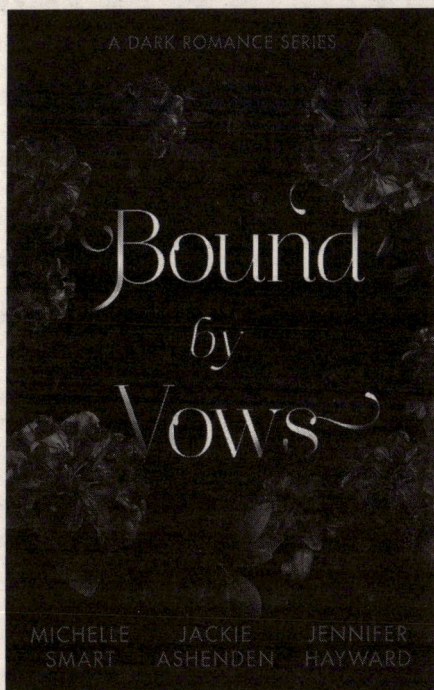

LET'S TALK

Romance

For exclusive extracts, competitions and special offers, find us online:

f MillsandBoon

X @MillsandBoon

◉ @MillsandBoonUK

♪ @MillsandBoonUK

Get in touch on 01413 063 232